THE HOPE LIST

*The Difference Between What's Good For You
and What's Good For Everyone Else
Is Happiness*

BY CHRISSY ANDERSON

ISBN: 978-1-5005-1215-6 (sc)

THE LIST TRILOGY

The Life List

The Unexpected List

The Hope List

For Dana...Whose death taught me how to live.

And for all of the Forsaken Francescas...I think about you every day.

TABLE OF CONTENTS

Zero Time
Going Home
Restructuring
Full Circle
Coming Clean
Tuesday Night Dinner
Saphalhos
Epicenter
So Close
Second Chance Barbie
Husband & Wife
Like a Virgin

<u>NEXT</u>
Anniversary Day
Do Over?
Not Funny
He's *Baaaaaaack*
~~Francesca~~
Lover of Horses
Sweet Symphony

Pres*ent (adjective)
Being, existing, or occurring at this time or now

Devoted

September, 2013

"...and it sure seems like this cellular telephone thing is becoming all the rage."

Her skin is as pale as those little white butterflies you see fluttering around in early spring. Her severely cracked lips are a distracting bluish color, and for every five words she speaks she has to take two labored breaths. She's having a hard time swallowing and gets noticeably agitated when she can't remember basic words and facts. Aside from the perfectly positioned bright red scarf wrapped around her bald head, everything I'm looking at and listening to is in painful disarray. My beloved best friend from childhood, Kelly, who died thirteen years ago, is giving this life lesson every ounce of energy she's got, and just like all the other lessons on all the other videos before it—it's absolute torture to watch.

"...But just ask Ki-Ki, even a milkshake in your hand is enough to cause a distraction when you're driving. I swear, that woman never could tolerate a brain freeze...damn near killed us that day. I hate to think of the damage she would've caused if there were actual cell phones in cars when we were younger. Promise me you won't ever talk on one of those things while you're operating a vehicle."

My daughter, Kendall, hasn't called me Ki-Ki for nearly ten years, and her hand instantly goes to my knee at the mention of the term of endearment she used to sing at the top of her lungs every single time she saw me when she was a small child. As always, the memory of the silly name makes her smile. Then, as always, the memory is immediately hijacked by the bitter reality of why she stopped using it. Her face morphs from a sweet smile into something resembling a tightly scrunched-up troll doll, and I see her mind teeter between wishing everything happened differently and being happy that everything turned out exactly like it did. It's a guilt-ridden battle I don't wish on anyone. Can you imagine the mental struggle of being sad your parents are dead, but at the same time, happy your life turned out exactly as it has? I can't. With that thought I squeeze her hand to let her know I sympathize with her battle.

"I'm not gonna lie to you, your Ki-Ki, Auntie Nicky, Auntie Courty and I used to break a lot of rules when we first got our drivers licenses. We even stole beer from our parents, parked at the top of Mission Peak, drank it all, and then drove back home like we were invincible. But we weren't...we were just dumb and incredibly lucky we didn't kill ourselves."

I purposely avoid eye contact with Kendall to dodge the shame of one of my many poor adolescent choices. Even so, I can see the critical look on her mature-beyond-its-years face out of the corner of my eye. I wanted to be the first one to tell her about all of my near-misses with cops that took place back in the day, but it looks like Kelly beat me to the punch on this one. Glancing over at the box containing only a few remaining videos, and listening to the strain in her voice, it's highly unlikely my beloved old friend will get around to too many more of my mess-ups.

"Don't think for one second you'll get lucky like my friends and I did with the whole drinking and driving thing, Kendall. In fact, there was a boy in our high school who died from doing it. It literally destroyed his family and they were never the same. Obviously, when that happened, my friends and I stopped playing with fire. But what if one of us had been him instead? I beg you to respect yourself and your life enough to take the privilege of..." She stops for a long while to catch her wheezing

2

breath, before continuing. *"...to take the privilege of driving a car seriously."*

Kendall and I let out a simultaneous sigh, silently acknowledging the morbid correlation between what Kelly just said and the fatal drinking-related car accident that *literally* changed *our* lives forever. At the time Kelly made this video, she had absolutely no idea the very heartbreaking scenario she just spoke of would take her husband's life, too.

"Now, let's talk for a minute about curfews..."

Kendall hastily reaches across the bed, grabs the remote, and presses pause. Then, in her usual grown-up and concerned nature, she lays in on me.

"Mom, *really?* Auntie *Courty*...Auntie *Nicky?*"

Actually, it is a little silly considering...

Now pointing at the television screen, she interrupts my thought and continues, "*And, would you look at her?* This is getting beyond brutal, don't you think?"

The thing is, I completely agree with her. It's been brutal for four years now, ever since we watched the video titled *Twelve Years Old,* when Kelly damn near threw up in the middle of talking about super absorbent tampons. However, I don't think it was the chemo making her sick. The woman never could discuss feminine hygiene without gagging a little.

"I know, Sweetheart. It's just that...I made a promise."

"Mom, *puleez*. I might only be fifteen-and-a-half, but I'm smart enough to know you've broken a few promises in your day."

A few? Ha! She doesn't even know the half of it.

Pointing back up at the television screen, she protests, "I appreciate that she made these for me, I really, really do. But you and Daddy have already talked to me about this stuff, and well..."

"Yes?"

3

Lowering her head, she whispers, "It's kinda hard to say."

Lifting her chin up so our eyes meet, I gently press, "It's okay to tell me what you're thinking, Kendall. Besides, we're probably thinking the same thing."

After a long pause she lets it all out.

"It's just that…It's like we're a perfectly normal family for three hundred and sixty-*four* days a year and then one day a year, on this stupid video day, I get reminded we're not. I know she was your best friend, and I know you made a promise to show me every last one of these things, but can't we just stop at this one? I mean, geez, I don't even want a car, I want a horse. Something, you know about and she doesn't…because *you're* my mom."

Kendall's right. For three hundred and sixty-*four* days a year we have swim meets, equestrian show-jumping competitions, theatre productions, dentist appointments, flu shots, backyard barbecues, wardrobe malfunctions, temper tantrums, and end of the school year pool parties. We wake on Christmas morning in our matching footy pajamas (*including* my mortified husband), we hunt for Easter eggs, bake cookies, participate in school talent shows, have slumber parties, and meticulously tend to our much-loved vegetable garden. For all but *one* day of the year, it's normal family operating procedure, and I adore every single second of every single one of those days. But then comes this day—video day.

Video day is on auto-reminder in my Outlook calendar. On this same day every year I'm prompted to pull the archaic VCR out from under my bed and plug it in. Then I glumly saunter over to my closet, uncover a large box of dust-covered videos, and summon Kendall to come into my room so we can watch the latest installment in private. I tried to leave the ritual up to whenever the mood felt right, but that only resulted in a lot of procrastination (and a lot of potential promise breaking). So one day, many years ago, a day was picked at random by playing pin the tail on the calendar with Kendall, and this was the day selected as the one day every year we'd watch the recorded life

4

lessons her mother made for her before she died of pancreatic cancer in 2001. It was a task originally appointed to Kelly's husband, Craig, but unbelievably he died too. So that left me, Kendall's legal guardian, as the one showing her the sixteen videos—one made for every year of her life beginning at three years old and ending at eighteen. But they're becoming incredibly difficult to watch and quite frankly I'm not so sure it's fair to ask that Kendall does…regardless of the promise I made.

Yes, Kendall and I were thinking the *exact* same thing. We both want to be a perfectly normal family for three hundred and sixty-*five* days a year and not get reminded on this one day that we're different. In fact, aside from a few individuals who know otherwise, you'd *never* know her father and I weren't her biological parents, and you'd never *ever* know she wasn't the full-blooded big sister to the ice-cream-stained-smiley-face who just barged into my bedroom.

"Whatcha guys doin' in here, Mama?"

Like the great team we've been since the very beginning, Kendall hurriedly turns off the television while I distract the little mess.

"Your sister and I were just talking about the big party we're gonna have later today. And speaking of party…looks like someone raided the ice cream!"

"Hey, Smudge! Did you save any of it for the guests, or did you just slather it all over your face?"

Ice-cream-stained-smiley-face just turned into ice-cream-stained-grumpy-face.

"Daddy said it was okay! I promise!"

Kendall scoots off the bed and wraps her arms around the little mess she so lovingly nicknamed Smudge just hours after I gave birth ten years ago.

"C'mon Smudgy, I'll help you get cleaned up before everyone gets here."

Before she leaves the room, Kendall turns to me and with hope in her voice asks, "So, are we good with boxing up the videos, Mom? Cuz I'm ready to…I mean, if you are."

"We'll talk about it later, okay, Hunny?"

"Okay, love you."

For a second I want to enlighten Kendall on the meaningful difference between saying "love you" and "*I* love you," but quickly file the discussion away for a more impactful time. Like, when she has her first serious boyfriend. It'll make more sense to her then. At least that's what her father keeps reminding me.

"I love you too, Sweetheart."

Just then, a chocolate covered hand grips my white bedroom door, and a sweet little chocolate covered mouth says, "And I love you too, Mama!"

"I love you too, Smudgy. Now go get cleaned up. We've got company coming! Oh, and quit stealing money out of Mommy's swear jar! Last count was over twenty bucks short!"

Once I hear my kids in the kitchen, playfully cleaning up what sounds like a much bigger mess than Kendall expected, I gently close my door and tackle the enjoyable task of making my bed. Yes, I just called making my bed an enjoyable task. Unlike pretty much everyone I know, straightening my pretty duvet cover just so and strategically positioning my nine shabby-chic pillows *every...single...morning*, is something I love to do. It's a fresh start to my day that makes me feel organized and accomplished. It's a task I check off of my daily mental to-do list (yep, lists are still a part of my life), and it's an addiction I'll never shed. And I don't have to. Unlike my addictions from the past, it's not like me, or anyone else, can get hurt or heartbroken from a crisp white sheet and straightened dust ruffle.

Normally I take my time making my bed, as it's when I mentally work out the logistics of my day, but not this morning. Right now, I'm doing it a little quicker than usual because I'm eager to peek out of my bedroom window and check on how things are coming along in the backyard for the evening's festivities and...to surreptitiously watch my husband. It's cute to spy on him when he's fixing things...thinking about things...worrying about things. He gets this concentrated look on his face that produces a little crinkle in the middle of his

6

forehead. It wasn't there when he was younger; it developed over time with all of the fixing, thinking, and worrying that's occurred over the last ten years with parenthood, work...and perhaps marriage. Whatever the reason for the crinkle, I love it. It represents our history and there's something about it that makes me feel incredibly loved. It's scary how close I actually came to never seeing that crinkle.

I quiver, like I usually do, when I remind myself of how close I came to blowing it with my husband. I stopped beating myself up years ago for all of the messes I made, but every now and then a quiver will catch me off guard and it feels like a punch in my gut. Well, this quiver didn't exactly do that, it merely made me stub my toe on the bed frame. Instead of hightailing it to the window like I planned, to spy on my better half, I limp to the bathroom to get a Band-Aid. After cleaning myself up, I turn to head back to the window, but pause when I notice the early afternoon sun shining on the mirror too perfectly for me to pass up. I step up to it and closely inspect my reflection. Once I'm satisfied my eyebrows are exactly how they should be, I take a few steps back to scrutinize the sight my husband insists age has treated pretty damn spectacularly. Me...I'm not so sure.

Every single overly sun-kissed spot on my face and arms is looking right back at me—compliments of the irresponsible pleasure of drowning in baby oil in the '80s. (I swear, nobody told me it would come back to bite me in the ass...until it was too late anyway.) Day after day I aggressively fight the brown freckles with hundreds of dollars worth of products that promise to sustain my youthful appearance, but I'm no dummy. They're full of shit. Whatever youthful appearance I've got left in me is courtesy of good genes. Even so, I'm a sucker for an infomercial with a beautiful middle-aged supermodel (who's no doubt had more laser surgeries than I'll ever be able to afford) convincing me I can look just like her. So to my wallet's condemnation, I spend, and spend, and spend, to try to erase what I naively permitted the sun to do to me so many years ago. All the while,

I'm telling myself I'm merely erasing big brown freckles—not, *gulp*, liver spots. Freckles are cute. Liver spots…not so much.

Blocking out the sound of a dish breaking in the kitchen, I take a step closer to the mirror and trace my index finger along the fine lines at the edge of my eye, and then slide it down to meet their counterparts which have just recently cropped up on my chest—the other area of my body I let the sun assault in my youth.

"*Son of a…*There's like a new line every day."

At this pace, my body is going to look like a road map in ten years! After I make a mental note to start looking for a better, stronger, more magical cream to eliminate my newfound enemies, I lift my tee-shirt to expose my stomach and then turn to my side to re-examine the mirror, exhaling a sign of relief that at least something's holding up.

Patting my tummy, I silently admit….With all of the wine I drink, this thing wouldn't have stood a chance without yoga. Dropping my shirt back down, I then cup my breasts and push them up and in to give them the look of life they no longer enjoy without the help of a very well-crafted Victoria's Secret bra.

I always wanted big boobs and on several occasions came very close to surgically altering mine, but I'm damn thankful I kept everything as it was meant to be. Miraculously, these suckers are still fairly perky, and if I was in a wet t-shirt contest with women my own age (okay, *gross*), I don't think I'd get ejected first. I try to take good care of the little bit of booby breast-feeding left behind on my chest, and, I guess you could say, I've become somewhat of a nip-nazi over the last few years. I abhor…no, wait! I am *revolted* by unevenly positioned nipples. You know those crazy ones pointing in completely different directions that you see running all over town doing errands and what not. Hey look, I'm a mom…I get the fact that nipples triple in size and become rather unruly after all of that breast-feeding. But can't everyone just take a few seconds to do a nip-check before heading out of the house? Does everyone have to run around looking like they're pointing people in opposite directions? I think not.

I release my breasts and let them drop back down a quarter of an inch to where they're happiest these days and then take an even closer step to the mirror to inspect my hairline for a stray grey.

I shake my head and wonder out loud, *"Oh, Chrissy, why do you care so much?"*

I mean, seriously, how hot *are* you supposed to be at this stage of your life? Quite frankly, it's almost odd that anyone would want to be.

A thunderous crash and a boisterous swear word coming from the backyard make me giggle and turn my attention away from the mirror and my timeworn exterior. My eyes travel in the direction of my husband's voice, and my mind drifts away from marveling about how astoundingly fast the first forty-four years of my life have gone.

Suddenly not caring a bit about liver spots, crow's feet, jumbled nipples, or grey hair, I make my way toward the window to spy on the man who, defying all odds, made all of my dreams come true. With each step, I find myself twisting my wedding ring and wondering if I really want to go through with the surprise I have planned for this evening. Scared that my good intentions could easily be misconstrued as a massive Chrissygan the likes of which my husband hasn't seen for nearly a decade, and turn what's supposed to be a monumental celebration into a total clusterfuck—a clusterfuck I'm worried might just break his heart for good and ruin everything we fought so hard to have.

Smitten

September, 2013

He's attempting to assemble his third heat lamp of the day in preparation for the party this evening, and he's stumbling through every step of the process, doing a terrible job of hiding his frustration from me and the kids. Even so, he's perfect.

He doesn't know I'm looking at him through the shutters in our bedroom. As usual, they're barely open when I spy. There's something I find nostalgically sexy about watching my husband on the sly. It takes me back to the way I watched him before I knew him—before I ever spoke a single word to him. I did some extremely childish things to make him fall in love with me—the most childish, of course, was pretending to be someone I wasn't. Consequently, we both suffered because of that foolishness, and so much more foolish behavior on my part after that, and I almost lost him…forever. But even when I thought he was completely out of my life, he was always in the background, dreaming about me, longing for me…hoping for some miracle to happen before he felt the pressure to move on with his own life. As I now watch the younger of our two children run into the backyard and playfully squirt him with a water gun, I get another one of those quivers thinking about just how close I came to losing him to that pressure. I'm not kidding, I came about as close as a girl can get to losing a dream dude. But I got lucky for like…the millionth time in my life, and an extraordinary visit to him resulted in an unfathomable roll in the hay. And that unfathomable roll in the hay miraculously produced a baby. And the baby miraculously produced the kind of reconciliation between a man and a woman that only seems to exist in romance novels. Yep, against all odds, the astonishingly forgiving man I'm spying on right now gave me the life I always dreamed of—

the kind of dream life I naively tried to construct on binder paper when I was a dumb sixteen-year-old girl.

Things weren't immediately wonderful after that unfathomable roll in the hay, though. Nope, I still managed to screw up a lot for myself. There were still lots and lots of lies by omission on my part, and there was one big flat-out lie that nearly cost me everything. But in the nick of disparaging time, I became the Chrissy Anderson I was meant to be, and the love of my life was able to put the past behind, and forgive me for the hell I put him through for over five years…and he asked me to marry him one more time. Like I said, he's perfect.

Physically, he hasn't changed much at all since we tied the knot, let alone since the day we met. Watching him effortlessly lift a potted plant that probably weighs more than an automobile, I think, *he's as beautiful as he ever was*. Age has done nothing to curb my attraction for him and the wisdom that fatherhood has brought has only intensified that attraction. For a long time I lived in fear that he wouldn't be able to tolerate the mistakes I made. But the second the ice-cream-stained-water-gun-toting-child popped into our lives quite the opposite occurred. His heart softened. If that metamorphosis didn't happen, we wouldn't have lasted. So I guess you can say, not only has fatherhood intensified my attraction to him, it saved us.

Startled by a heavy-duty squirt of water on the bedroom window, my loud scream blows my cover, and the man whom I fell head-over-heels in love with the moment I laid eyes on him is now laying his eyes on me. The jig is up.

He points to the heat lamp and nods his proud head. Instead of merely offering a thumbs-up to show my praise, I open the window to tease him a little.

"Hey, those things look like they might actually work, Mister!"

The crinkle in his forehead makes its first appearance of the day when he lowers his eyes and fakes despair. As he makes his way over to me, I ask, "Getting excited for tonight?"

"I am, but I'm more excited for what happened last night. Kind of makes me want to postpone this whole shindig and have a do-over."

What we did in bed last night *was* pretty damn spectacular. I won't fool you, though. We can't compete with the red-hot passion we experienced when we were first together. Can any couple who's been together for as long as us? Not likely. But we're not supposed to compete with brand new relationship kind of love-making, it would be almost unnatural. We're older now and our relationship has matured past that. We have kids, and one of them is a teenager who knows exactly what's going on behind a locked master bedroom door. We have job stress and *almost*-middle-aged exhaustion. We have bills to pay, worries about paying them, and sometimes too many cocktails to numb the worry. *We have normalcy.* But it's spectacular normalcy, the kind I dreamt of as a young woman, and feared I'd never have. The kind where we take pleasure in the stability of our marriage and the security in knowing we have each other's back—at all times. Where we have shared dreams that have come true, ones that have been shattered, and ones we're still trying to make happen. And on nights like last night, when both of our kids are at sleepovers, and we're not stressed out, exhausted, or inebriated, normalcy can be pretty damn spectacular.

"Those were some good moves, Mister. You'd think after all this time you wouldn't be able to surprise me like that."

And you wouldn't. Even after all of this time, he's attentive to my needs, and makes me feel like the most beautiful woman alive when we're in bed, and I still try to give him in return everything he gives to me. But it wasn't like that immediately after we reconciled, and not because we had a newborn and a five year old who exhausted us. There was understanding what transpired when we were apart, forgiveness, and needing to feel safe within the relationship; these needed to happen before there could be the kind of love-making that happened last night. Surprisingly...not by him, by me. I know, I know...given what I put the man through, one might find that incredibly hard to understand. And trust me, there was once a period in my life where I'd painstakingly try to explain it to people I care about because I needed their approval. But I don't live my life by others expectations anymore. The need to do that died right along with my best friend…and I've been mastering the technique ever since.

"You okay? Seems like I lost you there for a minute."

"Oh, I'm okay. Just wrapped up another awkward video moment with Kendall, that's all."

No need to tell him I'm also stressed out about the surprise I have planned for tonight.

He speaks tenderly, choosing his words carefully because he knows it's a sensitive subject.

"Maybe it's time…you know, to put them away for good."

His heart's in the right place and so is Kendall's. If it were anyone other than Kelly's dying wish, I'd even agree with both of them and tape the damn box up for the attic. But, it's Kelly…who up until that dying wish *never* asked me for a damn thing in her life. It's really, really hard not to fulfill the obligation and show Kendall every single video her mother made for her.

Annnd, there's that word again—obligation. Obligation haunted me for so many years of my life—damn near prevented me from being the woman I was meant to be. Damn near turned me into Francesca from *The Bridges of Madison County*! But with the help of my lovely old therapist, Dr. Maria, I learned how to kick obligation's ass. And I can honestly say obligation left my life, and in no way, shape, or form has it returned in the same heart-wrenching manner in which it previously existed in my life. Except for once a year, on this day, when I have to pop in a stupid video.

Now standing on the other side of the bedroom window, my husband places his hand on the screen. I reciprocate with mine so that I can feel his touch. It is tender gestures like this that I hope my children notice and seek out in their future love lives.

14

"I just don't want you guys to get hurt. Seems like that's all those videos have done, for what...four years now?"

"Yeah, they're getting pretty bad. Kelly's giving them all she's got, but she's struggling," I pause to take a deep breath before continuing, "I wonder if it's fair to make Kendall watch someone she doesn't even know suffer."

"Not if she doesn't want to. I know it's hard, but she's not a baby anymore, and we have to respect her opinion on this. Sure, you made a promise to Kelly, but if anyone has the right to break it, it's Kendall. You know that Kelly would never hold that against you."

"Maybe you're right. We'll talk about it later." Pointing behind him, "Someone's coming up from the rear. WATCH OUT!"

Smudgy runs up and starts squirting the water gun like a crazy person—or a kid who just ate a gallon of chocolate ice cream. Then the two of them run off to the garden where I assume there will be some sort of retaliation with the hose.

Left alone at the screen, I take in the magnificence of my younger child as she runs off. I can't help but think of the hard, distinct, and LONG overdue line Smudgy drew into my life. Almost every day since I gave birth, I've been calm in the present...I've lived and loved in the moment, and I've tried very hard not to question my past or get dragged back into it. But because of the wrench I'm throwing into today's festivities, it's hard for my mind not to get dragged into the past.

It's been so many years since we've seen him. All of our lives have changed, and for the better. Several times over the last few weeks I've questioned the decision to disturb what my husband and I have going on right now, and I've been beating myself up for opening a can of worms that's been harmoniously sealed shut for ten years. And I wonder, am I righting a wrong or wronging a right by inviting him back into our lives? With the clock now ticking down the time until his arrival, I still don't know the answer to that question, and it has my stomach in knots. We're living a fantastic life, and from what he told me on

15

the phone, he is too. After all of these years, it was surreal to hear his voice and I was shocked that, while a little apprehensive at first, he was pleasant and open to the idea of coming to my home this evening. And several times since I've heard his voice, my mind has drifted back to a time that was exciting, terrifying, intense, and chaotic—wondering all the while if the drifting is counter-productive to the spectacular normalcy I've worked so hard to have.

I've been feeling sick to my stomach for keeping the first secret in ten years from my husband. But I had to. He NEVER would've signed off on who's planning to ring the doorbell in five hours. Turning back to the mirror that I walked away from just minutes ago, I stare at myself and think, *and I can hardly believe the person who's planning on ringing the doorbell agreed to ring it.* Not after what happened all those years ago. Yep, because of my soon to be unleashed Chrissygan, it's definitely hard not to get dragged back into the past, and as Smudgy skips into my view with a handful of white roses just clipped from the garden...that's exactly where I get dragged for the millionth time this week.

Past (adjective)

Of, having existed in, or having occurred during a time previous to the present.

Near to you, I am healin'
But it is takin' so long
Cause though he's gone and you are wonderful
It's hard to move on
("Near To You," *A Fine Frenzy*)

Freefall

April, 2003

Leo can't see what I see, which is a stunned Kurt, standing motionless behind the glass door of the meditation room. His back is to everything I'm forced to look at. His green eyes and strong hands are fixated on the wonderment of my pregnant belly. After the initial shock of seeing me in this condition wears off, he pulls my different-than-he's-ever-seen-it body up from the meditation room floor, and says the words I've imagined hearing him say since the moment I met him.

"I'm gonna be...*a dad?*"

I came into work today with the expectation that Kurt would be the only man from my past to make an appearance. He's back from his trip to Nepal where he went with Megan to do God-knows-what for God-knows-how-long. I lost track. Needing more understanding of the phone call he made from Kathmandu—the phone call in which he confirmed we slept together—I asked Kurt to come to the studio at ten o'clock this morning. Granted, the phone reception during that call was so fuzzy it seemed like we were talking through two cans tied together with a string, but I heard what I heard...and it wasn't good news for me. In fact, it was so God-awful to hear Kurt say, "The baby's mine, I'm sorry I didn't tell you sooner" that I farted, fainted, and ended up in the emergency room. And for thirty days since that phone call, Kurt's words have been all I can think about. So last night, when I got an email from Megan

19

telling me they were back home, and a bunch of other stuff I ignored, I promptly drafted my own email to Kurt asking to see him right away.

I arranged the meeting to take place here, at my yoga studio, and I planned to tell Kurt I slept with Leo two weeks after our trip down memory lane. And as disgusting as it sounds, I planned to ask him to submit to a paternity test so that I could rule him out as the father of my baby…at long, long, long last making me trashy *Jerry Springer Show* material. When I entered the studio this morning I was calm, and I intended to remain that way during my conversation with Kurt. And I also decided, no matter what the outcome of that test, I would remain calm for the duration of my pregnancy…and my life for that matter. And to kick off that promise, I arrived to my yoga studio early to take one of Slutty Co-workers classes. But surprisingly she was nowhere to be found. Just as surprising, Barbara, the woman I've come to rely so heavily on for sane advice, business and otherwise, was M.I.A. too.

To kill time until my big Jerry Springer moment, I settled into a relaxation pose in one of the cathartic, water fountain-filled meditation rooms for some calm. But fifteen minutes ago, all plans to stay calm were squashed when Slutty Co-worker barreled into the meditation room to tell me that Leo, whom I haven't seen for seven months, was waiting for me (courtesy of her meddling self) in the lobby. And ten minutes ago, calm was clinging on to dear life when the both of us heard Kurt's car pull into the back parking lot. And five minutes ago, calm was nowhere to be found when Leo entered the meditation room to find out what Slutty Co-worker deemed so vital that he had traveled all the way from New York to see with his own eyes. And three minutes ago, calm was completely taken over by panic when he saw my seven month pregnant belly, seemingly figured it out, and asked me if he was the father. And one minute ago, panic turned into insanity as I succumbed to a massive Leo-love-drug overdose and said whatever I had to say to keep him here with me, which was "Yes." And five seconds ago, insanity became sheer terror when I saw Kurt round the corner to the meditation room and come to an abrupt halt. Then, as if in slow motion, I watched the seven white roses he was carrying drop out of his grip and to the ground, as his eyes squarely focused on the man he was not at all prepared to see.

Leo, in obvious shock from the news I just gave him, moves closer to me now and asks, "Why didn't you tell me sooner we were having a baby, Chrissy? I never would've...things could've..."

Then he moves even closer and rests his forehead on mine. The familiar scent of his citrusy masculine cologne washes over me like a drug-laced waterfall. It causes my eyes to drowsily fall shut, and I totally forget about the man on the other side of the door. For a second, I get the sensation Leo's about to kiss me, and I tilt my head slightly in preparation for it. Instead his lips glide past my own and settle against my neck. When he speaks I can feel the warmth of his breath as his lips brush up against my skin.

"Jesus, I missed so much of this. Why on earth did you keep this from me?"

Is he really standing in front of me right now? Is it really his hopeful voice asking me these questions? I'm stunned that any of this is even possible. He met another woman. His best friend told me he's in love with her. My God, I even saw her long brown hair with my own blue eyes at that restaurant in February. He looked like he had moved on. I convinced myself he had. *And now this?*

"Chrissy, please, I have to know. Why did you keep this from me?"

My eyes open and gaze subtly over Leo's left shoulder to find Kurt still standing there...frozen. My heart begins to beat as loud as a college marching band. I can only imagine the horrible damage it's doing to my unborn child's ear drums.

"I...I...I was scared, Leo. There's the Kendall stuff, and Kurt still having a role in my life because of her. I knew how much it bothered you. I mean, the last time I saw you at your loft

21

in New York your exact words were, 'I'm not *that* guy, Chrissy. I'm not someone who can share the scene with your ex-husband.' You asked me to set you free. I guess I was just trying to give you what you wanted."

He looks like my Leo—the same intense man I fell in love with and left, along with my engagement ring, in his New York loft after we made love for what I truly believed was the last time ever. There was love that day and ironically almost more than we had ever given to each other before. I remember he was wary of being intimate with me at first. He felt it was counter-productive to getting over me. But I convinced him it was the closure I needed to move on, and he surrendered. Everything we did that day was tender and slow and accompanied by long gazes into each other's eyes. We were apologetic and full of heartache and wishing we could go back in time and do things differently. There were moments we felt meant to be…followed by the tragic realization that we weren't. And when we were done and he fell fast asleep, I left him…unknowingly taking his baby with me. Yes, regardless of the death stare Kurt's giving me right now, I stand by intuition. With all of my heart, I know this baby is Leo's.

"Chrissy, you thought his visitation with Kendall would bother me so much that I wouldn't want to be a part of my own child's life?"

"It's just that…it's just that he'll always be close by."

Looking over his shoulder again and into Kurt's piercing eyes, I silently freak…*and he's a lot closer than you think.*

This is a nightmare. And I have Slutty Co-worker to thank for it. I mean, dammit, if I just could've had the conversation I planned on having with Kurt when I asked him to come here today…if I just could've confirmed my intuition with the paternity test *and then* reached out to Leo…none of this would be happening! I wouldn't be getting a death stare from the other side of the glass door, or a quizzical one on this side. Things would be calm! I don't care if that woman has been my closest companion, and most reliable confidant, for as long as I've

22

known Leo, I don't think I can ever forgive her for this nightmare. She screwed with my plan...my quest for calm. She's so fired. No, more than that, she's dead to me!

Clearly angry at himself for the things he said to me in New York all of those months ago, Leo shakes his head in shame and his voice cracks when he says, "I'm so sorry I acted like such a fool. I should've dug deeper to get over my jealousies. I love you and I never stopped loving you. And I love Kendall, too. It's been *killing* me that after everything she already went through with her parents, I deserted her like that. I guess I thought it would be better for everyone if I backed away. But I was wrong and I know that now. I had everything I ever wanted and I threw it all away because of...because of your fucking ex-husband."

Dropping down on his knees to get even closer to my stomach, he then gently places his hands on my tummy, looks up at me, and confesses, "I guess I had to touch my future to realize how foolish it was to let your past get in the way. But I realize it now, Chrissy." And then resting his forehead on my large belly he whispers, "Please tell me you believe me."

With Leo on his knees, Kurt's in my direct line of vision. His eyes are now off of Leo and set firmly on me. He's not budging. Clearly there's no way he's leaving here without taking everything he thinks is his.

There's no way out of this. With my eyes not leaving Kurt's, I slowly nod and concede to myself that there won't be a happily-ever-after ending to this nightmare moment. I won't be getting away with the deplorable betrayal I just tried to pull over on Leo when I impetuously told him the baby was his. I won't be able to get quiet confirmation from a paternity test of what I know to be true. There is no avoiding the shame of the last seven months, and mostly, the last seven minutes. Nope, the plan I had when I walked into the studio this morning—to find the answers I needed to avoid chaos—is blown to smithereens, and probably right along with any chance of a future with the man kneeling before me.

The time has finally come to tell Leo the truth about the night I spent at my ex-husband's house, and the truth about what I've really been worrying about for the last seven months. Then right after that I have to get down on *my* knees, beg for forgiveness, and hope to God he can give it right back to me one…more…time.

Tit for Tat

April, 2003

So dumbass, how the hell is this going to go down?

For starters, you're going to do what you should've done seven months ago when you found out about this baby. You're going to channel Dr. Maria's words of wisdom, and follow your heart. When you do, the pieces of your life fall into place.

My heart? My heart is telling me to grab Leo's hand, jump over that water fountain, bust through that glass window, and make a run for it.

Don't be stupid. You have to just calmly tell him the truth.

So what you're saying is after every beautiful thing Leo *just* confessed to me, I'm supposed to tell him I made a stupid mistake by getting drunk with Kurt, ended up in his bed with no pants on, and have been living in fear for seven months that I might've cheated on him? And I'm supposed to tell him Kurt confirmed that fear in a phone call from Kathmandu? *I'm supposed to tell him that this baby might be Kurt's?*

Yep, that's it! Tell him that! Rip the damn Band-Aid off of your life and tell him now, Chrissy!

Oh sure, no problem. And while I'm at it, should I also tell him Kurt's standing right behind him, or should I save that little nugget of information for phase two of RUINING LEO'S FUCKING LIFE?

My baby suddenly gives me a hard kick, interrupting my internal Good-Chrissy/Bad-Chrissy tirade. And the tapping inside of my stomach persists right along with the agony about the secret I've been keeping for seven months and am now forced to reveal. A few minutes ago, I thought I was insane when I told Leo for a fact this baby was his, but I'm certifiable if

25

I think for one second his truly, madly, deeply heart will ever forgive me for the deplorable deception I just tried to pull over on him. And with that thought, the tapping in my tummy turns into mild cramping.

"Leo...there's something I have to—"

Still sweetly kneeling in front of me, he looks up and interrupts.

"Hold on. If it's about Kendall, she'll never know I had a problem with Kurt. And for her sake, I'll never have one with him going forward."

That's the first time I've ever heard him say my ex-husband's name out loud. Jesus, he really means everything he's saying. He wants me back. He wants to be a family. He actually wants shared dreams with me again. I hate me so hard right now.

"I swear to God, Chrissy, I'll make everything up to the both of you. I've missed so much already and—"

"No, it's not that, it's—"

Slowly rising from his knees, he worriedly asks, "It's Lauren, isn't it?"

Oh God, 'L,' with the long brown hair. I *never* wanted to know her name. First Kurt's here and now I get hit with this friggin' name bomb. This is NOT my day.

"...She was a stupid mistake, Chrissy. After we broke up, I couldn't get you out of my mind and she was just a distraction that spiraled out of control."

Awww yes, a destructive distraction. I'm familiar with those. In fact, one of them is staring at me outside of a glass door right now.

"But I can fix it, Chrissy. I mean, I was going to anyway. I just needed to find the right words. I'm just glad I got the email last night and I'm here right now before it became a bigger mess to clean up."

Forgetting that *my* destructive distraction could very well walk through the glass door at any minute and make things a whole lot worse for me than they already are, I turn all attention to Leo and the ambiguity of what's coming out of his mouth.

26

"What mess? I mean, if you're talking about moving in with Lauren…" I take a few deep cleansing breaths to keep myself from throwing up after saying her name before I continue with, "…I already knew that was happening. Taddeo told me."

"Wait, you talked to Taddeo?"

"Yes."

"*When?*"

"I called him about five weeks ago, after I saw you at that restaurant. He told me that you were moving in with her. I sort of assumed it already happened."

"And that's *all* he told you?"

"Isn't that enough?"

All of a sudden his mind is racing even faster than it was when he saw my stomach. He takes one tentative step away from me and speaks uncomfortably slow when he admits, "Actually, she wanted me to move in with her, but it hasn't happened yet."

Holding back large chunks of the pancake I ate this morning at the thought of him snuggling up next to her in bed, I forge on with my questions. I mean seriously, how much worse can this moment possibly get? My ex-husband/potential baby daddy is throwing eye-daggers at me from the other side of the glass door, and my ex-fiancé/potential baby daddy just told me he's about to shack up with another woman. Might as well suck it up and get all of the facts. There's no way things can get any worse!

"I don't understand. If you're not living with her, then what mess are you talking about cleaning up?"

He speaks even slower than before, like he's delaying some kind of horrible inevitable truth.

"For some reason…I thought you might've already known."

Unlike him, I *don't* speak slowly. In fact, I talk like I'm hopped up on caffeine, paranoia, and hormones when I blurt out, "How would I know anything about your life, Leo?"

"I thought Megan might've…I mean, I know she's given you updates about me before and…"

In conjunction with another sudden sharp shooting pain in my stomach, I bark back, "Megan's been in Nepal for…for…for fucking ever! Just tell me already, Leo, what mess do you have to clean up?"

I was so unbearably wrong a few seconds ago. Things are about to get a million times worse than I ever could have imagined. And the cramping that's been building in my belly intensifies as I conceive in my mind the exact words he's about to speak.

"Chrissy, I'm so sorry. You have to believe me, it was all a big misunderstanding. I never wanted to marry—"

Grabbing my stomach because the pain is getting more and more excruciating with every word that comes out of his mouth, I cut him off mid-sentence.

"STOP! Don't tell me what I think you're about to tell me! I mean it, Leo! Do NOT tell me one more word!"

Restlessly running his fingers through his jet black hair, he squeezes his eyes closed, and agonizingly mumbles, "Fuck me. I can't believe this is happening."

My eyes are wide open and pleading, *don't say the words, don't say the words, don't say the words*, and he doesn't until I can't help from apprehensively and breathlessly begging in disbelief, "Please tell me you didn't...*Leo?*"

Shaking his head in defiance of the reality of what he must admit, he finally opens his now watery eyes and confesses, "I'm engaged."

I take a step away from him as I comprehend more than just the engagement.

"That's why you didn't kiss me when you first walked in here—when your lips brushed past mine and landed on my neck. You won't cheat on her."

And he wouldn't. He's just that loyal. He has just that much integrity. I hate Slutty—NO! I hate The-Woman-Who-Is-Now-Dead-To-Me for inviting him here and reminding me of how wonderful he is and how close he once became to being *my* husband—not L's. Indeed, The-Woman-Who-Is-Now-Dead-To-Me, who will hereby be referred to as TWWINDTM, is most *definitely* dead to me!

"Chrissy, I have to fix it first. She doesn't—"

"She doesn't what, Leo? She doesn't deserve what I did to Kurt? She doesn't deserve to 'go out of business' because she's been 'taking care of business' since she met you? I mean, that is your motto I'm paraphrasing, right? You know, the one you so proudly proclaimed when I was having an affair with you!"

Vomit is literally making its way up my throat at the thought of her 'doing business' on his body.

"No, that's not what I mean."

"Please. You never lied to me before, don't start now."

It's quiet for a long time, long enough for me to totally forget about Kurt on the other side of the door.

"I'm not lying to you. It's a huge fucking mess, but I'm gonna fix it, and then we're gonna fix us. We're gonna have everything we always talked about going all the way back to that barstool at Buckley's. You, me, Kendall...and now this baby are gonna have everything we ever dreamed of."

Now in a daze, I whisper, "But you fell in love with her."

"No! Chrissy, listen to me! I was just pissed about what happened with us...everything I thought was good fell apart, and for the millionth time! But the engagement was an accident, and I can clean it up. I promise you."

"But you loved her enough to ask her to marry you."

"No! I love you!"

Head is spinning. Cramping is tightening. Heart is breaking. Voice is softening.

"If this baby didn't exist, you were gonna marry her."

In my Chrissy-world, full of Chrissygans, Chrissy-doubt, and Chrissy-fuck-ups, where everything is a mess all of the Chrissy-time, there's only one thing I know for sure, and I tell him what it is.

"I can never be with you knowing that."

And I can't. All of those hallucinations that have been haunting me ever since I saw the two of them canoodling at that restaurant in Lafayette...*they all happened*. His lips have been all over her. He buried his face in her hair and he did with his body all of the delightful things he used to do to me. His eyes looked passionately into hers as his deep voice whispered over and over again, "I'm never letting you go." And most sickening is that her dreams magically aligned with his. All of it had to have happened. He never would've asked her to marry him otherwise.

"No, Chrissy, she has nothing to do with how I feel about you! I'm the fool here! *Don't you see that?*"

"I can't see anything."

And I mean that, literally. The cramping is so bad now that it's making everything blurry.

Grabbing my shoulders, Leo jolts my body causing my hazy eyes to snap wide open and align with his fiery ones.

"SEE ME! SEE THAT I'M STANDING HERE RIGHT NOW...BEGGING YOU TO FORGIVE ME! SEE THAT I'M IN LOVE WITH YOU AND I WANT BACK EVERYTHING I FOOLISHLY THREW AWAY! SEE IT, CHRISSY, BECAUSE IT'S ALL HERE...STANDING IN FRONT OF YOU RIGHT NOW!"

Hearing Leo yell causes Kurt to explode through the door and rush him like a wild Papa-bear protecting his beloved Mama-bear...and the cub he thinks is his.

Mayhem

April, 2003

I knew it was about to happen. I mean, how could it not? Papa-Bear was in murder-stance from a distance for the last ten minutes as he watched protectively over those he thinks are his family. And Leo was doing the exact same thing but from a closer position. They were bound to attack each other. They were bound to try and protect what each of them thinks is theirs.

Just like at Craig's memorial when the two went at it, I close my eyes and press my hands to my ears to block out the noise. This time though, I don't scream to make them stop. The pain that's been building in my stomach will only intensify if I do that.

Right before I closed my eyes though, I saw Kurt bash through the door, his shoulder leading the way, and I heard the collective gasp of about fifty well-paying yoga patrons from down the hall when it happened. My eyes quickly went from that scene to Leo's stunned face, which didn't stay stunned for long. In the blink of an eye, he also turned into a crazed animal, one resembling a Papa-Lion, protecting his pride. Everything went dark for me the instant they punched each other in the face. I felt the floor vibrate and I heard powerful muffled voices. But I couldn't open my eyes. Even though I have a lot more weight on me now to stand in the way of their destructive path, it's weight that needs protecting, not exposure to violence. So I stood still, silent and blind until the powerful muffled voices came to an end—terminated by a very shrill domineering one.

"GET THE FUCK OFF OF EACH OTHER!" Separating Bear from Lion, TWWINDTM barks like a hyena as she

31

continues to scream, "For God's sake, get a hold of yourselves! Do you boys want her to give birth right here and now?"

I swear, it feels like I'm in *Mutual of Omaha's Wild Kingdom*.

Sensing the end of the mayhem, I open my eyes to take in the carnage of Kurt and Leo's rage. Unlike Craig's memorial, no draw this time. Lion kicked Bear's ass. Frantically, I rush to Bear's side.

"Oh my God, Kurt! Are you okay?"

Then, turning to whom I once thought was the love of my life, I scream, *"Are you fucking insane?"* so viciously it must seem like he's the hate of my life...knowing full well my words and my tone would be different if he didn't just tell me he was engaged.

All Leo does is spit blood on the floor and stare me down as he tries to catch his breath.

Then I join the gang in *Wild Kingdom* when I morph into the most feared animal in all the world—the honey badger—and lock eyes with TWWINDTM.

Clenching my fists and my jaw, I snarl, "See what your meddling caused? Why couldn't you just mind your own damn business...let me figure this out on my own?"

"Hunny, I was only trying to help. How was I supposed to know you invited..." pointing to Kurt on the ground, "...this one here last night?"

"You weren't. You wanna know why? BECAUSE IT'S MY GOD DAMN LIFE!"

Hitting her limit with my theatrics she retaliates with, "Oh yeah? Well, look at your stomach Chrissy...and look at his fucking face and his fucking hands...how's that life working out for you?"

She's right. TWWINDTM is right. It's not working out for me, and I'm reminded by the cramping in my stomach and the battered men in the room that the clock is running out on hoping my life, and more specifically, my baby-daddy debacle, will magically work itself out. Still though, I say nothing. Other than

32

the animalistic heavy breathing all around me, the room stays quiet until TWWINDTM starts to meddle again. I'd get mad at her interference, but truthfully I've got nothin' to say. So I just stand in shocked silence as she takes hold of Kurt's arm and nudges him to walk away with her, encouraging him to give me and Leo some space. But he's not having any of it.

"*Space?* She doesn't need space! She needs my help."

Confused she barks back, "What the hell are you talking about? What about what you just told me in the lobby?"

But both men ignore her questions.

Leo, incensed at Kurt's audacity to stick close by me, tightens his grip when he talks.

"You actually still think you have a chance? Look at her! We're having a baby, Man!"

Ignoring Leo, partially because I think he knows it'll annoy him; Kurt looks at me and says, "I should've called you sooner to explain everything. It was selfish of me not to."

Wait, selfish because he knew he was screwing with my head or selfish because he thought I was possibly pregnant with his child this whole time and chose to ignore it? Which one, dammit? It has to be the first one! It just has to be! Oh my God, I feel like I'm gonna pass out. I feel like...Oh, no...no, no, no, no, no! I feel a little...gassy. Shit, shit, shit. NO! Don't shit! Do NOT shit your pants Chrissy!

Noticing my wobbling body, both men take a step closer to me and simultaneously express their concern with, "Chrissy, are you okay?"

That's all Leo's patience can take. He shoves Kurt in the chest and demands him to back away from me.

Kurt shoves him back and warns, "Don't fucking touch me, Man. You have no idea why I'm here."

Oh, God...there's the monkey. The same monkey I always see when I'm about to faint. His sadistic symbols are banging, and they're getting louder by the minute. I can barely hear Leo when he begins to talk again.

"Tell me then, Asshole! *Why are you here?* Seriously...I'm back in her life for five minutes and SURPRISE, you are too. When's this shit gonna stop?"

"Just get the hell out of here so I can talk to her alone."

Thirsty. I need...water. The monkey...so loud.

"What makes you think she even wants to talk to you? She divorced you. Or don't you remember that?"

"I don't have to explain anything to you."

Now back in Kurt's face, Leo warns, "I think you do."

TWWINDTM jumps in between them again and scolds "Shut the fuck up, the both of you. Can't you see what this is doing to her?" Now turning to me, "Hunny, are you okay? You don't look so good."

Swallowing hard to try and find a drop of moisture in my mouth, I roll my head up and reprimand her.

"I told you I wanted calm in my life. And I was about to have it. Now look what you did."

"Hunny, please don't be mad at me. Everything's gonna be okay now." Then she lowers her voice, but not so inconspicuously whispers, "He told me...Kurt told me."

Turning his attention away from my ex-husband, Leo demands, *"He told you what?"*

Before I can get my wits about me to shut her meddling-ass up, she blurts out, "There's no way the baby is his." Then she turns back to me and says, "Did you hear me, Chrissy? You didn't sleep with Kurt! It's all out in the open!"

I want to feel relief. No, I want to feel joy at that news, but there's none to be found as Leo's homicidal eyes slowly lock with my dizzy ones. And after what seems like silence forever as he processes the truth of what I've really been struggling with for the last seven months, I turn to TWWINDTM and bitterly chastise, "No, Dumbass. *Now* everything's out in the open."

Whatever focus I have left shifts back to Leo, where I internally scramble to come up with some kind of explanation for what was just revealed, but before I can think of one, he's literally in my face.

"Is this really something you needed confirmation of, Chrissy?"

I've got nothin' but extreme cramps to offer him, so I keep my mouth shut.

"So the truth is you've been keeping this baby…*my baby*, a secret because of what *you* did. Or, as I guess we're all finding out now…what you *didn't* do?"

"But Leo, I—"

"But nothing, Chrissy! Ten minutes ago you tried to make me think I didn't know about this baby because of something *I* did…because of the things *I* said to you in New York about not wanting to share a life with your ex-husband. But this whole time…*for seven months,* it was really because you thought you fucked him."

At a loss for words, I begin to look for help from Kurt and TWWINDTM, but they just lower their eyes to the ground. The move makes me feel like an even bigger piece of shit. It's uncomfortably quiet for a long time, before I take a cautious step toward Leo to say something…anything to fix the damage I've done, but when I do, he takes a giant step back.

"I just need to understand one other thing. Did you just tell me this baby was mine even though you didn't know for sure it was until…*five seconds ago?*"

Finally ripping off one very old, very dirty, and very adhered Band-Aid off of my life, I nod my head in deplorable shame.

With more sadness than I've ever seen in Leo's eyes, he repulsively wonders out loud, *"Who does that?"* Then he turns and walks out of the meditation room, but not before bashing into Kurt's shoulder, nearly knocking him back to the ground.

Faster than my queasy body can handle, I whirl around to try and tell him, "Someone who follows her heart" but the words fizzle out as soon as I begin to say them.

Something's seriously wrong with me…and not just mentally. Something is very wrong with me physically and I have to let Leo go right now to take care of it. I reach out to

Kurt, because TWWINDTM is, well, dead to me, and cry, "I need…water. Everything's blurry…"

Just then Megan and Barbara, who must've seen Leo storm out of the building, come running into the meditation-room-turned-*Jerry Springer Show*. Barbara's eyes immediately zoom in on my mid-section and as they travel lower she screams, "Oh my God, someone call 911! SHE'S BLEEDING!"

Haggling

April, 2003

Dear Lord Jesus, who I wish so badly I believed in so that you could comfort me, please let my baby be okay. This baby is the something good to come out of something deplorable. This baby is my redemption from past pain and mistakes. I need this baby. Kendall needs this baby. This baby is my family…This baby is my hope.

Shocker. There's no answer from Lord Jesus, or whoever the F is calling the shots up there, only the encouraging sound of a tiny heartbeat emitting from one of the machines I'm hooked up to. *Or, maybe that sound is the answer.* I have no idea how all that metaphysical religious shit works. I guess you have to be a true believer to understand.

I'm alone in my hospital room. Being alone is something I have actually gotten used to over the last month. After Kurt called me from Nepal, my focus became all about Kendall and the baby. I also became sort of resigned to the fact that I had officially become some kind of mutant strain of Francesca—the tragic woman from *Bridges of Madison County* who found the love of her life but let him go out of obligation to her family. The woman I tried so hard not to become but always felt a little fucked-up kinship with. Yep, before this morning I was actually living quite peacefully. Aside from obsessing about Leo and his new girlfriend, Kendall and I had settled into a nice little routine. The yoga studios were thriving. My household was manageable. Life was strangely calm. Obviously, I would've rather not been alone for the last seven months. I would've rather been with Leo, living out our shared dreams, but that didn't happen…

Leo was supposed to become my husband this past September. The west coast division of T.L. Capital that he'd been working on tirelessly had finally opened, and he was supposed to have moved back from New York and into the home we bought together in Lafayette. We planned to raise Kendall there.

Rubbing my stomach, I sigh, "And all of the other kids we planned on having one day."

But none of that stuff happened because of that stupid night at Kurt's house last August when I decided to take a drunken trip down memory lane—a drunken trip that resulted in a shared bed with no pants on, and the likelihood of an overly-intoxicated-mercy-fuck with my ex-husband that I never had the guts to substantiate. Nevertheless, without knowing for sure what transpired in Kurt's bed that night, I ran to Leo and begged him to believe me that nothing happened. Miraculously he did, but unfortunately it was the last straw in our chaotic and convoluted love-story. That drunken trip down memory lane paved the way for Leo to tell me he'd never be okay with Kurt in the picture. And since I can't cut Kurt out of the picture because of the visitation he was awarded with Kendall, it meant the end of the road for me and Leo. So we made love one last time, I left my engagement ring on his nightstand, and walked away—destined to live my life without a man because no one would ever be able to take his place. Then, a few weeks later, I found out I was pregnant. And ever since I found out I was pregnant, I've lacked the balls needed to determine who the father was. I know, I know, it seems incomprehensible that I'd procrastinate on something so huge. But I had two really good reasons why I was so scared to find out who the father was...

I moved giant mountains of fear and shame to end my relationship with Kurt so that I could start a new one with Leo, and the idea that it might've been all for nothing was too much to bear. To ask Kurt what really happened in his bed that night might have revealed I cheated on Leo...*my honorable, loving, adoring Leo.* The thought of coming so close to having everything I ever wanted and throwing it away with reckless abandon like that made me sick with disgrace. And so that's why I could never bring myself to ask Kurt what really happened that night. That's why I never found out if the baby might be his.

To make the procrastination worse, Leo had already ended things with me and he made it perfectly clear we were over. I think his exact words were, "My love for you fucks me up." To find out the baby was his would've meant forcing him to live a life with me in it, a life he told me he no longer wanted…a life that fucks him up. The thought of forcing Leo to have a relationship with me made me feel overwhelmingly guilty. So, you see? No matter who the father was, it was a no-win situation. So I procrastinated on finding out. Obviously, at some point, shit was going to hit the fan and the father of my child was going to be revealed. I just hoped…I just hoped…Shit, I have no idea what the hell I was hoping for. All I know is, it wasn't what just happened.

I got to the hospital about three hours ago. I don't remember much about the ambulance ride or the minutes before I tumbled to the ground. I do remember telling Leo the baby was his and for a minute everything became dreamlike and idyllic. With one word, "yes," I went from being a single mother of two, to becoming Cinderella. No wait, it was more like I became Julia Roberts in Pretty Woman. (I'm more of a whore who was given a fairytale life than a loveable fairytale character given a fairytale life.) I remember Leo told me he loved me…that he never stopped. Instantly all of the scary fears I had about forcing him to live a less than desirable life with me in it floated away. But I also remember Kurt appeared with a bunch of white roses and my minute-long fairytale life came to a screeching halt. I remember being very mad at Slutty Co-worker for ripping the calm right out from under me, and I remember Kurt and Leo getting mad at each other…there were vicious punches. I remember getting dizzy, and then I remember seeing the symbol-banging monkey, and getting scared, very scared. But then, mercifully, I remember being told *I never...slept...with Kurt.*

Wrapping my arms around my tummy, I say, "But, you already knew that, didn't you?"

But mostly I remember the blood. When Barbara pointed to it, it was difficult to understand why no one in the room had noticed it sooner. I had on light grey yoga leggings and the dark red fluid had made its way about four inches down my inner thighs. I remember a loud scream, it could've been mine or maybe it wasn't. And then finally, I remember Kurt catching me as I fell to the ground...the monkey deliriously laughing, his huge symbols banging, the predictable fart exploding, the room blackening.

Now here I am in the hospital (which, pathetically, is the second time in the last thirty days I've been here due to a farting and fainting spell), wondering what's going on with my unborn child...Wondering what's going in Leo's mind now that he knows the real reason I kept it from him. Now I know why none of us had noticed the blood sooner, we were too busy noticing Leo abruptly disappear from my life...once again.

It remains quiet for a very long time—just me and my remembering. I've toyed with the idea of pressing the button to summon the nurse, but resisted for fear of hearing bad news. So I just lay with all of my remembering and the hopeful sound of my baby's heartbeat. But just now my thoughts are interrupted by the soft creaking sound of the door opening. I do what brought me calm the last time I was alone and interrupted— when Leo entered the meditation room—I close my eyes.

"Chrissy?"

You.

"We need to talk."

Bad, bad things happen when there's exposure to you. I can't talk to you. Shit, I can barely look at you. Eyes are staying closed—tight.

"Okay, it's obvious you have nothing to say, so I'll do all of the talking."

I hear him place what sounds like a bouquet of flowers, perhaps the ones he brought earlier to the studio, on the table next to me and then settle into the chair by the side of the bed. It's quiet for a long time before he speaks.

"The doctors won't tell me what's going on with you. You know...because I'm not family."

It's quiet again for a few seconds before he continues with, "That's still settling in, you know...that we're not family. I should've realized it by now, but I haven't. I guess that explains why I'm here."

My eyes are still closed...The baby's heartbeat is the only sound coming from my body.

"You might find this hard to believe, given the fact you think it's the thing I failed at the most in our relationship, but it feels like I need to protect you."

And now my eyes are wide open.

"Yep, thought that'd get your attention."

I didn't notice it back at the studio because so much was happening at the time, but in the seven months since I last saw him, he's changed dramatically. His crew cut is the same and his eyes are still vibrant and young at heart. His physique is still powerful and prepared for whatever physical challenge lies in his path, (minus Leo's fists, of course). But his behavior is different. I noticed it a little bit the few times I saw him after 9/11, and at his house the night of my drunken trip down memory lane, but I couldn't put my finger on what it was about his behavior that was different, but I can now. What's different about it is, it isn't *indifferent*.

"I can't believe you're pregnant. I mean, I knew you were. Everyone told me...Courtney, Nicole...Megan whenever she dropped Kendall off at my house when you were avoiding me. But to see it for my own eyes a few hours ago, it really blew my mind. But you know what blows my mind more than that?"

"What?"

41

"Well, for starters, that you actually thought we slept together. C'mon Chrissy, you were drunk. You know me better than that."

I do. *How could I have doubted him?*

"But what blows my mind even more than that, is you actually thought I'd run away from a baby you thought that I thought could've been mine. Man, I must've been a really shitty husband to have made you think that."

Realizing the enormity of how much I screwed up my life, Leo's life, Kendall's life, and now my baby's life by thinking those ridiculous thoughts, I hang my head low and admit, "No, I'm the shitty one Kurt."

"Nah, you're just a shitty drunk."

And there it is, his million dollar smile, once again appearing at just the right moment to save me from well-deserved shame.

"You definitely waited a lot longer than necessary to find out the truth, but I understand the delay."

"You do?"

"Totally. You fought so hard to get out of our marriage because you didn't want to have kids with me, only to find yourself back in the hot seat. I can only imagine the mental torture you put yourself through."

Now that I'm so far on the outside of his life, he's nothing like the controlling dick I built him up to be. I see him now how everyone else has always seen him...as an endearing man. And as long as the next woman he falls in love with doesn't portray herself to be something she's not just to land him, and then confuse the shit out of him when she suddenly decides to be herself, he has a good chance at being endearing to her too.

"Kurt...I...I don't know what to say. I feel terrible."

"You gotta stop that...that beating yourself up stuff. It's taking over your life."

Not knowing how else to be, I keep my mouth shut.

"You don't remember anything from that night at my house after you found the picture of us from my college graduation, do you?"

42

"I remember there was a kiss—*a really good kiss.*"

My head now hangs even lower because while I may not have slept with Kurt, in truly, madly, deeply Leo-land, the kiss I shared with my ex-husband is *still* a betrayal. Even though the full scope of my betrayal is infinitely smaller than originally feared, it's a betrayal nonetheless, and it's something Leo would never forgive if he ever found out about it. We're doomed on so many levels. With the exception of his engagement, sadly all of the levels were created by me.

"You know why that kiss was so good?"

"Why?"

Before he continues on he clears his throat, which is his usual way of signaling he's uncomfortable.

"Do you remember when that song, 'Only The Lonely' played on the stereo and you sang that part out loud about *kissing altogether wrong* and then made jokes about it?"

"It rings a drunk-bell."

"It bugged me, Chrissy. Not a lot does, but that did. We might've kissed altogether wrong for a lot of years, but we didn't in the beginning...we had good intentions. We wouldn't have gotten married otherwise, right?"

It feels like he needs to be okay with the failure. I get it. I was stuck there for a long time myself. Damn near got the best of me. I never want him to beat himself up like I did. I mean, for a long time I did. I wanted him to beat the shit out of himself for not being the man I needed him to be, but not anymore. He's a wonderful man whom I fell madly in love with as a young girl. None of the crap that happened after I fell madly out of love with him matters anymore, and I don't want it to matter to him either. We never would've gotten married if we had always kissed altogether wrong, and he needs to know that.

"We had great intentions. I loved you more than you'll ever know, Kurt...more than I still think you're able to comprehend, and more than I'll ever be able to understand. I loved you so much that I couldn't even see how wrong we were for each other. I said 'I do' to you with nothing but dreams of growing old together, and I know you did the same. But we grew up and our amazing kisses could no longer mask how wrong we were for each other. There are regrets…a lot of regrets…things I wish I would've realized earlier, done differently…said sooner. And I certainly could've handled myself with more dignity when I realized our kisses had lost their magic..." Placing my hand on top of his, "…But there's no bad guy here, Kurt. We did the best we could with what we knew at the time—going all the way back to when I was sixteen and you were seventeen."

"I'm ready to agree with that. And I was ready to agree with it that night at my house. I guess I kissed you like that because I wanted to end things as good as they started."

Like I wanted to do with Leo in New York…seven months ago.

"But I thought we already had our final kiss, when I brought you home from the hospital after your motorcycle accident, remember?"

"Final for you, maybe. Kayla was a rebound for me, Chrissy. I wasn't ready to move on—at least not with her. And you…well, you were happy with your new life. I guess I still needed the period at the end of our sentence…that final kiss. I guess it couldn't happen until I met the right person, too."

He found her. And it doesn't feel like a punch in the gut anymore. It feels like bittersweet relief.

"Chrissy, I didn't kiss you that night because I was trying to reignite a spark that went out a long time ago. I just wanted to kiss you good-bye the same way you got to kiss me good-bye that day you brought me home from the hospital. I needed you to know how much I really did love you, and you needed to hear it from me, not Dr. Maria. I also wanted you to know I'd never make the same mistakes again."

"Really?"

"Yeah, we were just happy and having a good time talking about stuff we should've talked about years ago. Well, actually I take that back. We were happy and having a good time until you pushed away from the kiss and got pissed at me. I tried to

44

explain why I did it and that I met someone new, and I tried to thank you for my second chance, but you were too far gone. You just grabbed two more bottles of wine and hunkered down in the first bed you could find. You were passed out by the time I found you. I turned on the TV, drank the rest of the wine, and that's all she wrote."

"That's all?"

"That's all. And I told you nothing happened the morning after when you were freaking out."

"But you have to admit, you weren't that convincing about it either."

"I agree. I'm sorry, but there was something kinda satisfying about that guy thinking you cheated on him."

"I suppose I deserve it—all of it."

"Nah, you deserve to be happy. But there's something about you, Chrissy. It's like you're the queen of sabotaging your own happiness. You wanna know why I think that is?"

"Not really."

"Too bad. I think it's because you feel guilty about what happened with us, or rather…your part of what happened to us. But don't feel guilty anymore. I'm the happiest I've ever been."

"Wow. So it's official, huh? You totally moved on?"

"Yep."

"No more guilt, no more calling me a quitter?"

"Nope. And there hasn't been for a really long time. You would've known that if you didn't go into hiding for the last seven months."

"When did all of this happen?"

"At the coffee shop right after 9/11…when I tried to apologize for things I should've apologized for a long time ago. Clearly you had left the past behind, or at least you were trying really hard to. That's when I started to do the same. No, wait. I think it officially-officially happened when I got to punch what's-his-name in the face at Craig's memorial." With a huge smile, he gloats, "That was some good closure."

45

"Why didn't you tell me all of this stuff when you found out I was pregnant? Didn't my friends tell you I was agonizing about possibly cheating on Leo? Or, did you enjoy it?"

He lowers his eyes at me in a give-me-a-break kind of way.

"I'm serious. I can see how you'd want pay back like that after what I did to you."

"Actually, the total opposite."

"What?"

"It's kinda hard to move on when someone you care about is hurting. Made me realize how you must've felt for a long time after we split up. But, Chrissy, I was only doing what you told me to do. Your exact words the morning you bolted out of my house were, 'Never talk to me about our past or tell me about your future, but mostly *never* talk to me about what happened last night.' So that's exactly what I did. The whole time we were together I never gave you the right Christmas gifts, the vacations you wanted to take…the attention you needed. But I finally listened to you, Chrissy. I finally gave you what you asked for…and then I decided to take a sabbatical and go with Megan all the way to Nepal so I didn't have to hear from Courtney and Nicole about how miserable you were. You know me; I don't like the bad stuff."

But he sure did learn how to cope with it since we split up. I mean, look, he's sitting here with me right now.

"Well, can I just tell you your timing sucks? Couldn't you have started listening later?"

Happier than I've seen him in a long time, he smiles and says, "Nah, it was time."

"But wait…what about the phone call from Kathmandu? I heard what I heard!"

"You should've heard me telling you the baby's not mine and I'm sorry I didn't tell you sooner. In fact, I said it three times in a row."

"All I heard was you telling me once that it was yours and that you were sorry you didn't tell me sooner. After that the line went dead."

46

"Weird, because when I finally hung up I even asked Megan if I got my point across, and she didn't think I could've done a better job of putting you out of your misery."

I let out an exasperated sigh when I admit, "Nope…been consistently miserable for some time now. And after what just happened, I don't see things changing anytime soon." Jolting up in my hospital bed, "Hey, if you knew this baby wasn't yours, then why did you bust down the meditation room door like that?"

"I was stopped in the lobby by that freak you work with. She explained you still didn't know what happened at my house that night—that you thought I told you on the phone the baby was mine. Megan and I were both a little shocked. Anyway, she threatened to cut my dick off if I didn't come clean and immediately put everyone out of their misery. I didn't know who 'everyone' was until I walked down the hall. Naturally I was a little shocked to see him. You might be in love with him, and I might've moved on with someone else, but I still hate the guy for what he did. I mean, c'mon, he knew you had a husband the whole time he was—"

"Hold on. To be fair, he thought you were just my fiancé for awhile."

"Okay, one, you're weird…" Then with *almost* Leo-like intensity in his voice, "…and two, I don't wanna know the specifics of any of it, ever. Got that Chrissy?"

"Got it. Sorry."

"Anyway, once I got to the meditation room and saw you pregnant, it was a little hard to walk away. I just wanted to watch you for a while—make sure you were okay. Then when I heard him yell at you, I kind of forgot why I was there and I sprang into action. We might be over, Chrissy, but I'll never let anyone hurt you."

I let out a heavy sigh and slump into my pillow.

"Leo wasn't trying to hurt me. He was begging me to forgive him."

"Forgive *him?*"

47

"I know, right?"

For what?"

"He's engaged to someone else."

"Oh, man. I don't know what to say."

"There's nothing you can say."

"I guess I should've listened to your friends and said something to you sooner. Maybe—"

"No, it's my fault. Everything's my fault. I should've listened to my heart sooner. But maybe like you...and everyone else for that matter, says, maybe I'm queen of sabotaging my own happiness. Maybe I'll always feel some ridiculous need to feel guilty about *something* to the extent that I ruin everything."

"But you never felt like that before you met him."

"Exactly. Maybe meeting him, and my less-than-stellar behavior as a result of meeting him, is the thing that will forever make me feel guilty...insecure..." My voice trails off as I continue with, "...undeserving."

"You gotta get over that. Like I said when our divorce was final, what good is your freedom if you're not gonna use it to go after the things you didn't think you could have with me?"

It's quiet for a long time as Kurt mulls over something that's obviously causing him some internal conflict.

"Remember that call you begged me to make the morning you woke up at my house—the one to what's-his-face telling him nothing happened?"

"Yeah."

"If it'll help, Chrissy, I'll do it for you now. Maybe I can talk him down."

I'm overwhelmed with his sweetness, and semi-resentful that there's some chick out there that's benefitting from all that he learned from our break-up. But I guess in healthy divorce-land that's exactly how it's supposed to be. Maybe we've officially arrived.

"Thanks, but I don't think there's anything anyone can do to fix the damage I've done, not even me. Besides, what is there to fix, really? He's engaged."

"Probably not much I can do about that."

He stands to leave, but not before he kisses the top of my head and says, "For what it's worth, you make a beautiful pregnant woman."

In barely a whisper, I mock, "You know me...it's what's on the outside that counts."

"C'mon now, that's not true. If it were, you'd still be married to me. You're all heart; don't let anyone ever convince you otherwise. Got that?"

Squeezing his hand, I say, "Thanks, Kurt."

"Anytime. Hey, make sure to let me know how you and the baby are doing. I'm sure everything's fine. Man, though...what is UP with that gas, woman? You freakin' crop-dusted the meditation room!"

Before he pulls the door open, I blurt out, "But Kurt, wait! Tell me...who is she...this woman you're so crazy about? Please, please, please tell me she's nothing like Kayla."

"Actually she's—"

"Oh dear God, and please don't tell me it's some Nepalese tribal woman! It's not is it? That would be just plain strange."

But, before he can answer, my OB gently pushes the door open from the other side and enters looking grim enough for my ex-husband to take five steps back and stand by my side again.

Placenta-*what?*

"**P**lacenta previa."

Knowing I crumble in situations like this with big words and blood, Kurt steps up and takes over the conversation with my doctor.

"Will they be okay?"

Remembering the out-of-control conversation me and TWWINDTM had with him at my very first doctor's appointment, my OB is quick to ask, "And you *arrrrre* the ex-husband or the ex-fiancé?"

Suddenly grasping the gravity of how fucked-up my life has been for seven months, Kurt murmurs, "The ex-husband."

Glaring at Kurt over the rim of his glasses, my OB continues to berate us both.

"*Annnd* did everyone figure out if that made you the father of the child, or have we not had that essential conversation yet?"

I butt in with, "He's not the father, but he's the only one here with me right now, so please just get to it, Doctor, because the look on your face is scaring the crap out of me. Is my baby okay?"

"Yes. You and the baby are just fine."

I exhale, feeling more relief than ever before in my life.

"Here's what's going on. The placenta is usually attached to the upper part of the uterus, away from the cervix where the baby passes through during delivery. But in your case, Ms. Anderson, it's lying low and if we aren't careful, it could completely block your cervix."

"Is that why I've fainted so much in the last month?"

"No. Fainting isn't a side-effect of what's going on in there. That probably has more to do with fatigue...stress. Any of that playing a role in your life right now?"

51

"A starring one, actually."

Kurt butts in to ask the next critical question, "What was with all of the blood?"

"With placenta previa, bleeding often occurs as the lower part of the uterus thins during the third trimester of pregnancy in preparation for labor—which is where Ms. Anderson is now. The more of the placenta that covers the opening of the cervix, the greater the risk for bleeding. Make sense?"

Now I worriedly wonder, "Is this common?"

"It occurs in about one out of two-hundred pregnancies, but you don't exactly fit the bill for it. It's more common in women who have an abnormally shaped uterus, who have had many previous pregnancies, and multiple pregnancies...like, for instance, twins and triplets. You have none of those things. However, it could also be caused by scarring on the lining of the uterus, due to a history of surgery, previous pregnancy, or abortion. But in looking at your medical history in these forms you filled out, I don't see evidence of any of that stuff either."

My heavy eyes fall on Kurt's mournful ones and we stare at each other for an eternity before he sits next to me on the hospital bed and pulls me into his chest, saying the words, "I'm so sorry, I'm so sorry" over and over again. In response, I cry, "I wish I could take it back...I was just a young girl...I didn't know what else to do..." over and over again. My usually insensitive doctor realizes the tragic meaning behind our sorrow and takes a soft step back to give us some privacy.

Then finally, for the first time ever, Kurt and I grieve the loss of our unborn child...together. He says the heartfelt words I've needed to hear for so long and cradles me with the protective arms that I needed wrapped around me all of those years ago. For too long I forced myself to be tough—to say I had put the awful experience behind me—but I never was and I never did. It might have taken sixteen years for Kurt to realize those things, but he does now, and that's all that matters. There is truly nothing indifferent about him anymore.

After the doctor clears his throat, signifying we've taken up too much of his time, we wipe away each other's tears and then Kurt motions for him to return to the conversation.

"I take it there was some information you failed to disclose, Ms. Anderson?"

For the second shocking time today, Kurt steps up to protect me.

"You make her feel bad about that for one second, and I'll break those fucking hands you need to do your job."

Feeling like we're *finally* the team I always wanted us to be, I chime in with, "He will too. He's pretty pissed. See his eye? My baby's dad did that to him."

After my doctor settles down to our theatrics, I feel it's necessary to set my medical records straight about what happened to the inside of my body all of those years ago, so that I can get the best care for what's growing inside of it now. With fresh tears welling up, Kurt prepares himself to hear for the first time in his life the horrific details of the shoddy abortion I received as a young girl.

I begin by recounting the dreadfully hot waiting room, and how I fainted amongst all of those irresponsibly pregnant strangers. I try not to notice when, for a split second; Kurt and the doctor lock sympathetic eyes. I describe the grey and artless room where the procedure took place, and the loud whirring sound of the terrifying machine that I gave the green light to turn on. I try not to notice when their eyes mournfully shift toward the ground. I explain the anxiety from not having any anesthesia, not even a valium, and I weep when I tell them about the heartless and mean man who thrust equipment in and out of me without regard for how young and scared I was. And I shake when I tell them how I screamed at the heartless and mean man to stop—I changed my mind—but it was too late. Then, slowly and vividly I detail the contents of the blue bucket where the carnage of my poor choices ended up...*my price to pay*. And I try not to notice when both of their heads delicately shake in revulsion. I tried really, really hard not to notice all of their painful gestures, as I recounted the biggest mistake of my life, but it was impossible, and when I'm done I lose it once again…blaming myself for being a murderer.

"Chrissy, please don't cry. Like you said earlier, you…*both of us*…did the best we could at the time. We were young and scared. It's not the choice we'd make now, so please release yourself from this guilt—that image. You're not a bad person…neither of us are. We're good people who just made a bad choice, that's all, okay?"

"Your husband—"

With stuffy noses and wet faces, Kurt and I simultaneously interject, "*EX*-husband!"

"Right. Your *ex*-husband is correct. What you're doing to yourself now, Ms. Anderson…what you've been doing to yourself all of these years, it's not healthy."

Once I'm calm and willfully agree to use my pregnancy as a way to reconcile the one I painfully got rid of, my doctor proceeds to give me the lowdown on placenta previa and how scar tissue from the biggest mistake of my life is most likely the reason I suffer from it. But he also reassures me it has the potential to fix itself, and that the baby and I will be just fine, even if it doesn't resolve before I deliver. I need to stay off of my feet as much as possible, stay away from stress (problem) and sex (no problem). My pregnancy is now considered high-risk, and I'll have to get bi-monthly ultrasounds to track the placenta to make sure it's heading to the top of my uterus where it belongs. If it doesn't, I'll have to have a c-section, which is exactly what I wanted anyway. Think about it. I won't have to push a Leo-sized baby out of my huha, or a Chrissy-sized poop out of my ass. I saw those videos in Lamaze class! I heard my instructor say on more than one occasion, "Push like you're having a bowel movement and don't be surprised if you have one." Uhhhhh, HELLS NO! I can barely crap in the privacy of my own bathroom! I ain't doin' the deuce in front of an audience.

Kurt stays for a while after my doctor leaves, stroking my hair, and making jokes to lighten my mood, like how my baby will probably grow up to be an ultimate cage-fighting champion.

"What are you talking about?"

"Look at my freaking eye, Woman! I hate the son-of-a-bitch, but damn…the father of that kid of yours packs a serious punch."

Once Kurt's satisfied that I'm not going to meltdown after he walks out the door, he reassures me that Kendall's in good hands with Barbara back at my house, and he'll check in on both of them on his way home. Then he tells me there's one more person outside of my room who desperately wants to see me.

"Is it—"

But before I can finish, he's shaking his head.

"If he was here, Chrissy, do you really think he'd be patiently waiting in the hallway this whole time knowing I was in here with *his* baby?"

Now I'm the one shaking my head.

Then he opens the door to reveal TWWINDTM.

Before she can open her mouth, I turn my head away.

"I don't have anything to say to her."

"C'mon, Chrissy, everyone makes mistakes. Just let her talk to you."

I can't. Yes, I know her big fat slutty heart was in the right place, but in this instance it was at the wrong time. It cost me everything…*everything* I ever hoped for. If I could've just had my meeting with Kurt this morning like I planned, I would've gotten all of the answers I needed to make things right again with Leo. He never would've had to know about the shame I'd been carrying around with me for seven months. And it wouldn't have been a lie when I told him the baby was his.

But what about Lauren? TWWINDTM is certainly not the one to blame for Leo getting engaged. I'm the one who opened the door for the girl with the long brown hair to walk through. And now that she exists…now that I know Leo gave himself to her in ways I never thought he'd be able to give himself to another woman…*we'll never be what we could've been.* Our shared dreams have been shattered. And none of that is TWWINDTM's fault. But…finding out about all of it this morning is! I guess that's why I don't have anything to say to her…that's why I can't look at her. She's the one responsible for the moment I realized Leo and I will never happen. She's the one responsible for the moment I lost all hope.

"Get her away from me—now."

Not wanting to upset me, he sympathetically shakes his head at TWWINDTM and begins to close the door. But before it closes all the way, I holler, "Tell her to clear out all of her stuff at the studios! She's fired! I never want to see her again!"

Home Crap Home

April, 2003

"You know you have to tell him, right?"

After twenty-four long hours in the hospital, I'm finally home. Barbara, or as Kendall now calls her, Bar*nana*, dropped the kiddo off at school this morning before going to the hospital to pick me up and bring me home. The two of them have gotten quite close since their awkward first introduction a year and a half ago, just before Kendall's father's memorial. Up until that moment, Barbara had done nearly everything she could to avoid children—especially little girls—since the tragic loss of her own. But from the get-go they've had some kind of unspoken bond, a closeness that their flip-flopped losses cultivated, a connection that's grown leaps and bounds since that awkward first introduction. In fact, there's almost no one Kendall would rather be with than her Barnana.

I begged the doctor for permission to take Kendall to school myself since today is her big Easter celebration and I was supposed to help her class dye eggs, but he gave me the big thumbs down. Per his orders, I'm supposed to lie in bed for at least a week—until my next ultrasound. I guess I'll just add the missed Easter egg experience to my long list of failures…should put it somewhere around number three thousand five hundred. Anyway, after filling me in on how much fun the kids had, and bragging about *every-little-detail* of *every-little-egg*, Barbara tucks me into bed all nice and cozy. Then I *thought* she went to the kitchen to make a snack. Instead, she stuck her head back in the doorway to advise me of what, deep down, I already know needs to happen.

57

"Did you hear what I said? I mean, it's his baby too, Chrissy. He needs to know what's going on."

Leo never showed up to the hospital. I have no idea where he is or what's going through his mind. Shit, for all I know he's already back in New York professing his love to 'L' and thanking God he found someone normal to share his truly, madly, deeply life with.

Leo used to share that life with me. I remember when we would make-out like sex-starved maniacs in the alleyways of Mill Valley, and when he'd rescue me from seedy bars like The Red Devil Lounge and The Round-Up, and take me back to my cottage and show me what it felt like to be a woman. There was that time he pointed out a pregnant woman and told me he couldn't wait until the day I looked like her. And, of course, there were all of the days and nights he worked non-stop on his new business so that he could make all of my dreams come true. Looking around my soon-to-be-mother-of-two-bedroom that's sans any semblance of a family photo, or a man, my blood starts to boil about how far away that truly, madly deeply life is.

The thought of Leo confiding to that 'L' girl all of the deplorable betrayal I bestowed upon him for the last five years makes me crazy. He'll fail to tell her I did it all because I was scared. He'll fail to tell her I did it all to protect his feelings. He'll fail to tell her how much I loved him. And with that single thought—how much I *loved* him—I pick up a pretty little frame from my nightstand, one that I bought for the very first picture of my baby, and I chuck it against the wall.

Never one to get flustered by my theatrics, Barbara composedly says, "Penny for your thoughts?" as she walks over to the broken glass and begins to clean up.

"It's a mess, isn't it?"

"Well, you definitely can't put a picture in it anymore, that's for sure."

"I'm talking about my life."

"It's not the prettiest picture, but there's still time to repaint it."

"He asked another woman to marry him, Barbara. I can't paint over that."

"And *you* were married before…can't you just call it even and believe everything he told you back at the studio? Gee whiz, not a girl in the world who wouldn't want some tall, dark, and handsome green-eyed dude shouting, 'SEE ME! SEE THAT I'M IN LOVE WITH YOU!' Holy Hannah…gave me hot flashes."

"Hey, wait a minute, how do you know what he said at the studio?"

"Megan turned the intercom on."

Good Lord, does everything that happens in my life have to be on display? Seriously, why doesn't someone just write a friggin' book about it!

"So can you do that, Chrissy…Can you call it even?"

"It's not how I'm wired."

And that's putting it mildly. I fell in love with Leo's intensity, the reckless stubble he wore on his dangerously handsome face without regard for how intimidating it made him look…his serial killer-esque gaze. I felt special the whole time we were together because I was the only one to have access to the other side of those characteristics…the side that was emotional…sensitive…adoring. *I was the only one who knew the soft side of Leo.* If he's become soft for anyone else, I can never be with him…even if this is his child.

"Barbara, I can't expect you to understand the way Leo and I love." And then my voice trails off when I say, "I mean *loved*."

"Did you ever think that's *why* you two belong together?"

"It's all I ever used to think. But you can only repaint a picture so many times before the paper turns into a big grey gooey blob."

And there's that damn color again—grey. First Kurt and I were grey when we were married, then Leo and I got grey for a while right after we got engaged, and now this muddled mess. No good comes out of grey. But, that's my life—grey. Always has been, always will be. And then I pull the covers over my head to hide from my self-made grey muddled mess.

59

From underneath I mumble, "Leo knows where I am. Wait. Scratch that...he knows where *we* are, right little baby?"

"Exactly...the little baby! Chrissy, he needs to know about the placenta pre—"

"No way, I can't make the call. Not right now anyway. I'll wait and see how the ultrasound is next week and then maybe we can talk about it."

Barbara, who went from being Sad Frumpy Lady to Smart Sassy Lady in the last two years, pulls the blanket off of me, and lets the motherly love rip.

"You did drop an awful lot on the man, you know."

I give her my best pouty face when I say, "Aren't I supposed to be taking it easy?" But again, she ignores my theatrics.

"Oh, whatever...I know how tough you are and you're going to listen to me, dammit."

I let out a deflated, "Fine."

"Two days ago, Leo was living a quiet life in New York...trying desperately to forget about everything he left behind here, and then BOOM, he's got a baby on the way, a relationship with Kendall he needs to restore, an ex-husband he needs to make nice with, a mortgage payment, your needy—"

Picking up another item on my nightstand, I chuck it against the wall and scream out, "DON'T FORGET ABOUT THE FUCKING WEDDING HE WAS PLANNING JUST TWO DAYS AGO!"

"Okay, okay, okay! Maybe we should remember what the doctor said after all and take it easy."

"I can't, Barbara. I thought he was the love of my life. But the love of my life would never rush into a marriage like that. Our relationship is tainted."

"Well you better find a way to un-taint it because that baby right there deserves better. And you know what? So does Kendall. Yeah, I'll say it. Leo would make an amazing father to that little girl. When I used to see them together I could feel their bond—almost like he needed her just as much as she needed him. Sure, they didn't get a heck of a lot of time together, but when they were together, they related on some kind of cerebral level that no one else could replicate. They had their snipe hunting, board games, and long walks along the reservoir where they'd talk about wild life and ocean creatures. Do you know, because of that man, that kid knows the name of damn near every type of shark in existence?"

Rather sarcastically I scoff, "I didn't even know Leo knew the name of damn near every type of shark in existence."

"Well he does. And together, the three of you had the potential to be a family, and a damn good one. And here's another thing to marinate on while I make you a snack...The love of *his* life would never do what *you* did. Tsk-tsk...Keeping a baby a secret...thinking you slept with your ex-husband...hoping it'll all just work out. Good Lord, what is it with you young kids these days? Life's not supposed to be a soap opera, you know. " Shuffling off down the hallway she yells out, "No relationship, Chrissy, I don't care how truly, madly, deeply it is...No relationship survives on hope. It's forgiveness that keeps it alive."

Notalotaloveslala

April, 2003

"Yeah, right there."

"You like that?"

"Omigod, Omigod, Omigod. Do NOT stop!"

"No way, Baby. This is all about you. All I want is for you to be happy."

The sheets are a crumpled mess, as if the sex has been going on for hours. Everything is stripped down, and sweaty, and it doesn't seem like the euphoria is going to end anytime soon.

"Omigod, your body is so amazing, Leo. How it looks…what it's capable of doing to me...for me. It's like you can protect me from anything."

"And I will."

"How did I get so lucky?"

"Are you kidding, Baby? How did *I* get so lucky?"

Everything comes to an abrupt halt as positions change and he's the one on the bottom now. His head cradled in his strong hands, arms flexed, chest swelling with each pulsating gift given to him. His luminous green eyes locked on the most important person in his life.

"My God, you are so beautiful."

"Shhhhhh, just enjoy what I'm doing to you."

And he does exactly that as his hands reach out to fondle the sexiest thing he's ever touched while receiving every man's ultimate dream—a strikingly beautiful naked woman doing all of the work.

"It all had to happen, you know."

"What had to happen?"

63

"All of it, all of those shitty experiences with shitty people had to happen for me to be exactly where I needed to be so I could meet you."

"I love you so much, Leo"

"Not as much as I love you, Lauren."

"Notasmuchasiloveyoulauren. Notasmuchasiloveyoulauren."

"Mommy, wake up."

"Notasmuchasiloveyoulauren."

"MOMMY! WAAAAAAAAKE UP!"

A big jab in my arm jolts me out of my horrific nightmare. After I get my wits about me, I look over to find Kendall dressed up as a fairy princess, pointy magic wand and all.

"Whose Notalotaloveslala?"

"Huh?"

"You kept saying dat ova and ova again."

My sweet, sweet, Kendall. Five and a half years old now, and despite the heartbreaking loss of both of her parents, and my colossal screw-up that no doubt cost her *ever* having a father, she's living a pretty fabulous life. She's in the best pre-school my single-mom-ass can afford, she's got a bedroom full of toys I wish I had as a kid, and the love of six of the most amazing women in the world. Damn, I guess that number actually just got cut in half. Her Auntie Courty and Auntie Nicky are moving far away in the next month and TWWINDTM is…well, her name says it all. That leaves me, her Barnana, and Megan. Eh, that should be good enough to mold her into something kind of close to what her Mom ever hoped for. At least I hope so.

Anyway, our nighttime prayers continue to include *all* of our angels in Heaven (including my Grandpa and all of the ants she squashed on the playground that day), but unless she wants to specifically talk about her mother and father, I don't bring them up. There will be a time later in her life when she'll ask questions about them, and of course, I have all of the videos

Kelly made to help me answer them. Right now my goal is to make Kendall's life as normal as possible and be the best mom in the world. I'm sure there are a lot of people who are fiercely debating my success level in both categories, but whatever. Until you have an affair, hack voicemail accounts, get a divorce, quit your career, start a new one, lose your best friend to cancer, obtain custody of her child, get engaged, lose your fiancé to a drunken night of supposed sex with your ex-husband, get pregnant, not know who the father is, then find out who the father is only to discover that he's engaged to someone else and wants nothing to do with you *or* your unborn child…who are you to judge?

Wiping drool off my chin and still a little out of it, I probe, "Was I really saying that?"

"Yep, and loud!" Twirling around in her princess dress she yells, "Notalotaloveslala! Notalotaloveslala! Notalotaloveslala!"

Even though her pronunciation of what I know I was mumbling is way off, I plug my ears with my fingers and tell her, "Okay, okay, okay! I get it."

And I get the dream. I gave Leo to 'L'. All of the shitty experiences he had with me drove him straight to her. She's all my fault. All of that glorious stuff he used to do with me…for me…to me, it all belongs to her now. And I'm reminded of it almost every time I fall asleep. There they are, professing love…making love….making plans…making me sick.

It used to be my best friend Kelly who would come to me in my dreams. She talked of babies, love growing inside of me, and how I haven't figured out my life yet. Mostly, she warned me if I didn't make a choice, one would be made for me. All of it was so confusing. I remember being so freaked out by one dream in particular that I rushed to the cemetery and had one of those fake conversations with her…you know, where I'd answer myself as if I was her. I asked her, "What do you think dreams really are anyway, Kel?" She said, "Maybe they're the release of our deepest secret desires, or maybe they're the place we go to solve the problems we couldn't solve when we were awake…maybe

65

they're just a montage of bits and pieces of our day mixed in with the crap we watch on TV." Then she asked me, "What do you think they are?" And I said, "I have no clue, but I have a weird feeling you're gonna teach me."

And she did. What she taught me was to listen to them and listen well…But I didn't do that until it was too late. If I had just listened to Kelly's advice, *if I had heeded her warnings in my dreams*, if I had stopped for ONE second to wrap my head around what it would feel like to lose Leo forever, I wouldn't be having these new dreams about him fucking the shit out of that bitch. He'd be fucking the shit out of this one! Well, not for the next eight weeks anyway—Doctor's orders. But, yeah, I listen to my dreams now and I listen well. And what they're telling me is Leo and I are over.

My beloved Kelly hasn't been back to see me in my sleep since last month when she made a quick visit to me in my slumber. It was right after Kurt called from Kathmandu when I cataclysmically confused his dialogue, farted, fainted, and ended up in the hospital. (It's quite tragic how that sequence of events is becoming a reoccurring theme in my life.) Anyway, the last time Kelly appeared she was quiet and reflective. She made a quick mention of my baby when she said it's "beautiful and has the most stunning eyes and brilliant smile I've ever seen." Which is why, even with the placenta previa, I'm calm. I know everything will be okay…Kelly told me it would be. But as soon as she came to me in my sleep that night, she was gone. Tenderly whispering as she left, "Kendall needs you," she vanished and hasn't been heard from since. Perhaps she got tired of my Chrissygans, decided to take a well-deserved hiatus, and she's hiding under some heavenly rock with my Grandpa. Who could blame her? I miss her, though. Glancing over to the corner of my room where the box of videos resides that she made for Kendall just before she died, I think, thank goodness I still have those. No matter what, she's never too far away.

"Mommy, are you even wistening to me?"

"Oh! Yes, of course, Sweetie!"

66

"So *when?*"

"When what?"

She puts her hands on her hips and stomps her foot on the ground in frustration.

"I *saiiiid*, what time will Ku-Ku be here? Barnana said he bwought me somedin' back from Nupul!"

My first deflated thought is that I pray to God he didn't bring back a wife, and my second is that it's Friday. The first one since Kurt returned home, and time to re-establish his weekend visitation. Despite the little kumbaya moment I shared with him the other day, and how excited Kendall is that he's back, I'm deflated that I have to let her go for the next forty-eight hours...and forty-eight hours next weekend, and the weekend after that, and the weekend after that. Wow, with every day that passes and every new dream I have, that perfect little family life I always wanted slips farther and farther away. I wonder what Dr. Maria would have to say about that?

I also wonder where Leo is and what's going through his mind. Even though his engagement and my deplorable betrayal have officially ended all hope of a happily-ever-after ending to our love story, I don't think anything will ever kill the desire I have for him. Nope, that's about as permanent as this baby.

I hear a car pull up outside and for a second my heart drops. *Could it be?*

Kendall scrambles to the window and yells out, "Yay! It's Ku-Ku time!" and then runs to the front door, leaving me to pick my heart and my desire up from the ground. Scared that it's a feeling I'll be stuck with for the rest of my life.

I slump back into my pillows and wonder...*Where are you Leo...What's going through your mind?*

By Design

April, 2003

"Well, well, well...I didn't expect to see you! Get over here and give me a hug!"

Megan bounces over to my bed, wraps her arms around me, and rocks from side to side, clearly missing me as much as I missed her.

Finally she breaks away and with big eyes exclaims, "You got HUGE!"

When I focus on her my eyes get big too.

"And you got TINY! *What happened?* Shitty food in Nepal, or what?"

Blowing me off with an eye roll, she puts the focus back on my stomach.

"But seriously, look at the size of that sucker! I noticed it for a second when I saw you at the studio the other day, but you fell to the darn floor faster than I could zoom in on ya!" Placing her hands on my stomach, her eyes widen again as she exclaims, "It's a beast!"

"I know, it's probably a boy, huh? Gonna be forced to look at a mini-Leo the rest of my tortured life, aren't I?"

Laughing, Megan settles in next to me in bed and admits, "Well, there are worse things to look at."

"True...true. Damn him and his good looks."

"I only saw him for a second the other day—rushed past me so fast to bolt out of the studio! But the boy has clearly been taking his work-out supplements!"

"Either that, or New York, and more specifically a particular female in New York, has been treating him exceptionally well."

I was going for nonchalant when I said that but, of course, it came out as cynical as ever.

"You wanna jump right into this mess...talk it out?"

69

Of course I do. But since the amount of women in my life is dwindling faster than the chance of me ever having sex again, I figure it's a good time for a non-selfish moment.

"No, you first! How was Nepal? Tell me everything! Did you get the charity bug out of your ass? Are you ready to be my little capitalistic money-grubbing designer again? The yoga collection has come to a complete halt without you, ya know."

With a sparkle in her eyes I don't think I've ever seen, not even on the day I told her she could be my one and only clothing designer, she turns to me and exhales, "It was... it was...Oh Chrissy, it was unbelievable...life changing!"

Preferring a root canal over the prospect of traveling to Nepal, I question, *Really? Life changing?*

"Oh my Gosh, yes! Almost as soon as we arrived, we settled into this little orphanage in Bijayanagar that was in desperate need of help. I mean, this place was in shambles—needed everything cleaned and organized! I was a little scared to dive in at first, but it was as if Kurt had been doing stuff like that his whole life. And, of course, he was a champion with all of the medical stuff. He brought along so many supplies from his company. I swear, I would've thought he was a doctor if I didn't know otherwise. It wasn't long before I pitched in with teaching the kids English and setting up a library. And they LOVED the clothes I brought. There was this one little girl in particular named Bimata. We bonded almost instantly and..."

The more Megan rambled on about her life-changing excursion, the more I began to realize her heart might not be as committed to clothing design as it once had been, something much bigger than the Fall line has taken over her interest. And with the recent death of TWWINDTM, I foresee a serious bump in the road ahead for Forever Young, Inc.

"...So anyway, I had to be dragged away from Nepal kicking and screaming, but here I am. Guess it couldn't have come at a better time too, huh? Noticed someone's desk at work has been cleaned out."

Despite my rage, the thought of never again seeing TWWINDTM at work is a depressing thought. Even so, I just shrug my shoulders.

"I had coffee with her yesterday."

"I don't want to talk about her."

Ignoring my childishness, she continues with, "She's already putting some feelers out for a new job. She's thinking about going back into clothing manufacturing. *Blech!*"

Trying not to sound like I care, but needing to ease my curiosity, I ask, "Why not just go work for another yoga studio? I mean, that's what she loves doing, after all."

"Near our studios? Duh, she knows she'll put you out of business. She would too, you know. Chrissy, once our customers find out she's not coming back, they won't either. Everyone loves her. *You* love her!"

"No, I hate her. And I want to change the subject."

"Alrighty, we covered Nepal...how our business is about to go under. Guess that leaves just one more thing to talk about. Your lover...Leo."

"There's nothing to talk about. I don't even know where he is or what's going through his mind."

"What if I told you I did?"

For three days I've been sitting here not knowing anything, agonizing about the what-ifs and what-happens-nexts. I've been throwing things against the wall and anxiously listening to cars pull into the driveway. I've had nightmares about Leo making love to that girl and waking up in a cold sweat. All of it has been pure torture. But I fear it's a walk in the park compared to what I might now be told.

"I made a call."

Bracing myself, I mutter, "What kind of call?"

"To the Guggenheim Museum."

Confused, I bark, "Who the frick at the Guggenheim would know anything about anything?"

"I'm joking, Dumbass! To Leo! I called Leo!"

"Dumbass?"

"Eh, I figured you can't fire me since you fired everyone else. Thought I'd have some fun."

"Not funny! Not having any fun!"

"Okay, okay, okay! Let's bring it down a notch." Handing me a glass of water, she continues, "Take a drink and calm down. I'll continue when you're ready."

I don't think I'll ever be ready to hear what she has to say, so I just sit in silence until she can't stand it anymore.

"Okay fine. He's pissed."

"What's he *mostly* pissed about?"

"That you told him the baby was absolutely his when you absolutely didn't know for sure it was. Crap, I'd be mostly pissed about that too. I mean, *Jesus*, what if you were wrong, Chrissy?"

The tiny sip of water I just took sprays out of my mouth.

"Are you kidding me right now? You knew I wasn't wrong! Geez, you were standing right next to Kurt when he called from Kathmandu to set the record straight! Oh my God, Megan, how can you sit here and talk about potentially being wrong when you, of all people, know I wasn't?"

Lowering her gaze, she chastises, "I was standing next to Kurt in the lobby the other day when my fired friend told him that there was a bad connection on that call from Nepal—that you thought Kurt told you the baby *was* his, and you've been thinking it might *be* his ever since. Apparently, you didn't know what I knew! So there, Dumbass, that's why I'd be mostly pissed!"

"Okay, that's your second dumbass. I'll give you one more because I deserve it, but anything after that and you'll be back to working for that pervert at the old clothing company right next to TWWINDTM. Got it?"

"Yeah, yeah. Anyway, that's what he can't wrap his head around, and quite frankly, I can't either. It just didn't need to come to this."

"You're right...he's right...Barbara's right. Everyone's freaking right. It didn't need to come to this. And if I ever had

72

the chance to explain to Leo why it did, and apologize for it, I would. But I don't think he cares what I have to say because he moved on with someone new."

Megan's silence makes my heart feel like it's jammed in the middle of a paper shredder and I can't leave it like that that. I have to either pull it out or push it through.

Tentatively, I ask, "Because that's what he did, right? He moved on with someone new, didn't he?"

Frowning, she lets it drop, "Looks like it."

"Like, what does it look like, exactly?"

"He said she still has the ring. But I don't know if it's because he still wants to marry her or if he hasn't figured out how to tell her he doesn't. He didn't seem willing to go down that road with me. He sounded annoyed, like he was in over his head."

"Christ, we just broke up like seven months ago. *How did she even happen?*"

"I'll give you one guess."

"Taddeo."

"Bingo."

"He always did think I was bad news, didn't he?"

"Was never a fan. Not because you were married before, or any of that, it's because of the lies and stuff. Leo had a lot of rough years before he met you, and Taddeo's just super protective of him. His intentions are good, but he's a lot like Leo. Once you end up on his bad side, it's damn near impossible to get back to good."

"So he pushed 'L' on him?"

"You sure you can handle all of this? I mean, aren't you supposed to be taking it easy?"

"Just go."

"You guys were still together when she met him through the new Texas office. Apparently everyone but Leo could tell how attracted she was to him. He was totally blinded by you..." I'd pick something off of my nightstand to throw, but it's all been broken. "...but the morning when he called your cell and you were in Kurt's bed, the blinders came off and she swooped in for the kill."

"She hit on him when we were still together?"

"She tried, and probably with Taddeo's encouragement, but absolutely nothing happened until after you guys broke up in New York."

"But how did the engagement happen so fast?"

"I have no idea and I didn't push for the details. I could tell he was getting a little agitated."

"Agitated?"

"Well, yeah. He's hurt and confused. He's engaged to a woman on the east coast, who in my opinion, it doesn't seem like he's in love with, and he's about to become a father to a baby on the west coast. He's a simple, no-nonsense guy surrounded by a lot of complicated foolishness. To be honest, I think he's traumatized."

"Does he know what happened after he left the studio the other day—about the placenta previa and bed rest?"

"I didn't say anything. I mean, clearly he didn't see the bleeding. We both know if he had, he never would've bolted from the studio. But I thought I'd leave the medical stuff up to you, I didn't want to scare him. I just wanted to be able to come here today and give you some hope that this can all work out. It's not too late."

"Megs, you just said yourself the girl is wearing an engagement ring."

"No. I said she still *has* the engagement ring. Big difference there."

"Semantics. Trust me, it's so late for me, it's laughable."

Reaching out again to grab something...*anything* to throw, I give up and then nauseatingly ask, "When are they supposed to get married anyway?"

"July 5th."

Two weeks after my delivery date.

"He won't go through with it, though. I just know he won't. He's in love with you, Chrissy, always has been, always will be.

74

I know he wants to be a father to this child, I can hear it in his voice. How can he be that involved in your life and not be with you?"

That right there is my biggest fear...that Leo will be involved in my life…with a different wife.

Just then Kendall bounces into the room with her backpack full of supplies for the weekend, over-the-moon to see Kurt.

"Got everything all packed-up, Love-Bug?"

"Yep!"

"Promise you'll call to say good-night?"

"Yep!"

"Get your cutie-booty over here and give me a kiss then."

After our usual fancy lady kiss, a kiss on the left cheek, one on the right, and then one smack dab on the lips, Kendall lifts up my t-shirt and plants a wet one on my belly and says, "Bye, Baby Weo! I'll be back in two days!" And then she runs out of the room.

Megan raises her eyebrows and inquires, *"Baby Weo?"*

"She's adamant it's a boy, and that his name will be Leo."

She can't resist saying, "Never a dull moment with you, Chrissy Anderson, never a dull moment!" as she laughs and shuffles off of the bed." Then she blows me a kiss and yells, "We'll have her back Sunday by five!" as she makes her way down the hall.

Lost in the overabundance of information Megan just dumped on me, and the pain of my heart that's still feels like it's jammed in a paper shredder, I completely forgot to ask where Kurt was, and why she's the one still transferring Kendall back and forth between us now that the truth is out about what happened at his house seven months ago.

Moving on

April, 2003

"I can't believe it, Chrissy! Not even one stinking phone call?"

"I know! Geez, Man, I had to hear about your bed rest from Kyle!"

The truth is it didn't even occur to me to call them. And it didn't occur to me how weird that was until this very moment. Can't admit that to them, though.

"You guys are way too busy with your moves and all to be bothered with this stuff. Just trying to be considerate for once."

"C'mon, girl, we're never too busy for something this big!"

My best friend from childhood, Nicole, slaps my other best friend from childhood, Courtney, in the arm and says, "Dude, it's not ONE thing, I think it's more like FIVE! That's the impression Kyle gave me anyway."

"You're absolutely right, Nic, and that's exactly why I didn't call. The two of you have way too much going on in your lives to deal with any more of my messes."

And boy, do they ever. My besties—the remaining members of the A-BOB.'s, the club we started when were young girls in high school—are moving away. Courtney to Zimbabwe, which I still can't find on a map, and Nicole to Arizona...which I can *sometimes* find on a map.

Courtney's on some big mission to rebuild a hospital, or teach medical students...or maybe to dig ditches for clean drinking water. Shit, I have no idea what her mission is or why she's moving there. But it makes her happy, so it makes me happy...Sorta. You see, Court's been my touchstone...my problem-solving stabilizer for over half of my life. When I freak out (and, as everyone knows, I freak out a lot) she's one of the few people able to calm me down. Sure, she talks to me in an

77

annoying placating whisper when she soothes me, but for whatever reason, it works. Courtney always leads me in the right direction, and always gives me sound advice, and now she's leaving.

And Nicole's leaving too, to pursue a job as a junior high school science teacher. Apparently her career change has to take place in Arizona because of all of her medical school loans. She's adamant it's the only place cheap enough to live as she pays them off while pursuing a new, not as lucrative, but infinitely more satisfying occupation. This is bad for me because Nicole's the only person who can make me laugh, I mean, *seriously* laugh. Even in the midst of some of my most extreme chaos, the woman has something so sarcastically funny to say that puts me in check, and makes me realize how freaking ridiculous I am. I've always trusted Nicole to talk me off of a ledge with a giggle, and now that giggle is moving to the desert.

Despite how busy the two of them are with their impending moves, they came to my house tonight because Kurt told their husbands what happened the other day at the studio. But, as usual, their dopey husbands didn't have the detailed scoop they were looking for, so they drove straight to my bedside to get it.

"Do I have to rehash *every* little thing or can I just sum up?"

"You can sum up, but don't skip over the good parts." And then, in true Nicole style, she claps her hands and adds, "Especially if there's sex involved!"

"Sorry, Nic, no sex to speak of. I have placenta previa. Hence the bed rest. I guess that would be the biggest item on the list, and we should start with that. My doctor said I have to—"

Brushing me off to get to the supposed good stuff, Nicole barks, "Yeah, yeah, previa's no biggie—totally manageable. C-section will probably be the worst of it. So where's Leo right now?"

Rolling her eyes, Courtney mocks Nic when she says, "Someone's horny, as usual." Then she puts her hand on my leg, and asks me if my previa is serious.

"Nope. Doctor seems to think it's pretty minor. Just have to lay here for a week, until my next ultrasound when—"

"See! Told you she's fine, Courtney!"

"Alright, alright! I guess we're moving on to item number two—the father of your child."

Clearly excited that my baby-daddy mystery has been officially solved, Nic unknowingly stabs me in the heart as she fires off question after question.

"I bet he's at Babies-R-Us making up for lost time, right? No! I bet he's at Tiffany's buying back that fabulous ring you idiotically gave back to him! Yep, that's where he is, huh? No, wait…I bet he's at the bookstore buying every single book there is on fatherhood because he has a lot of catching up to do. The way you described him, all intense-n-shit, he seems like the kind of guy to do that."

And she keeps on going and going and going with the dreamy possibilities. Hitting my limit, my hand searches the nightstand for something to throw at the wall. Coming up empty handed, I open the drawer, and grab the only thing in it—my Hitachi Wonderwand. I raise it above my head and just as I'm about to lob it across the room, Courtney grabs my forearm.

"What the hell are you doing?"

"Yeah, Chrissy! Are you crazy? That thing does God's work!"

Looking like a crazy woman, I threaten, "Either you shut the fuck up, Nic, or the vibrator takes a beating."

Courtney moves slowly as she reaches for the Wonderwand, acting almost like she's taking a loaded gun from my hand. Once she has it safe in her possession, she says, "Tell us what's going on, Babe."

"I have no idea where Leo is. I haven't seen him since he found out about the baby."

Confused, their eyes dart back and forth.

Court's the first to chime in with, "But…that was three days ago."

Nicole's not far behind with, "And he's having a baby...with *you*."

"Right, but I kept this from him for seven months, and then I lied to him about why I kept it from him. I also stretched the truth about some other stuff. Not hard to see why the guy would need a little space. Oh, and I guess the fact that he's engaged to marry someone else might also be contributing to his absence."

Both of their jaws simultaneously drop in shock.

"Yep, *annnd* that would be item number three. Would you guys mind if I fast-tracked right along to number four, or do you want me to go all classic Chrissy and cry?"

Their non-responsive stunned faces tell me it's okay to move right along.

"Okay then, number four. Kurt's in love with someone else. Probably some Nepalese woman with a bone through her nose, or some funky shit like that. And lastly, number five. I fired the woman who's responsible for over half of my business, and for almost all of my sanity, and if she paid attention to anything I said I'll never see her again. We all caught up now?"

Almost as if I'm not in the room, Nicole turns to Courtney and declares, "I always knew it was Leo's baby."

Courtney's turn with, "Totally, me too."

I'm looking at the two of their selective-memory asses like they've lost their ever-lovin' minds.

"Uhhhh, NO you guys didn't! The two of you bounced all over the map of who you believed this baby belonged to!"

Wrapping her arms around me, Courtney lowers her voice to a whisper to calm me down.

"We're just playing with you, Babe...Trying to make you laugh is all."

"There's nothing to laugh at, Court. I can't fix this."

"Sure you can."

"How?"

"Admit you made a mistake, and tell him you love him. Right, Nic?"

"Right. Chrissy, if he loves you, I mean *really* loves you, it's as easy as that."

It's of no use to explain to the two of them how Leo and I love. In fact, it's useless to explain it to anybody. In our world, he can never forgive me for what I did, and I can never forgive him for what he did. We're so over, and it's almost laughable that anyone even thinks apologies and confessions of love can fix us.

"So when can you break out of bed?"

"I'm on lock down for four more days."

Talking to Courtney like all of a sudden I'm invisible, Nicole divulges, "It's gonna be a long four days for someone like her, with all of these big problems, to be handcuffed to a bed."

"You got that right, Sister."

"What should we do to help?"

Lovingly grabbing my hand, Courtney smiles down at me and says, "Absolutely nothing. She's a mom now. Only she knows what's right for her family."

Typical Nicole takes the tender moment and pulverizes it when she howls back, "*What family?* She's got a kid over at her ex-husband's house right now, a fatherless bun in the oven, and an ex-fiancé who's engaged to…what was her name again, Chrissy?"

"I hate you so hard right now."

Then, doing what Nicole does the very best, she kisses the top of my forehead and says, "Oh Sweetie, I bet not as hard as you hate yourself."

And then my besties, the two women I literally grew up with, and relied on so heavily to give me the maternal love I so desperately needed my whole life, quietly leave me to solve my big problems all on my own. When they arrived, I thought it was weird that I forget to call them when all of this shit went down. But just now another weird thought occurs to me. Until this very moment, I never realized how truly wonderful the two of them are at this motherhood thing, and how lucky their husbands and children are. I don't think I'll ever be able to measure up.

81

Now alone in my bedroom, I sulk at the silence. At a time when it feels like I need them the most, my two best friends are not only leaving my house, but essentially my life. To which they'd probably say, "When have you ever NOT needed us the most?" To which I'd say, "Go to Hell." They'd give substantial examples to back up their claim, I'd relent, and then we'd kiss and make up, and go have a cocktail where we'd talk about the good ol' days that included Kelly. But I can't have a cocktail right now and they don't have time for one. And you know what? It's probably a good thing. I have a lot to figure out, and as I scan my empty bedroom/prison cell, I think…*and a lot of alone time to do it.*

Ugh, alone time. I remember those dreadful hours I spent alone in Leo's Moraga apartment back when he was temporarily living in Monterey and I was still married. I forced myself to lie in his bed and come to terms with the fact that my life had become nothing more than a non-stop blur of semi-fake therapy, pretend marriage, and compulsive cheating. Wow, cut forward five years, and I'm now forced to lie in *this* bed and come to terms with the fact that my life has become nothing more than a non-stop blur of semi-fake happiness, pretend authenticity, and compulsive screwing myself. A step up from how things used to be, but definitely nothing to write home about.

Anyway, the more I forced myself to sit in the silence of Leo's apartment and 1) come to terms that I was a mess and 2) find a way to fix the mess, the more restless I got. I'd hop out of his bed and swarm the place to find something else to occupy my mind. It didn't take long before I called off 'Mission Silence' and ran to Dr. Maria's office with my tail between my legs…begging for help. But there's no one left to ask for help. I've either cut them out of my life, or they've cut me out. Sure there's Barbara, but the woman had her final say when she stormed out of my room yesterday, mumbling something about hope and forgiveness. And I guess as a last resort, there's always Dr. Maria. But I'd rather be chained to this bed for the rest of my life than admit to my old therapist I can't stop screwing myself.

So that leaves…that leaves…

Scanning the room, my eyes lock on the box containing my voice of reason.

"Ha! I'm not alone after all."

Barbara would kill me if she knew I was violating my bed rest, but she's off at a yoga class right now, and I don't feel like waiting for her to get back to help me. Carefully, I crawl out of bed and make my way over to the box, grab a video, and pop it into the VCR. Once I tuck myself back into bed, I look down at the case and study Kelly's teacher-perfect handwriting that says *Five Years Old*. Memories stir. I could really use one of her good slaps in the face right now. A tough talk on her front porch…a letter addressed just to me…something telling me to get Leo back, or telling me to let him go. I'd listen. She was just that good. Abruptly setting the video case down in my lap, I think…*or maybe she wouldn't do any of that*. And maybe Barbara wouldn't care that I'm helping myself. Maybe that's what everyone's waiting for me to finally do…even my friend in Heaven. With that thought, I press Play.

Crossroads

April, 2003

" " *...Since Kendall hasn't even turned five yet, and I can't
remember what it was like to be five, the best I can do is
read as much as I can about the age in the short time I have left.
So bear with me, Sweetheart, I'm struggling through this
probably as much as you are right now."*

She's struggling with a lot more than that. The effects of chemo,
and whatever else she's got going on to prolong her life, have
begun to take their toll. I couldn't tell much of a difference
between healthy Kelly and cancer Kelly in the last video, but her
treatments in the interim got the best of her. Her eyes are sunken
in and she's obviously been crying—in physical or mental pain,
or both? I don't know. In classic Kelly style she doesn't give
you a clue which one; and she makes no mention of anything
bad happening to her. Even though so much time has passed
since her death I'm still in awe of her strength.

You'd think the thing that kills me the most about these
videos is watching Kelly cram in as many life lessons for her
daughter as she can before she dies. But it's not. The thing that
really gets to me is that she's talking to the camera like she's
talking to her husband, Craig. Kelly's relying on him to
implement her lessons. She's relying on him to mold Kendall
into the type of woman she wants her to become. But he's dead
now, too. I imagine at some point Kelly's dialogue will switch,
and she'll begin to address Kendall directly. But there will come
a day when Kendall will view these earlier videos, and Kelly's
dialogue with Craig is just one more thing that will make
showing them to her that much more difficult. Thank God I still

have a few more years to wrap my head around how to even do that. For now, these are all for me.

"According to what I've been reading, Kendall should know right from wrong at this stage of her life, so don't let those big blue eyes and that pouty lower lip of hers trick you into letting her off the hook. She needs to take responsibility for her actions and endure the consequences of her bad choices. Tough love will be the way if you want her to mature into a young woman who's able to stand on her own two feet."

My gaze shifts from the television screen to the mirror across my bedroom where I'm confronted with my own big blue eyes and pouty face. It's a puffy and pathetic sight. Then it shifts to Barbara, who just walked in from her yoga class. She caught wind of what Kelly just said and from down the hallway mumbles, "Gee, who's she talking about, you or your daughter?" Ignoring her mockery, I turn back to the screen.

"...Oh, I can already see this coming with the way she circles her stuffed animals around her and pretends to train them, she's gonna play a lot of make-believe. I really want you to let her imagination run wild and encourage her to dream big. But promise me you won't lead her to believe that just because she hopes and wishes for something to come true or to be real, that it'll magically happen. There's a big difference between dressing up as a movie star and being a movie star...or whatever it is she aspires to be when she grows up. Nothing magically happens. She's got to know it takes hard work and dedication to get what she wants in life...and I guess in love too. But that love stuff is a conversation I can have directly with her in one of the later videos."

I reach out for the video cover and check the age written on it again, making sure it really does say "Five Years Old," not thirty-two. Barbara walks by my bedroom door, notices the

86

repulsed look on my face, and asks, "How's it feel to be five?" Ignoring her again, I shift my attention back to the television screen.

"Another thing I can already tell with Kendall is that she's gonna be an enthusiastic problem solver. Remember last night when she was trying to button up her own shirt and she freaked when she couldn't do it, but then freaked even more when we tried to help her?"

Kelly's giggle makes me giggle too.

"You're in for a bumpy ride, my love. Gently steer her in the right direction, and as frustrating as it might get, let her solve her own problems. It'll get easier as she has new experiences. She'll begin to ask more questions and weigh her choices..."

Problem solving? For the love of Pete, I'm nowhere near that level of maturity! I'm actually starting to get nervous that Kendall's gonna mature faster than me and *she's* the one who will have to watch these damn things and teach *me* how to grow up.

"...I realize my illness throws our whole good cop/bad cop thing out of whack and you were relying on me for all of that tough love stuff, but it's all up to you now. You're all she has left." She blows him a kiss and says, *"I'll always be here for you, Craig. You might not be able to see me or touch me, but know that I'm always here—sending you the strength you need to do the right thing for our daughter."*

Kelly reaches forward and her very shaky finger turns off the camera. Lost in the static buzz of the blank television screen, I don't notice when Barbara walks in and sits on the bed.
"She was a pretty cool chick, wasn't she?"
"Yeah, she was."

"Tough too, huh?"

"The toughest."

"And damn smart."

"We didn't call her 'the voice of reason' for nothin'."

Pensively shoving a handful of chips in my mouth, I think, Kelly was all those things, cool, tough…smart. Then, stopping mid-chew…come to think of it, we both used to be all of those things. I know why she's not any of that stuff anymore, but what happened to me? Was it Kurt or was it Leo? Was it letting Kurt down or letting Leo in? Was it letting Leo in and then letting him go? Was it losing Kelly? Was it winning Kendall? Was it getting pregnant? Was it when I started keeping secrets again? When did I lose my cool…when did I get so off-track that I couldn't get back on? AHHHH! Forget it, there's no time to figure it out anymore! I've got to just reclaim it all before it's too late—before I wither away into the un-coolest, weakest, dumbest girl alive! That kind of person can't raise Kendall properly. That kind of person isn't who Kelly trusted with her daughter's life. That person can't be the best mom in the world to the new baby. And that kind of person certainly doesn't stand a chance at experiencing the kind of truly, madly, deeply love she craves. Get your shit together, Chrissy, and get a clue! When Kelly tells Craig she's counting on him, she's *really* counting on you. You know that! And initially you even handled the responsibility quite well. You nurtured Kendall through the darkest days of her life all by yourself. But look at you now. You're a freaking mess, and over what? Your own lies! Your own weakness! For God's sake, you can't tell Kendall to take responsibility for her actions, to work hard and dedicate herself to the causes and people she loves, to solve her own damn problems, when you don't even do those things for yourself! And if you don't do those things for yourself, you'll fail. And if you fail yourself, you'll fail Kendall! And if you fail Kendall, you fail Kelly!

Barbara, who can see my wheels spinning, says, "Oh, boy…What you're thinking?"

I'm thinking about all of them. TWWINDTM, when she pitifully asked me the other day at the studio, "How's that life working out for you?" I'm thinking about Kurt, when he reminded me that my freedom is useless if I'm not gonna use it to go after the things I didn't think I could have with him. Courtney and Nicole, when they said I can fix things with Leo if I simply admit my mistakes and tell him I love him. Megan, when she said, "It didn't need to come to this."

"*Chrissy?* Spill it."

Focusing on her face, but not comprehending her words, I think, *and you Barbara*, I'm thinking about you when you said, "No relationship survives on hope; it's forgiveness that keeps it alive." And lastly, Kelly, when she once again made me feel like a child as she spoke about her own. *All of their insights and insults are correct.* And I've known it. I just needed to be handcuffed to this bed long enough to sit still and deal with it, accept it, and believe it. As anyone can probably tell by now, sitting still has always been a weakness of mine. But I'm tired of running…tired of not feeling as cool, smart, and tough as I can be. I've got to reclaim all that I'm capable of being in order to show Kendall and the new baby that you can have everything you want in life if you work hard enough for it. And hell, if you don't get what you want, at least you can hold you head high and say you died trying…Just like her incredible mother is demonstrating in these gut-wrenching videos.

Well, if this isn't the biggest aha-moment of my entire freaking life. And shockingly enough it didn't take a trip to Dr. Maria to have it. It merely took hitting rock bottom.

"Darling, you look like you're either shitting your pants or having the baby. Which one, so I know what kind of towels to line the bed with?"

With a sense of urgency I haven't felt since the day after I met Leo in 1998, when I giddily ran to the phone to call him and fell flat on my face, I hurl the bag of chips on the floor, turn to Barbara and cry out, "Quick, get me my computer!"

Alabaster?

April, 2003

In a genuine attempt to reclaim not only my cool, toughness, and smarts, but also my manners, I *profusely* thank Barbara for getting my computer lickety-split and then I tell her my plan.

"Well, well, well, at this pace you might just turn six before Kendall after all."

Then backing out of the room, she wishes me good luck and reminds me, no matter what, she'll always be there for me. She's family.

While waiting for my computer to fire up, a million overwhelming thoughts fire through my mind, and for a minute they almost get the best of me. In fact, they almost make me want to be five years old forever and hide under my covers with nothing more than hope that everything will magically work out for me. But I know what I have to do for a chance to have everything I ever wanted—the man, the family, and the freedom to be the kind of wife and mother I always wanted to be. And thanks to the tough love of everyone who ever loved me, and those who love me now, I'm ready to give my overwhelming thoughts the middle finger and do it.

Obviously there are a few major hurdles in my way of having everything I ever wanted, but the one that worries me the most, the thing I fear could be the ultimate roadblock to putting the pieces of my life back together, is my pile of humiliating feelings about Leo's engagement. I just don't know where to put them. But I guess that's another good reason to do what I'm about to do. I'll never find a place for them if I don't ask for help. I'll stew in them until I turn into a sad frumpy lady.

I brush my fingertips across the cover of the video I just watched, and I can feel Kelly encouraging me to move forward with my plan. I can hear her voice of reason saying the same thing it said to me on her front porch almost three years ago. *"Stop taking each day of your life for granted and spend it with the ones you love the most, the ones that make you feel the most loved."* And then I hear her voice telling me the same thing it just told Craig, *"It's all up to you now...I'm here for you— always."*

Double-clicking on Outlook to open up my email, I think...my days of running on hope are over. I'm smart enough to know that the difference between doing something and doing nothing is everything, and I'm aware of the fact that the difference between being calm and being chaotic is clarity. I've practiced those mottoes, and witnessed the advantage of doing so. I've overcome too damn much to live one more day of my life with my fingers crossed. I'm too cool, too tough, and too smart to be a fool.

When my dial-up finally connects and my new emails flood in, the first thing I notice is twenty new messages from TWWINDTM. I delete them all. I'll reclaim whatever's needed to deal with her later. No time now. There's a baby on the way.

As I start to type in Leo's email address, the auto-fill in feature fails me. I deleted him, and all of his emails, right after my return from New York when we broke up. I needed to get all of his emails filled with plans of the future as far away from me as possible for fear of turning into creepy-old-email-re-reader-person-crying-about-what-could've-been. I'd rather go back to being one of those self-help book reader freaks than EVER become that! (F.Y.I., I didn't delete the emails completely. I backed them up on a floppy for posterity. I mean, I'm not insane. It's Leo we're talking about.)

Hmmm. Was it tlcapital.net or tlcapital.com? Was his middle initial in the address?

My new Mommy brain has turned into baby batter, and for the life of me I can't recall his exact address. It's been seven months since I used it. I minimize the screen and search the internet for T.L. Capital. I can't chance this email ending up in the wrong hands...I have to be absolutely sure it gets to him.

The second the *contact us* page of his business opens up, I'm confronted with the next thing that almost gets the best of me—the most debonair picture I've ever seen of the man who was supposed to be my husband. It's situated right at the top of the list of employees, and his bold name and bold title are in bold letters underneath...*Leo S. Armstrong, Managing Director.* His posture is as powerful as his last name: his eyes penetrating, and his mouth curled just so that if you were a man you'd think he was the shit, and if you were a woman you'd shit your pants. It's just that titillating. Quickly, I copy his email address. But before I exit out of the screen I do the worst thing, *the most un-cool thing*, imaginable. I scroll down to look at the other employees and it doesn't take long to land on 'L'—the *next,* next thing to almost get the best of me. Her full name is finally revealed...*Lauren Alabaster, Director of Corporate Relations.*

"Yeah, I bet you're the director of corporate relations, alright. Specifically, *Leo's* corporate relations."

And what about that name...*Alabaster?* Are you even kidding me right now? Who has a name like that, and furthermore who has freaking skin that matches their last name? Seriously, she's drop-dead gorgeous. So much so that I can't imagine there's a woman in the world who truly likes her.

Don't do it, Chrissy. Don't do it! But, it's no use, I can't help myself. Disparagingly, I get out of bed and walk to my full-length mirror. My hair hasn't been washed in two days, my tank top has a four inch long spaghetti stain down the front, my hands and ankles are swollen, and my eyes are wearing bags the size of caterpillars. And don't even get me started on the thirty pounds of new weight that I'm beginning to think will never go away.

Stop! Ignore the face and the body, *hers and yours*, and press on!

Shell-shocked at my reflection, I get back into bed, and timidly, almost like it might bite me, move my computer to my lap. Here goes what I should've done seven months ago...

Send

April, 2003

My fingers are shaking. Literally shaking so hard that I have to retype the word "Dear" three times before I can proceed with what I know I have to do to get my life back. From the kitchen I hear Barbara yell, "You're doing the right thing, Hunny!" And with that encouragement, I type away…

Dear Leo,

Ever since the day I met you, I tried to convince myself I would be okay if we didn't work out. Yet, each time we don't work out, I never make it to okay. I know eventually I'll make it there. I mean, I have to for me and the kids. But I don't want to sit around and wait for eventually. It hurts too much to get there. So I'm fighting for what I want. I'm fighting against that eventual moment when I have to be okay without you, and I'm writing this letter to ask if you want to fight with me.

Before I get to why I think we should fight for us, I should tell you about the baby. First, and most important, it's healthy. Despite the unnecessary complications I added to my life for the last seven months, everything with the pregnancy has gone smoothly.

Okay, some might disagree with me on this, but he doesn't need to know about the placenta previa, more specifically, the reason for it. At face value, one might think it manipulative to keep it from him, like that I'm purposely excluding any mention of Kurt for fear it'll push him further into L's arms. But that's not the case. I simply don't want to be dramatic—another ugly characteristic of mine it's time to shed. Let's face it, dramatic is very un-cool. Besides if I follow the doctor's orders, everything

95

will be fine. If at next week's ultrasound I hear different, I'll let him know the situation.

I don't know what I'm having, but Kendall is adamant it's a boy, and his name will be Weo. It's painfully cute, and a testament to how much you meant to her in the time you guys had together. She still misses you a lot and I hope, despite the damage I've caused, that the two of you can find a way to have the kind of relationship you had before.

Here goes nothing...or everything...

You probably want to know the real reason why I kept the pregnancy from you. It was fear, Leo. Despite what I told you in New York, I didn't actually know what happened the night I spent at Kurt's house because I had too much to drink, and I ran away from finding out for seven months. There's no apology in the world that can erase the stupidity surrounding my decision to hide from the truth, so I won't even offer one up. The only thing I can do now is try to be honest with you.

Taking a deep breath in, I continue to nervously type, shaking my disgusted head with every brutally honest word, but oddly at the same time, feeling calmer by the minute for letting all of the chaos out.

The morning you came to the studio was the morning I was to get all of the answers from Kurt, that's why he was there, too. But you arrived before him and something snapped inside of me when you walked in, that same something that snaps every time I get near you. Once you were close to me I couldn't bear to let you go, and so I said whatever it took to make sure that didn't happen. I'm sorry, but it's true, Leo, I didn't know for absolute fact that the baby was yours when I told you it was, but from the bottom of my heart I knew I was right. I knew this baby was yours. Even though it's a foolish excuse, and something you

96

probably can't forgive, it's the truth and it's all I have to give you.

I stop for a moment to tell myself this is the last time I will ever ask for forgiveness for telling a lie.

There is one other disturbing thing you should know. If I had been able to do what I planned the other morning, which was to have a confidential talk with Kurt and get assurance that the baby wasn't his, I was never going to tell you what I had been struggling with for seven months. I was going to make you think that you, specifically the reason why you broke up with me, were the real reasons why it took me so long to tell you about the baby. To get you back I was going to lie to you, something I vowed I would never do again.

The words I'm writing now are as mind-blowing and eye-opening as the ones I wrote five years ago in my journal about my affair. Kurt ended up stumbling upon those secrets and chose to ignore them. I wonder if Leo will do the same.

For a second it seemed like my plan would work. I naively thought Kurt would see how happy I was and walk away...I'd get the proof I needed from him later. But then everything came to a screeching halt when you told me about your engagement. In an instant, my plan no longer mattered. The only thought racing through my mind was I could never be with you knowing you gave yourself to another woman like that, but...

It's okay Chrissy. Be authentic...be vulnerable. They're the two best characteristics taught to you by two of the most amazing people you've ever met...Dr. Maria and Leo, himself. And being those things is the only way you'll ever get what you want. And who cares if what's-her-Alabaster-face gets hurt by what you want? The difference between what's good for you and what's good for everyone else is happiness.

97

...now that I've had a few days to think about it, I'm not so sure that's the case.

Since this might be my only chance to ever tell you how I feel about your engagement, I have to take it, and I have to be shamefully honest. So here it goes...She'll never break your heart like I did, Leo, and I don't mean that in a good way. You'll never be that in love with her. Everything you told me at the yoga studio the other day convinced me of that. You deserve truly, madly, deeply love, and the idea that you could enter into a marriage without it brings me to my knees. Maybe I screwed up too much to ever be the one you marry, but don't choose her. She's not enough for you. The safe route won't be the right route, and you'll end up being unsatisfied, and like you said at the studio the other day, there will be a bigger mess for you to have to clean up. I've been there and it's the worst place imaginable. It's so bad that it's easier for most people to stay in the mess than try to clean it up. And what kind of life is that?

Thinking back to the one raw and tender gesture Leo made early in our relationship, the one that convinced me of his intense love for me, I wipe away a solemn tear and press on.

If you've ever placed her hand on your heartbeat so that she could feel your love and commitment to her beating inside your chest, then I'm wrong about everything. I'll graciously move on and treat you with nothing but respect and admiration while we weather the storm of raising this child. I promise, Leo, I'll never get in the way of your heart.

I close my eyes and pray for a miracle before I sign off.

I know I've wronged you in the worst way imaginable, and I'm not sure you can ever forgive me, but I'm begging you to let me help you. And I'm begging you to help me forgive your engagement. For people like us, these seem like insurmountable tasks, but there's no one else in the world I trust more to help me mend my broken heart. I hope you feel the same way. Please, Leo, please decide to dream with me again. Please decide to fight for us.

Chrissy

I sit in the silence of my bedroom, reading over my long overdue words, pausing midway through when I begin to reflect on someone else's—Dr. Maria's. I'm clearly at one of those crossroads in life that she spoke to me about a few years ago. And like she advised, I have to make a life changing move before too much time passes, before it becomes too hard to accept the fact that I wasted precious time and energy, and am forced to pretend everything is okay. As if I'm back on her couch, I make a promise to her.

"I notice the crossroads, Dr. Maria, and hard as it is, I'm taking action."

But just as I'm about to hit the Send button, I hurriedly minimize the screen, and open up a blank Word document. At the top of the page I type, *The Hope List*. Now, I've made a lot of convoluted lists in my time, *The Life List* I made when I was sixteen being at the top of the pile. I've also been the recipient of some complicated lists, *The Unexpected List* that Kelly created being at the top of that pile. But as far as lists go, this new one will be uncomplicated. It won't be a list of silly pipe dreams, foolish material things, or one detailing the precious gift of a child. In fact, it won't be a list of anything tangible at all. My hope list will just be a simple list of all the things I've learned over the past five years and know to be true, but sometimes, like right now, need reminding of.

The Hope List

The difference between doing something and doing nothing is everything.
The difference between being calm and being chaotic is clarity.

The difference between what's good for you and what's good for everyone else is happiness.

My hope for you, Chrissy Anderson, is that you will never forget these simple things. For it is these simple things that will furnish you with more love, happiness, peace, and strength than anything money could ever buy.

After I save my hope list, I return to the email. With my cursor hovering over the send button, I contemplate all of the things that almost got the best of me tonight. There were my daunting thoughts, my hideous reflection, the horror of my mistakes, probable rejection, humiliation, Leo's dashing picture on T.L. Capital's website…Alabaster's insanely beautiful one.

So many things almost prevented me from typing these grossly honest words and right now they're almost preventing me from sending them. After a super huge deep breath in, I hit send and think…*Almost.*

As I watch the email casually leave my Outbox and settle into my Sent file, I realize something's missing. For the first time ever, I don't feel the warmth and tingle of the love-drug that always courses through my veins when I make contact with Leo. Right now all I feel is shame of my behavior, and bone-penetrating fear that it was so vile that Leo, and quite possibly Kendall and my baby, will never forgive me for it.

Unknowingly

May, 2003

B ed rest sucks. But you know what sucks even more than that? Professing your love…begging for forgiveness…pouring your heart out to the love of your life and getting zilch in return. I take that back, I didn't get zilch. I got an out-of-office-assistant. Yep, immediately after I electronically sent my heart to Leo, I got this:

Until further notice, I'll be out of the office. Please contact Taddeo Pascali, with any urgent matters.

I have an urgent matter, alright, but I'll be damned if I contact that son-of-a-bitch to ask for help. He'd probably just consider it "corporate relations" and gleefully patch me through to Lauren.

When I got the auto-reply, a million questions shot through my brain. Did he set it up *before* he showed up to the studio or *after* I shattered his heart with more of my lies? Did he set it up because he's in shock over becoming a father, or because the news encouraged him to quickly elope with Lauren? Did he set it up because he's busy moving his life back to the Bay Area to be closer to the baby, or because he's meeting with attorneys to fight for full custody to move the baby to New York because I'm a despicable human being who has no business raising a child?

Today is my first productive day following my week of bed prison and the freedom couldn't have come soon enough…for me *and* my belongings. Out of frustration, I threw nearly everything I could find within arm's reach against the wall— even digging into my nightstand drawers again for more ammo. For a second time, I was stopped just short of annihilating my precious Wonderwand. Thank God Barbara entered my room when she did and reminded me that I'll probably need that thing if Leo never shows up. I'm so lucky to be surrounded by such wisdom.

I just dropped Kendall at school, and am heading into my yoga studio in Lafayette. It'll be my first time back since my deplorable behavior in the meditation room seven days ago. Rolling down my window for much needed air, my eyes wander the streets, and my mind races with questions.

Where are you Leo?

What's going through your mind?

Little did I know he was unknowingly three cars behind me, searching for an office space in beautiful downtown Lafayette.

Merely hours after *Mutual of Omaha's Wild Kingdom* played out at my yoga studio, and Leo found out he was about to become a father, he was back in New York to take care of important business. His first order of business was to talk to Lauren. It was a delicate conversation that took less than thirty minutes, and one that resulted in her acceptance of a lot of things, but unfortunately, her refusal to do one *very* important thing. His next order of business was dissolving his T.L. Capital partnership with Taddeo. After a maddening conversation that took ten times longer than the one he had with Lauren, Leo finally convinced Taddeo to buy him out. Then, he packed up what little belongings he actually cared about and shipped them back to California.

It took less than three days to make all of the necessary steps to transition his life back to the Bay Area, and with all of the heavy lifting behind him, today is his first productive day of finding a home for his new company which will simply be called, Armstrong Financial Services. Spotting a vacant office space that looks like it'll fit the bill, his car unknowingly splits off from mine.

I'm looking forward to getting back to work and keeping my mind busy, and the Lafayette studio is the best place for those two things. It's where all of the big decisions get made, clothing designs get approved, and plans for growth are born. It's the first studio I opened with my motley crew from the old clothing company. Man, that was such an awesome day when Megan, TWWINDTM, and I quit our jobs at the clothing company and made the old owner of the studio an offer she couldn't refuse. The following weeks were some of the best of my life as we demolished and rebuilt what would become the first of three thriving studios. Barbara joined our team shortly after we started and the four of us have been an entrepreneurial yoga-match made in Heaven ever since.

"What the?"

Ever since last week I guess. Pulling into my parking space I'm hit hard with another harsh reality of my poor decision making—an empty lot.

Under my breath, I mumble, "Wow, who knew the departure of a forty-something-year-old-slut could have such an immediate effect on business."

Brushing off the irritation of TWWINDTM's influence on our bottom line, I think…Well, at least I have two other capable women to help me figure out a fix to this problem. But when I get inside the studio, I worriedly wonder…*or are there?*

I arrive at Barbara's little nook first. As usual it's spotless, but not like usual, it's empty. Duh, Chrissy, she's running errands! Remember, she's out shopping for the last of the crap you need to keep the baby alive after you bring it home from the hospital. Recalling my conversation with her last night about where she'd be this morning, I relax and move onto Megan's tiny office. As usual it's a freaking mess, but not like usual, it's littered with stuff from Nepal, not design paraphernalia.

Walking over to a paper pile on her desk, I flip through mounds of handmade cards and letters from Nepalese children profusely thanking her for their library and professing their love for her. Then I move over to stacks of boxes marked *"For the kids"* and open the top one to find more clothes made out of scrap fabric.

"Oh, Jesus, here we go again."

Apparently Megan's focus is elsewhere these days. After I put a sticky note on her computer screen to find me when she returns, I head down the corridor to my office that's tucked away in the back of the studio. On my way I pass a yoga class in session and gasp at the sight. It's a class usually taught by TWWINDTM and it's usually so full it has a waiting list. Not today. Today it consists of seven very confused people, and it's being led by a rather large twenty-something-year-old aspiring hippy with more body hair than Big Foot. The girl can barely settle into a crisscross-applesauce pose, let alone a revolved half moon.

"We're in trouble."

Startled by Megan who crept up behind me and gave me the news I pretty much just figured out on my own, we walk the rest of the way to my office together.

"Is it worse than I think it is?"

"What do you want first, the good news or the bad news?"

"I guess the good."

"Well, so far we're only seeing the effects of her absence at this studio. Moraga and Alamo are still performing as usual. Probably because she teaches way less classes there."

"What's the ba—"

The second we hit my office door I'm hit hard with the most horrible smell in the world. I'm hit even harder when I open it. My desk is over-flowing with vase after vase of days-old flower deliveries. A few are hanging on to dear life, but most are wilted and stink with mold and old water.

My mind is on over-drive.

Leo!

Maybe these are from him and he wants to dream with me again! Maybe he wants me to help him forgive and he wants to help me do the same! Nearly diving for a card attached to one of the vases, Megan cuts my over-active imagination off at the pass.

"Nope. Not from him."

Dejected, I plop down in my chair.

"Then who?"

But before she can answer, I figure it out for myself when I open a card and see "I'm sorry" written in my old slutty friend's handwriting.

Ignoring it, I toss it in the trash and get right to business.

"What's up with Sasquatch out there?"

"She's the only person we could find on such short notice to fill her spots."

"You're telling me you couldn't find one single skilled yoga instructor in all of Contra Costa County?"

"None who want to fill the old instructor's shoes! Chrissy, I tried to tell you it was a mistake to fire her. She's legendary. Half of her classes were filled by people from her old studio who drove all of the way here from San Francisco. Once she left, we lost all of them."

"Well then, we're just gonna have to figure out a way to get them back."

"I agree and I know an easy way to do that."

"See? That's the spirit!"

Grabbing my pad of paper and a pen, I teeter on the edge of my seat, eager to get started. God, I missed stuff like this when I was stuck in bed! It's definitely a nice little distraction from having a fatherless child.

"Give it to me! Whatcha thinkin'?"

"I'm *thinkin'* you call the freaking sweatshop we escaped from a few years ago, the sweatshop I know she's working at again, and beg our yoga meal-ticket to come back to work so we can eat!"

I drop my pen and paper on my desk, point at my stomach and say, "Until I figure out what's happening with this, I can't deal with that. So drop it, okay?"

She replies with a clearly disappointed, "Fine," and then gets up to walk back to the Red Cross...I mean, her office. But before she closes my door all of the way, she hesitantly pops her head back in and asks me one more question.

105

"Is there anything you want to talk to me about…anything else bothering you?"

"How much time have you got?"

"No, I mean, is there anything bothering you about *me*?"

I suppose I could mention her campaign to save the children of the world, but that would be very un-cool and opposite of all of the goodness I'm trying to reclaim.

"Not at all, why?"

"I dunno…Like, you read your emails, though, right?"

"All but the four thousand TWWINDTM sent the last few days. Why? Did you guys forget to pay a bill while I was on bed rest or something?"

Pausing for so long it makes me think her and Barbara forgot to pay *a lot* of bills while I was on bed rest, she eventually, and seemingly regretfully, says, "No…nothing like that. Just wondering." Then she closes the door.

The second she leaves, I immediately log on to check our finances, and quickly confirm that other than the Lafayette studio coming to a screeching halt, everything is on the up and up. Then I open up my email to see if Leo has anything to say. There's nothing.

Dammit, Leo, where are you?

I'm about to close out of my email, but stop and click back on my Inbox, wondering what the heck Megan was talking about. I start to scroll through the list of all incoming emails for the last month and it's business as usual until I land on *Mutual of Omaha's Wild Kingdom* day and Kurt's email telling me he'd meet me at the studio. I quickly re-read it, feeling a slight stir in my stomach as I relive the anxiety I felt that morning. Then, my stomach settles when I remember our long talk at the hospital later that day. So many shitty things happened to me that morning, not one of them being Kurt's confession of love for a new woman. As sad as I am for myself right now, I'm happy for him. I quickly draft an email telling him so and I ask when I can meet the new woman, promising not to go all Kayla on her ass. I trust his judgment, but it's important for Kendall *and* harmony

106

for me to meet her. Gee whiz, look at me doing mature things and turning all six years old over night!

When I'm done with Kurt, I click on the email Megan sent me the night before *Mutual of Omaha's Wild Kingdom* day—the one alerting me to the fact that she and Kurt had arrived home from Nepal—the one I never completely read. Just as I'm about to re-read it, an appointment reminder pops up on my screen. I promptly shut down my computer, rush out of the office, and drive like a maniac down Mt. Diablo Boulevard to get to where I need to be…unknowingly passing Leo, who's standing outside of the office he just signed a lease on.

Mr. Wonderful

May, 2003

"So how's everything looking down there, Doc?"

It's been a week and a half since I was diagnosed with placenta previa, and time to see if the time I had spent in bed had made a difference. It's also time to see if it's necessary to email Leo and let him know what's going on…even though he hasn't asked me to.

"I see slight movement of the placenta, which is good, considering it's only been a week. The shift, combined with the fact that you only had a mild case of placenta previa from the start, is reassuring."

"How reassuring is it?"

"I'm giving you the green light to resume a light workload, but I want you off of your feet by three o'clock every day. And all of the other stuff I told you before still applies. No sex and no stress."

"So I'm still on target to deliver on June twenty-second?"

Pulling out his calendar he says, "Yes and no."

"What's that supposed to mean?"

"I'm scheduling a c-section…" He begins to flippantly flick though his datebook, "…and my schedule dictates your baby will come on June nineteenth."

That certainly gives me a good reason to email Leo.

"Okay then. June nineteenth it is."

Wow, this couldn't be any better…I get another reason to contact Leo to ask for his forgiveness *and* no chance of crapping on a delivery table!

Slapping his datebook closed, my doctor curiously asks, "So, what's your birth plan?"

"Uhhhh, to get it out."

109

"No, I mean, have you decided who will be by your side at the birth? Who would you like to cut the umbilical cord? Who will go with the baby if it needs special care...drive you and the baby home from the hospital? Stuff like that."

I want to hide under a mountain of un-cool, un-tough, and un-smart, and break down at the thought of bringing this child into the world without Leo. I feel the tears swelling, and for a second it feels like I might have to rely on the doctor with no bedside manner to give me a shoulder to cry on, but instead I clear my throat and answer like I've got everything under control.

"Oh, I was just...I was just kidding with you. I...my friend...the one who came to my very first doctor's appointment...you remember her, right?"

Rather contemptuously he answers, "How could one forget?"

"Most can't. Anyway, the plan is for her to be by my side and do all of that stuff."

It *was* my plan. But now that she's out of the picture I have to come up with back-up birth plan.

As he makes a note in my file, he mutters, "Then I guess I'll inform the rest of the hospital to be on high alert for a crazy person, I mean, your friend, on June nineteenth then."

Gathering his notes and walking to the door without offering any kind of good-bye, my grumpy old OB pauses when he turns back to find me hunched over with my gaze locked on the ground.

With his eyes piercing over the top of his reading glasses, he asks, "Any chance the baby's father will join us on June nineteenth, Ms. Anderson?"

Being asked a question like that was never on any list I made.

"I'm working on it."

"It's none of my business, but is he a good man? A man you'd like to be a part of the child's life? I'm only wondering because you haven't included him in it so far."

110

Feeling one more kick in my shamed pants, I softly tell him, "He's the most wonderful man in the world. He's hard-working, loving, and loyal. He's everything I hope my baby becomes."

"Strong too, huh?"

Raising my head, I ask, "Yeah. How did you know?"

"That ex-husband of yours was wearing a pretty nice shiner. I believe you said it was compliments of the baby's father."

Cracking my first smile of the day, I divulge, "I think it's his way of showing love."

"Perhaps he'll take a break from that primitive method, and choose to hold your hand on the nineteenth?"

All I can do is put on a brave face and shrug my shoulders.

"Bringing this baby into the world will be one of the most monumental tasks you've ever performed, Ms. Anderson, and there are no do-overs. It'd be a shame not to have the people by your side that matter the most."

Hanging my head low again, I whisper, "No matter how wonderful the baby's father is, I might've messed up too bad for that to happen."

"Well now that you have an official date, the clock is ticking for you to track down Mr. Wonderful, make things right, and get him involved with things. You might regret it if you don't." Closing the door behind him and leaving me all alone with nothing more than a belly smeared with KY jelly, a fistful of tissues to wipe it off, and my shameful thoughts, I think…It'd just be one more regret swimming around in an ocean of them.

Unglued

May, 2003

"You told him the date then, right?"
            "Yeah, a week ago."
"And?"

"And I just got another one of those out of office messages. He's probably on his honeymoon or something."

I'm picking at my food and wanting to throw up at what I just admitted to my two oldest and dearest friends. It's our final meal together before Courtney jets off to wherever and Nicole drives off to who-fucking-cares. I don't know what hurts more right now, our last official girls' night out, or that Leo has apparently turned his back on me forever.

"Well, Mama, can't you just call him? I mean, this is one of those special circumstances that warrants an interruption— honeymoon or otherwise."

"Court's right, Chrissy, I think it's time to suck it up and make the call. At the very least you need to ask him to support you financially with this."

My swollen fingers drop my fork.

"How can I possibly ask him to give me something he doesn't want to willingly give?" Then shaking my appalled head, I make my feelings clear with, "No way, I don't want anything from him."

I started considering the scary certainty that I'd be bringing up not only one, but two, children on my own the minute I got Leo's *second* out of office message. Sure I'd already adapted to raising Kendall on my own, and I'd already been without Leo for my entire pregnancy, but most of my anxiety about being a single mother of two had been safely tucked away in the back of my mind since the moment I found out I was pregnant. But the minute Leo's *second* scripted out of office message hit my

113

Inbox, all anxiety was unleashed and it took over my whole being. I scrambled to my bank statements and calculator and started working the numbers. The overhead of my dream house has been hanging *over* my head since the moment I moved into it and now with the Lafayette studio going down the drain, reality set in that I might have to let it go. I was so focused on making ends meet during my anxiety attack that I didn't notice when Barbara walked in on my freak-out with a bag of groceries. I also didn't notice when she turned my laptop around to read the unanswered email that started the mad scramble.

Dear Leo,

Every second since the email I sent to you last week has been torture. Between beating myself up for what I did to you and imagining you getting on with your life...I'm miserable. Understandably, this must make you and a lot of other people happy.

I'm sending this email to tell you the baby will be born on June 19th. I was diagnosed with something very minor. It's nothing affecting the health of the baby, but it's something that warrants a c-section. There's a part of me that can't blame you for not wanting to have anything to do with this, but there's a much bigger part of me that can't fathom you blowing this off. This is your child, Leo, and something about your absence since you found out about all of this, isn't adding up to me. I did a lot of things wrong, but not even the worst of it would keep you away from this baby. I just know it.

I still want to fight to save us. Please say you feel the same.

Chrissy

In the middle of my number-crunching Barbara walked up behind me, wrapped her arms around me, and whispered, "He'll come around, Hunny. I just know it." But her words of encouragement had the opposite effect that she intended. In that moment, I realized if Leo was going to come around, he would've done it by now. I became convinced that he had, in fact, moved on with Lauren. And this is exactly what I just got done explaining to Courtney and Nicole.

"But Chrissy, you don't know that for sure."

"I agree with Nicole. Your delivery date is still seven weeks away. Technically, he still has a little time left to process all of this."

"Yeah, I mean, he already missed, like, thirty-two weeks of this thing. What's a few more?"

"Guys, if Leo's anything, he's all business. Trust me, if this was something he wanted to take care of, he'd take care of it, and he'd separate his feelings about me from it. In fact, his motto is, 'If you don't take care of business, you go out of business.' His absence since finding out about all of this is crystal clear. I'm so out of business it's not even funny."

The sympathetic looks in their eyes tell me they believe what I'm telling them. After a long pause my best friends do what they've been predisposed to do since the day I met them.

"You know what, Chrissy? Since Kyle and I sold our house we have a butt-load of cash. I'm giving you some to get you through that first year, and I won't take no for an answer. Diapers are a bitch on the budget and I want to help out."

Court's not far behind with, "I'm in, too. Whatever you need, Chrissy."

Being a charity case was never on *any* list I made, EVER. If these offers came from anyone other than the two of them, I'd die of embarrassment.

"I love you both so much, but I'm fine, really. My heart may be broken, but so far my bank account isn't. Barbara's pretty much moved in to my house to help out, and the studios are doing great."

Well, two out of three of them anyway, but they don't need to know that.

"I live in a beautiful home, I have a beautiful career, and I'm about to have one more beautiful child. I'm the luckiest single mom in the world."

The two of them roll their eyes.

115

"Guys, I'm serious. Comparatively speaking, I know how good I have it."

I don't, but why ruin our last meal together?

The rest of our last convenient dinner together is peppered with talk of Nicole's new teaching job waiting for her in Arizona, Courtney's funky housing accommodations in Zimbabwe, and some funny old stories about Kelly that on any other night would've had us laughing a lot more. Once the last of Kelly's place setting is cleared from the table, and we get our usual confused look from the server as to why we requested it (along with her untouched cocktail), we sit in silence, tears welling up in each of our eyes. Nicole's the first to break the silence.

"No good-byes, okay? Nothing changes."

Then Court with, "I'm down with that, besides nothing *does* change. A-BOB's forever, right girls?"

Even though I join them in saying, "Right," I know otherwise. It *is* good-bye and everything does change. Life is crazy hard and without the ease of having your best friends close enough to visit on a regular basis, life kind of moves on. Dinner slots get filled with convenient friends, and you suddenly find yourself telling those convenient friends the things you used to tell your best friends. Don't get me wrong, Courtney will forever be regarded as my problem-solver, and Nicole will always hold a sarcastic place in my heart, but without the convenience of these dinners and having the two of them close by, we will drift apart. And I fear, one day, we won't really know each other anymore. My package is officially broken. There's no glue or tape left to keep it together. These depressing thoughts are why I am, and always will be, the emotional core of the group.

"Chrissy, you leave first, okay?"

I shake my head in dynamic defiance.

"Court's right, Chrissy. If you don't leave first we'll just sit here and cry until they force us to leave the restaurant. Then we'll just prolong the agony out in the parking lot. It won't be pretty."

"But you guys are the ones deciding to leave me! Why are you making me do the hard part?"

It's quiet for a long time before Courtney admits, "Because I can't."

And then Nicole, "I can't either..." Taking a deep breath in, she continues with, "...I talk all tough, and make all of my dumb jokes, but it's all a defense mechanism to protect me from crying like a baby."

Courtney places her hand on top of mine and admits, "Deciding not to leave here first is the same reason we couldn't give Kelly's eulogy. It's too fucking hard. Emotional wreck and all...you've always been tougher than us when it comes to matters of the heart, Chrissy."

I slowly gather my purse and rise from my chair, keeping myself remarkably composed until Courtney asks me to send pictures of the baby the minute it pops out. I bite my trembling lower lip and nod my head. In an attempt to protect her heart with her sarcasm, Nicole reminds me not to forget to bring the baby home from the hospital. I keep biting, trembling, and nodding.

"Just go, Chrissy."

"Yeah, before we start to talk about all of 1987, *The Price Is Right*, MC Hammer's house, or some other completely ridiculous memory that'll take us into tomorrow."

Then Courtney does something extremely rare, she asks for reassurance.

"We'll be back, Chrissy. This isn't forever, right Nic?"

"Right. A-BOB's forever."

My overly emotional ass wants to correct Nicole by reminding her that if we really were forever, Kelly would still be here, but I don't. Instead, I tuck my chair in, and stand at the table for a moment longer, taking both of them in. The moment is reminiscent of my last minutes standing at the podium at Kelly's funeral. Except this time, a tiny smile doesn't form on my perfectly lined lips and I'm not overwhelmed with any guiltless knowledge about anything. I'm not wearing a stitch of make-up, and the only thing I'm overwhelmed with is gas and bloating—compliments of the last stages of pregnancy.

My crackling voice whispers, "I love you guys and I'm so proud of the big moves you're making. I am, and always will be, in awe of the both of you." Then I blow them a kiss and walk out to my car.

Instead of immediately leaving, I sit and wait for the two of them to exit the restaurant, which they do about five minutes after me. After a tight embrace, and assisting each other with the removal of smudged mascara, I watch my maternal love, my very best friends since I was a fourteen year old girl, get into their own cars and drive in opposite directions, painfully comprehending the symbolism.

Light Bulb

May, 2003

It was a long and brutal drive home from the restaurant as memories of all of my years with Courtney, Nicole, and Kelly whirled through my mind. Tears slid off my face and plopped onto my large belly as I remembered some of our best…and worst…times together. There were memories of stalking our first boyfriends, stealing beer from convenience stores, driving without licenses, proms and, of course, atrocious prom dresses. There was our covert trip to Los Angeles to try out for *The Price is Right*, getting on *The Price is Right*, and then getting kicked out of *The Price is Right*. There were wild spiral perms, pathetic bob-style haircuts, insane bachelorette parties, wonderful wedding parties, and surprise twenty-ninth birthday parties gone awry…thanks to me. Memories of all of our girl talk throughout the years brought me smiles and giggles that had me looking borderline cuckoo on my drive back to Lafayette—the most cherished memory of all being when the four of us would cut class in high school, drive to Santa Cruz, and listen to "Forever Young" on our boom box. We'd sit in a tight circle in the sand, the wind whipping through our big Eighties hair. We'd hold hands and address each other by our fake names, you know, the good ol' fashioned slut names we really wished our parents had given us. Nicole was Charlotte, Courtney was Tiffany, Kelly was Ginger, and I was Vanessa. While our names might've been phony, our conversations were always real…especially the ones we had on the beach as teenagers. The four of us would talk excitedly about the future and we'd dream out loud about the boys we wanted to marry one day…and we promised to stay tight, no matter what. And we were tight for a very long time.

As I pull into my driveway, the memory of the last time my friends and I held hands jars me. There were only three of us and it was while I was giving Kelly's eulogy. I thought I'd have Kelly, and all of the A-BOB's for that matter, in my life until the day I died. Additionally, I thought Kendall would have both of her parents her whole life. Christ, I also never thought I'd be pregnant without a man in my life or without a father for my baby. Goes to show ya, things just don't turn out how you think they will…no matter how many lists you make or how much planning you do. By the time I exit my car, I look as if I had poured an entire glass of water on myself.

The A-BOB's will always be the A-BOB's, but the girls I grew up with are gone. Obviously, one a lot more gone than the other two, but all feeling further away than they ever had before. Kelly hasn't been back in my dreams since last month and I get the sense she's never going to return, and now Courtney and Nicole are embarking on these amazing journeys that will change their lives, and our friendship, forever. Depressed and way too drenched to immediately go inside and recap all of my losses to Barbara, I plop down on the front porch and recap them alone.

Leo…gone.

Best friends…dead and gone.

Lafayette studio…almost dead and gone.

Mid-recap, the lawn sprinklers pop on. Lost in the haze of their rhythmic movement I mull over everything…Listing things out as usual.

1) I'm doing all I can with Leo. I was authentic and vulnerable in my emails and I will continue to be. I won't quit on him until he tells me to. *But what else can I do?*
2) Courtney and Nicole are gone, at least in a geographical sense. I'll feel the loss of their nearby friendship and the maternal love they gave me, but I'll replace it with someone else. *But who?*
3) Something must be done to turn my yoga business around and quick. The only idea Barbara and Megan continue to throw my way is to bring back

TWWINDTM. But there's no way. I didn't rename her for nothin'. *But how can I generate the kind of business she did?*

Paralyzed in some sort of emotional vortex, I continue to sit, unable to give myself any reassurance that everything will be okay. Fortunately my mini-life coach erupts through the front door to lend a hand…and I am so grateful that she did.

"Hi Mommy! Whatcha doin'?"

"Oh, just thinking about Auntie Courty and Auntie Nic. They're leaving soon to start their big new adventures."

"Are you sad?"

"A little bit."

"But you still have Barnana, and Megan, and—"

Cutting her off before she can say the name I no longer want to hear, I put my arm around her and shout out, "And you! I have *you* and you're all I need!"

"Don't forget about baby Weo! You need him too!"

"Kendall, about that…I'm not so sure baby Leo is…a Leo."

I wish I had a camera to capture the look on her sweet stunned face.

"You mean…he might be a *guuuuuurl*?"

"It's a possibility we have to be prepared for. Are you okay with that?"

She lets out a big ol' exasperated sigh and moans, "I guess. I'll just have to teach her about snipe hunting and sharks. A baby Weo would already know dat stuff."

"A baby *anything* would have to be taught that stuff, Love. I'll help you, though, okay?"

"Do *you* even know about any of dat stuff?"

"Of course I do!"

Not a clue.

"More than Weo?"

"So much more than Leo, it's not even funny."

My life is so off course, it's not even funny.

For a minute we both get lost in the meditating motion of the sprinklers. The tranquil moment is interrupted when Kendall wonders, "Mommy, will this baby have a daddy or will it be just like me?"

Ouch. I look up to the Heavens and silently scream, "KELLY! GRANDPA! *HELLOOOOOOOOOOOOOO!* ANYONE WANT TO HELP ME OUT WITH THIS?"

Knowing full well that no one will save me, I place my fingers on her chin and delicately shift her focus to my face.

"Kendall, this baby is going to have you and me. And *we're* going to have this baby. The three of us will make a family. If someone else comes along and they want to be a part of our family, the three of us will have a very important meeting and we'll decide together if we want to let them in. How's that for a plan?"

As quickly as a smile appears on her face, it disappears.

"But what last name will this baby have?"

"I'm not...I'm not sure yet."

"Can we all match?"

Kendall still goes by her parent's last name, which is Wilson. It never occurred to me how badly she wanted all of us to be the same.

"I don't...I don't think me or the baby can have your last name, Hunny. But it doesn't mean we aren't—"

"Then, can I have yours?"

Shit, I don't even want mine, I want Leo's. But as each day passes it seems like Lauren has it now and there's not a damn thing I can do about it. Great, I'm gonna be that *The Jerry Springer Show* slut who gets mail at her house for a bunch of kids that all have different last names and not one of them matches hers because none of her baby-daddies wanted to marry her. Technically that wasn't the case with Kendall, but my mailman won't know that. He'll just lick his lips when he sees me for the baby-maker that he, and everyone else, will assume I am.

122

"Sweetie, you can have anything you want. How about this…we'll name the baby after it's born and then we'll decide on the same last name for all of us?"

"Really?"

"Really!"

Hope she likes Anderson because all signs point to it as the only option.

Kendall bolts up and runs back in the house to deliver the news to Barbara, and I wipe a bead of sweat off of my forehead from the tricky conversation. It suddenly occurs to me that one day, probably very soon, Kendall will outright ask who the father of this baby is. How will I tell her it's Leo? And how in *theee hell* do I explain to her why he's not a part of our lives? Jesus, how do I explain all of that stuff to his own child?

Where are you, Leo?

What's going through your mind?

Actually, screw this! My besties were right. With just a little over seven weeks left of this pregnancy, it's time to track Leo down and confront him with those questions. I'll tell Kendall and the baby whatever *he* wants me to tell them. Criminy, I told him what I wanted in my emails; it's time for him to do the same.

Then something else occurs to me.

Fuck feeling like I need to be taken care of. I'll miss Court and Nic like crazy, but I'm a maternal love-giver myself now, and I have to admit, I'm kind of good at it. In fact, I make a pretty damn good single mother. Look how happy I just made Kendall.

I sit up straight and proud and think, look at me…sitting here in the midst of all of these crossroads…deciding where to go! But then I immediately slouch back down when I think about the damaging drop in business at my beloved Lafayette studio. I've been racking my brain since that dreaded day I saw the empty parking lot, and still no solid plan to boost business. I might be a damn good single mother, but I'll be a *struggling* single mother if something isn't done fast!

I know! First thing tomorrow morning I'll drive over to the Moraga studio and sit in on a class from one of our better instructors. Of course, I can't participate in the class...doctor's orders. But just being there will get my creative juices flowing and inspire me to get out of my money-crunching corner. I wish all of the single mommies of the world had as much access to the calming benefits of yoga that I do. They probably *never* have a moment alone to contemplate crossroads, let alone take action on them. When their children are in school, I imagine they're trying to make ends meet, and when their children aren't in school, I bet they're waiting on them hand and foot...Never a moment to achieve a clear head...Never a moment to—

Whoa...wait a minute!

I slowly sit straight back up.

Oh my God, could that actually work?

The wheels of my brain, the ones that fell off when I got pregnant, begin to reattach themselves. Ideas start shooting around, and one of the biggest smiles to hit my face in eight months appears out of nowhere. New lists start forming in my head and my baby wobbles all around at the excitement. Just like Kendall, I bolt up from the porch and barrel through the front door, screaming out, "Barbara, I just had the best idea, EVER!"

The moment the front door slams shut the sprinklers abruptly shut off and water that once covered the dusky evening air like a misty veil settles onto the grass...revealing a contemplative Leo across the street leaning against his old red Jeep.

Game Changer

May, 2003

"**B**ut what about the liability insurance costs?"

"Yeah, Chrissy, that's gonna take a nice chunk of the profit you're expecting."

"Guys, I don't care if there's only a penny left at the end of the insurance costs, it's a penny more than we're making now. Besides, this isn't about the money."

As if my unborn child just slid out of my huha and landed on the ground, the two of them snap their heads in my direction and stare at me in shock and disbelief.

"Not about the money?"

"Who are you and what have you done with our Chrissy?"

Addressing their ridiculousness, I cradle my hands under my belly because it really does feel like this thing is going to slip out…I'm just that huge.

"Megan, you're not the only charitable bitch in town, you know! And Barb, I'm right here and more myself than I've been in a very long time. So let's get to work!"

And that's exactly what we did. With just seven weeks left of my pregnancy, and probably only seven weeks left of the Lafayette studio, there was no time to waste. I tackled all of the non hard-labor-related activities like securing financing, interviewing new staff, and of course, negotiating the most kick-ass, affordable liability insurance policy in the world. A policy that guaranteed a heck of a lot more than a few pennies if my projections pan out! (I have my pregnancy cleavage to thank for the outcome of that negotiation.) And strictly following doctor's orders, I did all of my work from the comfort of my desk before three o'clock, and on my couch at home after that.

Megan took care of the nitty-gritty demolition crew, and cracked the whip on the guys hired to build my vision, and she did it even better than I could've done it myself. For the first time ever I could actually envision her on that strenuous trip to Nepal, and unselfishly, I even wanted the experience for her again. It's become abundantly clear to me that her interest in clothing design has dwindled. A fire is burning in her to do something more meaningful than dress middle-aged soccer moms. While my little vision is satisfying her need to do good, it's still *my* vision. I can tell she wants her own.

Barbara was in charge of purchasing all of the supplies to fill the newly constructed space, and for developing a program to engage our precious new clientele. Talk about attacking a task with gusto! In all of the time I've known Barbara, I've never seen her so happy. Not even when I introduced myself to her in the parking lot of our old therapist's office and got her creative juices flowing after many years of hibernation. Barbara's enthusiastic dedication to the huge undertaking at the Lafayette studio reassured me we were on the right path. She even enlisted Kendall's help in the process, making all of us feel more like a family than ever before.

Then, after three very productive weeks, the three of us hit the marketing road. We placed fliers on every car in every elementary school parking lot, dispersed them in every pediatrician's office, and even went the extra mile by lining Mt. Diablo Boulevard with signs advertising our bold transformation. If I hadn't been so focused on the task at hand I would've noticed I taped a flier right outside the front door of Armstrong Financial Services, and I would've noticed Leo sitting at his desk watching me do it.

Finally, on the last day of May, exactly twenty days after the light bulb moment on my front porch, Club NiCo had its grand opening. In classic Chrissy-style I invited the local media and bragged about the expansion of Forever Young, Inc. The article that ran in the paper the next day looked like this:

Chrissy Anderson, owner of three Forever Young Yoga studios has much to celebrate these days. There's the upcoming

126

birth of her second child, and the grand re-opening of her Lafayette Studio where Anderson recently added Club NiCo. Named after her two best friends from childhood, Club NiCo is a customized yoga program, day spa, and childcare facility specifically focused on the single mom.

Anderson says, "It's fairly easy for me to schedule time to take care of myself—I'm in a yoga studio every day. But I'm also a single mother, so it's very easy for me to see how that can be a challenge for a lot of women." Anderson's objective with Club NiCo is to offer women with limited time and resources the opportunity for some much needed TLC. With affordable prices, and the luxury of built in childcare, Anderson has artfully and skillfully tapped into an oftentimes neglected market.

"I want all mothers to enter this space and truly relax, and I know that's not possible unless their children are well taken care of. With an art studio that's staffed with the most fun and creative people I've ever met, our goal of taking care of mothers and their children will be met."

Additionally, Anderson promises the overall nature of her business of relaxation for all clientele won't be compromised by the changes at the studio. "We've created a separate outside entrance for mothers and their kiddos. Once checked in, the children will remain in that space and the mothers will pass through another door, gaining access to the calming studio where they'll be able to unwind, reflect, and rejuvenate along with everyone else."

Dedicated to two women in her life who gave her unconditional love and support, Chrissy Anderson is paying it forward with Club NiCo in a clever and thoughtful way.

What my scaled-down motley crew has been able to achieve in such a short amount of time is truly remarkable. Ninety-nine percent of that article was to hopefully benefit them, and of course, the woman we're now able to service. Truth be told, one percent of it was for Leo's mom. I remember Leo told me she read the last article that had ever been written about me—when

127

my first studio opened in 2000. She even sent a copy of it to him in New York. At least that's what he told me when I not so accidently ran into him at P.J. Clarke's. My hope is that she'll do the same with this article and he'll see me for the "clever and thoughtful" person I am, and not the stupid and reckless woman he knows me to be.

While my focus has mainly been on three things for the last four weeks, Kendall's happiness, the baby's health, and Club NiCo's success, my hunt for Leo hasn't been far behind. I continue to email him every single day and tell him I won't stop until he tells me to. And every day I get that damned out of office auto-reply. His absence is baffling me. I saw his face the day he saw my pregnant stomach. He loved this child on impact. He might be mad as hell at me, but there's no way he'd take that anger out on the baby. Something very, very weird is going on.

As I now leave the Lafayette studio on its first full day (well, half day for me…doctor's orders) of brand new business, I rub my very large and very aching belly, and declare, it's time to get creative in my search for Leo. Time is running out.

Tick-Tock

May, 2003

"Hunny, you up *again*?"

"Yep. It's like every ten freaking minutes with this thing."

It's five o'clock in the morning, and it's the fifth time I've been up to pee since I went to bed last night. Ever since I got pregnant it's been my goal to keep the baby inside of me for as long as it took to sort out my life. But as of a couple of days ago, my bladder is beginning to make me rethink that plan. And it's not just my bladder, either. I'm psycho-bitch irritable, my nipples are the size of marbles, my face is puffy, my back achy, I have heartburn, can't breathe, and there's no doubt in my mind that a hemorrhoid or two is sticking out of my ass. Things are becoming annoyingly uncomfortable. If I knew what I know now when I made that life list when I was sixteen, item number six would've only mentioned getting pregnant once!

Another thing I'm rethinking is my ability to fix the damage I've caused with Leo. I've been giving the emails all I've got. I've been repentant, willing to accept the consequences of my actions, and even seemingly tolerant of his decision to move on with another woman. I stopped asking him to fight for us and started focusing on his relationship with the baby. All I want for him is to know his child. But still no word as of two seconds ago when I sat down at the kitchen table and checked my empty email box. Well, technically it wasn't completely empty. There was one email from Courtney. She and her family arrived safely in Zimbabwe, and her crusade to save, rebuild, or create whatever it is she went there to save, rebuild, or create is underway. She attached a darling picture of her, Guss, and their son outside of their new home and it's that image of the perfect family that Barbara walks in and finds me staring at.

129

"I'm never gonna have that, am I?"

She settles in next to me and lets out a heavy sigh.

"I'm surprised...disappointed actually."

My head drops low into the defeated position it's become so familiar with over the years and I let out a heavy sigh myself as I apologize to her for being such a huge disappointment.

"Not at you, Chrissy, at Leo. I expected more from the boy. To be honest, I wasn't sure if he'd be willing to give you another chance after what you did. That would've been a lot for even the most forgiving person to get over. But to turn a blind eye to this baby...Well, it's just disappointing. That's all I can say."

"And all I can say is, it doesn't make any sense."

I struggle to get up from my chair, waddle over to the front window, peer into the darkness, and think for a really long time before I say, "Or...maybe it does make sense."

"What do you mean?"

"I bet my last tube of stretch mark cream he's struggling with doing the right thing and the thing that feels right. That kind of struggle can take a prideful person, which we both know Leo is, a long, long time to work though. I know this because I've been there."

"With your divorce?"

"Yep. I remember the night after I met Leo...sitting on my hearth in Danville, with a ginormous glass of wine, debating whether or not to call him. I was struggling between doing the right thing and the thing that felt right. It was horrific, Barbara. Here was this person who made me feel more beautiful, *more wanted*, than I'd ever felt in my entire life, but it wasn't permissible for me to do something as simple as pick up the phone and talk to him. I couldn't have the thing that made me feel alive because I was married. That's why I always referred to Leo as my drug; he represented some kind of heavenly detrimental influence. He felt *so* good, but at the same time he was destroying my life."

Turning away from the window to face her, I share a revelation I got a while back.

"Falling in love is the best high you can get without breaking any laws, don't you think?"

"Absolutely."

"But when you made a vow to be in love with someone else, that high can disorient you. It can make you do scandalous and irrational things. It can also prevent you from seeing truth and postpone the inevitable..." Turning back to the darkness outside, "...Anyway, like the drug addict I became the minute I looked into Leo's eyes, I naively convinced myself I'd only make one call to him and then I'd go back to my life as Mrs. Kurt Gibbons." Laughing into the darkness, "I thought the right thing to do was to keep on pretending my life as Kurt's wife was everything I ever wanted, and I continued that prideful struggle for way too long." My bitter laugh dies down as I contemplate a sad thought. "I wonder how many women sat on their hearths last night with a ginormous glass of wine and struggled with doing the right thing and the thing that feels right."

"Sadly, probably a lot. But why did you continue that struggle so long after you and Leo fell in love?"

Turning from the window to face her again, I confess, "Because Kurt never betrayed me. It made it easy for me to be a coward and cling to what I thought was fair and right."

"Looking back, what would have been the right thing to do after that first phone call to Leo?"

"Ironically, the thing that felt right. I should've confessed my love for Leo to Kurt and the rest of the world the minute I felt it. For Christ's sake that's what I ended up doing anyway. There never needed to be a choice between doing the right thing and the thing that felt right. They were one in the same."

"But you think Leo's trying to choose between the two of those things right now?"

"I do."

"What does his struggle look like?"

"The right thing would be to follow through on his commitment to marry that girl. The right thing would be to stay as far away from me until the baby's born, and then come

131

forward, but only to have a relationship with the child, because my lies by omission and my deception were so horrific he can't wrap his head around forgiving them."

"And what's the thing that feels right?"

Imagining Leo in the scenario I'm about to describe, I let out a little chuckle.

"To bust down that front door and punch anything standing in the way of having everything he ever wanted."

"Any idea which way he'll lean?"

Peering back out into the darkness, I acknowledge the only thing I know for sure.

"All I know is Leo always does the honorable thing."

"Well, Hunny, both of those choices display some kind of honor."

"Exactly."

"So what you're saying is—"

"What I'm saying is I have absolutely no idea where he is or what he's planning on doing. I just know he's struggling."

"Based on that big mystery, what do *you* plan on doing?"

Just then my baby gives me the biggest and swiftest kick in the gut, reminding me that time is of the essence. If it could kick me in the ass I bet it would.

"This may come as a shocker, Barbara, but I don't plan on giving up." Turning back toward her I ask, "Can you please hand me the phone."

She curiously grabs it and walks it over to me.

"Chrissy, it's five-thirty in the morning. You'll wake up whoever it is you're about to dial."

Thoughtfully taking receiver, I correct her, "It's not five-thirty in New York."

Dickhole

May, 2003

I slowly dial the number that will forever be tattooed on my mind. Not even the worse case of pregnancy brain could erase it. Hearing Leo's voice will most likely induce labor, but I can't go on one more day wondering where his head is. I cannot sit at this crossroads for one more single second. The line only rings once before his deep voice starts speaking.

"This is Leo Armstrong. I'm not able to take your call right now. Leave me a message and I'll get back to you as soon as possible. If you need immediate assistance, press zero for the operator."

The voicemail beeps and prompts me to begin speaking, but before I even say his name, the voicemail beeps again and tells me the mailbox is full.

"What the?"

I end the call and immediately dial it back. Barbara's standing across from me in nervous anticipation. I can tell she's doing her best to stay quiet, knowing that any slight sound or move could make me blow. For a second it makes me wish TWWINDTM was here. She had a magical and amusing ability to relax me in even the most intense circumstances—like when she told me I was pregnant, or when she coached me through various perverse sexual acts to practice on Leo. She always knew how to lighten things up and teach me stuff no one else ever could. I have to learn how to live without her charisma though, because I hate her dead guts.

Leo's voicemail pops on once again. This time I press zero for the operator after savoring the sound of his voice.

"T.L. Capital, how may I help you?"

133

"Leo Armstrong, please."

"Who may I say is calling?"

Looking down at an old newspaper, I pick the first two words I see and piece them together.

"Uhhhhh, Angie...Couch."

"Angie Couch?"

"That's right, I was referred to him by a friend of mine."

"Please hold, Ms. Couch."

Omigod, omigod, omigod! I'm about to talk to him. Do NOT get emotional, Chrissy. The man has been through enough. Just ask him where his heart is after reading your emails. Tell him you can handle it...even though you totally won't be able to if his heart doesn't include you. Just accept the outcome of this mess and make the very best of it. You're a mother first now. And that's what moms are supposed to do best, *aren't they*?

I hear the line click over to an extension and a seriously ticked-off voice says, "This is Taddeo Pascali, what can I help you with?"

Why is Taddeo taking Leo's calls?

"Hello?"

Should I ask him or just hang up?

"*Hello? Ms. Couch?*"

Ask him what, though? All he's going to do is laugh at me, or worse, yell.

He's quiet on the other end of the line until he finally asks, *"Chrissy?"*

Huh? My eyes begin to dart around the room, and then frantically out of the window, Barbara's puzzled eyes following mine.

What the heck? Can he see me?

"Chrissy, I know it's you, so just say something already."

I've come this far...might as well get all of the information I can so that I can get on with that crossroads path picking bullshit.

Giving in, I groan, "How did you know?"

134

"I knew you'd eventually come looking for him. Well, that, and I asked the receptionist for the prefix of the call...took a guess from there."

"Why are you taking Leo's calls?"

"He's not here."

"Where is he?"

"Look, I'm not getting involved with this, okay?"

"Taddeo, please, I'm less than four weeks away from having his baby, and I have to know if he's okay. I have to know that I haven't destroyed him."

"You haven't destroyed him."

Fucking dickhole.

"Taddeo don't make me feel like I didn't mean anything to him! You weren't in our relationship! You weren't—"

"He quit, okay? He's not in New York anymore. To tell you the truth, I don't know where he is."

"What do you mean, he quit? He gave up everything to start that company...why would he leave it all behind?"

"Why do you think?"

I have no clue what I think. Did he leave it all behind for Lauren? For me? For the baby? Can someone just tell me what the hell is going on?

"You tell me, Taddeo, because I have no idea where Leo's head is."

I just hope to all that's Holy it's not in Lauren's crotch right now!

"Honestly, I don't either, so I'm not really sure why we're even talking."

"Please. I know you have a way to reach him. I don't even care if he married that girl. He just needs to know that I want him to know his child. I'm different now, I swear I am."

"Yeah, right."

"I AM! YOU HAVE TO BELIEVE ME!"

"I don't have to believe anything, I'm not in a relationship with you, and the last time I checked, Leo wasn't either."

"How can you be so cold?"

Barbara is suddenly and noticeably worried about the effect this conversation could have on me and the baby, and she silently instructs me to hang up over and over again.

"I don't like you, Chrissy. From the minute I met you at his apartment in Moraga that night, I knew you were wrong for him. He deserved better."

"Good God, who's in love with him, me or you?"

"Fuck you, Angie Couch."

"Okay, okay, okay, I'm sorry. I don't want to fight with you. I just need your help."

"Chrissy, get a clue. He knows where you are. If he wanted anything to do with this, he'd have something to do with this. Obviously his mind is made up."

He's right. The bastard is right. Leo knows I'm having his baby, he knows where I'm working, and where I'm living. Yet...nothing. To my absolute shock and horror, he's acting just like Kurt did when he found my journal—apathetic. My deplorable behavior did the unthinkable...*it made them the same*.

Fighting back tears, I wave off Barbara as she steps closer and attempts to put an end to this train wreck of a conversation.

"Look, I know your allegiance lies with Leo, and I'm actually glad he has someone like you to have his back. But one day you'll regret talking to me like this, Taddeo. Trust me, we will cross paths, and I'll probably have this baby in my arms when it happens, and you're going to feel horrible. But don't worry, I won't rub it in your face, and I won't make you feel worse than you'll already feel. I won't *ever* make you feel like how you're making me feel right now—like a piece of shit."

And then Barbara saves me from additional potential humiliation by taking the phone and hanging it up.

"I'm okay, Barbara. It was mean, but it was what I needed to hear."

"What was what you needed to hear?"

"It doesn't matter if Leo didn't get the emails. He knows where to find me, yet he's nowhere to be found."

136

"Maybe he—"

"Barbara, it's over. He's going to do the right thing, not the thing that feels right."

"Refresh my memory..."

"He's never going to forgive me for the betrayal, and he's going to follow through on his commitment to Lauren and marry her, if he hasn't already. He will come forward, because he's a good man. But not until after the baby is born, and it'll only be to have a relationship with the child."

Barbara catches on to what most would not have.

"Wow. You finally said her whole name, out loud...Lauren."

Turning back toward the window where dawn is just breaking over the horizon, I whisper, "For everyone's sake, I probably need to start getting used to it."

"Come on, Darling, let's get you back into bed for a little more rest. It'll be another busy day at the Lafayette Studio and Kendall will be waking soon. You'll need your energy for that stuff."

In acceptance of where my focus is required, I break away from the window and shuffle off down the hall with one of the best women I've ever met in my life. Had I waited just fifteen more seconds for the sun to rise, I would have noticed Leo who had been jogging back and forth on the street for the last thirty minutes.

Apology Tour

June, 2003

It's quiet. I like quiet. I ran and ran and ran from it for a long time, but when there's nothing to run from, quiet is quite nice.

Nicole and Courtney are settled into their new habitats and loving everything about their new lives. Their emails are full of excitement and energy, and I couldn't be happier for the both of them, especially because they credit me for taking the risks and following their hearts. The three of us will most likely never go to Chili's for a shitty meal ever again, we won't ever sit on the hillside adjacent to M.C. Hammer's old house and drink booze out of a paper bag, and we will gradually, and naturally, begin to share the day to day facts and funnies of our lives with people who reside closer to us—convenient new friends. Two out of three of those things are just fine with me, and the third...well, that's just life. Maybe if I had stayed put with my old life with Kurt, I'd be paralyzed by the change, but I've moved on, too.

And Kendall is the one I credit most for my moving on. She keeps me busy as a bee and forces me to look forward. I love her more than anything in the world, and to be honest, I can't wrap my head around sharing that love with another child. Some people have told me it happens magically when you hold your new baby, and I have to take their word for it because quite frankly, I'm too damn tired to research the subject.

Another thing keeping me busy as a bee is my little Lafayette studio project. It took off *way* better than projected and I'm literally every single *single* mother's BFF. While I'm still obeying doctor's orders and home by three o'clock to rest, I'm like a chicken with my head cut off the nine hours before it. I had no idea there were that many single women out there who needed a break, and that many who needed someone to offer one to them they could afford. In fact, Club NiCo has performed so well, I'm inspired to expand the concept to the other two studios. It's an undertaking that'll have to wait a few months though because I have a much bigger one to undertake before then—the birth of my child.

I'm one week away from the big c-section and my revised birth plan is set in place. Most would include their mother in on theirs, but I'm more than happy for my mom, and her big ol' sunglasses, to hang in the waiting room until my baby is born. So, the plan is Kendall will stay with Barbara and Megan will go with me to the hospital. Both women continue to beg me to talk to TWWINDTM, and I still get a half a dozen emails a week from the meddling tart begging for a conversation, but no, I just can't do it. As far as I know she's working back at the old clothing company, and as far as I'm concerned she can stay there. Okay, okay, I'd be lying to you if I said I didn't miss her, and that I could've used her wit to get me through the last month, but like I said, I just can't do it. My life exploded, and while I set the stage for it to happen, she's the one who pulled the rip cord.

Kurt's been M.I.A. since he popped into see me at the hospital last month. I suspect he's off falling deeper in love with the mystery woman, who, despite my email asking to meet, remains a mystery. I'm fine with it for now. I have enough on my plate. And to help me with all that's on my plate, Megan continues to transport Kendall back and forth to Kurt's. She insists she doesn't mind, and reassures me the "new girl" is amazing, and I'll love her to bits. Kendall, though, she hasn't said a word about the "new girl." I asked a couple of times if Ku-Ku had a new friend, but she just shook her head and said everything's the same as it's always been over there. As long as she's happy, same is good.

I stopped emailing Leo the day I spoke to Taddeo. What's the point? Everything he said is true and my heart tells me Leo has made the decision to move on with Lauren. She will be a part of my life and my kids' lives. The only thing I can do now is pray to God her beauty extends to the inside and she's a good and loving role model to my children…and tolerant to the fact that I'll always be in love with her husband and won't rest until I get him back.

With that thought, I sway myself out of the rocking chair.

I'm standing in the new baby's room and everything's ready to go. The beautiful wrought iron crib is set up, teeny tiny little diapers are piled high in a wicker basket sitting atop a cozy changing table, and there are calming bunnies everywhere to be seen. Unbelievably, it's only a matter of days until there will be a baby in this room. I've had roughly two hundred and eighty days to wrap my head around that fact, but am only now feeling the magnitude of how hard things will be. I'll be getting up in the middle of the night to feed the baby, take it to its first doctor's appointment, change all of the poopy diapers…all alone, and all while, Leo is starting a new family.

I remember feeling very alone the day after I met Leo, five and a half years ago. I remember thinking of how comforting it would be to surround myself with women who've been at that same adulterous crossroad, to question those who have made the same mistake as me and get reassurance that I'm not a failure. I wish the same thing for myself right now. I wish there was someone out there who could make me feel better about the position I'm in—*the position I put myself in.* Unfortunately, though, just like back then, it's a free pass from resolution I'll never have. Sure, I can find a bunch of single mothers to surround myself with and have pity parties with, especially now that I have Club NiCo. But I can't imagine there's anyone out there who wouldn't shake their head in repulsion over what simply didn't need to be.

Shaking my own head, I make my way back to the rocking chair, look up to the Heavens and apologize.

"I'm so sorry."

My remorse doesn't stop there. In fact, it doesn't stop at all. Just like the night I subconsciously knew my marriage to Kurt was over and I screamed, "I FEEL DEAD INSIDE" over and over again, the same thing happens now.

"I'm so sorry, little baby. I'm so sorry I did this to you and Kendall. I'm so sorry, I'm so sorry, I'M SO SORRY."

Head still pointed up to the Heavens, I beg, *"What can I do? Please tell me something, anything.* I'll do whatever it takes. Please, please just give me one more chance."

I apologize to Kurt again for the agony I put him through, to my Grandpa for having to witness it, to Kelly for being so selfish when she was sick, to Barbara and Megan for being so selfish...always. Even to Taddeo, because he was right from the beginning...Leo would've been better off without me.

"And I'm sorry, Leo. I'm so, so sorry. I never meant to hurt you. I was scared. And in a way I think I've been scared my whole life. But I don't want to be scared anymore. I want to be happy. Please be happy with me. Please give me one more chance." I drop my head in my hands and continue to beg over and over again, "Please forgive me...Please. I'm so sorry. I'm so sorry."

Barbara catches my apology tour as she's walking down the hallway, and swiftly attempts to stop it.

"Chrissy! Oh my goodness, what is it? What's the matter?"

Near hyperventilation, I gasp for air as I tell her, "I'm apologizing...to everyone. I know it's too late...but I don't know what else to do!"

"Hunny, this baby is coming in four days! You can't do this to yourself right now."

My crying comes to an abrupt halt as I start to do the math in my head.

"Oh my God, what's the date today?"

"June sixteenth. Why?"

Horrified, I bury my face back in my hands and resume blubbering like a child.

"It's Kelly's birthday. I should be at the cemetery! I forgot and you want to know why?" Without waiting for an answer, I blurt out, "Because I'm a deplorable, selfish bitch, that's why!"

Kneeling in front of me, Barbara tries her best to console me.

"Oh, Hunny, please don't do this to yourself! It's not good for either of you."

It's too late, I'm a wreck the likes of my twenty-ninth birthday surprise party when Leo called me from the restaurant where I planned to secretly meet him. Kurt was supposed to be out of town. Instead he surprised me with a stupid party. I remember standing in my bedroom in a slutty outfit, surrounded by Courtney, Nicole, Kelly, and Kurt, my cell phone rang and it was Leo...worried about my whereabouts. I freaked then like I'm freaking now.

"I can't do this, Barbara. I can't. Every day will be torture. Leo's supposed to be with us. Why doesn't he know that?" Looking up at her, "Please someone find him and tell him he's supposed to be with us! Someone has to tell him how sorry I am!"

"I would, Chrissy, you know that. But I don't know where he is. No one does."

Just then we hear a car pull up in the driveway.

Through my tear and snot encrusted face I wonder out loud, "Great. A visitor...*Now*?"

"It's probably just Kendall."

Checking my watch I correct her.

"Can't be. She's not due home from her playdate for two more hours."

Given the conversation we we're just having, both of our eyes zoom to the window and listen intently as a car door opens and then slams shut. Even though the shutters in the baby's room are closed nearly all of the way we're able to see the outline of a man as he walks in front of the window and to the front door. Seconds later the doorbell rings.

143

The Torture Device

June, 2003

"**O**migod, Barbara, do you think it's Leo?"

"I don't know, but you better go and wash up. If it is him, I'd hate for that to be your reunion face."

But as soon as the doorbell rings, the man walks back in front of the window, gets in his car and leaves.

"Wait! Where's he going?"

"Sit tight. I'll be right back."

Seconds later, Barbara returns with a ginormous floral arrangement.

"What the fuck is that?"

"Chrissy…the language! We talked about this, like, *a zillion times.*"

"I'm sorry. I'M SORRY! Dammit, when will I ever stop being sorry?"

As she hands me the card, she says, "How about we shoot for today?"

Hand shaking, I take the card and say a little prayer before I open it.

Also anxious, Barb blurts out, "Read it! What does it say?"

And then I read the disappointment out loud.

"Chrissy, I miss you guys so much. Can I please come back to work now?"

Barbara takes the card, smiles and says, "Bless her heart." Then looking disapprovingly at me, she pleads, "Can't you just call and make up. Lord knows you could use another friend."

"No. Dead to me…And that's something I'm NOT sorry about."

I pick a white rose out of the assortment and settle back into the rocking chair. The flower takes my mind back to that nightmare day at the studio, and my deplorable betrayal that lead to this sad and lonely predicament.

Softening her tone, one of the only friends I have left in the world assures me, "He'll come around, Chrissy. Like you said, he's just waiting to do the right thing."

"But I want him to do the thing that feels right."

Now primping the crib, Barbara's mind travels back to her own nightmare day. Her tone turns reflective and regretful.

"Take it from me, Hunny, we don't always get we want."

Annnd, here I go again with the "I'm sorrys."

"Jesus, I'm so sorry Barbara. I know this isn't the family you always dreamt of having either."

"No, no it's not." And then her mood quickly transitions back to a happy place. "But, it's a very close second! Now, go get cleaned up. We're going to have a nice quiet dinner when Kendall gets home. Take it from me; they'll be harder to have after next week." Then she sings as she walks down the hallway, *"Life is about to get very busy around here!"*

I walk to the window, open the shutters all the way and wonder for the millionth time, *where are you Leo? What's going through your mind?* Then I pick up the stupid flower arrangement and begin to walk with it down the hall, stopping dead in my tracks when I feel my soaked pants.

"Goddammit!"

From the kitchen, Barbara yells, "Can't you just say 'shoot' or 'aw shucks' for a change?"

After examining the mess, I gripe back to her, "Well this is just *faaantastic*! The water in this cheap thing is spilling out from the bottom. Everything, including me *and* the floor, is completely drenched!"

As fast as a fifty-something year old woman can move, Barbara rounds the corner with a towel and panics as she gets closer to me.

146

"Don't move a muscle! I can't have you slipping and falling!"

After she wipes the floor all around me, she grabs the flower arrangement to inspect it.

"Uh, Chrissy?"

"Yeah?"

"The vase is completely dry."

"That's impossible. Look at me, I'm soaked!"

"Sorry, Babe, can't find a leak anywhere."

Pointing at my pants I say, "Well then, what's all this?"

Her eyes travel from my knees to my crotch, an area of my body I haven't been able to see for months without standing in front of a mirror. Even then, I try as hard as I can to avoid eye contact with the vicinity. Shall we say…it's become a bit unruly. A wax is definitely on the menu after this thing pops out…or, maybe not. It's not like anyone other than my doctor will be rooting around it. Might as well let it go to pot right along with my love life.

With a mile wide grin her face, Barb continues to stare at my crotch as she exhales, "Well I'll be darned."

Bending from side to side, I try to look over my huge belly to get a glimpse of whatever it is she's looking at.

After giving up on the pointless task, I ask in embarrassment, "Aw geez, has the hair grown out so much that it's popping out of my freaking pants?"

"Nope, your water broke!"

"Say what?"

"The little bugger is ready to join the world!"

Stunned, I rephrase the question.

"Come again?"

"We're having a baby, Chrissy. Today."

I violently shake my head from side to side.

"No, no, no, no, no, no, no! I'm the mom and I say it has to stay there until next week!"

Laughing and clearly enjoying the moment, she puts her arm around my shoulder.

"Sorry, my Dear, but these things cannot be controlled!"

Then she begins to rattle off tasks, plans, and priorities.

"We have to call the hospital first and then we have to figure out what we're going to do with Kendall...she'll be home from her playdate soon."

She then nudges me in the back to get me to walk down hallway, which I do in a total daze.

Still shaking my head from side to side, I mumble, "It's not supposed to happen like this. My c-section is scheduled for next week...Leo's supposed to have more time..."

Ignoring me, she gets right to work gathering my belongings that have been neatly packed for weeks, right beside the box of Kelly's videos.

With bags in hand, she suddenly stops in the doorway and informs me, "You do realize we have a little problem, right?"

Still in a daze, I mumble, "A *little* problem? That's nice for a change."

"Well, we all know the plan was for me to stay with Kendall and for Megan to accompany you to the hospital, but—"

In the blink of an eye, I go from dazed to distressed.

"Oh shit! Megan's in Oregon!"

"Oh *shucks*, Chrissy. It should be 'Oh, *shucks*, Megan's in Oregon.' At least *try* to stop with the swearing, would you?"

Ignoring her plea, I resume my mumbling.

"When she asked me for time off to visit her parents, I thought I had another week. What was I thinking letting her go?"

"You were thinking you had another week. But, it's okay! We can go with another plan."

Kicking into panic mode, I belt out, "You're right! We can call Kurt! He'll stay with Kendall and you can come with me. I wanted to keep him out of this, but it's a better plan anyway...You'll be a much better coach than Megan. What does she know about this stuff anyway, right?"

As I wobble over to the phone Barbara tells me to stop, she has something to tell me.

148

"There's no time for chit-chat, Barbara! Kendall will be home in an hour. I need him here now!"

"Hang up the phone, Chrissy."

"What? *Why?*"

Obviously struggling with her words, she blurts out, "Because he's gone, too."

"How do you even know that?"

After she mutters something about "You kids these days..." and "I need a break from this nonsense" she explains that two days ago, when Megan dropped Kendall off from her weekend with Kurt, she mentioned something about him also being out of town this week. Then, she followed up the quick explanation with "That's all I know, okay?"

After I put the phone down I wonder out loud, "I get why Megan is still dropping Kendall off at Kurt's house...she said she wanted to help me out, and she said she also liked to spend time with her. But why is she still dropping Kendall off over here when Kurt's visitation is over? It's not like he's is on bed rest with placenta previa or anything. And I'm not hiding from him anymore, *remember*?"

The anxious way she's shoving unnecessary things like cans of soup and old bananas into my hospital bag tells me she *absolutely* remembers.

"Alright Barbara...Something really weird is going on and I think you know what it is. Start blabbing!"

"I don't know what you're talking about."

"Yes you do, and I want to know right—"

In the blink of an eye, my curiosity takes back seat to the sharp pain shooting right through the middle of my stomach and straight out of my back...No wait, let me rephrase that. It feels like a medieval torture device, one resembling a pry-bar covered in spikes, is being shoved up my huha, between my hips, and it's spreading apart *everything* in its path...showing no mercy in its demolition.

My eyes shoot wide open and I grab onto Barbara's shoulders and freak.

"What the F'n hell was that?"

"That would be labor. Now can I tell you what my plan is, so we can get going?"

Wanting any and all drugs in my system as quickly as possible to prevent feeling the wrath of the medieval torture device, I urge her to, "Spill it."

It takes less than a nano-second after she gets done talking before I say, "No freaking way! I'll go it alone before I do that."

"Darn it, Chrissy, listen to me! The minute that baby is born they might take it to another room to clean it up, perform some tests, or whatever, and you won't want it to be alone. But you won't be able to go with it, and it'll rip your heart out. Trust me, feeling guilty about EVERYTHING kicks in bad enough when you have a baby, don't make it worse for yourself than it's already going to be by not doing what I'm asking you to do. You need to have someone by your side that can also go with the baby after it's born. You've got to believe me on this."

Grabbing my crotch as if I can control the speed at which all of this is going to go down, I beat myself up.

"Goddammit, I knew I should've gotten my mother involved. Sure, she would've looked down at me disapprovingly while I was giving birth to my fatherless child, but when it was over she'd command control of the situation and—"

"It's too late for do-overs, my love. Can I just make the call so we can get this plan in motion?"

Like a child throwing a temper tantrum, I defiantly shake my head no. But all movement comes to a screeching halt when I feel the medieval torture device begin to rev up.

The experienced and self-controlled mother she is, Barbara takes a step back, offers no assistance, and waits out the painful moment—obviously playing hardball.

My eyes bug out in terror and panic sets in as the torture device begins to plow through my entire body. I reach out to grab Barbara's arm for support, but she takes another step back, crosses her arms, and raises her eyebrows.

Wow, she's got this mother thing down.

150

Mid-torture, I blurt out, "Do you know what you're asking me to do?"

She says nothing. Just patiently waits for me to tell her what she wants to hear.

Finally, the torture device backs off. I'm relieved, but also scared to death I won't have a hand to hold the next time it fires up.

Knowing Barbara has me beat, I breathlessly exhale, "Make the call."

Welcome Back

June, 2003

Twenty minutes after Barbara made the call, TWWINDTM is alive, jumping up and down, and grinning from ear to ear as she asks me the dumbest question ever.

"It was the flowers, wasn't it?"

Standing in the doorway holding my hospital bag, irritated, and scared out of my mind, I correct her.

"No, it was desperation, and Barbara made me do it."

Trying to hug me she teases, "C'mon, you want me here, and you know it."

I push her away.

"No! I don't want you here and you need to know it! You and you're meddling cost me everything...EVERYTHING! Do you realize that?"

Pissed at my stubbornness, she snorts and retaliates with, "I realize one thing, Chrissy, and it's that you wouldn't have truth in your life if I didn't do what I did."

Silence takes over the room. And in anticipation of the next words spoken, Barbara's eyes bounce back and forth between me and my old partner in crime,

Frustrated with the fact that the baby is coming days earlier than expected, that there's no father in sight, and that TWWINDTM is 100% right, I stomp my feet, and scream at the top of my lungs, "Oh, God! I hate you so hard right now!"

She grabs the hospital bag and comes back with, "Ha! I bet not as hard as you hate yourself!"

Snapping my bag from her grip, I mumble, "Why the hell is that everyone's new favorite thing to say to me these days?"

Without waiting for an answer, I make my way over to the swear jar, take sixty bucks out of it, hastily stuff it in pocket, and

153

whine, "You know what? I don't need this, not right now! I'll just take a cab to the hospital!"

But it's the swear jar, not my theatrics, that grabs the attention of TWWINDTM. Shocked that it's filled to the rim with cash, she steps closer to it, points at its contents, and worriedly asks Barbara, "Is that how bad it's been since I got cut out of the picture?"

"I'm afraid so. I think it was at half capacity the last time we saw you. And now…"

"…Now there must be over three hundred dollars in that thing!"

After she finishes Barbara's sentence, TWWINDTM turns my way and barks like the hyena she is.

"Chrissy…what the hell happened to have made the swear jar get this out of control?"

"It's more like what *didn't* happen. But please, spare me the surprise. You know perfectly well what's going on over here."

I look at Barbara who shakes her head and says, "Not from me. No time for gossip! I've got a household to run…a granddaughter to take care of…"

It slipped off of her tongue so naturally…*granddaughter*. I want to walk over and hug her, but with the medieval torture device lurking in the background, and a resurrected dead friend standing in front of me—no time.

TWWINDTM chimes in with, "And not from Megan, either. I haven't heard squat from that girl since we had coffee shortly after you gave me the boot…Something about a new boyfriend." And then she gives Barbara a creepy wink, which under normal circumstances I'd get to the bottom of. But again, no time!

"You want to know what happened to have made the swear jar get this out of control? Fine, I'll tell you what happened…NOTHING FUCKING HAPPENED!"

Frustrated, I take five of the bucks I just took out of the swear jar and throw it back in.

"Doh! Now see what you made me do? You just can't stop costing me, can you?"

154

Once again ignoring my theatrics, my slutty old friend turns into concerned old friend as her eyes leave mine and begin to suspiciously scan the house. Not satisfied with what she finds from her vantage point she begins to search my home, room by room. She's mad as hell when she makes her way back to us.

"Why is there no sign of a man in this house?"

Glancing over at Barbara, I tell her, "I've got this." And then I smugly let it rip, "Because *you* scared him away."

"*I* scared him away? Last I checked I'm not the psycho pregnant one!"

"Newsflash, the pregnancy isn't what scared him away, it's what you told him in the meditation room that did!"

"I made things right!"

"Not for him! You don't get it, do you? I told him the baby was his! Then you walked in and made him realize I didn't know for sure! But it was his, I mean, *is his*, but none of it even matters now, because he hates me."

Softening back up, she says what I wish in my wildest dreams were still true.

"Give me a break, Chrissy, he could never hate you. The man adores you."

"Oh yeah? Well if he adored me so much, then why did he marry Lauren Alabaster?"

Genuinely shocked at the news I just delivered, TWWINTDM screams, "HE'S MARRIED?" so loudly that Barbara places her hands over her ears.

"All signs point to yes. And now you know why the swear jar is so full."

"Jesus Christ, Chrissy, I'm shocked. And not just about the marriage…I mean, how about that stupid last name. C'mon, Alabaster? *Seriously?*"

Appreciating the snide comment about Lauren's stupid last name, I forget for a second that I hate her guts when I confirm, "Seriously."

Like a truly, madly, deeply girlfriend...I mean, a truly, madly, deeply *ex*-girlfriend, she then regretfully inquires, "Do I even have to ask?"

Wishing it weren't true, I confirm again, "Yep, the skin matches the name. How's that for the icing on the...the icing on the..."

The medieval torture device is back and digging into my gut like it hates me just as much as Leo does. As I'm doubling over in pain, Barbara puts a shocking end to our childish nonsense.

"Alright, that's it! I've had enough of this bullshit! Kendall's going to be walking through that door in less than twenty minutes, and I'll be God damned if she sees her mother in this much pain. It'll scare the crap out of that child and she's been through enough in her life." Pointing at TWWINDTM, "You, grab that fucking hospital bag!" Now pointing at me, "And, you, get your big fat pregnant ass in her car, go to the hospital, and have that baby. I don't want to hear one more word spoken about what happened between the two of you. For however many hours it takes to get that child out, I expect you guys to pretend like you're best friggin' friends. *Capisce?*"

Scared straight by Barbara's out-of-character profanity-ridden rant, we're speechless.

"I said, *CAPISCE?*"

Like we're children, in unison we nervously promise, "Capisce."

Rushing past me with my bag and grabbing my hand, my old friend whispers, "Holy cow, how much would the swear jar have charged for all of that?"

"Twenty-five large. Easy."

Holy Shitballs

June, 2003

So this is it. This is the moment I've been waiting for my whole life. Well, at least since eleventh grade chemistry class when I created item number six on my life list. I remember so vividly sitting in the third row, right behind Courtney and all of her brains, pretending to listen to my teacher…lost in my dreams with a purple pen. I spent thirty-five minutes thoughtfully planning out my entire life, and then ceremoniously sealed the deal by folding my seven point list into a fancy pocket-sized triangle and decorating it with heart doodles. Now here I am, seventeen years later. I'm not married to Kurt anymore, and there's no fashion career, or home in Danville left to speak of. Yep, items number one through five on my life list are shot to shit, but item number six is about to come to fruition and unlike those other things, it'll never go away. I'm about to have a baby.

The hospital room is beautiful. The nurses…caring and attentive. I'm in my light blue hospital gown, tucked cozily under warm blankies, and the music playlist I specially created for the whole experience, can be heard humming softly behind all of the bells and whistles of the equipment in the room. Everything is here. Almost.

Patting my tummy, I muse…*But he still has a little more time. You're not out yet.*

My grumpy doctor made one small visit in which he let out one large sigh at the site of TWWINDTM. Then he put his hand deep inside of me, inspected the goods, and made the determination that he's going to "let me" go the vaginal delivery route.

Freaking at the prospect of that, I jolted up from the bed and reminded him, "No! That wasn't the plan! I have placenta previa, remember?"

To which he reminded me he's the boss by growling, "Things look okay right now, Ms. Anderson. I'll pull the plug and move you into surgery if I foresee a problem."

And then he was gone.

Oh, sweet Jesus whom I really, really must start believing in...Please don't let this baby be six foot two and two hundred pounds like his father. I'm not built for it! Christ, I'm barely built for what that six foot two, two hundred pound man put into me to make this happen!

Mid-internal-freak out, I try to yank my hand away from TWWINDTM, who grabbed it when the doctor was inspecting my goods, but she won't let it go from her grip.

"You can let go now, I'm fine."

Disgusted and pale-faced, she gasps, "Well, I'm not. Did you see how far he stuck his arm up there? Surprised the damn thing didn't come out of your mouth."

I just look the other way.

She takes a concerned deep breath in, and on exhale her tone softens to a gentle nature hardly ever heard.

"Honestly, Chrissy, I had no idea you haven't spoken to Leo or that he wouldn't be here. I swear, no one told me anything."

Still looking away, I update her on the unanswered emails, his engagement to Lauren, his resignation from T.L. Capital, and my disturbing phone call with Taddeo."

"Tsk-tsk. How can that man be so good looking and so mean at the same time?"

I mumble, "Which one, Taddeo or Leo?"

Ignoring the question, she fires off another one of her own.

"Did you try to call his mom? Maybe she can—"

"She can what? Make Leo love me again? Should I call and ask her to tell Leo to dump Lauren and pick me even though I screwed him over? And what if she doesn't even know about the baby? I mean, I thought for sure she'd see the newspaper article

158

about Club NiCo, read about the pregnancy, put two and two together, and intervene, but nothing. Or maybe she did see the article, and she's relieved her son didn't end up with a pig."

Instead of one of her usual quick fire responses, she remains quiet for a long time, presumably lost in some kind of slutty thought. Just as she opens her mouth to say something, the medieval torture device—a *new and improved* torture device— interferes. It's like…It's like, The Torture Device 2004! It's pulverizing and relentless, and meant to cause ten times more pain than the older model.

I grab the only hand in the world that's extended to me, squeeze it, and scream "HOLYYYYYYYYYYYYYYYYY SHITBALLS!" so loud that three nurses rush into the room. Two of them tend to me and one of them hands TWWINDTM a form to fill out. She glances at it for two seconds before she starts mumbling expletives. Clearly she's not happy about what she's looking at, and her discontent is about as vocal as mine is about the medieval torture device.

I look over the heads of the nurses who are taking a field trip in my crotch, and call out to dead girl, "Problem over there?"

"Uhhh, yeah! A big one! Apparently, I have to fill out this form to get one of those identification bracelets. It's the only way I can stay in the room."

"So then fill out the damn form!"

She rushes over to me and in a hushed voice whines, "But Chrissy, take a look at the first line."

"You want me to review paperwork…*now*?"

Not budging from her stance, I snap the form out of her hand, zoom right in on the problem, hand it back and assure her, "No one will even notice. Just jot it down so you can get the bracelet. Really, it'll be okay."

"No. I can't. It's too hard."

"IT'S TOO HARD?" I point at the two nurses whose heads are still buried between my thighs and growl, *"Have you ever done this?"*

"But Chrissy, you know how uncomfortable it makes me, right?"

"DO *YOU* KNOW HOW UNCOMFORTABLE IT IS TO HAVE AN ENTIRE HUMAN BEING BEARING DOWN ON YOUR VAGINA?"

I can tell she's actually mulling over all of her steamy sexcapades, and considering a debate on the subject, so I remind her exactly what I'm talking about when I yell, "FROM THE *INSIDE,* YOU BIG HO!"

"Well...no."

"Then write your freaking name down!"

She snaps the paper out of my hand, scribbles in the required information, and then hands it back to one of the nurses, who after examining it, bites her lower lip to prevent laughing, and then rushes out of the room.

In a huff, TWWINDTM barks, "I'll be right back. I have to make some calls."

"Hold on a second! First you want me to review paperwork, and now you have to make some calls?"

"Yes, important ones, actually. Oh, and by the way...After making me fill out that form, you might just be dead to me too!

Auntie M

June 16, 2003

Shortly after TWWINDTM left the room to make her "calls," the torture device began to repeatedly rip its way through my body. It got to the point where I just couldn't take the pain any longer, so I had an epidural put in. It would've been nice to have a hand to hold during the procedure…someone by my side to comfort me, but I didn't. So I just picked a spot on the wall, focused on it, and blocked out the fact that I'm alone. Shortly after that, my doctor paid me another quick visit (so quick that I'm beginning to wonder if those guys even work) and told me I'm whizzing though labor. It could be less than a few hours before I'm pushing…or fingers crossed, before I'm cut open. If that's true, the baby will miraculously be born on June sixteenth, Kelly's birthday.

I've been at the hospital for five hours and it feels like I've been alone for most of them. Heck, I guess I could've taken a taxi after all. In fact, it might've been better. I probably could've paid the cabbie a little extra to hold my hands through the epidural. But alas, my hands are empty. I place them on my stomach and wearily say, "Not for long, huh little baby?"

It was then that TWWINDTM reentered the room. It seems like forever since she left to make her so-called "phone calls." So long that there's no doubt in my mind she spotted a hot doctor and decided to get a "check-up."

Winded and frazzled, she plops down in a chair next to the bed and apologizes.

"Sorry that took so long."

I mock her apology by snorting, "Yeah, right."

"What's that supposed to mean?"

I stare at her for a long time, so many derogatory words dangling on the tip of my tongue. Before I get a chance to vocalize any of them she snaps out of her chair and stares right back at me. And then she lets it rip.

"*Really?* Do you honestly believe I'm that big of a piece of shit that I'd leave you in here all alone, at a time like this, for a fuck with some guy? Tell me, Chrissy, because if that's what you believe, then I have no business being here at all!"

Oh my gosh, she has tears in her eyes. Real honest-to-goodness tears that look like they come from a real honest-to-goodness place. I have no idea where she was for the last hour or so, but nothing about her demeanor points to going down on some random dude while locked up in a dirty janitorial closet. Just like so many of my other reactions in the past, the one I just had when I snorted was completely out of line.

With a loud sigh she plops back down into the chair and wonders out loud, "Why is it so damn hard for you to let people love you, Chrissy?"

It was in that moment that I gave up being mad. I have no anger left, at least none that should be directed at anyone other than me.

"Seriously, what's it gonna take for you to stop being mad at me? I made a mistake, okay? But it was a well-intentioned one. Need I remind you…just like so many of yours."

With tears now in my own eyes, I grossly admit, "You didn't make a mistake. I did. It's just been easier to blame you for it. I'm so sorry, can you forgive me?"

She looks over her left shoulder, and then her right shoulder, like she can't believe I'm the one in the room who just admitted she made a mistake, apologized for it, and asked for forgiveness.

"It's the new me. I've been trying her out in all of those emails I sent to Leo, clinging to hope that he'd respond kindly to her…but no dice."

"Is she temporary or here to stay?"

"She's permanent. It's always been in me to be that person. I just got so lost. It took a while…a long time, but I found her, and she's a good person. She even has a hope list. Want to see it?"

"Oh no, another list? I'm not so sure that's such a good—"

162

"No, this one's different."

From under the covers I pull out a copy of the hope list I made when I sent that first email to Leo. I've been carrying it around for luck ever since I made it.

Reading down the list, she asks, "Which one of these things are you trying to bear in mind right now?"

"I guess I'm searching for a little clarity by being calm."

"I like it. It's a real nice list, Hunny."

"It's nice, but unfortunately I think I waited too long to practice what I preach. I'm afraid Leo's so far down a path with Lauren that it's making it nearly impossible to find his way back to me."

"Well, you know that old saying, 'it's not over until the pregnant woman gives birth.'"

My old friend's attempt to cheer me up fails miserably.

"It's over. I gave up the best thing to ever happen to me because I was too afraid to tell the truth." Disgusted with the damage I've caused and all that I've lost, I sob, "*Why dammit? Why on earth would I have kept this from a man I truly, madly, deeply love?*"

"You really want to know?"

I was asking more of a rhetorical question and wasn't really expecting feedback. I shrug my shoulders like *give it to me*, but before she talks, I enlighten her, "Kurt thinks it's because I'm queen of sabotaging my own happiness."

"Kurt's hot, but he's an idiot. Doesn't he realize the reason you abandoned him and all that stupid life list crapola, is because you *wanted* freaking happiness and you *knew* you deserved it. Good Lord, if you were queen of sabotaging your own happiness you wouldn't have shoved your tongue down Leo's throat the night you met him, and you'd still be married to that fucker."

The woman never has and never will sugar-coat anything. She reminds me of Kelly...a potty-mouth Kelly.

"Here's the skinny, I think you kept this baby from Leo for one of two reasons. I think you either *thought* you were showing your devotion to him by giving him what he told you he wanted on the day he broke up with you—total distance from your relationship with Kurt. Or maybe—and this might sting a little—maybe you did what you did because you thought Leo gave up the best thing to ever happen to *him* when he broke up with you that day."

"What do you mean?"

"Maybe you thought his love for you should've been greater than his jealousies over Kurt and Kendall's relationship. Maybe it was rejection that stopped you from telling him about the baby."

"Who knows, maybe it was all of the above *plus* what Kurt thinks."

Shaking my head in disbelief I ask her when she thinks screwing up things became second nature to me.

"Oh, Hunny, other than this little snafu..." looking down at her watch, "...which I still think we can fix, what else have you screwed up?"

"You're kidding, right?"

Then I quietly and horrifyingly chuckle as I start to list off the names of people I've screwed things up with, in the order in which they all occurred.

"There's Kurt, Kelly, Courtney, Nicole, Kendall, Leo, Megan, you...and I guess I can toss Barbara into the pile. Why not, right? Everyone else is in there."

"Okay now, you just stop right there! *Kurt?* He screwed himself up. Yeah, yeah, I get that the adultery thing was a bit harsh, but Chrissy, without it, think of where the two of you would be today. Well, actually you'd probably still be here, but instead of pooping out your *first* child, it'd be like your seventh little outdoorsy-bike-riding-kayaking-Gibbons-freak-baby. And I bet even *he* didn't want that! I know for a fact that man is happy as can be that everything happened as it did."

"How do you—"

Brushing me off, she interrupts with, "More on that later. I want to know why you think you screwed up with Kelly."

I reflect on all of the hours I spent on Kelly's porch and all of the letters I wrote to her.

"I wasted so much of her time those last months of her life…she even told me so."

"Peeshaw! The way you sat there on her front porch day after day…all tenacious and what not! You gave that woman peace of mind that her husband would have the help he needed once she was gone. In fact, I bet my last buck those hours you put in on that porch are the very reason she changed her Will to give you sole custody of Kendall in case anything ever happened to him. And thank God you were the kind of friend you were to her, because look at what happened to the guy. Think of what that child's life would be like if she were with anyone other than you. Poor kid would be kicking cans down some dirt street in Zimbabwe, or sweating her ass off in Arizona, that's where she'd be! And before you even get started on how you think you screwed up Courtney and Nicole, those two screwed themselves up by moving to those God-awful places."

Chuckling, I ask, "How do you know they're God-awful? Have you ever been to Zimbabwe or Arizona?"

"No, but the heat, Hunny! Would wreak havoc on my hair."

God, I've missed this woman.

"And you think you screwed up me, Megan, and Barbara? *Really?* This, I've got to hear."

"I treat you like a punching bag, Megan like a taxi driver, and Barbara like a nanny."

"Yes, yes, and yes. But it's all temporary. And besides, we wouldn't have it any other way! You know why?"

"Why?"

"Because you took a chance on us, Chrissy, that's why. I *hated* that damn job at the clothing company. For years all I wanted was to teach yoga and have a chill life. And thanks to your guts to buy that old studio and transform it, and your willingness to take a chance on my skills as an instructor, my dream came true." She pauses for a second before she continues

165

with, "And speaking of my dream, can I please have it back now?"

Disgusted with myself for acting like I did and firing her, I squeeze her hand, and apologetically nod my head.

Placing her hands in Namaste pose, she bows her head and squeals, "Yay!" before continuing with, "Now let's move on to Megan. You know damn well that girl would still be counting buttons and waiting for a low-pay slot to open up in some shitty design department if it wasn't for you. Seriously, what girl her age gets to call herself head designer of a yoga collection *and* take weeks off at a time to go gallivanting all over Nepal? "

Tilting my head, I think, *no one actually.*

"And Barbara...What you did for her, Chrissy, well...it's truly inspirational. What was it you used to call her?"

Shamefully, I admit, "Sad Frumpy Lady."

Leaning into me she whispers, "Yes, and by the way, we'll never tell her that, okay?"

I whisper back, "Of course not. I love her."

"And she loves *you.*"

Then she leans back into her chair and continues to enlighten me.

"Let me explain something to you, Missy. You reached your hand out to a woman in *desperate* need of friendship, a woman who lived the last decade of her life in heartbroken seclusion, but look at her now. You brought Barbara back to life, Chrissy. You're giving her the family she never had, so please, please, please see what I see, and never think for one second you screwed her up. In fact, it's quite the opposite. You screwed her in, my friend."

She places her hand on top of mine.

"And the same can be said about Kendall. That little family of yours is all she knows, and what she knows, is she's the happiest girl in the world. I mean, you tell me, what kid in this day and age gets God damn cookies and milk after school, and probably enough money in a swear jar to buy a car *before* she turns sixteen?"

166

"I'm not sure if one of those two things is something to be proud of, but to answer your question, not many."

Proudly winking at me she proclaims, "Damn right about that."

Feeling as hopeful as a child on Santa's lap, I sit up in my hospital bed, and ask, "But what about Leo?"

She's quiet for a long time, almost long enough for me to give birth, get pregnant, and give birth all over again, before she sheds much needed light on the fall out of my deplorable behavior.

"Well, you definitely baby-bombed him and it shocked the shit out of him. And then you tried to pull a well-intentioned fast one over on him, and it kicked him in the gut...kinda like a one-two prego punch. But I wouldn't say you screwed him up as much as you beat him up."

"Kinda the same thing, aren't they?"

"Nah, you can stay screwed up forever, but everyone has the potential to rebound from a little ass-kicking."

"I just hope he didn't rebound with another woman."

She looks down at her watch again and says, "Me too, Hunny. Me too..."

It's amazing really. Here I am, sitting across from a voice of reason, a problem-solver, and a whole lot of sarcasm all rolled into one. My package never broke, it just got...well, it got repackaged. It makes me think back to something Dr. Maria said when I was sitting on her couch. She said, "If we open our hearts and minds, I mean *really* open them to the point that it feels uncomfortable to do so, there's an opportunity to find some good stuff we never knew existed."

Just like in the past, I've been so focused on what I was losing, that I couldn't see what I had the potential to gain. There is so much good, *so much to gain*, sitting across from me right now, and it needs to know how grateful I am for it, and mostly, how sorry I am that I treated it like shit.

"Thank you."

"Thank *me*? For what?"

167

"Being the whole package."

"Ha! I've been called a lot of things in my life, but 'the whole package?' That's certainly one I've never heard before!"

"I'm sorry for being such a bitch these last few months. You didn't deserve—"

"Say no more. Not necessary."

"It is necessary. I beat you up when you were only doing for me what I didn't have the courage to do for myself."

"That's what friends are for."

"Correction. That's what *best* friends are for."

"Best friend? *Really*? What about—"

"The A-BOB's?"

"Well, yeah. Those are your girls, Hunny."

"They'll always be my girls...my sisters, and I'll do anything for them. But life has taken us in different directions. Not just with their moves, either. We've been going in different directions since college. There's no doubt in my mind that each of them has a new bestie in her life. Poor girls have probably just been too scared to tell me so. But it's okay and I finally realize it's okay because my direction introduced me to a new best friend, too."

Getting the sense she's not buying what I'm selling, I throw some friendship facts at her that she might've forgotten about.

"Think about it...Who did I confide in first when I was falling in love with Leo?"

"Me?"

"Yep. And who did I trust with the knowledge I was unhappy with my fashion career?"

"Me?"

"Yep. And who did I call on that scary day when I was feeling all alone and needed help moving into my cottage?"

"Me!"

"Yes...and you promptly told me you didn't perform manual labor, and then you hung up on me!"

Through her laughter, she defends herself.

168

"That may be true, but let's not forget months before that I let you stay at my apartment, and I gave you a shoulder to cry on for days on end! That makes up for the cottage mess, yes?"

"Sure. Let's call it a wash."

My tone softens and my voice cracks as I reflect on the most overwhelming thing to have ever happened to me—the most precious thing I entrusted this woman to share with me and guide me through.

"And who held my hand during that pregnancy test, and reassured me everything would be alright after it came out positive?"

"Good ol' Auntie M!" Suddenly serious, she clarifies, "You do know that's what your kids will be calling me, *right?*"

"I do now."

And then I get suddenly serious as well.

"But you know the best thing you ever did for me?"

"What's that?"

"You forced me to rip the damn Band-Aid off of my life and live honestly. For that, you're the best friend a girl could ever ask for. Scratch that...You're the *bravest* best friend a girl could ever ask for."

"It took some balls, alright! Thought you were gonna rip my arms off and beat me over the head with them when I revealed the truth about what happened, or rather, what *didn't* happen, at Kurt's house!"

"I wanted to!"

"I only did it because..." She looks away from me to hide her watery eyes. "...Dammit, now look what you're making me do!" Taking a deep breath, she shakes off the rare emotional reaction before looking back at me, and admitting, "...I only did it because you're my best friend too."

Then she clears her throat, reclaims her cool, and her wit, and lays out the best friend rules.

"Now, I've never had one of those before, and I've certainly never been called one, so we're gonna have to take this slow...No need to shout 'I have a BFF!' from a roof top, or start

169

buying those gushy 'you're my other half' Hallmark cards for each other, or matching engraved necklaces. We want to act sort of cool about this, right?"

"Of course! Needy girls are pathetic!"

"Oh, Sweetie, no need to insult yourself…Especially at a time like this!"

As soon as we erupt in laughter, we're interrupted by a nurse who barrels through the door and screeches at the top of her lungs, "Alrighty Mommy! It's baby time! Are we ready to start pushing?"

Everything stops…even my breath it seems.

I close my eyes and whisper, "I'm scared" to whoever can hear me.

"Squeezing my hand, my bestie whispers back, "I know you are. But I'm here and I'm not going anywhere, okay?"

The stupid nurse interrupts the tender moment with, "Now where's the proud papa? We sure don't want him to miss the big moment!"

Throwing in the towel on any and all hope of a truly, madly, deeply life ahead with the man I love, I ask for one final confirmation of my worst fear.

"He's not coming, is he?"

Looking down at her watch one more time, she looks almost as dejected as me when her voice of reason exhales, "It doesn't look like it, Doll."

Then like the great repackaged best friend she is, the great Auntie M promptly diverts me from heartbreak with some problem-solving and sarcasm as she gets busy prepping and primping everything around me.

"Now, enough about him. Let's get those swollen feet in those stirrups where they belong and start pushing like you have to take a seven pound poop."

A Good Thing

June 16, 2003

I always thought labor and delivery would be loud and violent. Like I'd be screaming at the top of my lungs, doctors and nurses would be yelling at me to calm down, metal objects would, for some reason, drop to the ground, and chaos would fill the room. But it's nothing like that. Well…at least not as it relates to child birth.

Just as one of the crotch-inspecting nurses confirms I'm fully dilated and ready to go, she summons for my doctor. Unlike before, the old grump doesn't ignore my friend when he enters the room. This time he takes one look at the woman holding my hand, and a mile-wide grin appears on his face. I think it's the first time I've ever seen his teeth. I'm pretty sure I know why he's suddenly jolly, but for fear of the truth, I stay focused on the task at hand.

"Any chance we can drag this out another couple of days, Doc?"

"We can if you don't mind exploding. But I don't think your insurance covers human detonation."

"It's just that…if we could just give him…Well, I was hoping…"

When my doctor realizes what I'm trying to say, his smile diminishes right along with my hope.

"I gather you weren't able to track down Mr. Wonderful?"

"The thing is, I don't think he knows this is happening today. I told him I was having a c-section on the nineteenth. Any chance we could pump me full of something to postpone this until then?"

"Not possible, Ms. Anderson. These things cannot be controlled."

"…And besides, Chrissy, you're not even sure if he got all of those emails telling him about the date of the c-section anyway."

My doctor's face becomes cheery again as his focus shifts from me to my supportive-voice-of-reason-spewing friend. He caught a glimpse of her earlier when he was shoving his fist up my huha, but he had to run out, there was no time for a verbal exchange. The last time they had one of those was at my first prenatal appointment when she was yelling expletives at him. And it looks like it's about to be payback time.

"Well, well, well, look who we have here! Ms. Anderson mentioned you might be assisting with her delivery and I apologize for ignoring you earlier…had to rush off to deliver another baby."

My doctor walks over to where my friend is standing and with more glee that I've ever heard in his voice, says, "It's lovely to see you again…" He then pulls an identification bracelet out of his pocket and fakes as if he's reading it for the first time. I can see the unpleasant moment coming a mile away, and it makes me want to crawl up my own crotch and hunker down with my unborn child until it's over. "…Let's see, let's see…what does this say here? Ah, yes…lovely to see you again, *Ms. Stewart.*"

Without lifting her eyes from a tray of medical instruments, the nurse who made the bracelet does all she can to contain her laughter. Not amused, my friend snaps the bracelet out of his hand and moans, *"Here we go."*

But then it looks like we're going to brush past the name on the identification bracelet, because my doctor turns his attention back to me and the remarkable rate at which my placenta previa corrected itself just enough to give the pushing thing a try. I even give my friend an encouraging nod like *it'll be okay…* Wishful thinking.

"Everything looks A-okay down here Ms. Anderson. Once Martha puts on her bracelet, we're ready to get this baby out."

At once, the entire room erupts in laughter. One nurse drops a medical instrument and shouts, "HOLD ON, YOUR NAME IS

MARTHA STEWART?" so loud that another nurse pops her head in the door and asks, "Are you serious, Martha Stewart's here, *where?*" It only makes the commotion in the room grow louder. It's exactly the kind of volume you'd expect to come from a labor and delivery room, except it's not coming from me.

My friend, Martha Stewart, who hasn't been called Martha Stewart since the person famously known as Martha Stewart came onto the scene twenty years ago with all of her arts-n-stupid-ass-crafts and totally unattainable domestic bliss, nods her head in mortification as she snaps the bracelet on her wrist and addresses the group.

"Okay folks, for your information, I go by Marti…and the bracelet's on now so you can all stop laughing."

Sadly, it does nothing to curb the chaos.

She yells even louder, "…Did you hear me? The bracelet's on! Joke time's over!"

My doctor, who obviously hasn't had this much fun in his entire life, can't contain himself and roars, "BRACELET'S ON! WELL THAT'S A GOOD THING! GET IT…*A GOOD THING?*"

The group bursts out in laughter once again.

I remember laughing my ass off, too when I found out her name for the first time. It was years ago at the clothing company when I pulled her employee file to do a review. That's when my dickhead boss pointed out Marti was short for Martha. We literally rolled around on the ground in amusement (officially making us both dickheads) as we spouted off all of the ways our slutty Martha Stewart was different from Martha Stewart the media mogul.

Dickhead boss: Hey, here's a good thing…Save your toilet paper rolls! They're perfect for drying and shaping used condoms.

Dickhead me: Oh, and don't forget to check for leaks by filling with water, bottled of course!

Dickhead boss: And how about that turkey baster? It's not just for adding flavor to your holiday meat!

Dickhead me: Nope! Now your man meat can taste however you want!

And the jokes went on and on and on.

I can't think of a better time to make amends with my insensitive and childish behavior...with some more insensitive and childish behavior.

"ENOUGH! All of you!"

At once the room becomes silent.

"Shame on you for making my friend feel bad about her name. She came here today to help bring my baby into the world, not get made fun of for a name she didn't even give herself."

Pointing at a nurse in the corner of the room, I let it rip.

"Hey, Joan Jett, what if I started cracking jokes about your circa-seventies haircut? How would that make you feel, huh rock star?"

The Joan Jett lookalike turns beet red and starts to apologize, but I cut her off as I turn my attention to the next Martha-hater in the room.

"And what about you, Snaggle Fangs? Your teeth are so crooked you probably need a map to find your tongue."

Her hand quickly covers her mouth to hide the butt of my joke. I add salt to the wound when I blurt out, "Girlfriend, you're gonna need two hands to hide that mess."

Then my eyes lock on the big man.

"And you, Doctor! You're so mean you make Hannibal Lecter look like Santa Claus, and you're so fat you make Santa Claus look like...look like..." I shout over to Marti, "Hey, who was People Magazines last sexiest man alive?"

"Ben Affleck."

"*Blech.* Really?"

"I know. I was super surprised myself. I mean, where's the chest on that man?"

"I was thinking it would be more like Clooney, Crowe, or Pitt. Shit, I'd even take Damon over Affleck."

"Girl, you're preaching to the choir on this one."

The shamed group's eyes are darting back and forth between the two of us while we go round and round on the sexy man subject. Finally, mean ol' Hannibal Lecter attempts to speak but I put my finger in the air to silence him.

"No! Not one word from any of you until you apologize to my friend." Pointing to Marti, "That woman right there has had to deal with so much crap just for knowing me, and it ends now! I mean it. No more crap for her! Do you understand me?"

Everyone, including my doctor, murmurs a piss-poor apology to Marti. It's not good enough for me.

"I CAN'T HEAR YOU!"

Louder, and now in unison, they exclaim, "We're sorry."

I clear my throat and continue with my list of demands.

"Good then. Now that we've got that taken care of, someone turn up the volume on the music and let's get this baby out."

I turn to Marti and with all of the happiness I can muster up say, "Let's do this."

With my eyes glued to the ceiling, I lean back and place my feet back in the stirrups.

Marti, formerly known as TWWINDTM, formerly known as Slutty Co-worker, grabs my hand and asks, "You ready?"

My heart says no because Leo's not here, but my body says...

"Yes."

And then the sounds of the labor and delivery room turn into what they're supposed to sound like as Joan Jett gently tells me to put my chin to my chest, hold my breath, and push while Snaggle Fangs begins to count to ten.

Countdown

June 16, 2003

"Six…Seven…Eight…Nine…Ten…*aaaaand* relax."

My head collapses onto the pillow and sweat drips down my temples, mixing into hair already drenched with perspiration.

After an hour of pushing, Marti took over as the push-counter-person. I don't think Snaggle Fangs was too comfortable being that close to my face following my attack on hers and almost as soon as we started pushing, she excused herself to go and help another pregnant woman…a *nicer* pregnant woman.

"Hunny, are you sure you're doing it right? It's been like forever and I don't see anything coming out."

Aghast at Marti's comment, I snap, "*Forever?* It's a human being, not a tampon!"

Hannibal Lecter lifts his head up from down below and chimes in, too.

"Far be it for me to agree with Martha Stewart, but I think you're holding back a little on us, Ms. Anderson."

I am. I know it's completely insane, but I'm still holding out hope that Leo's on his way. That somehow he found out about this and he's knocking over buildings and people to find me. If I take this slow…

"*Ms. Anderson?* Are you sure you're trying as hard as you can?"

I don't want to lie because it goes against new and improved Chrissy's lifestyle, so I just shrug my shoulders and bob my head around in all kinds of yes and no directions.

"Then I need you try a little harder…like how they taught you in Lamaze."

Hannibal's head then disappears back into the abyss of what used to be a very lovely destination. Ugh. Given the last sixty

177

minutes, I can only imagine what that thing looks like now…and a baby hasn't even come out of it yet. No man will ever want me again. I'm doomed to a lifetime of emotionally detached sex with my boyfriend, Wonderwand.

Marti's back in my face with, "You heard the man, start pushing like you have to take a—"

"I know, I know, I know, you don't have to remind me!"

Just then her cell phone rings, and she hastily leaves my side to pick it up.

I sarcastically mumble, "That's fine, it's not like we have anything important going on here."

Hannibal uses the interruption as an opportunity for me to take a break…or for him to go eat a sandwich. Not sure which one. He says he'll be back in ten minutes and abruptly leaves the room.

With Marti in the corner whispering into her cell phone, I close my eyes and pray like I've never prayed before.

Grandpa, Kelly…Craig? Gosh, there are so many of you up there now. Normally I'd think that was a really bad thing, but at the moment, I need the numbers for things to work in my favor. Okay, okay, that was really morbid humor…but I thought we could all use a laugh right about now. Seriously though, Guys, I need your help finding Leo. Something really strange is going on. No matter how awful I was, or how horribly I mishandled news of my pregnancy, he'd never miss this. Not in a million years. Please remove whatever barrier is standing in his way so that he can be here for the birth of his baby. This isn't about me, Guys. I swear it's about him. He'll never forgive himself for missing this moment. Okay, that's it. Amen…or God Bless…or whatever it is you or your keeper up there need to hear to make this work out for my family.

I divert my attention from the Heavens back to Marti as she wraps up her call and returns to my side.

"Who called that was so important it interrupted the miracle of life?"

"That was my Ho-Bag. Remember him?"

"How could I forget?"

And how could I? He was there the night I met Leo at Buckley's. The memory of that fateful night, and all The Ho-Bag's cigarette-behind-the-ear nonsense, brings a much needed smile to my face.

"Oh, so he's *your* Ho-Bag now, huh?"

"Hey, after meeting me, could he be anyone else's? Anyway, I sent him on a little mission."

"The Ho-Bag on a mission?" Laughing out loud, "That's priceless. I'm not so sure that guy can walk and chew—"

And then it hits me mid-sentence. Earlier...before my epidural went in...Marti left to make some calls! She got so mad when I questioned her intentions! Maybe that's because they were really good ones and not the slutty ones I accused her of having in a janitorial closet. *Has she been meddling again?* God, I hope so!

I'm about as happy and hopeful as I've ever been. And those two things skyrocket when I see a mischievous smile appear on her face.

"Miss Marti...Do you have something you'd like to share?"

Clapping her hands she boasts, "He found Leo, Hunny. Well, I guess technically Leo found The Ho-bag."

Feet still in stirrups and sweat dripping everywhere, I nudge myself up as fast as I can.

"What are you talking about?"

"Leo called him when he moved back to Lafayette...in April."

April? Oh my God, he's been here the whole time.

So many thoughts are swirling through my mind. Why did he move back? Is Lauren with him? Is she now his wife? Does he know I'm here right now?

"I see you're about to explode..." Placing her hand on my belly, "...in more ways than one, so I'll cut to the chase. After the little incident in the meditation room, Leo went directly back to New York to quit T.L. Capital, but you already knew that, right?"

"Yes."

"Well, he came back here and opened up some kind of office. I'm assuming it had to do with finance because that's what he does, right? I mean, it's not like he'd go into dog grooming, or open a bar, or—"

"Marti, cut to the chase!"

"Right! Anyway, his office, whatever it is, is right there on Mt. Diablo Boulevard." Slapping my leg, she loudly proclaims, "Two freaking blocks from the studio! Can you believe that?"

Feeling a tightness in my belly I hadn't felt since before the epidural, I clench my teeth in discomfort as I ask, "Where exactly?"

"The Ho-bag said somewhere between Oak Hill Road and Dolores Drive."

"Oh my God, I placed fliers all over that vicinity when we launched Club NiCo."

How did I miss him?

"Where's The Ho-Bag right now?"

"I assume somewhere between Oak Hill Road and Dolores Drive."

"What are you talking about?"

"Hunny, he just left Leo's office."

Just then my doctor bursts into the room, and starts barking orders left and right to get started again. I block out the commotion to get more answers.

"Did The Ho-Bag tell him where I was? Did he tell him I'm having the baby?"

Cautious because she's afraid I'll morph back into a honey badger, the likes of which she saw that day in the meditation room, and rip her face off, she slowly asks, "That's…what…you wanted him to tell him, right?"

"Yes, Marti, yes!"

A clear sign of relief washes across her face.

"Thank God. I mean, I knew you did, but lately you've been all hormonal and super scary and—"

"MARTI! IS HE COMING?"

"He didn't know."

"What do you mean, he didn't know?"

"He said the second he mentioned you were in labor, Leo bolted out of the office, jumped in his jeep, and drove away. I assumed it was to come here, but..."

"But what?"

"Sweetie, that was almost thirty minutes ago."

The hospital in only twenty minutes away from Leo's office, at the most. If this is where he was headed when he bolted out of his office, he'd be here by now. My spirits fade as fast as the pain in my stomach grows. Hold on a sec...Why *is* the pain in my stomach growing?

"Ms. Anderson...*Hellooooo*. Are you and Martha Stewart ready to get going again?"

I stare at my grumpy doctor for a second before turning all of my attention back to Marti.

"Did The Ho-Bag tell you *anything* else?"

"Yes and it's super cute. He said Leo has been calling the hospital every single day since he moved back. He's been checking to see whether or not you were admitted."

"What time did he usually make the calls?"

"Hunny, it's The Ho-Bag, not Magnum P.I. I don't think he dug that deep."

Clearly irritated, the doctor stands and clears his throat.

"Ladies, you think we can get this baby out before it decides to walk out on its own?"

Ignoring him again, I keep at the questions.

"Marti, go out there and ask whoever you have to if Leo's been calling here for the last two months. I have to know if it's true. I have to know if he still cares!"

"But what about the baby? You heard the doctor. It's time, Chrissy!"

"Go! And tell Snaggle Fangs to come back in here. I need a push-counter-person!"

It's a...

June 16, 2003

"Ms. Anderson...Ms. Anderson! I need you to listen to me very closely."

Disoriented, I attempt to lock eyes with my doctor to take in what he's saying.

"We've been at this for longer than I'm comfortable. The baby's not in distress or anything, but the bleeding from the placenta previa is picking up, and I'm not going to let this go on much longer."

I'm dehydrated and tired as all hell from acting like I'm pushing harder than I am. It makes me wonder how dehydrated and tired I'd be if I were actually doing things right. And after what the doctor just said, I'm not really sure it's safe or wise to drag this out any longer. Marti's been gone for thirty minutes in search of something she might never find, and Leo still hasn't shown up, despite knowing I'm in the hospital. It's starting to look like I'm going to be stuck bringing my baby into the world with Snaggle Fangs, Joan Jett, and Hannibal Lecter.

"Ms. Anderson, did you hear what I said? I'll give you a few more contractions, after that I'm moving you into surgery."

That's what you think. Sorry Doc, there will be no c-section. I know I had my heart set on one, but my huha is already shot to shit and all of that half-ass pushing has got to count for something. If I have any control over things, this baby is coming out the old-fashioned way. And boy oh boy, it's sure starting to feel old-fashioned. My epidural is definitely wearing off. The pain is mounting and making me wish I hadn't been farting around for the last couple of hours. It's starting to look like that

183

pilgrim-style childbirth Kurt encouraged me to endure all those years ago might come to fruition after all. Mother F…

Just as Snaggle Fangs is instructing me to put my chin to my chest to have another go at it, the door to the delivery room flies open and Marti hurries over to my side, shoving Fangs over, and assuming her position as push-counter-person.

"I'm back and I've got good news!"

Hannibal yells, "Shut up and do your damn job, Martha Stewart, or I'm kicking you out!"

For the first time in the life of our friendship she pokes fun at her name and whispers, "Well, that certainly wouldn't be a good thing." And then quietly asks me where we are in the process.

"I'm just about to push."

"Okay, okay, okay, head up and here we go. Deep breath in, hold it, and one, two, three, four, five, six, seven, eight, nine, *aaaaand* ten. Let out your breath and relax, Hunny."

Still whispering, she asks, "You're not holding back anymore, are you?"

"Not on that one."

I thought we were sly, but Hannibal heard everything.

"And I can tell. I see a head…and a lot of hair. Dark hair, must take after Mr. Wonderful, eh?"

With news of the hair and the progress we're finally making, Marti grabs my hand and squeezes with all her might. I'm biting my quivering lip and nodding my head a million miles an hour. I'm overcome with joy I can't describe.

"Did you hear that, Marti? The baby has Leo's hair."

"I did, Hunny!" Then, yelling down to Hannibal, "She take a crap on that one, Doc, because it sure felt like she did from up here?"

From down below, Hannibal yells back, "No bowel movement yet, Martha Stewart. Let's give it another shot and see if we can get one out of her yet."

On news of the head and the hair, the two of them are all of a sudden acting like some kind of weird team.

"Quick, before we go again, what's the good news, Marti?"

"Well, it looks like The Ho-Bag got it right. Leo *has* been calling here. You should've heard the nurse out there go on and on about his sexy voice. You woulda punched her! I thought about doing it for you, but—"

"Marti, stay focused. What time did he call here?"

"She said he called twice every day, once at six in the morning and once at six at night."

He really has been looking after us.

I can feel my long lost Leo drug slowly begin to churn in my system. Actually a lot more than I want to feel it, thanks to the waning epidural.

"Let's see...You were admitted at eleven this morning and it's just now five o'clock. Based on the timing of his calls, he wouldn't even know you were here if it weren't for my little Korean lover boy!"

I take her optimism down a notch when I remind her, "But Marti, even for The Ho-Bag...Leo's still not here."

What's does this mean?

"Alright Ladies, let's give this another shot. You ready, Ms. Anderson?"

Wanting to see this baby more than anything in the world, but hesitant to give it another shot without Leo, I'm torn about just how much effort I should give. Something has to be delaying him...Maybe if I...

Knowing the exact thoughts racing around in my mind, my new voice of reason delicately intervenes.

"Chrissy, you can't hold back anymore. With or without Leo, this baby has to come out." She gently guides my face to hers, "Stop trying to control the outcome and let things happen naturally. Who knows? Maybe the result will be better than anything you ever could've hoped for."

She's right; I have to stop controlling things. It seems like since I was sixteen years old I've tried to control the outcome of things, and almost everything has backfired on me. Marti was right to blow the lid on my secret in the meditation room and she's right again now.

185

"Do you think he'll ever show up? You know…to see the baby?"

"Of course! C'mon, it's Leo we're talking about. Remember what I told you, you didn't screw him up; you just beat him up a little. It'd take a lot more than an ass-kicking to keep that man away from his child. There's a reason why he's not here, and I bet my rock-hard yoga ass it's a good one. Okay?"

Relenting all control, I offer up a meek, "Okay."

"Ladies, the clock is ticking. You know the drill. Up and at 'em!"

"Wait, Marti, turn the music up. I know it's silly, but this is the exact song I envisioned playing when the baby's born."

"Ladies, my patience is running low!"

After she barks back, "Keep your scrubs on, Doc, we're almost ready," Marti rewinds the song and then gives me a hand lifting my head to my chin.

"I can't believe you're about to have a baby, Chrissy."

"I can't believe I'm about to have *two* kids. It's gonna be great, right?"

"The best."

"You really think I can do this? I mean, I won't screw them up because I'm, you know…alone?"

"Chrissy, the risk of you screwing up these kids isn't any greater than that of a stay-at-home mom with an adoring husband and enough cash in her wallet to make it look like she has the perfect life. In fact, as far as I'm concerned, the children of those moms are *most* at risk of a screw up. Bitches have nothing else to do than mess their kids up with all of their time for meddling and money for doting. *Blech!* We hate them!"

Even though she just trashed my dream life, I love her for what she's trying to do.

"…And besides, do I need to remind you that you're *not* alone? You've got a punching bag, a taxi driver, and a nanny waiting for you at home, remember?"

"Marti?"

"Yes, Doll?"

"Will I ever stop loving him?"

My new and improved voice of reason doles out what I already know to be true.

"No. In fact, the second you see this kid's face, I'm afraid you'll fall deeper."

Her honesty is refreshing. She's going to make an excellent Auntie...and an excellent best friend.

I nod my head and give Hannibal a shaky thumbs-up, instructing him I'm ready. My thoughts immediately go to Kelly and the shaky thumbs-up she gave me through her living room curtains the last time I saw her standing. I close my eyes and see her giving me that same thumbs-up right now and I'm immediately overcome with a sense of calm. The kind of calm I tried so hard to create for myself since the moment I found out I was pregnant, but struggled to sustain. With Kelly's image it's like a calm spell has been cast over me and my worries about Leo's whereabouts vanish completely. It's no fluke that this baby will be born on June sixteenth. Kelly's here with me now and always, and my baby's birthday is her way of telling me so. My entire family is being watched over and protected by her. I'm far from alone.

Happy Birthday, Kel.

"Alright Ms. Anderson, two more contractions is all I'm giving you, so make them count."

Looking fiercely into my eyes, Marti instructs me to take a deep breath in and then she starts to slowly count to ten. When she hits number six, the door to the hospital room flies open once again.

187

Breathe in, breathe out
Move on and break down
("Breathe In, Breathe Out," *Matt Kearney*)

...Giant Crap

June 16, 2003

Exactly two minutes and forty-one seconds into the song I thoughtfully picked as the one I wanted playing when my baby was born...at the *exact* moment it hits its crescendo, Leo startles us all when he storms through the door, frantically calling out my name.

He found his way back to me.

My worried eyes quickly find their way to his ring finger. His anxious ones unmistakably explore my body to make sure everything's okay.

Without lifting his head, Hannibal Lecter screams, "I don't know who the hell just barged into my delivery room, but do NOT let it distract you, Ms. Anderson! Complete the push!"

But it's nearly impossible to focus on the task at hand.

Leo's here.

Hannibal continues to yell, "Keep her focused, Stewart! This is a good push and I don't want to lose what I've got down here!"

With a smile on her face that's probably as big as my vagina is at the moment, Marti finishes the count.

"Seven...eight...nine, *aaaaaaaaaaaaand* ten! Good one, Chrissy!" Then turning her attention to Leo, "...And good to finally see *you*, handsome."

The reckless stubble he wore on his chin when we first met is now neatly-trimmed facial hair, complete with one of those sexy patches right below his lower lip. I can also see teeny-tiny specks of gray in his hair, the ones I caught glimpses of when I

189

showed up at his apartment in New York nine months ago. It's the kind of gray that makes a man appear stable, sexy, and successful. He's wearing khakis and a light blue button-down dress shirt that's completely unbuttoned, revealing one of his classic white t-shirts. There's a circle of sweat on his chest and one under each armpit. Yet, like usual, he smells like Heaven. His green eyes are on fire with worry, and I can tell there are as many questions shooting through his brain as there are shooting through mine. I want to stare at his face forever, but I can't take my eyes off of his left hand. He takes a cautious step forward and asks Marti if he can hold mine.

Happy for the break from my death grip, she answers, "Gladly, I think mine is about to fall off. I'm warning you though; the girl's got a grip!"

I thought I'd seen the worst of mean old Hannibal, but not so. Pissed at the millionth interruption of the day, he blows up.

"NOW THAT'S IT! In case you've all forgotten, this is supposed to be the birth of a child, not a Goddamned cocktail party, or a missing persons investigation...or bleeping date night!"

"I'm sorry Doctor. No more disruptions, I promise. It's just that this is…" Looking up at Leo, I attempt to make the introduction. "…This is—"

"Well, I certainly know it's not your ex-husband! Already met that one. Let me guess…This one must be Mr. Wonderful."

Knowing Leo's short fuse when it comes to any and all mention of Kurt, Marti mutters, "Well, that takes care of what could've been a very lovely reunion." And then she takes a giant step back in anticipation of all hell breaking loose.

I take my worried eyes off of Leo's ring finger and lock them with his confused ones, praying my sweaty, stinky, swollen, and disgusting appearance will be so much of a distraction that he'll completely forget about what the doctor just said.

"Kurt was here?"

Damn. Guess I don't look as bad as I thought.

Finally succumbing to how tired I am, I don't backpedal, I don't make up excuses…I don't lie. I just humbly answer, "No. Not today, Leo."

"When?"

"In April, after that day in the meditation room…There was a problem and I had to go to the hospital. Kurt followed me over just to make sure I was okay. That's all."

Everyone, including my now intrigued doctor, pauses for reaction.

"What happened?"

"He just stopped in for a minute and—"

"No, not with him. Why did you have to go to the hospital?"

Look at that! Focusing on what's important…So far, so good.

"I…I was bleeding. Everything's fine though…And it had nothing to do with what happened that day. I just had a little condition that some bed rest and forced relaxation fixed. That's all."

My doctor, who noticeably softens a little, adds, "Long story short, because that's all the time I have given your delayed arrival, something was blocking the area where the baby passes during delivery. Chrissy did as she was told to correct the problem so that she could avoid a c-section…" He clears his throat before proceeding with, "…But given her half-hearted attempts at pushing for the last couple of hours, which I can only assume were to give you enough time to bless us with your presence, she's nearly shot her epidural to bits. I don't like what I'm seeing down here, and I'm not going to allow this to go on for much longer. One more contraction, to be exact."

Even though I can tell Leo wants to defend himself and explain why he hasn't been around for most of the pregnancy, he stays on point with what's most important.

"Are she and the baby okay?"

Back to his mean ol' self, Hannibal mumbles, "Given there's been nine months of this pregnancy, it's curious to me that you're suddenly so concerned."

Leo glances at me first and then at all of the other curious and judgmental eyes in the room. Holding back his frustration, he places his hand to his forehead and pinches his fingers into his temples, staying silent.

He's been through enough.

"Doctor, please…It's not his fault he wasn't around. It's my fault. I kept this from him. He didn't know about the baby until just recently."

Deservedly, all curious and judgmental eyes now shift to me.

Hannibal breaks the silence with, "You certainly do live a jumbled life, Ms. Anderson. Perhaps Martha Stewart over here can put her name to good use and help you organize it."

Ignoring everyone's obvious disdain of my decision to keep the baby from Leo, I turn my attention to the man I love. Even though I have no idea where he's been for the last sixty days, I give him the benefit of the doubt…Lord knows he's done that for me a million times.

"Trust me though, he's been concerned from the second he found out about the baby, and he's gonna be a wonderful father, so please, Doctor, tell him everything he needs to know." Now turning to Snaggle Fangs, "And if it's alright, he'll need one of those bracelets. You know, so he can stay with the baby after it gets here."

Throwing his hands in the air, my doctor caves in.

"Okay then, to answer your question, *Mister?*"

Leo's voice cracks when he answers, "Armstrong."

"Fine, Mr. Armstrong, here's what's happening. The two of them are okay right now, but her bleeding is intensifying and so is the baby's heart rate." Now addressing the entire room, "…So, if we're not expecting anymore ex-husbands, fathers, or private investigators called Ho-Bug…"

The entire room, excluding Leo, corrects the doctor by yelling, "*Bag!*"

"I don't give a damn what the guy's name is, my point is, I want to deliver this baby before its first birthday." Then, he barks at Snaggle Fangs who's getting started with the identification bracelet paperwork, "There's no time for that right now…we'll deal with it after we deal with this."

Pissed, Marti shouts, "HEY! NO FAIR! I had to fill out a form…Tell all of you my damn name! Get laughed at!"

Hannibal shouts louder, "Stewart! I swear to God, one more disruption from you, and I'll kick you out of this room faster than you can say 'color coordinated bath towels.'"

Tenderly brushing hair out of my sweaty face, Leo smiles down at me and says, "Have they been at each other like this the whole time?"

"Pretty much. The only time they make nice is when the baby crowns."

"You're that close?"

Looking deep into his green eyes that have always mesmerized me, I gently nod my head. Then I tell him what I know will shake him as it shook me.

"The baby has a head of dark hair."

Near full on tears, he gushes, *"Really?"*

"Really. Let's hope he or she has your eyes, too."

"Oh, I dunno…I was kind of hoping for your baby blues."

Is it gross that I want him to impregnate me again, *right now*? Seriously, I love this man so much it crushes my heart. I'm such a fool to have done what I did. I hate me. I hate me. I hate me.

Still brushing my sweaty hair back, he asks, "Are you okay?"

"I'm alright. It's exactly how I always imagined it would be…" My voice trails off, "…Well, the labor pain anyway."

"Chrissy I—"

"No. I've hurt you terribly, Leo. So terribly, I don't think I can ever forgive myself."

I want to ask him about the emails…why he didn't respond to my countless apologies and pleas to fight with me to save us. I want to ask about his ring finger, and where he's been since the meditation room meltdown, but I don't have the right to ask him for a damn thing other than his forgiveness.

"I can never get the time back…The pregnancy is over."
Laying back down for my final push, I regretfully declare,
"Well, almost anyway. And you didn't get to experience it, Leo.
You missed everything because of me."

"But I'm gonna try my best not to miss anything going
forward, and that's what matters most, right?"

Hard as it will be to tell him this, I have to let him off the
hook.

"Leo, I respect why you ended things with me. Really I do.
Truth be told, I couldn't be with you either if you had an ex-wife
milling around…" Criminy, for all I know I'll now be forced to
deal with an *actual* wife. Payback is such a bitch. "…And well, I
don't want to pressure you to have to be there for everything. I
mean, I was planning on doing this alone anyway. I just want
you to be happy…That's all."

He looks shamed.

"Chrissy, that's my baby in there. Don't let a foolish
decision I made nine months ago cause you to think I'd make
another one now. I'm not going anywhere."

"But this is gonna be so complicated with Kurt hanging out
with Kendall on the weekends and you and…Lauren…"

I was hoping Leo would finish my sentence. I was hoping
he'd give me some idea if he meant what he said in the
meditation room about still being in love with me, and that his
engagement to Lauren was a mistake, but Hannibal's forceful
grunt causes me to immediately lie back down. I've pushed my
doctor's patience about as far as it can go. This baby has to come
out NOW.

Marti steps forward and asks Leo if he wants to take over her
spot.

Nervous, he answers, "I'm not really sure what to do."

"Can you count to ten?"

"Yes."

"I know it can give one, but can your hand take a beating?"

Smirking, he takes hold of my hand and says, "I think it can
handle it."

194

"Then she's all yours." Walking over to stand next to the doctor, she boasts, "I've been *dying* to get a bird's eye view of this party since it started, and…" Stopping dead in her tracks when she arrives at his side, she gasps, "YOWZA!" Then slapping the doctor in the shoulder, "How the hell does that thing go back to what it's supposed to look like when this is all said and done?"

Dear Lord Jesus, I'm never having sex again, am I?

Hannibal actually chuckles a little before going back to his grumpy old self and griping, "Alright, alright, date night *and* comedy hour is over. Everyone get in to position. One more push Ms. Anderson, so make it count."

From his side, Marti repeats, "Make it count, people!"

Rolling his eyes, he continues, "Listen up, Mr. Wonderful, I need you to help her lift her chin to her chest."

Marti repeats, "Chin to chest, baby!"

"Then on my mark, you'll slowly count to ten, Mississippi style. Hopefully by the time you hit it I'm holding a baby in my hands. If not, we're moving to plan B."

Marti sings, "Movin' to plan B!"

Gazing up over the rim of his glasses, he adds, "If not for the health of Ms. Anderson and your child, so that I don't murder Martha Stewart."

Marti opens her mouth to mimic the doctor, but quickly realizes the joke was on her and snaps it shut.

"Ready, Ms. Anderson?"

I nod my head.

"Okay, deep breath in and here we go…"

I've been imaging this moment forever…Leo holding my hand, looking deep into my eyes, lovingly encouraging me to have the strength to deliver our baby. And I haven't just been imagining it for the last nine months; I've been imagining it for the last five years. Watching him now, slowly counting to ten, I block out everything around me and think about all of the magical things that led to this very moment. It all started in 1998, with my out of character decision to go to Buckley's, and the random choice to sit on a barstool right next to him. After that, I tried so hard to get him out of my mind…forget about the way he made me feel that night, but then there was my fortuitous drive to the Lafayette reservoir where I came across him sitting on that bench. Just six hours later, we were in his bedroom exploring each other's bodies. Even after that, I foolishly thought I could shake my feelings for him, but with dreamy day trips to Mill Valley, sensual picnics on the floor of his apartment, and that trip to Monterey when he said of the pregnant woman sitting next to us, "I can't wait until you look like that," he continued to take my breath away. Every single thing I learned about Leo from the moment I met him made me fall deeper and deeper in love. Even after he moved in to my cottage, our romance stayed red hot. Had I not gone and blown everything up with my trip down memory lane at Kurt's house, there's no doubt it would still be flaming. *The moment I met Leo, I became lovestruck.* Looking at him now, attentively counting to ten as I do my very best to push out our baby, I'm still lovestruck, and it hurts so much.

Finishing his count to ten, Leo cradles my neck and assists me back down to the pillow, praising my effort. I can't let him *ever* do this with Lauren. I have to get him back. He needs to know he's mine. He might've ignored my emails, but he can't ignore this…

Tired and breathless from what was apparently a failed push, because I don't hear a baby crying, *I cry*, "Leo, I need you with us. I don't want to do this without you." I grab his left hand, rub his ring finger and beg, "Please tell me it's not too late."

Is the look on his face one of pure torture or tremendous relief? Are those tears of joy or tears of torment? Are his eyes overjoyed or…over me?

"Please Leo, say something…"

Just as it seems like he's about to, Marti interrupts from down below.

"Hey, Doll…Remember earlier when you said you were done being a shit-show?"

I look at her like *now's not the time*!

Of course she totally ignores me and continues her cryptic diatribe.

"Well I'm pretty sure you meant *after* this."

"What are you talking about?"

"No baby down here yet, but *ho-ly* shit! And when I say shit…I mean it and a lot of it!"

I can feel my face turn beet red as she high-fives my doctor, and they praise my gigantic poop.

"Now that's what I was looking for during the last two hours, Ms. Anderson! I tell you what, you promise to give me one more push like that and I'll give you one more push! Deal?"

I pooped…*Oh my God*…practically in front of Leo…I pooped. Ever since he came into my life I tried so hard to conceal the fact that I poop—even prided myself that I was able to hide all trace of it from him while we lived together. No man wants a pooper. It's what sets the average girl apart from the Victoria's Secret models. Those girls don't poop—ever, at least not in any guy's fantasy. I wanted to be Leo's fantasy. Now I'm just a shitty ol' reality. Oh Jesus, does labor and delivery poop stink? Seriously, does it smell in here right now? I could die. Oh my God, my life is over. I'm the disgusting, pooping single mom who will forever be in the background watching as the love of my life adores his gorgeous non-pooping Alabaster wife.

Forgetting about the love I just professed, I look away from Leo and mumble, "That was supposed to happen, by the way. That's what they teach you to do in Lamaze. You know…in case you were wondering."

I can tell by the tone in his voice he has a grin on his face.

"I know all about it, so don't worry, okay?"

"How do you know all about it?"

"You think after I found out I was gonna be a dad I didn't do any research?"

"I kind of thought you were busy doing other things these last two months."

"I was busy doing a lot of things…"

197

I roll my eyes and think, *great*.

"…But the most important thing was reading about all of this."

I turn back to him, relieved.

"Really? I sort of thought you were on some tropical beach with a blue drink in your hand."

"C'mon, Chrissy, it's me we're talking about."

"But your commitments—"

"Are right here."

Is he talking about just the baby, or me, Kendall, and the baby? What's he saying, dammit?

"Leo, I can't take it anymore. I need to know about Lauren."

My doctor chimes in with, "Well, you're going to have to wait to know more about her for at least one more push."

"Yeah, come on, Doll! I saw the head! You're almost there!"

Leo reaches out to gently pull me up. When our hands meet, his eyes contemplatively shift from our touch to my face.

"We'll talk about everything, Chrissy. I promise." And then, so adoringly it melts my heart, he says, "Let's just do this first, okay?"

Without saying another word he begins the count. I bear down with all my might and by the time he hits the number eight, the room goes strangely silent for me. I see Leo's hand cover his mouth in amazement. I see Marti clapping her hands and jumping up and down. And I see Hannibal's mouth excitedly barking orders at everyone. Snaggle Fangs is even wearing a mile-wide grin, showing off way more of her mouth than she really should. But the intensity of what's happening to my body drowns out all sound. On exhale I feel an extreme amount of relief, but don't completely realize why until Leo gets in my face and cry's out, "You did it, Chrissy! Oh my God, you're incredible! You did it!"

It's over?

Then he gets down lower and whispers in my ear, "It's a beautiful baby girl."

It takes several seconds for the information to hit me.

I have two daughters.

As imperfect as my life has been, it's perfectly perfect now.

Thank you Kelly, Grandpa, Craig...Thank you, thank you, thank you.

Smiling from ear to ear, Leo boasts, "Kendall is NOT gonna be happy about this!"

That's strange. The only thing I told him in my emails was that Kendall thought the baby would be a boy, nothing about being unhappy if it wasn't. I want to ask him how he knows this, but the commotion, or rather lack thereof, at the end of the table consumes my focus.

Worried because I don't hear the typical spank and cry I grew up watching on television, I ask, "Can I see the baby? Is she okay?"

Just then, my doctor carries over a tightly packed pink blanket, hands it to Leo and say's "She's a beaut. You guys did good."

Leo stares into the blanket for what seems like an eternity before kissing what's in it. Then he gently places the bundle in my arms.

I close my eyes and absorb the weight on my chest. My thoughts immediately go to Kelly and what she must've felt like when she held Kendall for the first time. I feel my beloved best friend, and her first born, on me and in me, and am overcome with gratitude. For so long I couldn't imagine my life without Kelly, now I can't imagine it without Kendall. She's just as much my daughter as the one I'm holding right now, and I cannot wait for her to meet her baby sister.

My eyes slowly open and peek into the tightly packed pink blanket. When they land on my baby my heart stops and skips a beat before it begins to thump louder than ever before.

Her head is full of fluffy dark hair. Her skin is pale, pink and pristine. Her eyes, though hard to tell what color, are attention-grabbing. She smells heavenly...just like her daddy. And Marti was absolutely right, the instant my eyes landed on my baby, I fell deeper in love with her father.

Looking up at the man who started it all, I marvel, "She's you, Leo."

And then my pale, pink, pristine perfection starts wailing so loud glass could shatter.

Over the piercing noise, my best friend boasts, "She might look like her father, but she sure as hell sounds like her mother." And then Martha Stewart and Hannibal Lecter get in their second, and final, high-five of the day.

Happy Birthday

June 16, 2003

Not long after my beautiful bundle arrived, the hospital room cleared out. Hannibal had to go yell at other pregnant women/deliver more babies, Marti ran to convey the good news to Barbara, and Leo left to make some calls—God-willing to his mother, not his wife. Right now it's just me and the baby.

I glide my finger tip along the delicate features of her sleepy face…taking in the tranquil moment, and the magnificence of the creation in my arms.

How did I do this?

And then it hits me.

You didn't, Dumbass.

For most of my life I've been all sarcastic and witty about all of that ol' Lord Jesus that I *don't* believe in, *should* believe in…*have to* believe in mumbo jumbo. But in all honestly, I never really felt like I needed to believe in a higher power. *Why would I?* I had my ghosts. But as I sit here, holding my baby's tiny hand in mine, a weighty thought crosses my mind…*My ghosts couldn't have created this life*, and I sure as hell didn't assemble all of her bits and pieces in all the right places. This had to take big God-like brain power and involvement to execute.

For the first time in my stubborn life, I go over my ghosts' heads and address you-know-who directly.

Hey there Jesus…God…person,

Nice to finally meet you. If it's alright, I'm gonna go with your image as resembling Molly Shannon, you know…from Saturday Night Live. I hope that's okay. It's just that the Holy image with the crown of thorns and the dots of blood is a little too intimidating for a heathen like me. I can't talk to that image. I'm sure you understand.

I want to thank you for Kendall and my baby. Up until this moment, it never felt right to thank anyone for Kendall, it seemed kind of gross...Like I was thankful Kelly died or something. But I am thankful for her, and if you're what's advertised, I don't have to explain why that is. You just get it.

My little pink perfection stirs in her sleep, and her lips pucker up before they settle back in to a relaxed position. It's amazing how I've only known her for an hour, and I'd jump in front of a bus for her.

I think I need to apologize to you, Molly-God. No need to go all the way back to when I was sixteen and made that stupid life list, and all of the damage I caused as a result of it. Neither of us have time for that. But I do need to apologize for wasting a lot of the last five years. I'm pretty sure you've been watching me screw up my perfectly good life, and in the process, hurt a lot of people. I need you to know, though, nothing I did was malicious, or motivated by anger. Other than being unnecessarily mad at Marti, and recklessly drunk at Kurt's, every single choice I made was inspired by love. I know, I know...it might be hard to recognize that, but it's the truth. And speaking of the truth, from this day forward, I promise to live my life by it. Of course, you already know I turned that tide back in April when I came clean to Leo in that email. But what you don't know is that I also promise to stop trying to control the outcome of things.

From inside my hospital room I can hear Leo receiving congratulations in the corridor. It makes me smile...until it doesn't.

Hey, how about a deal, Molly-God? If your crystal ball shows earnest effort on my part to live my life with truth, and that I have officially given up controlling stuff I have no business

202

controlling, can you give me one more chance with Leo? I don't care if that means he becomes my husband, or if it simply means I get his forgiveness...I'll accept whatever outcome as long as he and the kids are happy. I promise.

Just then the door to the room inches open.

Oh, and my promises mean something now too...Yep, my new life has begun.

Leo quietly steps to my side.

"Hey guys, how are you doing?"

"We're amazing. I can't believe she's here...and she's a *she*."

"You thought *boy* too, huh?"

"Is that what you thought it would be?"

"I was talking about Kendall..."

I really, really want to know what he thinks about the truths I confessed in all of those unanswered emails. But I don't want to overwhelm him with questions and information he no longer cares to discuss.

"...After The Ho-Bag told me you were in labor, I raced to the house thinking you were still there. Obviously, you weren't, but guess who was?"

"You saw Kendall?"

The look on his face tells me the reunion ripped his heart out.

"For some reason I thought she would've forgotten about me. I mean, I never forgot about her. She's amazing." His voice trails off in frustration. "I wanted things to turn out differently."

"I know what you wanted. I wanted it, too. I'm sorry for all of us I messed things up so bad."

It's quiet for a moment before I ask, "How was she...you know, when she saw you?"

"She jumped in my arms like it had only been a week since I left. Went on and on about how I'm just in time for the baby...was convinced it was a boy, would be pretty upset if it wasn't, and then she ran in the house to look for her night vision goggles. She went on and on about how she wants to make up for lost time, and hit the backyard hard tonight. I didn't have the heart to run out as quickly as I got there, so we hung out in the backyard for a while. I knew you were here...doing this...but I couldn't leave her that quickly. Not again."

News of that rips my heart out too. *Almost* as much as what I am about to say.

"I can let her know you aren't staying...or that you have to get back to...Actually, Leo, I'm not really sure what I'll tell her. The first time around was hard enough."

His eyes slowly travel from mine to the baby's face, and then back to me again before he says, "I think you should tell her—"

But just then Kendall and Barbara crack the door, and proceed to tippy-toe into the room, stopping him mid-sentence.

I should tell her what? I should tell her what?

But now's not the time. Now's the time for Kendall. And so all of my attention, and Leo's, turns to her.

"Hi, Lovey."

"Hi Mommy, Are you okay?"

"I'm super-duper okay. Come on over here and sit with me. There's someone I want you to meet."

Leo's never really seen me and Kendall function as a family before. In fact, he's never heard her call me Mommy. He was in New York for the first months I had her, and then I ruined everything before he had a chance to return to us. Kendall and I were always close, but the bond we formed since he left is unbreakable. If you didn't know otherwise, you'd bet money I was her real mother. And right now I can tell our natural connection is blowing his mind.

As timid as timid can be, Kendall walks over to the bed. As she gets closer I read the proud words, *'I'm a big sister!'* written in glitter on her little t-shirt.

"Wow, did you make that?"

"Barnana helped me. Do you wike it?"

204

"I love it. Know who else is gonna love it? Your baby sister."

Her heart was set on a boy, and the look on her face tells all, but it'll readjust itself. I just know it.

"Wanna meet her?"

Her big blue eyes widen and she nods her head.

As Leo sweetly helps Kendall onto the bed, thoughts of what could have been rip through my heart. Shaking off the loss, I smile over at Barbara and say, "You get over here too, Lady. Whether you like it or not, you're family, and you have to help us name this little one."

With tears rolling like a river down her face, she staggers over to my side, and settles in next to Kendall.

The second I adjust the blanket to reveal the baby's face, the *owwwing* and *awwwing* commences.

"So, what do you think, K?"

"Will she wike me?"

"Are you kidding? She's gonna adore you!"

"Can she do stuff like hunt for snipes?"

"Well not yet, but you can teach her. That's what big sisters are for."

With that news she perks up a little and peers into the blanket more intensely.

"She doesn't wook wike me and you, Mommy. Her hair is dark. She kinda wooks wike Weo."

Barbara leans into Leo and whispers the words, "She doesn't know."

He then locks worried eyes with me.

Deep breathe in.

"She does look like Leo. Want to know why?"

"Why?"

"Well, Sweetie, Leo is her daddy."

Deep breathe out.

"*She* has a daddy?"

"Well…yes."

"Will she live with him or with us?"

205

Eyes back on Leo, I apprehensively answer, because I have zero idea what he expects the living arrangements to be. We haven't had that, and so many other essential conversations yet.

"She'll live with us, Sweetie."

"Then why can't Weo be my daddy too?"

I'd still be looking deep into Leo's eyes if he didn't just close them tight as can be.

"Well Kendall, I…Mommy made a…uh…Leo and I are just…"

Barnana comes to the rescue with, "How about we go and get some ice-cream, Kendall? It looks like they have all your favorite flavors down there in the coffee shop."

"I don't want ice-cweam, I want a daddy just like the baby."

I'm the one who was awarded custody of Kendall—entrusted to protect her from heartache. But here I am, smothering her in it.

Kendall scootches off the bed and tugs at Leo's shirt.

"Can you wiv wit us at our house, Weo? We miss you. Mommy even says so all da time. I even hear her in bed at night crying to Barnana and everything."

Now it's my eyes that close tight as can be, and Leo who does the talking.

"Kendall, you know I—"

But I can't allow him to be the bad guy. Kendall's heartache is my fault, not his. I've put him through enough.

"Hunny, Leo has his own home, but—"

Then he shocks me…NO! He literally rocks my world when he butts in with, "But I can get rid of it in a heartbeat…I mean, if that's what you and your mommy want."

Barbara mumbles, "Well, I'll be damned."

Stunned, I block out Kendall's cheers, and mutter, "Whatareyou…whatareyou saying?"

"I'm saying we have a lot to talk about, but we can talk about all of it at home, right?"

What does this mean? Does he want me back or is he just putting off the inevitable conversation about his marriage to Lauren?

Grandpa, Kelly, Craig...Molly-God? What the frick is happening right now?

"Leo, can I talk to you for a sec?"

I delicately hand the baby to Barbara, who knows exactly what I need her to do, and carries her over to the corner of the room and occupies Kendall's attention.

"Leo, if I say 'yes' she'll think it means forever. As much as I want to, I can't promise you to her like that. What happens when you have to leave?"

As serious as the night I met him, when it sounded like he was reciting the pledge of allegiance and he told me he noticed me the minute I walked into that bar, he says, "Who said anything about leaving?"

"I don't...I don't understand. I mean, *I want to*, but I caused too much damage to have what I think you're offering. *Didn't I?* You left the studio that day...I haven't heard from you since. You moved on. *Didn't you?*"

"I think you forgot something, Chrissy."

Eternally hopeful, but thoroughly confused, I ask, "What's that?"

Unexpectedly, he takes hold of my hand and gently places it on his heart and says what I never thought I'd hear again.

"You forgot that I'll always be where I know you are."

The raw and tender gesture that he created just for me all of those years ago catches me by complete surprise. My long lost drug begins to percolate in my core and my lips begin to quiver.

"But...but what about Lauren?"

He holds up his left hand and says, "Do you see a ring on this finger?"

I rubbed the shit out of that thing during those last two pushes, searching for some kind of indentation. Even though I didn't feel one, I assumed my actions...*my lies by omission*, pushed him to her.

"Well no, but I figured after all of those truths came out in the meditation room that you'd follow through with the commitment."

"I always follow through with my commitment, that's why I'm here."

"You want to be committed? *To me?*"

Nodding over to the little girls, he says, "And to them. The whole damn package. I want it all, Chrissy. I've wanted it all since the day I met you."

The whole package…Kelly, did you hear that? Is this really possible?

"You're saying this even after I kept the baby from you?"

"Were you gonna keep her a secret forever?"

"Would you believe me if I said no?"

"Would you believe me if I said I believed you?"

"I want you to believe me because it's the truth, but frankly, people would think you're a fool to trust me with anything."

"Or like you said on those snowy streets outside of P.J. Clarke's, maybe I'd just be a fool in love."

There's so much more to talk about. Like, where Lauren went, where he expects me to put my feelings about her, and where he expects to put his feelings about Kurt, but the luxury of uninterrupted conversations is no more—we're parents now. And Kendall introduces us to this harsh reality when she cuts off our thoughts with one of her own.

"So can Weo wiv wit us Mommy? Pwetty *pweeeeeease!*"

I'm stunned he's here. I'm stunned with his forgiveness. I'm stunned at the question I'm about to ask him.

Shaking my head in disbelief, I skeptically ask, "Would you like to live with us, Leo?"

Scooping Kendall up in his arms he gushes, "I'd love to go home with my girls!"

My girls…Did you hear that too, Kelly?

Barbara's hand is covering her mouth like this moment is living up to every single love story she's ever read.

I ask him one more time, *"Are you sure?* I mean, she has her weekends with..." I pause for a super long time before I say "Kurt" expecting him to backpedal out of the answer he just gave us.

"Chrissy, I had a lot of time to think these past two months and I know exactly what I'm signing up for. I want what's best for Kendall, and if he feels the same, this will all work out just fine. I promise, no more fights, no more tension. I should've been saying all of this nine months ago when you came to New York, but I was an idiot."

"No, I'm the idiot."

Barbara steps forward, places the baby back in my hands, and lovingly says, "Awww, you're both a couple of idiots...idiots in love." And then she changes the subject to a very important one.

"So guys, what are we going to name this little girl?"

Leo interlocks his hand with mine and gives it a squeeze, reassuring me that everything will be okay, and that we'll talk later about all of the important things we don't have time to talk about right now.

He's here...and if I stay true to my promises to Molly-God, he'll be here forever.

Then he turns his attention to Kendall and asks, "What do you think? What does she look like to you?"

"Her face is all crinkly. I'm gonna call her...Smudge."

The nickname has me thinking back to my own use of the word 'smudge.' I first remember using it to describe my relationship with Kurt...

From the moment we met, Kurt and I were grey. Definitely not the best color to paint your relationship, but I didn't have any other colors to compare us to, he was my first one. And I foolishly tried to make the color work...for years and years. But ultimately our grey became distorted and we ended up as detached smudges of black and white. The contrast proved too harsh to coordinate, and finally, we went our separate ways.

Then the word 'smudge' came back to haunt me right after 9/11, when Leo and I got engaged in New York...

From the night we met, Leo and I were a bright and shiny color. A color so brilliant, there is no name to do it justice. But then all of a sudden we turned grey when he decided to stay in New York and help Taddeo rebuild the hedge fund business. As stupid as his decision was to stay in New York for as long as he did, it didn't compare to how stupid my decision was to spend the night at Kurt's house on my last birthday. Shortly after that bonehead move, we broke up...turning us into detached smudges of black and white.

I shake off the memories and look down at my new baby girl to get inspiration for the perfect name, and then I look back up at her father. He's aged a lot in the time we were apart. The grey that peppers his black hair is proof of the stress he's been feeling. While I feel bad for causing it, I don't feel bad for it being there. It's sexy as all get out, and looks amazing on him. Grey, though, it has never looked good on me, and I certainly have all of those damn smudges to back up that claim. Then looking back down at the baby laying on my chest, I think... *Hmmm, maybe it's about time for some good to come out of that damn color.*

"Guys, what do you think of Greyson?"

"Gweyson?"

"Yeah, how about, *Greyson Kelly Armstrong.*"

All eyes are on Leo, who after long deliberation, says, "I love it."

"Barbara?"

"It's beautiful, Hunny."

"Kendall?"

"Can I call her Gracie Smudge Cakes?"

"I don't see why not. So, do we have a winner?"

That we did. And after celebrating Greyson Kelly's new name, Kendall crawled up onto the bed in all of her big sister t-shirt-wearing glory, while Leo cautiously settled in next to me on the other side. Sinking into the nook of his arm is something I

210

never thought I'd get the chance to ever do again, and the idea that I might be able to do it for the rest of my life is mind-boggling. Unbelievably, after the chaos of the last five years, I might actually get what I always wanted...*the whole package*. And Barbara is busy snapping picture after picture of the snuggly moment...she even catches my first kiss in nine months on film.

Just before his lips touched mine, Leo whispered in my ear, "No more mistakes...by either of us." To which I replied, "No more mistakes." I so badly wanted to focus on what I was receiving. I had been dreaming about his kisses for nine months, after all. But it was impossible to block out the image of his lips on Lauren's, his body on top of hers...the engagement ring he slipped onto her finger. The images would probably still be there if it weren't for the one that replaced it when our lips parted. When I broke away from Leo's kiss, my eyes landed on Kurt who was standing in the doorway of my hospital room.

I Don't Think So

June 16, 2003

I've never seen any of my ghosts. Believe me, I wanted to. So many times I closed my eyes and wished that when I opened them my Grandpa, or Kelly, or Craig would be standing there for me to wrap my arms around. Even though Kurt's not dead, seeing him in the doorway of my hospital room was like seeing a ghost. He stood motionless and expressionless in his position, eyes locked on not one person in particular, but on the whole package that was piled up cozy in the bed. We never even made eye contact. Then, like a ghost, as soon as his image appeared, it was gone. The door to the hospital room closed as softly as it had opened, no one other than me realized he had ever been there at all.

Several curious thoughts crossed my mind after Kurt disappeared, one of which was...*I thought Barbara said he was out of town.*

Just seconds after Kurt left the hospital room, the door opened back up and in bounced Marti and The Ho-Bag, who was wearing a mile-wide grin, clearly crediting himself for saving the day and getting Leo to the hospital in the nick of time. He can have the glory. Other than what Marti gives him in the sack every other Friday, I imagine he rarely gets any.

Then to my great surprise, Megan followed behind the two of them.

"Megers! I thought you were in Oregon!"

"I was...five hours ago! Got a message from Barb telling me you were in labor, and caught the first flight home!"

Like the amazing women they are, Megan and Marti make their visit all about Kendall by showering her with gifts and attention, and then meet the baby when her big sister decides to make the introduction. After that, Megan stays by the bedside

213

with me and Leo, while Marti joins Barbara and The Ho-Bag in the corner of that room. As Megan's *owwwing* and *awwwing* at the baby, I take notice of the seemingly somber conversation the others are having. Apparently Leo does to, so he excuses himself to find out what the big deal is. When he steps away Megan dives in...

"*So*? He's back, huh? Is he alone or..."

"There's no ring on his finger, he put my hand on his heart, kissed me, and says he wants to come home with us...he's gotta be alone. Or, I'm the dumbest blonde on the planet and just invited his fiancé to live with me."

"Leo doesn't spark me as the threesome kind of guy, so my guess is he gave Lauren the boot."

The graphic images of him sexing Lauren up begin to flash through my mind. I have a scary feeling they're never going to go away, and if they don't go away...how will I ever let him sex me up?

"He didn't tell you what happened with her?"

"Not yet. Do you know?"

"Not a clue..." And then changing the subject, "...But what I do know is Marti's coming back to work!"

"It's good news, isn't it?"

"You bet! And I have some even better news to pile on top of it! Right before I came here I stopped by the office and sent out an email blast alerting all of our old customers she's coming back. Now that we have Club NiCo, we might have to add on to the space to accommodate everyone!"

"Oi, I hadn't counted on that."

"There's another thing you probably haven't counted on."

"What's that?"

And then she gives me some really bad news.

"I'm going back to Nepal."

On the inside I'm crying. Part of me feels like my oldest girl is growing up. Yes, I know Megan is quite a bit older than any child I ever could've had. But from the moment we made nice, I felt motherly toward her. I kind of feel like it helped her, and I certainly know it helped me. In fact, I never want what we have to come to an end. But she's finding her way…she's growing…she's changing. And all of that fashion and design stuff she thought she wanted, well, it doesn't look like that's what she wants after all. And who am I to stand in the way of anyone who wants to follow her heart?

"Wow, that's…incredible, Megs. I'm really happy for you in a not-so-happy-for-me kind of way." After sharing a little laugh, I reassure myself everything will be okay with, "We made it weeks without you before; we'll make it again."

She goes on to say something, but what, I don't know because my attention is directed at Leo who becomes seemingly somber himself after he listens to whatever it is Larry, Curly, and Mo just told him. Seconds later, he leaves the room.

"Megan, do you know what's going on over there?"

"What are you talking about?"

"With those guys in the corner." Now speaking to them directly, "Hey Guys, what's with the whispers?"

Marti and Barbara leave The Ho-Bag's side and walk to mine. But it's Megan who *sort of* answers the question.

"Kurt's here."

Even though I already know that because I saw the ghost, I remain quiet as three questions immediately come to mind.

1) How did Kurt even find out I had the baby today?
2) Why did he come here at all?
3) And what the hell did they just tell Leo to make him go into the corridor where my ex-husband is hanging out?

One question takes dire precedence over the other two, so I attack it first, and then I forget about the other questions when I find out the answer.

"What did you guys tell Leo to cause him to leave the room?"

Again, it's Megan who answers.

"Kurt wants to talk to him in private."

Oh, sweet Molly-Jesus! I'm just two hours into putting this relationship back together, and now this...

"Talk to him about what?"

With her darting eyes, she passes the torch to Marti.

"Well, Doll, given the birth of the baby, the *re*birth of Leo, and Kendall mixed into all of that, there appears to be some kind of peace treaty on the table."

"Couldn't these talks have waited until after we left the hospital? Why now, for Christ's sake?"

"Well, I was coming here anyway and—"

Megan stops mid-sentence and it bugs me. I've got boobies leaking all over the place, breast-feeding to learn, stitches from my back to my belly that hurt like a mother f'er, and I haven't eaten in...in...forever! I'm still calm, but the calmness is now sprinkled with annoyance.

"Megs, what does your coming here have to do with Kurt?"

Now *all* eyes are darting around. It's making me dizzy!

"I...I thought you could...that you could..."

To my shock, The Ho-Bag, of all people, steps in and calmly completes Megan's sentence.

"She thought you and Leo could use some time alone, now and for a few days after the baby comes home. So she asked Kurt to pick up Kendall here at the hospital and take her to his house for a couple of days. It'll also give Barbara a break before everyone comes back home. It makes sense that Megan would be the one to coordinate this type of thing. I mean, she is the one you put in charge of transporting Kendall back and forth between your houses during the pregnancy, wasn't she?"

The look on my face might as well have a stamp across it that says, "And how in *theeeeee* hell do *you* know shit from crap about any of this?"

As if Marti can tell exactly what I'm thinking, she busts in with, "Hunny, he knows a lot more than any of us give him credit for. He's a private investigator now, remember?"

"Uhhhhhhh, no he's not! He works in a freaking rock yard!"

"Well, technically, yes. But, he, he, he has aspirations!" Then turning to Megan, "And my little guy was right on target with the breakdown of the situation, *wasn't he?*"

Looking way too relieved that The Ho-Bag rescued her from answering my question she blurts, "Spot on. I called Kurt when my plane landed, and it just so happened that we got here at the exact same time."

"Fine then, but if Kurt's only intent was to take Kendall back to his house, why the peace treaty talks?"

"Well, Doll, guess he figured there's no time like the present to bury the hatchet."

"Jesus, hopefully not in each other's back!" Then yelling at The Ho-Bag, "Dude, put those Magnum P.I. skills to good use and see what's going on out there!"

After a quick glance into the hallway, he proudly proclaims, "All good. No body bags, blood, or stretchers. Just two dudes who used to bone the same chick having a friendly conversation."

Leo and Kurt...*in a friendly conversation?* I don't think so. And the way all of their eyes are roaming around the floor in clear avoidance of my own, confirms my doubt. Something very, very strange is going on.

Zero Time

June, 2003

The remainder of my time in the hospital was peaceful and uneventful, like it should've been. After my entourage left that day, Leo returned with a satisfied look on his face. He wasn't smiling, he wasn't pissed...just noticeably satisfied. I didn't have to ask him what happened in the corridor; he told me all on his own...

"Kurt's gonna take Kendall for a few days to give us time to settle in with the baby. Once we get situated, he'll bring her back. After that we'll all talk about a schedule that works for everyone."

"That's it?"

"That's it. Like I promised, no more fights, no more tension. And he feels the same."

"Really?"

"Yes, really."

I sat there, stunned. *Why couldn't things have been like this nine months ago?* But then I remembered...Oh wait, it's because I woke up in Kurt's bed without any pants on, that's why. And that blasphemous move paved the way for Leo to have a million blasphemous moves with Lauren. And then the images began to flash through my mind again...the sweaty, pulsating, euphoric images of them in bed.

Everything went down that day in the hospital as Leo said it would. Shortly after his conversation with Kurt, Kendall kissed us and Gracie Smudge Cakes good-bye, and then she happily went with Kurt to have fun for a few days. Correction. She went happily, but *only* after Leo pinky swore he'd be here when she got back. Just like Leo said, there were no fights and there was no tension. In fact, I never even saw my ex-husband after that five-second-long ghost sighting.

219

Barely forty hours after giving birth to Greyson, The Anderson-Armstrong family, if that's what you call us, was discharged and we headed home—a place Leo had never seen the inside of before. He wondered through the house with his new baby in his arms, talking to her, and getting to know the terrain of a residence he virtually bought over a fax machine. The home is solely in my name now, a transfer of ownership he requested after my boneheaded move at Kurt's house.

It's now two weeks after that weary first day home, and with Kendall home too now, my boobs exploding every hour with milk-a-palooza, and a baby that refuses to sleep for more than twenty minutes, we haven't had the time to talk about where ownership of the house should now stand. In fact, I still haven't asked Leo about what happened with Lauren, or where he was for the last sixty days. On top of not having the time, I haven't had the heart. He and Kendall have been reconnecting in the most essential way, with snipe hunting, shark trivia, and lots of swimming. And when they're not involved with that stuff, he's doting on his baby girl. I haven't wanted to say or do anything to disrupt the sweet harmony.

On our first night home, when it was just the two of us, we did what all new parents do. We stared into Greyson's bassinet, totally shell-shocked that the hospital let us take an actual baby home. We were scared out of our minds because we had no idea what to do with her when she moved or made a sound. Talk of our relationship and where his fiancée went took backseat to the human being we were expected to keep alive. Our focus was one hundred percent on the baby. Well, mine actually dropped to ninety-five percent when Leo asked where he should sleep for the night. Then it dropped to eighty-five percent when I suggested he sleep in my bed with me…you know, in case the baby woke up. Then it dropped to seventy-five percent when he agreed, took off his shirt, and crawled in beside me. As for me, I kept my shirt on…and my sweats. We're light years away from being skin on skin again. And it's not just because I'm tired as shit and my post-pregnancy body is hideous…it's those damn images of him and Lauren.

Like I said, it's been two weeks since that first awkward night home, and even though we've settled into a little bit of a routine now, there's still been no time to talk about *us*. But after waking up for the fourteenth night in a row in a sex-dream induced cold sweat, I ask Leo for that time. (And by the way…I'm not the one having sex in my dreams, Leo and Lauren are, and they're having a lot of it, and they're having it everywhere.)

"Baby, are you okay?"

He's here…And he's in my bed and he's shirtless and beautiful and adoring and attentive. I so badly want to grab onto all of it and forget the past, but I can't…

"No, I'm not. I want to be, because I don't want to invite anymore drama into our lives. But I have to know where you were for the last sixty days…I have to know were Lauren is…*I have to know how she even came to be*."

He takes a deep breath in and exhales before saying, "I know, and I want to tell you. I just didn't want to overwhelm you with that stuff right now."

"Leo, that stuff *is* the only thing overwhelming me."

Staring at me for a long time, so long it makes me scared about what it is he has to tell me, he finally says, "How about if Barbara watches the kids tomorrow and we go for a little drive?"

After agreeing to the plan, he pulls me into his chest where I fall back to sleep…for twenty minutes, until Greyson shits herself, cries bloody murder, and annoys everyone within a thirty mile radius. She's like a chip off the old block.

.

Spent enough time in your arms to know
Just where I want to be
I've heard your voice enough to know
Just what I need to hear…
("A Little More of You," *Ashley Chambliss*)

Going Home

June, 2003

Being my first time away from the baby, I had to write out detailed instructions for every teeny tiny potential incident that might occur in my absence. Like, if Greyson poops this color, it means this, and if she poops that color, it means that. And if she makes this sound, it means she's hungry, and if she makes that sound, it means she's gassy. And the list went on and on and on. Instead of simply kissing my two little girls good-bye, and going about my long overdue important business with Leo, I scurried around the house obsessing that I forgot something, and what should've only taken three minutes, took thirty. The great thing about Barb was that she indulged my new-mom anxiety. Kendall, though—she had no patience for it at all.

"Mommy! We got dis. Just go on your fun twip wit Weo!"

Fun trip? I wish. Something tells me there's not going to be anything fun about what Leo and I have to talk about on this drive. Partner that anxiety with my anxiety about leaving the baby, and it feels like I could break out in hives.

Once in the car, Leo puts his hand on my lap and reassures me, "It'll be okay, Chrissy. Barbara knows more about what to do with a baby than the two of us put together."

As we drive away I stare at three of the most important girls in my life and sigh, "I know…I wish she didn't have to leave."

"She's leaving?"

223

"Just back to Berkeley, but it might as well be to a foreign country."

"Well, that kind of is what Berkeley is, right?"

I love his dark humor.

"She thinks we need to be alone...that she's in the way."

"She's not at all, though. I like having her around, and Kendall is like her number one fan, that's for sure."

"She's been at the house since the night of my baby shower, when we saw you eating dinner in Lafayette with..." I shake off the horrible image and continue, "Anyway, she stayed with me that night and pretty much hasn't left since."

Looking and sounding as remorseful as one possibly can, he asks, "That was the day of your baby shower?"

"Yep."

"I'm so sorry, Chrissy. My mom picked the restaurant. It's one of her favorites."

"Did she like her?"

"Did who like who?"

"Your mom. Did she like Lauren?"

Clearly not taking pleasure in this, but knowing we have to put everything on the table before we can move forward, he answers, "Not as much as she likes you."

Staring blindly out of the car window, I mutter, "Then she must not know about all of the horrible things I did to you."

He still hasn't brought up all of the emails I wrote that went unanswered. Clearly there was something in them that disturbed him—made them either unreadable or unmentionable. I won't bring them up either. But I do feel the need to repeat what was in them. I mean, that is the point of this drive, for both of us to come completely clean, isn't it? How can we survive without the truth? And let's not leave out all of the forgiveness it's going to take once the truth is told. For a second I want to pull a reverse-Francesca, yank the door handle, and roll into oncoming traffic because that's how scared I am to voice the truth *and* listen to the truth. But I don't. Instead, I channel my hope list, and hold on tight for a miracle of epic romantic proportions.

Eyes still glued to the window, I slowly begin to verbalize everything I had already painstakingly written to him…and then some.

"I was never going to tell you I thought the baby might've been Kurt's…If Marti hadn't spilled the beans, I was gonna let you believe I stayed away because of the reasons you broke up with me."

"I know."

"In my heart of hearts, I always knew it wasn't his. But I also never thought I could be so stupid as to get drunk at his house and stay all night."

"I know."

"But what you don't know, Leo, is that I kissed him that night."

He's silent.

"I want you to know everything…every single thing that's been eating away at me."

I don't have the heart to look at him.

"It was my birthday…I was lonely and I drank too much. But I don't want you to think Kurt took advantage of the situation. It wasn't like that. I mean, for a while I thought it might've been like that, but that's only because my mind got the best of me. Eventually he cleared everything up, but obviously, it was too late."

He's still silent. I still can't bear look at him.

"It was just a good-bye kiss, and I pushed away from it as soon as it started." Now turning to him, "He said he found someone else…that he's in love. I think he just wanted to mark the end of us. Obviously, we were already over…and we both knew that a long time ago. But I think he—"

"Stop. I don't need to know anymore."

The request was sweet but stern.

"There's something you have to understand, Chrissy. All of those thoughts and feelings you have about Lauren, well you can multiply them by a thousand, and it still won't come close to how many thoughts and feelings I have…I'll *always*

225

have…about you and Kurt. There's nothing I can do to erase all of your years with him, not to mention the fact that you married him."

It's quiet for a long time before he continues with, "But when I'm near you, those thoughts and feelings matter less, because I can see in your eyes how much you love me. Maybe that explains why I melted down in New York and ended things with us. I went way too long without seeing your eyes, a lot of disturbing thoughts and feelings started taking over. Then, obviously, they spiraled out of control the day after your birthday. We had been apart for too long, and yes, that's my fault…but I was only doing what I thought needed to be done for you and Kendall. I wanted to make a better life for us, and that's why I stayed so long. You believe that, right?"

"I do, but I don't think it was worth it."

"I know that now. And I'll never go that long without seeing your eyes again."

"But I'm scared, Leo."

"Of what?"

"I'm scared *your* eyes, and how much they tell me you love me, won't make my thoughts and feelings about Lauren matter less."

"Chrissy, if you—"

"No. There's a big difference between our situations. I was married…until you came along. But she came along after you ended things with me. You replaced me with *her*, Leo."

And with those words, *you replaced me with her*, the waterworks begin.

"Please don't cry. There's some stuff you have to know, and—"

"Yeah, like where you went after the meditation room that day. I had two months left of my pregnancy, Leo. *Where were you?* I mean, were you with her trying to figure out your best option?" Now full-on hyperventilating, "Because I don't think I can handle it if you were, I'm not that tough. And, and, and…we were supposed to be special. But you were just…you were—"

226

"I was right here, Baby."

Looking up through my tears, it takes me a minute to process the view. I didn't pay attention to where Leo was driving. In my mind, I assumed he would take us to the Lafayette reservoir where so much of our history took place. But here we are, just minutes from the house…parked right in front of my beautiful old cottage.

"What are we doing here?"

"Come on. I have some things I need to explain to you."

After Leo opens my car door, he surprises me by putting a key into the front door of the cottage, and then he walks inside. Confused, I follow his lead. By the time I make it to the entryway, he's already opening the French doors to the deck. Unbelievably, they're still shielded by the adorable curtains I hung all that time ago. Once on the deck, he gets started lighting a fire in an outdoor firepit. I slowly make my way into the cottage, and then stop dead in my tracks at the kitchen where I nervously scan the entire space, scared I might find leftovers of Lauren. But there's no sign of her. In fact, the whole cottage is nearly void of furniture. From my position I can see there's a blow up bed in the bedroom, and other than two barstools tucked under the kitchen counter, a couple of suitcases, and a few boxes, the cottage is completely empty.

With Leo busy on the fire, I walk into the kitchen and glide my hands across the wall where he so boldly called the sex shots on "Holy Fucking Shit" night back in December of 1998. Then I walk over to the counter he so effortlessly placed me on. My body winces at the unabashed memory of wrapping my legs tightly around him. It quivers as I recollect that exact moment when the balance of power between us shifted. Then my eyes snap shut at the sickening memory of Kurt's knock on the door—a knock that sucked the power out of both of us. Shaking off the God-awful memory, I open my eyes and slide my hands along the cold counter tiles until they abruptly stop. I slowly reach up and open the cabinet where I engraved the words, 'I

227

loved here' on the day I moved out. Without hurry, my fingertips trace my heartfelt words.

"I saw that when I moved in...thought it might've been you."

I whirl around to find Leo watching me. I'm so confused, and at the same time oh-so-happy to be back in this space. This space represents courage, taking chances, and new beginnings. This space gives me hope.

"Leo, do you live here?"

As serious as serious can be, he nods his head.

"Apparently alone, because no woman would stand for these bleak accommodations."

I stated that as fact, but he knows it was more of a question.

Stone-faced, he clarifies, "Totally alone."

Eye to eye, and matching his seriousness, I ask, "Where did she go, Leo? No wait, before you answer that, *where did she even come from?*"

"Come on outside, we'll talk there."

Situated next to the crackling fire, alongside the roaring creek I've missed so much, he begins to explain it all.

"I bought the cottage when I moved back in April."

"I didn't even know it was for sale."

"Made the guy an offer he couldn't refuse, and here I am."

"But why here?"

"Figured if we couldn't survive the Lauren fiasco, it's still near you and the kids. Besides, I always liked this place."

After a long stare into the fire, he finally begins to tell me where she came from.

"Taddeo originally hired her for the Dallas office, but it wasn't too long before we needed her expertise in New York. I was hesitant to relocate her because I could tell how she felt about me, but you and I were still going strong. I thought she'd see that and back off."

I remain quiet. It's either that, or throw the most unattractive temper tantrum in the world, which would do nothing other than catapult him back into that "expertised" bitch's arms.

228

"So we moved her. That was right before your birthday, and we both know what happened with that."

The fire cracks...just like my heart.

"I started seeing her a few weeks after you left New York...you know, after we made Greyson."

I just nod my numb head.

"I woke up and you were gone...there was just the ring on the nightstand. I know that's what I told you I wanted, but I thought for sure you'd be there when I woke up, and it surprised me, given what we had just done in my bed, that you weren't. For weeks, all I could think about was what we did that day, and all that I lost back here in California. And the Kendall stuff weighed heavily on me. I really wanted to help that little girl...be a positive influence in her life. There were so many times when I almost picked up the phone and told you I made a mistake, but then visions of you sleeping in Kurt's bed stopped me every single time. I so badly needed all of those heavy thoughts about you and Kendall to go away. I don't know what I was thinking, really, but I asked Lauren out. Guess I thought it would help."

A piece of red hot wood breaks off in the fire and crumbles into pieces...just like my heart.

"She wasn't you, Chrissy, she was just a distraction..."

God damn those destructive distractions! When will they leave me alone?

"...Don't worry, I'm not gonna sit here and say one nice thing about her to defend my choices, because I've been on the receiving end of those when it comes to you and Kurt, and I know firsthand it does nothing to make you feel better. It just feeds the anger."

The wind picks up and the creek below roars louder...just like my heart.

"The trip to the Bay Area was for my mom's birthday...and I was supposed to go alone. Lauren sprang her involvement on me at the airport."

"Sprang her involvement on you?"

"She 'surprised' me and joined me on the trip. We fought about it—bad—the entire flight over. By the time we landed, it was clear to me she was rushing things…pushing a relationship on me I really wasn't looking for. But knowing I still had to fly home with her, I postponed the inevitable break-up conversation for when we got back to New York." He takes a breather before saying, "Looking back, that was a huge mistake."

"Why's that?"

"For starters, if I had broken up with her right then and there she wouldn't have been at the restaurant that night. I would've been able to talk to my mom about all of the things I flew to California to talk to her in person about."

"What did you want to talk to her about?"

"You. I wanted to tell her I still loved you. Then I wanted her to give me one of her infamous Italian bitch-slaps in the face, and tell me to forget about Kurt and get you back." Running his fingers through his beautiful black hair, he sighs, "Instead, I was in some nightmare dining scenario with Lauren as she talked to my mom about her ultimate dream honeymoon destination. Then to make matters a million times more agonizing, I saw you walking across the street. Oh man, I'll never forget the look on Marti's face, it was pure hate…I could only imagine what you were feeling. I felt like such an asshole for being in Lafayette with Lauren, and like a bigger asshole, I kept my mouth shut. I didn't chase you down, and I didn't set Lauren straight. It's like I was frozen."

Staring into the fire, I somberly remind him, "You didn't chase me down at Buckley's the night we met, and you didn't chase me down the night you saw me outside of that restaurant. It seems like I'm always just a little too easy for you to let go of."

"Ignoring you at Buckley's was just plain stupidity, but my intentions for letting you go that night in Lafayette weren't. I just needed to go back to New York, end it with her, and figure out my next move. But you know what, Chrissy; couldn't I say the same for you? Wasn't I always a little too easy for you to let go of? I mean, how many times did you try to end it with me when you were with Kurt?"

"That was different, I was mar—"

"Love is love."

"Right. Love *is* love. And I only tried to end my love for you because I wasn't free to pursue it. But you *were* free to pursue it, and you pursued it with her, and so soon after we split up. What's even worse is you didn't go back to New York and end it with her, you asked her to marry you. The truly, madly, deeply guy I know would never do that. *When did you change, Leo?*"

"I never changed."

"You did change! The man I know would *never* propose to a woman he wasn't in love with!"

He startles me when he yells, "I never asked her to marry me, Chrissy!"

Full on boiling over like the fire, I scream back, "*What the hell are you talking about?*"

Bringing emotions down a notch, he suspends talking for a long time before lowering his voice and saying, "I said…I never asked her to marry me."

"Then why did you tell me you were engaged?"

"Because I was."

Okay, I know I'm up every two hours feeding Greyson, but seriously, *how sleep-deprived am I right now*? What the F is he talking about?

"The whole thing is so unbelievably stupid, and it's why I said earlier it was a *huge* mistake not to have broken up with her on the flight to California…" Rubbing his tired face, he continues, "…When we got back to my loft after the flight home I was finally gonna tell her we were over, but she found the ring…*your ring*…in the nightstand where I put it after you left that day. I returned from the bathroom and there she was jumping up and down, screaming 'Yes! Yes! Yes!' over and over again. I was stunned. One, she was wearing *your* ring. And two, before I even knew what was happening, she had announced the news to all of Dallas. Within minutes of her

231

putting that fucking thing on her hand, I was on the phone with her Texas Ranger father who said he'd blow my balls off if I hurt his little girl—and then he congratulated me."

"But her misunderstanding and his gun would never prevent a guy like you from setting the record straight. Why didn't you end it right then and there?"

"I was worried about T.L. Capital. She was our Director of Corporate Relations, Chrissy. Here was a woman who I just got done telling on the flight out to California that I thought she was rushing things, yet she had no problem slipping that ring on her finger. She knew perfectly well that thing wasn't for her, and I knew perfectly well she'd make things incredibly sticky at work, and with our clients, if I told her so. It was a total nightmare that I spent every day after that trying to wake up from and fix."

"If it was such a nightmare, then why did you tell me in the meditation room that day, before you even saw my stomach, things were finally working out for you?"

"I knew I wanted you back, but a part of me didn't want to make it easy for you. I missed you, Chrissy, but I was still reeling from what happened on your birthday. But the second I saw your stomach, none of that stuff bothered me anymore."

"When did you finally end it with her?"

"Even though things didn't work out like I expected in the meditation room that day, I took the first flight back to New York to close everything out there. To be honest, I didn't know what would become of us after everything that went down, but I knew you were having my baby, and I knew I needed to move back home. The conversation with Lauren took less than five minutes. She had no choice but to accept the news I gave her, which was that we were having a baby, and I wanted to try to make it work with you. By then I also didn't care about her slandering me at T.L. Capital because I knew I was resigning." He stares into the fire for a minute before admitting, "I don't know how to tell you this, but I had to let her keep the ring. She said it was the least I could do given I made a fool out of her, and if I wanted it back I'd have to pry it off her hand. Whatever.

She ruined the significance of that ring the second she touched it."

Slowly he rises from his chair, kneels in front of me, places his hands on my cheeks, and coerces my eyes to come together with his.

"But I can get you a new ring. *A better ring.*"

He's a beautiful man who says and does beautiful things. But it doesn't matter. I know me, and it just...doesn't...matter. And I know exactly why.

"Do you realize it was just a little over two years ago that we were sitting in this cottage...I had just picked you up from the airport...you had just moved in your last load. We were sitting right in there, on the wicker couch. Remember?"

He nods his head.

"I was worried that you had been with other women while we were broken up. The idea paralyzed me with something I'd never felt before, and I knew I couldn't be with you anymore if you had. But you told me hadn't, and even more, you told me sex with some other girl would've only tainted what we had together...that your heart had to be in it, or it was a no go. I *believed* you when you said those things, Leo, and I felt the same way. That's what made us special...That was our truly, madly, deeply connection going all the way back to the night we met."

I wrote all of those emails, confessed my horrid truths in them, and despite knowing about his relationship with Lauren, I even admitted I wanted him back. I even begged him to choose us when I was delivering Greyson. And he has. But even though he's willing to start over with me, there's something standing in the way of our truly-madly-deeply-ever-after. It's something most people would think I'm nuts for letting get in the way, but it's the thing I always thought set our love apart from the rest. A single tear escapes my eye and slides down my cheek as I painfully admit what I've been too scared to even admit to myself.

"You slept with her, Leo, and it changed the essence of us. What we had…our love…is tainted."

He pauses for a long time before he very sweetly reminds me of something.

"I've never told a lie in my entire life."

"I know."

Reminding me of what a good man he is causes my lower lip to tremble, tears to trickle, and self-deprecation to snowball. I drove him to her. Lauren is my fault. And now I have two choices. Either I stay and feel the effects of her for the rest of my life, or I leave and feel the effects of her for the rest of my life. It's a fucked-up crossroads I'm at.

"Then you know I'm not lying about what I'm about to say so that we can have our truly-madly-deeply-ever-after…"

There's nothing he can say to mend my crossroads.

"…I never slept with her."

Except that.

"*Excuse me?*"

"You heard me, Baby. Never slept with her. Heart wasn't in it."

Okay, hold on a minute. I saw this Alabaster chick's picture. A Catholic priest—*a gay Catholic priest*—would sleep with her!

He's quick to deal with my skeptic face.

"Looks like I also have to remind you of just how different I am than most guys."

"But…the way you described her as being crazy about you, didn't that make her mad?"

"I think she thought it was gallant, but I never cared enough to ask. But I did know I needed to break things off before the wedding night. Would've had a hard time explaining that, huh?"

And then I reveal my first grin of the day.

Wiping my face dry, he declares, "Now that smile makes me a very happy man."

He never slept with her. Good-bye images, helloooo future! Geez, while I'm at it…might as well get all the facts. And this is definitely something I've been wondering for a very long time…

234

"Am I the only girl you've ever slept with?"

"No."

Goddammit.

"But you are the only woman I've ever slept with."

I'll take it.

"And there's been no one after you, Chrissy. I swear."

Can't ask for more than that. *Maybe…*

"Did you kiss Lauren?"

"Did you kiss your ex-husband on your birthday?"

"I think we're good here."

As funny as the exchange was, in our truly, madly, deeply world, there was no laughter to be found.

"So can we put it behind us, all of it?"

"To move forward, we're gonna have to. And I want to move forward, Leo. I want to have everything we always talked about."

"So how about it, then?"

"How about what?"

"I think we still have some time before we have to get home…How about some ring shopping?"

"So we're really doing it this time?"

"I think it's definitely time to lock this thing down."

And then right there on the deck of my cozy old cottage, he pulls me to my feet and tightly into his chest, where he kisses every inch of my head before tilting it up toward his so that he can kiss my lips. It was a kiss that made me believe we were going to make it this time. And the most magical thing about it was not one single image of what's-her-Alabaster-face popped into my head.

After I pull away from his sweet kiss I inform him, "I don't need a ring, Leo. You gave me a baby. You gave Kendall a sister. You gave me a family."

He boasts, "Nice try, but whether you like it or not you're gonna have a satellite dish on that hand. I want everyone from here to Siberia to know you're married."

235

"I'll be wearing spit-up on my shirt for the next three years…Trust me, I'll be unapproachable. *But you*? That's another story! I'm thinking something titanium strength that's the size of a tire, engraved with the words 'I love my wife!' and I want it super glued on your finger. Those female clients of yours will have to think long and hard before even batting an eyelash at you…Speaking of clients, what the heck do you even do for a living now?"

"We sure have been busy these last two weeks, huh?"

"Little bit."

"C'mon, Baby, let's go for another drive. I've got the family business to show you."

Restructuring

July, 2003

They say once you have kids you shouldn't blink or you'll miss everything. Now, I don't know who 'they' are, but those assholes were spot on. It's been one month since we brought Greyson home, and apparently I blinked too damn much, because I can only remember about forty minutes of her life. That's how nuts things have been. Yep, there's been a lot of restructuring over the past four weeks.

After Leo and I left the cottage that day, he took me to his new office where he finally answered the question...*Where were you for the last two months?*

When he left the meditation room that day in April, he was as angry as can be, and I thought for sure my lies by omission had officially put him over the edge, ruining any and all chance of us. But apparently, the second he saw my pregnant belly, he made it his mission in life to rebuild our relationship...and he knew the foundation needed to be strong, and it needed to be local. So he high-tailed it back to New York, dumped Lauren, and sold out to Taddeo so that he could start building closer to me.

Standing outside of his consulting business, Armstrong Financial Services, he told me about something that stuck with him after our first ever conversation. It was something I said in my car outside of Buckley's on the night we met. It was my confession...my secret desire to *maybe* be a stay-at-home-mom. I yearned for the choice to stay home with my kids, and if time permitted, perhaps I could do something creative like be an interior decorator...or a writer. My confession never escaped Leo. In fact, it motivated him when he was in college, at his first job as an investment banker, and when he was in New York rebuilding the hedge fund business. Sure, he was in a full-blown

237

rage that day he stormed out of the meditation room, but just like those first years we were together, he was also in full-blown determination mode. He needed to quickly build a business that could provide for our family and offer me the freedom to be whatever I wanted to be. Ever since our first ever conversation…it was Leo's mission in life to give me my secret desire.

He worked all day, every day, on his new financial business. He networked with his old colleagues at Robertson Stevens, the St. Mary's alumni association, and even flew back to New York a few times to rub shoulders with the big wigs he did business with at T.L. Capital—even managing to steal a few away. But he spent most evenings parked in front of my house where he watched me, Kendall, and Barbara through the window. Watching me rub my pregnant belly and talk out loud to his child made him forget about the jealous rage he always had for Kurt. Watching Kendall sit on my lap for story time made him miss what he wanted to do for her. Watching Barbara's valiant effort to keep up with the household chores made him eager to put the past behind so that he could help out. Night after night, he watched through the window, and what he watched compelled him to forgive. Forgive himself for putting the success of T.L. Capital ahead of me and Kendall, causing us to drift apart, and forgive me for that foolish night at Kurt's house, forcing us to break apart. He said there were several nights that he wanted to knock on my front door, but stopped just short for fear of confusing Kendall and upsetting her laughter. And just as Marti revealed, Leo admitted to calling the hospital twice a day to see if I was in labor. From the moment he stormed out of the meditation room that day in April, it was always his intent to show up at the hospital, put my hand on his heart, and get his family back.

Everything Leo said and did on the day we visited the cottage and his new office reminded me that I'm with a modern-day knight in shining armor—a man who makes it his mission in life to provide for the ones he loves—*his girls*. After profusely thanking him for continually doing everything he can to make all of our dreams come true, and promising, once and for all, to do the same for him in return, we went ring shopping.

While it'll still take some time for Leo and me to get fully familiar with each other again, the home life of The Anderson-Armstrong family is steadily falling into place, and for the first time in a long time things are calm. Well, with the exception of Kendall, who interrupts us every five minutes to ask if she can change her last name to match Leo's and Greyson's. It's a conversation I'd love to have with Kurt, *but how?* Craig and Kelly were his best friends, too. I don't have the heart to ask for his blessing and erase the last name of Wilson from his life. Maybe once Leo and I are married, I'll revisit the subject. But for now, the option is off the table.

Another option that's off the table right now is sex. Per Hannibal Lecter's orders, no sex for at least seven weeks. It wouldn't have mattered if he gave me the green light the night I came home from the hospital, though. My huha is light years away from wanting a penis anywhere near it. I haven't had the guts to take a mirror to that thing since I got home from the hospital, let alone allow Leo to go rooting around it. The look on Marti's face when she joined Hannibal at the end of the delivery table was enough to scar me for life. No need to add insult to injury by adding the look on Leo's face to the list. Only time will tell in regards to the restoration of Leo and Chrissy's sex life. For now, I pray to Molly-God daily that I'm not the only new mother out there who's scared to death that her newborn baby is the defining line between hot sex and ho-hum sex.

Hot sex, ho-hum sex, or no sex, it doesn't matter. Our wedding date is set. On September thirteenth, one year and one day shy of our previously set day, Leo and I will be tying the knot. We decided to throw caution to the wind and make an unlucky number a long-overdue blessing. Either we're completely fearless or complete dumbshits to roll the dice on the number thirteen.

Soon after that day Leo and I reconnected at the cottage, Marti returned to work, which meant two things: business exploded overnight, and we had a little capacity crisis at the Lafayette studio. I did what any business owner would do: I strapped on my Babybjörn and rushed back to work. I couldn't let anything interfere with the serenity of Club NiCo, and I sure as hell wasn't going to let anything prevent me from retaining the returning clients…and their returning money. My ragtag team and I immediately got busy with a plan, and it wasn't long before we implemented it. Serenity and cash flow were promptly secured. It felt so good to get back to life, and back to one of my true loves, Forever Young, Inc. I'd been ignoring her for way too long. But now that the pieces of my life are falling back into place, nothing will go overlooked anymore. In fact, from here on out, I'll be watching over and protecting everything I love like a Mama lion. Given the fact I had a baby with a Papa lion, the reference certainly works.

Now it's today, and sadly, Megan's last day of work before her return trip to Nepal. It's somber in the studio as Marti, Barb, and I go about our business—each trying to forget about the sweet young woman on the other side of our walls that we'll have to live without for the next…the next…Shit, I forgot to ask how long she'd be gone this time. How the heck did that escape me? Oh yeah…been doing lots of restructuring.

With Greyson snoozing away in her porta-crib, the three of us tippy-toe to Megan's office with a bottle of champagne and a bunch of dehydrated food for her to take on her *negative* five-star vacation in Asia.

To my shock, her normally thrashed office is curiously organized. What's even weirder is it seems like I'm the only one startled by this.

"Wow, Megs, it's just a little toast to send you off properly. No need to get all cleaned up just for us."

Just like that day at the hospital, her eyes dart from Marti to Barb looking for some kind of help.

"Okay Guys, is there something you need to tell me?"

Ignoring all of their mumbo-jumbo answers, my eyes scan Megan's desk where I notice the missing family photos that used to litter it. Her book shelves are eerily clutter-free, and the calendar on her wall ceases to list any appointments past today's date. Then my eyes land back on her.

"You're not coming back, are you, Megan?"

"I'm not...I'm not sure."

"It's not for another design position, is it?"

"Oh no, Chrissy! I would never, ever, ever leave what I have here for another design position. I love you guys, *all of you*, and this has been the best experience of my life." Reaching her arms out for me to take hold of, she chokes up as she says, "I can never thank you enough for what you've taught me...what you've given to me."

Marti releases a tiny chortle, but I take no notice of it because I'm stunned that this good-bye party is apparently...an *actual* good-bye party.

"Is this about bigger things you plan on doing in Nepal?"

Marti says, "That's an understatement" and snickers again. It's irritating and making me consider calling her TWWINDTM again.

"Are you choking over there or what, Stewart?"

Megan's eye's bug out at Marti, clearly telling her to shut up and ignore my question.

"Meg, you've been making googly eyes at those two ever since I gave birth, what are you so afraid to tell me?" Turning my attention to all three of them, "Can someone just tell me what the heck is going on?"

"I need you to...Chrissy, I just need you to understand..."

All chortles and snickers aside, Marti busts in to save her with, "She needs you to understand she's young and wants to fart around the world for a while. Nothing wrong with that, right, Chrissy?"

"Of course not! And I don't want you to feel bad about leaving here for one second. I want you to follow your heart, Megs. Always."

241

"Even if that means someone gets hurt?"

"The three of us are gonna miss you like crazy, but no one is hurt. We're happy for you, okay?"

"No…I meant…"

"Megan, I'm gonna tell you what Dr. Maria told me. If you're not happy, you'll never be able to make anyone else happy. Promise me you'll always put yourself at the top of your list. Promise me."

"I promise. It's just that—"

"No ifs, ands, or buts! Follow your heart and see where it takes you. There will always be a place for you here. I mean it, Megan. No matter how far your travels take you, you always have a home at Forever Young."

"But Chrissy, I think there's something you need to know."

Marti interrupts again with, "All she needs to know is that you set up everything nice and neat for whoever takes over your job."

And then Barb chimes in with, "Yeah, and Marti and I can handle *anything* that might pop up after you're gone. Let's not ruin this little send off with nitty-gritty details."

After Megan caves into their convoluted nudging, we pop the cork on the champagne.

The rest of our little good-bye party was quite drab with Megan offering suggestions for a replacement to take over the yoga collection. By the end of the champagne bottle, we all resignedly agreed to steal Jewish American Princess Trust Fund Designer from our old clothing company. And by the time Greyson woke from her nap, it was time to say good-bye to the young woman I used to love to hate.

"It's not forever though, right?"

"Nothing's forever, Chrissy. I just have to pursue some things, free from all of this stuff—you know, see where life takes me."

"I hope it leads you to love, Megan. I really, really do."

"You mean that?"

Diving in for my last hug, I whisper, "Truly, madly, deeply."

With Greyson snug in the Babybjörn, Marti, Barb, and I wave good-bye to Megan as she drives away and out of sight.

It's sorrowfully silent for a very long time before I ask, "Do you guys think she's ever coming back?"

"Not a chance."

Shocked at Marti's matter-of-fact response, I screech, "*Why?*"

Ignoring me, she asks Barb, "I think it's time, don't you?"

After scratching her head in deep thought, Barb finally says, "Yep."

"Come on, Doll. I think it's time to officially remove that blonde head from your ass."

Full Circle

July, 2003

Ten minutes later, with my blonde head figuratively covered in shit, I finish reading what's on my computer monitor, and then tilt *wayyy* back in my desk chair. Dumbfounded, I stare at the ceiling for what seems like hours before I mutter, "How could I have missed this?"

Marti starts with, "I think Kurt tried to tell you the night of your birthday, but you drank yourself pantless."

Then my eyes zip to Barbara who says, "Then, immediately following that there was the big bad break up with Leo. You were too preoccupied with that to see what was happening right in front of your face."

Then they zip back to Marti.

"Yeah, then there was the pregnancy shortly after both of those things. It was probably hard to notice anything other than that growing gut of yours."

Then back to Barb.

"Then right as things seemed to be calming down enough to break the news to you, there was that horrible scene with Lauren in that restaurant."

Then back to Marti.

"Then right after that Megan left for Nepal. I thought that was about the time you'd start to see the writing on the wall—but nope. Probably because of that misconstrued phone call from Kurt, when you thought he told you the baby was his, and then you farted, fainted, and ended up in the hospital."

After they begin to crack up, I tilt back in my chair again to avoid eye contact. It's just too embarrassing.

"Then, of course, not long after that, there was the disaster in the meditation room, which was quickly followed by the bed rest. Had to be hard to think about anything other than the baby."

"I don't know though, Barb. You think she would've had time to figure it out as she sat in bed every single day, with nothing else to do. I mean, didn't she wonder why Megan was the one still taking Kendall back and forth between her and Kurt? There was no need for it anymore. Chrissy and Kurt had become friendly again."

"Well to her defense, that was about the time Courtney and Nicole moved away. I think that sucked the life outta her—made it hard to concentrate on anything."

Leaning back up, I glare at the two of them and ask, "You two done having fun?"

Apparently not, because they carry on as if I'm not even in the room.

Marveling at the dysfunctional last nine months of my life, Barbara says, "Gosh darn, you don't even see this kind of drama on television."

"I know, and that's just what happened in the last year!" Pointing at me, Marti bellows, "That girl's got drama going all the way back to 1998. Remember how it all started, with the affair? Then she separated from Kurt, got back together with Kurt, and then left Kurt *again* after that surprise party nightmare…"

"…*Ugh*, the surprise party. She lost Leo because of that. That was so sad."

"But it got happy again, remember? Because she got her cottage right after that, hacked into his voicemail, tracked him down at The Round Up, and hooked back up with him."

Flabbergasted that I'd resort to phone hacking, Barbara pleads, "Oh Chrissy, please tell me you didn't listen to that man's messages."

All I can do is continue to stare at the ceiling. And after giving up on waiting for an answer from me, Barb goes back to their sick little ping-pong game.

"She might've 'hooked back up with him,' but she lost him again right quick because she lied to him about getting a divorce."

246

"Poop, that's right. I forgot all about that. But! She dated that tatted-up lawyer who wanted to buy her really nice shit, *and* made out with that Cal quarterback who wanted to say really nice shit...Hey that reminds me, I should call that defensive end I played with. Mmmm- mmm-mmm, that boy was hot."

It's quiet *just* long enough to make me think they're done. Wishful thinking...

"This is where my memory gets a little fuzzy, Marti. What happened next?"

"How could you forget, Barb? Kurt fell off of a damn horse!"

"No-no, I remember now...It was a motorcycle! Let's see, after that she sold her house in Danville, quit her job, opened the first yoga studio, lost Kelly, which is horrible so we'll gloss right over that...Then she went to New York to get Leo back."

"No, you have the order wrong. She went to New York to get Leo back *before* Kelly passed away. Remember...it was Kelly who told her to go."

"Ah! That's right. Everyone's intentions were so good, but the outcome of that trip was so sad. Remember, her attempt to get him back failed miserably. He left her standing in the snow on the mean streets of Manhattan."

"That's true, but she also came home determined to get on with her life."

"Which was fantastic, but what was even better was when Leo realized he wanted a second chance after all, and showed up on her doorstep."

It's all I can take. I throw my hands in the air and ask, "Are we full circle now?"

My new voice of reason playfully answers, "Technically we're not because there was still a lot of crap that went down between that second chance doorstep day and drinking yourself pantless at Kurt's house. But you were more of a casualty of the bad things that happened in that time period, not the instigator. So it's definitely not as much fun to talk about."

247

Coming to my rescue, Barb strokes my hair and says, "I'm sorry Sweetie, we're being mean. Forget about all that stuff. Life is good now."

Slapping me in the knee, Marti jabs, "Forget about it? Screw that! Good God, Chrissy, you should write a book about this shit."

"Yeah right, who would want to read about my train wreck?"

Barb interjects, "Anyone who wants to feel like they're not the only one going through a hard time."

"Yeah right. I think it's more like anyone who needs a good laugh, if you ask me."

"I'm serious, Hunny, show me one woman who can't identify with something you went through, and I'll show you a woman who is either very young, very much in denial, or the very luckiest woman on earth."

Like the new and improved voice of reason, problem solving, sarcastic freak she is, Marti hollers, "Or a woman who needs to be institutionalized!"

As the two of them continue to debate the sanity of the last five years of my life, I re-read what's on my computer monitor and then tilt back in my chair again and think…Yep, the last four weeks were a lot of work with the restructuring of Leo and Chrissy, the restructuring of the Lafayette studio, and the restructuring of my family, and I expected all of it. What I didn't expect, though, was the destruction of one of my most cherished friendships.

Coming Clean

July, 2003

What I learned three days ago literally rocked my world, which sucks considering my world *just* stopped rocking after five long years. I've been trying to block out what I read in my office the other day, along with all of the attempts made over the last eight months to show me the writing on the wall, but it's been difficult. It seems like every five minutes a flashback hits me. And when it does, I slap myself in the forehead and curse myself for being such a self-absorbed, oblivious idiot. I mean, seriously...*how did I miss this*? Even more, how does this news affect the dynamics of my family...*my recently restructured family*?

At first I didn't want to disrupt the sweet harmony that just kicked in at home with Leo and the girls, so I kept my worries to myself. But after three sleepless nights of wondering what all of the new changes mean for our family, I submit to my worry and toy with disrupting our sweet harmony.

"Leo, you awake?"

Groggy, but acting like the knight in shining armor he is, he rolls over to face me.

"I'm right here. Need help with Greyson?"

"No, no, she's fine. It's something else."

"Oh, yeah...what is it, Baby?"

After filling him in on the email and all of the failed attempts made to tell me what was in it, I sit and wait patiently for him to say something.

"Well, what do you think?"

"I think it's weird, but the same thing could probably be said about us."

"No, I mean what do you think it means for our family?"

Obviously that got his attention, because all of a sudden he sits up.

"What do you mean?"

"Kendall?"

"Chrissy, you're her legal guardian, and no matter what, that can't change."

"But I wanted to adopt her. I mean, not right now because I want her to be old enough to understand everything that's happening, but soon, though. You don't think this puts a hiccup in that plan?"

"Honestly, I don't see how that's possible. But if it'll make you feel better, we can talk to an attorney who specializes in this type of thing."

"You'd set that up for me?"

"I'd set that up for *us*. I want to adopt her too, Baby. When I told you I wanted to lock this down, I meant the whole damn family."

He's really here… And he's in my bed and he's shirtless and beautiful and adoring and attentive. I've said that same thing every night since he came home from the hospital with me and Greyson and I don't think I'll ever stop.

"I want all of us to have the same last name. That is what Kendall wants, right?"

"She wants nothing more, but I really can't imagine Kurt signing off on that."

"Does he have a say in it?"

Technically speaking, he doesn't. But compassionately speaking, I'd really like to give him a say. Not wanting to disrupt our sweet harmony, I keep that thought to myself and just shrug my shoulders.

"What do you think about everything, Chrissy? I mean, what you found out has to be pretty weird, huh?"

"I'm stunned. I mean, I want everyone to be happy, really I do. But I didn't know it would be so in-my-face."

"Well, maybe it won't be as in-your-face as you think it will be."

His reaction to everything I told him tonight is not at all what I expected. I guess his promise of no fights and no tension was no joke.

He lies down and pulls me onto his chest, which I can still barely believe is back for my enjoyment. My chest, though…those fire hoses are off limits to everyone but Greyson.

He then changes the subject to an uplifting and surprising one.

"I saw that Barbara started packing up the guest room. Is she moving back home soon?"

"Yeah. I keep begging her to stay, but she won't listen. She thinks we need our space. It makes me so sad though, Leo. I don't want her to go back to living alone in that Berkeley house. I don't think she ever changed anything on the inside since her family died in the earthquake fourteen years ago. I can't imagine her going back to that, not after being so happy here."

"Maybe she can give us the space she thinks we need without going back there."

"What do you mean?"

"I've been thinking about the cottage. Obviously I don't need it anymore."

"Yeah?"

"And it's five minutes from here…"

I jolt up in the bed.

"Omigod! Are you saying what I think you're saying?"

"What's that?"

"Barbara can live in the cottage?"

"She helped you so much when you needed it…when I wasn't here. I want to do this for the both of you. You think she'd be happy there?"

"I have no idea, but I can't wait to ask her!"

"It needs a few improvements. Will probably take a few months to get everything done…How about we ask her to move in right after we get married?"

"How about you're the most wonderful man in the entire world!"

251

I fire off about a hundred kisses covering the span of his entire chest, and in between each one I squeal, "Thank you, thank you, thank you!" With each kiss and each thank you feeling like the dynamics of my family will be just fine, regardless of the news flash I obtained three days ago.

Tuesday Night Dinner

July, 2003

When my cell phone rang at fog horn volume, it scared the crap out of me and I scrambled to answer it before it woke Greyson. That was the first thing to jolt my heart rate. The second thing to jolt it was the voice on the other line. I mostly just listened to what he had to say and then hesitantly agreed to his request. When I hung up, part of me felt like, *what's the point*? But to be honest, with my wedding to Leo less than two months away, and wanting to adopt Kendall, there were things I needed to talk to him about, too.

Once his voice was gone, I quickly put the conversation out of my head. There was something way more important that needed my concentration, so I clicked off my phone, shoved it in my back pocket, packed Greyson in the Babybjörn, and walked to the front door.

Once I land on the porch, Barbara looks at me eye to eye, and asks, "Are you sure you want to be here?"

"I'm positive. I want to help."

"It's just that…well, you might think—"

"I'll think nothing other than how happy I am that you're going to move into the cottage and continue to be close to us."

Leo and I offered the cottage to Barbara last week. At first it looked like it was out of the question because she just kept shaking her head no. But then all of a sudden she stopped and asked if it meant she'd have to get rid of her house in order to afford it. Leo put her worry at ease when he told her that wouldn't be necessary—it was a gift from us. She's been in deep thought since that conversation, and I think she's even been on Dr. Maria's couch twice in the last two days. Whatever my old therapist said must have convinced her that the move was a good idea, because here I am at Barb's house in Berkeley, prepared to help her pack up.

She stares at me for a long time, like she's second-guessing my participation, and it really makes me nervous about what I'm walking into. Even so, I give her a nod and a wink for encouragement. Hesitantly, she pulls her house keys from her purse.

After the door creaks open I try to get a good look inside, but all of the shades are closed tightly, making it too dark to see anything. Greyson and I wait in the entry way for Barbara to reach a light. When one finally clicks on, my focus becomes torn. It's torn between Barbara's agony, and the dining room table she's standing next to, a dining room table set for three.

As I walk toward the scene, I slowly and subtly wrap my arms a little tighter around Greyson. The closer I get to the table, the more in awe I am of what I see. When I reach the edge of it, I take in the crushing setting which is frozen in time.

The table is set for a normal Tuesday night dinner. There are two adult place settings, one for Barb, and one for her husband, and between the two of them, there's a place setting for her three-year-old daughter. It's complete with a booster chair and a Pound Puppy sippy cup. At one time, the wine glasses were filled with red wine. I can tell because there's dark sediment at the bottom of each. Either Barbara drank what was in them or the liquid has long since evaporated. In the center of the table is a basket filled with what looks like a green Styrofoam mold. I presume at one time it was bread. Slowly making my way around the circular table, I reach Barbara, who's also staring down at the scene, and lost in thought. I don't have the heart to interrupt. Curious, I leave her side and make my way into the tiny kitchen and then walk straight to the oven. I click the oven light several times to see what's inside, but it has long since burned out. Apprehensively, I open the door. Inside I find a fourteen-year-old lasagna.

Oh my Molly-God...She was making dinner when the quake hit.

Evidently Barbara followed me, because she's not far behind when she says, "Do you think I'm crazy?"

"Oh Barbara, I know you're not. If it makes you feel better, when Leo went back to New York after that fight at Craig's memorial, I never touched the last towel he used. I even kept it all crunchy from the water he dried off of himself."

"Chrissy, this is a little different. There's a fourteen-year-old meal on the table."

"And if it gives you comfort we'll leave it intact. None of this has to go in the garbage, Barbara. We're not here to dump the past; we're here to move all of it closer to me. Now I'm no therapist, and you might want to run this by Dr. Maria, but I think you can hang onto all of these things *and* have a fabulous life. I mean, isn't the last year and a half proof of that?"

Just a tight-lipped nod of the head.

"Obviously, most of the contents of this house won't fit in the cottage. So my suggestion is we move what you don't need to live with day-to-day into a storage unit. Leo found one just a mile and a half from the cottage. We can even set up everything to look just like this so that you can revisit these memories whenever you want."

She's quiet for a super long time. It makes me think I have no business saying all of the things I'm saying.

"You want to know what I think?"

Oh shit.

"I think we should throw away this old food. It's kind of stinky."

Oh thank Molly-God.

"Then I think we should go through some of...some of Annie's toys and see if there's anything the girls might like to play with..."

Her name was Annie. Sweet, sweet Annie.

"Are you sure about that, Barb?"

"It would be nice to see them get used after all of these years. I'd actually enjoy it very much, Chrissy."

"Kendall would love that. Thank you."

255

"Whatever's left over we can box up with Oliver's things and put in storage…"

The love of her life was named Oliver.

"…And as far as the dining room table goes, no need to set it up like it's Tuesday night dinner. I'll probably be having that at your house anyway, right?"

"Absolutely right."

Her eyes do a scan of everything in sight and it's clearly a poignant moment for her.

"Barb…you okay?"

"I am. It's time."

"For all of us, don't you think?"

"*Us*…I like that. Doesn't make me feel so alone."

"You're not alone, Barb. And you haven't been since that handshake outside of Dr. Maria's office. You have me, and Leo, and Kendall…Marti, Megan…everyone at the studios…" Patting Greyson's bottom and looking down at top of her head, I say, "And we keep adding more and more people to your family, don't we?"

"Yes, and it's like a gift from Heaven. Speaking of…would you like to see some pictures of my family?"

The rest of that afternoon, and the next three, were hard and emotional. After Barbara and I gently sifted through her old photo albums, and she shared her fondest memories of Oliver and Annie with me, we quietly dismantled the table setting. We disposed of the old food and tended to all of the other sensitive and personal items in the home before we called Leo and Marti to assist with us with everything else. (I was so proud of Marti when she didn't bat a fake eyelash at all of the manual labor that was required of her.) There were moments when Barbara was eager to share stories of her family with us, and then there were moments when she was so lost in thought it scared me. Like Kendall, Barb is a lone survivor, and the task of cleaning up and moving out of her home was eerily reminiscent of cleaning up and moving out of Kelly and Craig's home. There were many times when I had to join Barb on the couch and take an

256

emotional time-out myself. But when all of the work was said and done, we shared a big family-style meal at our home in Lafayette, and we even invited extended family—The Ho-Bag, who apparently really does want to become Magnum P.I. because he's now taking night classes in criminal justice. We'll see what happens with that...

Seemingly happy with all that she's accomplished in the last three days and a family she knows she can call her own, Barnana settles in nice and tight next to Kendall—the little girl she shares an extraordinary bond with—and makes a toast to the future.

And the plan for the future is that Barbara will stay at our house until Leo's able to make all of those "improvements" at the cottage. And I'm glad! I only have forty-five days to plan a wedding I've been dreaming about for over five years, and I can use all the help I can get.

("Swan Lake," *Chad Larson*)

Saphalhos

July, 2003

With Barbara's house behind us, and wedding plans underway, the time had come to address the phone call I received in Barb's driveway. But before I address it with the person who made it, I have to address it with Leo. On top of no more tension and no more fights, there will be no more secrets. Fully committed to my hope list and all of those promises I made to Molly-God, I open up about my plans for the afternoon as Leo and I sit in the backyard with our morning coffee.

"Kurt called me."

Without flinching, he asks, "Everything okay with Kendall?"

His reaction is refreshing. I wonder how long it'll stay like that after I say what I have to say.

"I think so. He didn't bring her up."

"What did he want then?"

"He didn't say exactly, but I have a feeling it's about all of that stuff we talked about in bed the other night. He asked to meet me in person…today. I think I'm gonna…I'm gonna meet with him. Are you okay with that?"

Now he flinches. Well, I wouldn't exactly call it a flinch, it's more like a twitch, but the twitch is in his gigantic bicep. Clearly a sign of annoyance. Even so, he surprises me when he says, "As long as he has Kendall every weekend, you guys should talk. Even if that means it's in person, I guess."

Impressive. Talk about taking the term 'digging deep' to the next level.

"But, just one thing…"

Wrapping my arms around the new and improved, not-needing-to-punch-his-fist-through-glass-at-the-mention-of-

259

Kurt's-name, guy I'm with, I kiss him on the lips before saying, "What's that?"

"Any mention of wanting you back and he's a dead man."

I'm flattered, but feel the need to remind him, "Baby, he moved on. He's in love with someone else."

"Yeah, well people thought that of me too, and look who my arms are wrapped around right now."

On the drive to meet Kurt, Leo's words repeated over and over in my head. Even though I'm ninety-nine percent sure there's zero chance Kurt wants me back, there's one percent of me that's nervous about this turning into another chaotic Kurt and Chrissy encounter. A small part of me will always feel like there's unfinished business between the two of us.

I finally arrive and park my car in the space that used to be so familiar to me…wondering why Kurt picked here of all places to meet. I see him in the distance, standing on top of the grass, grass that also used to be familiar to me. There were some months when I'd make two, sometimes three, visits to this place. But right now I can't remember the last time I was here, and for a moment I feel terrible about that.

But Chrissy, it's not how she wants you to spend your time.

And I know that. Even so, I feel like the quitter the man in the distance has labeled me so many times.

I get out of my car and slowly walk up to Kurt. His focus stays on the ground in front of him, his mind clearly lost in deep thought. I get it. It can happen so easily here.

When I make it to his side he doesn't look my way, just drops his hand down for me to hold. Out of some kind of tribute to the past we all shared, I take hold of it. Then we stand and stare at Kelly and Craig's gravesite for what seems like forever.

He's first to break the silence.

"The four of us had some good times together, didn't we?"

"The best. I wish video cameras were as affordable back then as they are now, so that we could have some of them on tape."

"What's your favorite memory?"

"You'd think it would be our weddings, but it wasn't. It was that time the four of us went sledding in Tahoe. Remember that?"

"Oh my God, when you and Kelly got in that inner tube together, that was hysterical."

Recounting the hysterics of the ride down the hillside makes me laugh all over again.

"...And then I jumped on her lap and off we went, cracking up, and peeing all over her with every bump we hit. We were beside ourselves when we made it to the bottom. I soaked the poor girl. Good Lord, I don't think I ever laughed so hard in my life. I bet I still have bruises from that day."

After we both stop laughing he turns to me and wonders, "Would you watch that memory if you had it on video?"

I think for a long time before answering, "I guess not, actually."

"Why not?"

"I'd never move on. I'm too nostalgic that way. You know me...the emotional core of the A-BOB's and all."

"So I take it you never watched our wedding video after we split up."

Still holding his hand, I turn to him, and admit, "Oh I did...night after night when I first moved into my cottage, along with sifting through all of our wedding pictures. Now you know why it took me so long to file for divorce...I was spending too much of my free time reflecting."

"Reflection can be good. I mean, I'd never want to be stuck in that state for as long as you were, but it has its good points. I'm just learning that."

Looking deep into his eyes, I tell him, "I'm really happy you're learning that, Kurt."

"Well, I hope what I'm about to tell you doesn't spoil your happiness."

Here it comes...I can feel it.

261

"Chrissy, I don't know how to tell you this so I'm just gonna come right out and say it. The girl I'm seeing…the one I fell for…it's…"

"Megan. I know."

He's quiet and apologetic-looking for a long time before he asks, "When did you finally figure it out?"

"You know, isn't it sad how people always ask me that question?"

After we share a mellow laugh, I tell him about the day Marti and Barb sat me down and made me read an email Megan had sent to me a long time ago.

"…Although, I guess I should've figured it out minutes before that when Marti was chortling and sniggering as Megan tried to explain why she was leaving Forever Young, and I guess I should've figured it out countless times before that when Megan dropped hint after hint after hint. The girl literally tried to tell me a million times."

And boy oh boy, did the girl try. Going all the way back to the day after my baby shower, when we were sitting in Greyson's room, and she asked me for time off for her first trip to Nepal. She tried to tell me then she was in love with Kurt, but I cut her thoughts off with my own. She tried to tell me again on my first day back to the studio after my bed rest…when she asked me if I read all of my emails. Looking back, she was hinting at the one she sent the day she returned from Nepal. The one in which she spelled out her love for my ex-husband. But I never made it to that sentence, I stopped with the one that mattered most to me—the one telling me Kurt was home. It meant I could now ask him face-to-face what happened that night at his house when I ended up in his bed with no pants on. In regards to that night, now I know why Megan was so mad when I was recapping it the day after it happened. I *thought* she stormed out of my office because Marti was talking about crunchy huhas and it disgusted her, but it was really because she was disgusted I thought Kurt and I had fooled around. And how about being clueless when it came to the pick-up and drop-off of

Kendall? Duh, only people in love have that much time on their hands. Speaking of Kendall…of course she shook her head when I asked her if Ku-Ku had a "new friend." Megan had been at Kurt's house *for months* before I asked that question...there was nothing "new" about her presence at all.

"Are you mad?"

"After everything I put you through, you're worried if *I'm* mad?"

"I just don't want you to think it's some kind of payback. It just sort of happened. I guess kind of like what happened to you, huh?"

Out of nowhere, an oddly maternal/Dr. Maria-esque side of me surfaces.

"Do you guys have the same interests?"

"Totally."

"The same dreams? I mean, are you sure she's not just saying she likes everything you like because of your brilliant smile? There have been girls who have been known to do that, you know."

Giving me a sliver of that brilliant smile, he sets the record straight.

"She definitely doesn't like everything I like, and she's super feisty about it…which is hot. You should've put your foot down more, Chrissy. Who knows where we'd be if you had been more vocal about not liking a lot of the stuff I asked you to do."

I lower my eyes at him in a *give me a fucking break* kind of way.

"Kidding! I'm kidding. Look, I love her, Chrissy, and she loves me, and all of that love came from liking and wanting *most* of the same stuff. I'm not an idiot…I won't be making the same mistakes in this relationship I made in ours, and I trust she's being…what's that word you threw at me every five minutes when you were seeing that therapist?"

"Authentic?"

"Yes. I mean, do you think Megan would pretend to be something she's not just to land me?"

263

I always considered Megan to be a mini-Chrissy. But while we're alike in so many ways, she's got something I didn't have at her age. She knows exactly who she is and what she really, really wants. Which is why I know she would never pretend to be something she's not just to land a guy. I slowly shake my head.

"It's pretty crazy, isn't it?"

"Just a little. So tell me, what does all of this mean?"

"It means we're happy and don't want to hide it anymore."

"Hiding is the worst."

"Brutal. Now I know why you lost all of that weight when you met Leo."

Did you hear that Kelly? He just said Leo's name. I think all three of us have finally grown up.

Smacking him in the arm with my free hand, I say, "I was wondering if you were ever gonna comment on that. Dude, it was like twenty pounds overnight and you never said a word!"

"To be honest, I didn't even notice it happened…I was too busy living in denial."

We both were. But all of that is in the past where I'd like to keep it.

"Chrissy, you need to know this has been tearing Megan apart. She didn't lose ten pounds because of the shitty food in Nepal. She lost weight for all of the same reasons you did. She was stressed out from living a double life. She loves you and she loves me, and she's scared she has to make a choice between the two of us."

My poor Megs. I remember the agony of having to choose between people I love. It's hell.

"It seems like she made her choice…she quit her job. But, Kurt, tell her I meant what I said at the studio on her last day. All I want is for her to be happy. She can have both of us in her life, and I'll never make it difficult for her. I mean, is it weird? Yes. But is it ideal for Kendall? I think it might be."

But he didn't hear a word I said.

"Hey you over there…Dare I ask if you're being reflective about something?"

Looking down at Kelly and Craig, he quietly says, "Now that I've met the right person, I feel bad that you wasted so much time protecting my feelings. You shouldn't have done that, Chrissy. You should've just moved on when you fell in love with Leo. I mean, look at our friends…look what happened to them…and so young. You need to make every minute count."

"But Kurt, just because I fell in love with him, it didn't mean I fell out of love with you. I couldn't move on until I figured out where to put my feelings for you."

"Where did you put them?"

"They're safely tucked away in a special place in my heart that no one needs to know about or understand."

"Our feelings can keep each other company then."

"I'd like that because sometimes that place gets a little lonely."

After another long pause in our conversation, and with some difficulty, he asks, "So this guy, Leo…Was he worth it?"

It's an emotional thing to admit to a man you once loved with all of your heart that the space he once occupied is full of someone else. So I just nod.

"Good. It's all I want for you." And then he clears his throat in that old familiar way that tells me he's uncomfortable. "When's the wedding?"

"September."

"Kendall's excited. We talk about it all the time."

"You talk to Kendall about *my* wedding?"

He nods his head and then surprises me with, "I talked to Leo about it, too."

"*You did?*"

"Yeah, the day you had your baby. I mean, you didn't know you two were getting married yet, but he sure did."

Another incident in a long list of them that should've been a smack in the face that Kurt and Megan were seeing each

265

other…*They arrived to the hospital at the same time…They were on trips at the same time…*Duh.

"I was pretending to help Megan look for you and…"

"Wait, *pretending?*"

"What guy wants to see his ex-wife and the dude he left her for on the day they have their first baby?"

"Good point."

"Anyway, I accidently opened the door to your room."

"I saw you."

"I didn't notice. The only thing I was aware of was the family on the bed."

He takes a deep breath in before continuing, "Megan and I had just come from Oregon. We were telling her parents about our plans in Nepal."

"Plans?"

"Yeah, we have plans, and after seeing all four of you on the bed together, it seemed like the right time to talk to Leo about them."

Apparently the conversation between the two of them that day was bigger than what Leo described—it was bigger than the "peace treaty." And now it makes sense why Leo was so calm about this face-to-face meeting...*he's aware of Kurt's plans.* Clearly they must benefit him or else I would've seen more than just a twitch of his bicep. The thought makes me smile on the inside.

"We're having kids, too, Chrissy."

Oh my Molly-God, Megan's pregnant.

"Actually, we're having seventy-five kids."

"I'm sorry, I'm not…I'm not following you."

"This is the real reason why I wanted to talk to you in person—here. Megan and I are taking over that orphanage we visited on our last trip, and we'll be gone for a very long time, maybe years."

"Wow, that sounds…unbelievably charitable, and at the same time a little bit like a death sentence. But if that's what you guys want…But, Kurt, what about…"

266

My mind immediately shifts to Kendall. He knows it and cuts me off.

"...And having a pool, a white picket fence, a routine, and a ranch home in Lafayette sounds like a death sentence to me. But I also know it's what every little girl wants."

"To clarify, Kendall's the little girl you're talking about, not me, right?"

He laughs while agreeing with me.

"I've talked to Kendall a lot about what you guys have going on over there, and she's really happy. She loves the guy you're marrying, and she adores her sister. In not so many words, she admitted she hates leaving them to come to my house on the weekends. Turns out she's more of a snipe hunter than a rock climber." Nodding his head at Craig and Kelly's graves, he says, "I know they'd want what she wants."

"What is it that you think Kendall wants?"

In a stunning move, he pulls the visitation agreement out of his pocket and slowly begins to tear it up.

"I've been thinking a lot about what's best for everyone, but I've been struggling with how to put it into words. So I'm gonna draw on something you said about our relationship right before you moved into your cottage, and try to put it into this context."

In complete shock over the last twenty seconds of this conversation, all I can do is barely mutter, "Okay."

"I don't want to be so consumed with meeting the terms of this visitation agreement that I can't see how wrong it is for Kendall. Kelly had really good intentions for setting it up, but if she knew then how your life was going to turn out, she never would've offered Kendall to me... We both know that." He hands me the torn up document, and continues. "...Quitting this agreement isn't a sign of weakness; it's admitting Kendall deserves a more fulfilling future. I wanted to meet here to tell you, and her parents, that I'm giving her what should have been all along."

Taken aback, I speak softly, "And Leo knows all of this?"

"Yeah, outside of your hospital room that day. I wanted to hear it straight from him that he's here to stay, and that he wants to adopt Kendall. I needed to see the determination in his eyes."

"Did you?"

"Fuck. And then some. The dude is intensely in love with you guys. I almost feel bad for whoever your girls want to date one day."

"We call it—"

"I know, I know…truly, madly, deeply."

"Do you have it, too now, Kurt?"

"I do. I get it, all of it."

"Then why are you still holding my hand?"

"Why are you still holding mine?"

"I think we both know why."

Letting the subject go, but not our hands, we say good-bye to our beloved old friends and make our way back to my car.

"When did you and Megan start this for real?"

"Last August, when we began talking seriously about Nepal. She's the one I tried to tell you about on your birthday."

"…The white roses you brought to the studio that day?"

"For Megan. One for every month we'd been seriously seeing each other."

Thinking back to the fourteen freedom roses he brought to me the day our divorce was final, I giggle and ask, "What is it with you and roses?"

"What can I say; I don't have a big bag of tricks. Anyway, that was the day we were gonna talk to you, but all hell broke loose and the opportunity was shot to shit."

"You're telling me, between that day and today, neither of you could find the time to tell me?"

"You tell me, between that day and today, when have you *not* had a mini-crisis to get in the way of us telling you? It just never seemed like the right thing to do. Besides, it all worked out for the best. We got the go-ahead on the orphanage at the beginning of June, and two weeks later you got your family. Everything fell right into place."

268

"So Leo and Kendall know *everything*?"

"Yep."

Hands still intertwined, we walk the rest of the way to my car in silence. Even when we arrive, neither of us says a word for a very long time. Delaying the inevitable is painfully obvious to the both of us.

"So…when do you leave?"

"Two weeks."

"Should I call Megan, or would that just be weird?"

"I think she'd like that."

It's been a long five and a half years, way longer than it needed to be to get to this inevitable moment. Actually, no, that's incorrect. The time it took to reach this moment was *exactly* how long it needed to take. It makes me think of that conversation I had with Courtney at Chili's in July of 1998, when she said my break up with Kurt is like a death and it'll take six months for every year we were together before I get on with my life. Look at me…I beat that estimate by six months! About time I exceeded expectations. I make a mental note to email the accomplishment to my friend in Zimbabwe.

Still hanging onto my hand, Kurt opens my car door. We both know what's coming and the moment is quite brutal.

"There's nothing left to say, is there Kurt?"

"There isn't."

Still, neither of us budges.

Now it's me that clears my throat when I ask, "You might think this is stupid, but before we leave, how about getting all truly, madly, deeply with each other?"

"What do you mean?"

"I mean tell each other one thing we would never expect to hear."

"Are you sure that wouldn't be crossing some kind of line? I mean, I don't really feel like getting punched in the face again."

"There will be no punch. We'll tuck our words away in that special place that no one needs to know about or understand."

"You know what, Chrissy? I think I'd like that."

269

He grabs my other hand so we're standing face to face. And just like all of the other times when I thought it would be the last time I ever saw him, I take in every one of his beautiful features. His tiny laugh lines that frame his perfectly molded mouth, his heavy brows that outline his trustworthy deep brown eyes, and his strong jaw and cheekbones that are flawlessly aligned on his golden skin. But this time is so much different than all of the other times. There's a depth to this moment that Kurt and I have never experienced, not even when we exchanged wedding vows.

After thinking long and hard, he finally speaks.

"Chrissy?"

"Yes?"

"Every single time I see you, I want to go back to the beginning and do things differently. I'll always wish I had treated you like a princess."

The vulnerability he just expressed is almost too much to handle, and my head drops down to avoid eye contact. Chrissy and Kurt have never done vulnerable.

"Look at me, Chrissy. No avoiding each other on this. I gave it to you straight from the heart, now you give it to me. This is what you said you always wanted, remember?"

I look back at him and realize I don't know this man. The Kurt I've known my whole life doesn't talk like this. Megan brought it out of him. What they have together brought out a side of him I've never known. I experienced a little of him on my birthday in August when we talked about his college graduation, and at the hospital in April when we talked about our mistakes, but I get the feeling there's so much more to Kurt that I'll never know.

"It's your turn now. Tell me something I'd never expect to hear, Chrissy. Something I can put in that special place in my heart."

I stare at him long and hard before I confess, "Every time…Every time I see you, Kurt, I wish I had shown you how strong I was, not by doing what you wanted me to do, but by

270

doing what I wanted to do. I'll always wish you could've fallen in love with the real me."

Moments like this are typically sealed with a kiss, but that would definitely be crossing a line. Nonetheless, Kurt lifts one of my hands to his mouth and kisses the top of it. When his lips touch my skin all of our unfinished business completely disappears. I am officially one hundred percent convinced that there will never be another chaotic Kurt and Chrissy encounter. Also, for the first time since finding out about Kurt and Megan's relationship, I now realize why I missed all of the clues...I wasn't focusing on them; I was focusing on me, Kendall, my baby, and Leo. I was focused on what was important.

After a very long look at each other, my very first love clears his throat one last time.

"You ready to get on with your life, Chrissy?"

"I am. Are you?"

"More than ready."

And then as if in slow motion, I watch as our hands slowly release, knowing beyond a shadow of a doubt, it will be the last time they ever touch.

He turns to walk away, but I stop him once last time.

"Hey, Kurt..."

"Yeah?"

"Saphalhos."

"Did you just say what I think you said?"

"Yeah, I had a feeling this meeting was about Megan and Nepal, so I brushed up on my Nepalese...I wanted to say good luck."

His mouth forms into his infamous million dollar half smile as he asks, "You really are something, aren't you, Chrissy Anderson?"

"You have no idea, Kurt Gibbons."

And then his smile widens so big I can feel ten thousand female corpses roll over in their graves. Then he turns and walks toward the rest of his life.

Saphalhos, Kurt. Saphalhos.

Epicenter

July, 2003

There were so many heavy things that came out of my meeting with Kurt, and I wasn't ready to stop thinking about any of them. But I knew if I went home I'd be forced to stop. Life as a mommy would suck all attention away from the things I want to think about right now. So I made a quick call to Leo to tell him I needed a few more hours alone. Without asking any questions (probably because he knew my time with Kurt totally worked in his favor), he told me he loved me and that he'd have something on the barbeque by the time I got home. After I hung up, I made a beeline for Danville.

Now that I live in Lafayette and my roots are blissfully planted there, I have no desire to live anywhere else. Yet, there will always be a mystical lure to Danville. Danville is the epicenter of all of my crossroads, and it will forever pull me in for clarity. I want to go there now to celebrate how simple and uncluttered my life has become. After that remarkable meeting with Kurt, I feel an overwhelming need to pay homage to my journey.

First I drive by my old dream house. I pull up alongside and think back to how hard I worked to buy it. Sure Kurt kicked in for half, but he never could've afforded it without me. I regret a lot of things on my life list, but item number five isn't one of them. Buying such a mature home at such a young age showed me that hard work pays off. It planted the seed in me that I can have anything I want if I'm willing to do the hard work. Even though everything else on my life list went up in flames, the proceeds from sale of this home gave me enough money to walk away without getting completely destroyed by the burn.

Everything looks so different than the last time I was here. Like the illusion I tried to plant, all of the beautiful flowers I put in place all of those years ago are long gone, replaced by rocks and a hideous water feature. The children playing in the street, whom I used to know and adore, don't even give me a second glance, which is a good thing. It means they don't remember me from that white trash day when I embarrassed myself and yelled at Kurt and Kayla on their bikes. I drive a little further down the street to the entrance of the trailhead I came to know as the start and stop of my morning jogs. I'll never forget the day I started jogging. For the life of me I couldn't figure out if I was running toward something or away from something. Either way, I liked it. This trail will always have a painfully special place in my heart. It's where I wandered around aimlessly in the rain the day after I met Leo. It was on this trail that I first realized my life was a complete mess.

I like coming back to this beautiful and sought-after neighborhood. Despite how hard it was to leave, doing so proved to be a courageous move and one that showed I'm more about heart than matter. But as much as I like coming back and reminding myself I made brave choices, I like leaving even more. It means I get to go home. But before I head there, I want to make a few more stops.

Pulling into the back lot of Buckley's, I park in the same spot Leo and I talked all night in my car on that January evening in 1998—the evening that changed the course of my life. Every single time I come here, I get the same feeling. It's one that reminds me to always be aware that something as seemingly insignificant as entering a bar can change my life. Even something as unimportant as choosing a barstool can lead to better things, or great pain and sadness, or as in my case, it can lead to both. I'd give anything to be able to look through the back door and see the barstools Leo and I sat on that night, but they're gone. In fact, all of Buckley's is gone. It turned into an

English pub a few years ago. I haven't been back here for a long time because it bothered me that I couldn't see our barstools…it bothered me that I couldn't relive that first seductive moment when Leo and I made eye contact. But I won't be bothered anymore by our missing barstools because now I get to go home and sit on something better—Leo's lap.

I leave the Buckley's lot and swing by Leo's friend's apartment complex where I dropped him off after we talked all night. It's where we shared our first kiss/rub of the penis/squeeze of the boob. The entire episode was a full-on feeding frenzy that ended with me in sheer mortification and him asking me to elope in Vegas. I blush all over again thinking about the gutsy moment when I asked Leo if he wanted to kiss me, and I giggle remembering how quickly he dove in. Then I shudder at the memory of driving away from him just as the sun was rising. It seemed so unfair that I'd never get to kiss his lips again. I wouldn't know it for another few weeks after that night, but kissing Leo was the love equivalent of shooting ten bags of heroin.

And where does an addict go for help? To a therapist. While Danville is the epicenter of all of my crossroads, Dr. Maria's office is the place where I was forced to evaluate each and every one, and it's my last pit stop before heading home.

Her office light is still on. In a freaky kind of way I'm jealous of whoever is on that old grey couch. Therapy is awesome. In fact, I might take it up again in the future. Not because I foresee any problems, but because I think it's a good idea to unload random shit on a complete stranger. Therapy is comparable to a solid maintenance plan for your car. You gotta check under the hood every now and then to make sure everything's running smoothly. And when it's not, it's better to be smacked upside the head by someone completely unrelated to your problems. Although therapy is pricey, I truly believe it makes life cost less in the long run. You know, I even—

The knock on my car window takes me by surprise, and impulsively I cover my face and I let out a giant scream. After my nerves calm down, I spread my fingers apart and peek at the fucker who startled me. Then I look back up at my old therapist's office…the light is now off. I snap back to the stranger and let out an even louder scream. Low and behold, the fucker is none other than Dr. Maria! I scramble to get out of my car and wrap my arms around her.

Struggling for air, she gasps, "You know, Hunny, I charge extra for these after-hours emergency visits."

"I'm not here on business…this is all pleasure!"

She pulls away to get a good look at me, and cheerfully asks, "Oh my goodness, when did you have the baby?"

"Last month, and on Kelly's birthday! Can you believe it?"

"Well, well, well…Look whose ghosts are talking!"

"I know, right!"

"Boy or girl?"

"She's alllllll girl."

"Name?"

"Greyson Kelly"

She raises her eyebrows and twirls her finger in the air signaling me to finish saying her whole name.

"Greyson Kelly *Armstrong*."

"Ohhhhhhhhhh. So the truth is out."

"*A lot* of truths are out. Honest living is good stuff, Dr. Maria. You know, you need to find a quicker way to emphasize that point to your patients…or is that part of your racket? To drag that detail out as long as possible in order to build up your bank account?"

"Good to see you haven't lost your wit in the midst of all of that honest living."

"I may have lost a lot in my life, but I'll never lose my wit."

"Let me think…The last time I saw you was in March, right?"

"Yep. I was six months pregnant and still hadn't told Leo. Boy, you were pissed at me."

"And I remember I told you Leo would be pissed too, and that he had every right to be. But I also told you to think about the possibilities with him once the truth was out. So, tell me…Are there any?"

"We're getting married on September thirteenth."

"See, I told you! Oh, Chrissy, I'm so happy for you."

"Hey, I have a little time before I have to get home, would it be weird if we had a post-baby, post-therapy, post-screwed-up-life celebratory drink?"

She laughs before saying, "I've never done that before, and there's a mighty good reason why."

"Why?"

"Patients should *never* see their therapists as real people with their own problems."

"And I won't! Forget about what happened in the past four months since I last saw you, telling you about today alone will take more time than either of us have. I won't have a chance to get to know you as a real person…I'll be too busy talking about myself!"

"You really are something, aren't you, Chrissy Anderson?"

"You know what's funny about that question?"

"What's that?"

"It's the second time today it's been asked of me. And guess who asked it?"

"Uh-oh, I'm scared. Who?"

"KURT!"

Dr. Maria looks across the street, points to a little bistro, and says, "I think I need that drink now."

"Yay! But just one…I'm breast-feeding."

"How about just one because that's what normal people do when they have to drive home?"

"Oh yeah…that, too."

Walking toward the bistro, she shakes her head and laughs at how dismissive I was of the whole drive home thing, and under her breathe she mutters, "What on earth am I going to do with you?"

"I don't know, Dr. Maria, but I'll tell you what you're NOT gonna do with me. For once you're not gonna charge me to sit with you for an hour."

One hour turned in to two as Dr. Maria and I sat there and chatted about my afternoon with Kurt and the events leading up to it. She asked very few questions. Mostly, she just sat and smiled at the how far not just I, but *everyone* in my life story has come.

"You know, Chrissy, for a man you used to call selfish, what Kurt did with his visitation of Kendall is one of the most selfless acts I've ever heard of."

"I know. Megan definitely brings out the best in him."

After tapping her nails on the side of her wine glass she sneaks a little of her therapist self into our conversation.

"I think she makes his life more adventurous, and we know how much the man likes a good adventure. But I actually think it was you, Chrissy, who brought out the best in Kurt."

Instead of questioning the compliment, I accept it and tuck it, along with my memories of my ex-husband, in that special place in my heart.

"Speaking of adventures…Sounds like Courtney and Nicole are following their hearts too, huh?"

"They are. Surprisingly I don't miss them as much as I'm happy for them. Does that sound weird?"

"Not at all, Dear. It sounds like it's exactly how things are supposed to be."

"Speaking of how things are supposed to be…Kendall is the light of my life, and I can't imagine my life without her. Oddly, I've never felt bad about that. The only thing I've ever felt was territorial."

"Good. Her parents made the right choice then by entrusting her to you."

"You know what? They did…they really, really did."

For a second, I consider telling Dr. Maria about all of the tapes Kelly made and that I'm scared shitless to show to Kendall, but I hold back. I don't have to look that far into the future anymore…I don't have to plan out the "what-ifs" of my life any longer. I'm all about my hope list and taking each day as it comes, and so we just sit and fill the rest of our time doing what most normal chicks do over a bottle of wine—we talk about how stupid everyone is.

"…What these men don't realize is if you don't have anything to say to them at the dinner table, and then you sit unmoved for hours in front of the television, with no entertainment between the two of you…that somehow you're miraculously into them in bed? Give me a break! I mean, how stupid are these guys to not think you're fantasizing about another dude while they're pounding away at you? Such idiots."

My wise 'ol therapist interjects, "But who's the bigger idiot, the man or the woman? I say the woman because she's the one not thinking about her husband while they're making love. She's the one with the knowledge, yet does nothing to change the scenario for herself."

"How many of those women do you see on a weekly basis, Dr. Maria?"

"Ha! You might've tricked me up when I revealed more than I should have about Barbara Cooper, but not this time, Missy!"

"Just a hint though…Would you say a majority of your clients are mini-Chrissy's or forsaken Francescas?"

"God, I *wish* a majority were mini-Chrissy's. It's a lot easier to enlighten someone about their future prospects than soothe someone with a broken past. But sadly, my couch is predominantly occupied by the latter."

"How many of those forsaken Francescas saw it coming…you know, their broken situation?"

"Almost all of them."

Blown away by the statistic, I sit in horrified silence.

"The look on your face tells me I should remind you of something. By your fourth visit to my office, you saw your broken situation coming, too. Even so, look how hard it was for you to admit you made a mistake and make the necessary changes to correct the mistake."

I think back to how close I came to accepting my broken situation, and I shiver.

"There is a *very* small window of opportunity to back out of a marriage before it becomes difficult, if not nearly impossible, to leave, and it's before children come along. Fortunately for you, you took that opportunity. But unlike you, Chrissy, most women on my couch have a couple of kids before they become painfully aware of how truly broken their relationship is. For those women…"

"…It's easier to stay with their 'Kurt' than upset everyone's lives because, after all, he's not a bad guy."

"Bingo."

Knowing I'm meant to be with Leo, and that Kurt is happier with Megan than he ever could've been with me, I can almost feel a bead of relief sweat trickle down my face. The two of us definitely dodged one huge-ass huge relationship bullet.

"Makes you feel pretty proud of yourself, doesn't it?"

"How did you know—"

"Your face. It's like an open book. You *should* be proud, though, Chrissy. What you did took some smarts and some guts."

"It's a weird concept to be proud of something society looks down its nose at."

"Well, in your situation, the disdain is probably less about the divorce and more about the lies and the cheating. But in your case, those two things gave you the critical time you needed to figure yourself out. Without them you'd still be married to Kurt, wouldn't you?"

"…Miserably married with a couple of kids, and at this very moment probably camping at a place without bathrooms."

"Then I for one don't condemn you for the lying and the cheating. And I promise you, a lot of other women won't either."

"Hopefully a lot of other women won't ever know what I did."

"You're too young yet to realize this, Chrissy, but one day you'll want to tell your story."

"No way! I want to put it all behind me and move on."

"Nah, it'll be too hard for you to resist. You'll see a mini-Chrissy sitting in some bar and feel compelled to tell her to run for her life—that it's not that hard once you're in motion. Conversely, you'll want to wrap your arms around a forsaken Francesca. You'll feel an overwhelming need to tell her you understand and sympathize with her heartache."

Laughing, I roar, "I can be like a truly, madly, deeply superhero who wanders from bars to park benches—changing messed-up women's lives wherever her travels take her!"

"Laugh all you want now, but mark my word…the chronicles of Chrissy Anderson are far from over."

I wish I could sit and talk with Dr. Maria forever. Alas, my boobs are about to explode, so we make our way back across the street and hug it out.

"You take care of yourself, Mrs. Armstrong."

"*Mrs*? That's not for another six weeks!"

"No time like the present to start getting used to it, don't you think?"

I'm not crying at the prospect of never seeing Dr. Maria again. In fact, I'm so far from a tear it's not even funny. My life has taken a very dramatic turn, and in a way I kind of do feel like a superhero. A super happy superhero who can't wait to get home to her family. I honk and wave at my much-loved therapist, wondering if or when I'll ever see her again, but also not obsessing about either outcome.

Everything has changed in the city I once called home, and essentially there's no trace that I ever even lived in it. For one of the first times in my life, I don't leave Danville with a heavy heart. This time I drive away eager to move on to where life has taken me.

So Close

September, 2003

"Stop fidgeting, Chrissy! It's making me nervous!"

Tomorrow's my big wedding day to Leo, and I can barely believe everything has fallen into place. Well actually not that much had to fall, really. The entire guest list is merely comprised of his mother and brothers, my parents, Marti, Barbara, The Ho-Bag, Kendall, Gracie Smudge Cakes, and...drum roll please...Taddeo. Yep, the fucker flew in for the occasion. Because there were so few, the invitations to the wedding were easy; the only thing that was a struggle to fall into place was my pre-baby weight. But after two months of hard-core yoga, a grueling running schedule, and excessive breast-feeding (resulting in one excessively fat baby), I'm back in business. And just in the nick of time. Though we haven't talked out loud about when we would ever have sex again, Leo and I both know the most poetic time to reconnect in that way is on the evening of our wedding. And with a clean bill of sex-health from Hannibal Lecter, a rockin' post-baby bod, a killer rack thanks to my blown up mammary glands, and thoughts of Leo doing to me what he used to do so well...I'm ready to go!

Leo spent the last two months preparing our backyard for the nuptials, and I went balls-out on a catered spread that cost so much it had better be fit for royalty. Everything, and I mean *everything,* will be absolutely stunning tomorrow. The only thing missing will be Megan. She and Kurt left a few weeks ago to raise their seventy-five *thousand* kids in Nepal. Obviously Kurt was never invited to the festivities, but Megan was, and her non-attendance will definitely be felt by me. I finally ended up calling my old designer/new lover of my ex-husband, but before I picked up the phone, I went back in to my old emails and re-read the one Barb and Marti forced me to finally take notice of. I still can't believe what a fool I was to stop at the sentence I stopped at on the evening I received the email. Had I just read on for two more I would've seen this…

"…Things have happened on this trip that I never planned, Chrissy. Not only did I fall in love with this country and its people, I've fallen in love with Kurt. And the kicker is I think he fell in love too. I know you of all people would want me to chase the love to see where it takes me, but in this instance I feel like I need your blessing…"

Obviously I didn't give her the blessing as quickly as I should have, resulting in a lot of unnecessary bullshit for a lot of people, but when I talked to her a few weeks ago, I finally delivered. In our conversation we never talked specifically about her relationship with Kurt. Don't get me wrong, she tried to bring him up…tell me she was sorry everything happened the way it did. But I cut her off and told her to NEVER be sorry for falling in love. After that, we kept things focused on our friendship and the future, and how both never looked so bright for the both of us. I reminded her that she'll always have a place at Forever Young, Inc., and in my family, and that we'd figure out the logistics of everything upon her return from Asia. I can't quite figure out what that picture will look like. You know…Megan and Kurt back from Nepal…popping in and out of my life…for the rest of my life. But I don't want to spend my precious time trying to figure it out. I want to spend my precious time doting on the ones I love that aren't in Nepal, and that's my focus at this very moment. Actually, I take that back. My focus at this *exact* moment is to dote on *two* of the people at this table tonight…the other one can rot in hell.

"I can't help it, Marti! Taddeo makes me fidgety. Nothing ever goes well when he's around."

"Then why are we having dinner with him?"

"Because he's Leo's best friend, and he flew in just to be here for the wedding tomorrow, and Leo has something…Well, *we* have something important to ask him."

"What?"

"You'll find out soon enough."

My last conversation with Taddeo didn't end so well. In fact, my last words to him were…

One day you'll regret talking to me like this, Taddeo. Trust me, we will cross paths, and I'll probably have this baby in my arms when it happens, and you're going to feel horrible. But don't worry, I won't rub it in your face, and I won't make you feel worse than you'll already feel. I won't ever make you feel like how you're making me feel right now—like a piece of shit.

Though I don't have Greyson in my arms right now, she will be the topic of conversation tonight, and given how poorly Taddeo treated me, that conversation is bound to make him feel horrible. I'm fidgeting because I'm torn between rubbing Taddeo's emotions in his face, and just letting go of our whole conversation from last March. I'd like to be the bigger person, but something tells me it's going to take all of my self-control not to make him feel like the gigantic piece of shit he made me feel like.

Slapping me in the arm and out of my funk, Marti gasps, "Fuck me if that New York lifestyle hasn't done that Italian boy well."

Walking toward our table is my beautiful Leo looking more proud and handsome than a man could ever possibly look on the evening before his wedding, and trailing behind him is the New York asshole Marti was just referring to—Taddeo. After Marti greets the big bastard with a hug that looks like it included a mini pelvic thrust, he nervously makes his way over to my side of the table.

"Hi Chrissy, I uh…I brought these for you."

Plop goes a stack of papers on the table.

Flipping through them, I scoff, "You brought me shares of stock?"

"I wasn't sure if I'd have time to pick up flowers between the airport and here, so I packed them just in case."

I look at Leo and ask, "Is he serious with this?"

"He's *seriously* trying, Baby. Can we just go with it and see what happens?"

And I did. In fact, I went with it so well that the entire meal wasn't completely objectionable. Taddeo was so over-the-top complimentary about everything from my post-baby body to the next day nuptials, that it was hard not to let him off the hook for his past treatment of me. And because all I ever wanted was for Leo's best friend to like me, I softened up. And several times throughout our surprisingly painless dinner, my mind even drifted back to that night the four of us spent at Marti's apartment in San Francisco, you know, after I "accidentally" bumped into Leo at The Red Devil Lounge. Everything about that night, from the music, to the cocktails, to the sultry temperature, was absolute perfection and just as I suspected would happen, I've oftentimes wanted to go back and re-live it. Tonight reminds me of that night, and just like then, chills trickle down the back of my neck at the splendor of it all. By the time dessert rolls around, I'm showing Taddeo pictures of Greyson…introducing us to the point of this meal together.

While it was a no-brainer to invite Marti here this evening and ask her what we're about to ask her, I offered up at least five viable options to take Taddeo's place. Leo had a rebuttal for each, and in the end I had no choice but to give into his wishes. But after the lovely effort Taddeo just put forth, it doesn't feel like I'm giving into anything. At the moment Taddeo seems like just as big of a no-brainer as Marti, so I give Leo a slight nod to proceed with the point of this meal together.

"So guys, I'm gonna cut right to the chase. The reason why Chrissy and I wanted to have dinner with just the two of you tonight is because we'd like to ask you to be Greyson's Godparents."

286

Heads everywhere turn in our direction as Marti leaps up in her chair, knocking it over, screaming in delight at the top of her lungs about how flattered she is. Taddeo though, he looks shell-shocked.

Leo slaps him in the shoulder and says, "Dude, don't worry, it won't cost you a thing. It's more of a formality to please my mother."

But Taddeo ignores Leo and turns to me.

"*You* want me to be your daughter's Godfather?"

"I want what Leo wants, and he wants you."

"But he wouldn't do it without your approval."

Placing my hand on top of his, I make a suggestion.

"Since it's going to be a weekend of vows, how about if we start now...I, Chrissy Anderson, do solemnly swear to give you, Taddeo Pascali, a second chance if you agree to give one to me."

Cracking a mighty handsome smile, he declares, "I do."

Then Leo joins in on the fun with, "Then by the powers vested in me I pronounce you, Martha Stewart, and you, Taddeo Pascali, as Greyson's Godparents."

The funny moment is made ten times funnier when Taddeo spews out red wine and hollers, "YOUR NAME IS MARTHA STEWART?" so loud that once again every head in the restaurant turns in our direction.

After our laughs die down, Marti does something incredibly uncharacteristic. She *completely* ignores Taddeo's ridiculing question, and turns the focus back on Greyson.

"I for one am honored by the request, and promise to be the very best Godmother in the world..." Her focus was lovely and noble until she said, "Oh boy, I'll never forget the look on Chrissy's face when I told her she was pregnant! Can someone say, 'shock and awe!' Oh and her first doctor's appointment was a total riot. Talk about a doozy you wouldn't have wanted to miss! And what about those Lamaze classes, huh Chrissy? Remember how everyone thought we were lesbian lovers, and we played the part for shits and giggles? Oh geez, I feel so fortunate to have been there for everything, and now this!"

287

Aware of the fact that he wasn't there for anything, it's hard for Leo to hide his sorrow when he says, "I bet it was nice to be able to share all of that with her."

Feeling terrible about her snafu, she backpedals with, "Oh but don't get me wrong, Leo, nothing *that* interesting happened until April. That's when all of the fun stuff kicked in with the previa and the once a week 3D ultrasounds, right Chrissy?"

Hoping to spare Leo's hurt feelings, I blurt out, "Absolutely right! It was nothing but dullsville until then. All of the real action started with the bed rest and all of those trips to the doctor. And I told you about all of that stuff in all of the emails, Leo. I promise, you knew everything."

For a long time, it was a mystery to me why the contents of those emails didn't compel Leo to join me for the last months of my pregnancy. And the mystery continued to nag away at me for weeks after I gave birth to Greyson. But then he finally explained his whereabouts and his intentions that day we visited the cottage—the day he asked me once again to marry him. After I said yes, it seemed appropriate to leave those unanswered emails in the past, which is where I thought they'd stay. But thanks to Marti's big mouth, I was just forced to bring them up.

Noticeably confused, Leo asks, "What emails?"

Confused right back, I ask, "You're kidding, right?"

"No, Baby, I'm not kidding. I have no idea what you're talking about."

"But that's impossible, Leo. I sent you like five emails a week starting three days after the meditation room fiasco. I came clean about everything…why I kept the pregnancy a secret, why I struggled with telling you about the baby. I told you about the Placenta Previa…the date I was scheduled to have a c-section. I even asked you not to marry Lauren. I literally begged you to fight for us. I must have sent over a hundred emails. C'mon, you have to have seen them. *Didn't you?*"

But he ignores my question and asks me one of his own. But he's not staring at me when he asks it, he's staring at Taddeo.

"Where did you send the emails, Chrissy?"

"To your office, of course. Leo, what's going on?"

In an unbelievably harsh tone, he answers, "Forty-eight hours after I left your meditation room, I was in New York quitting T.L. Capital. After that all of my emails were forwarded."

"Forwarded to who?"

But Marti answers the question I'm too dumb to figure out, and Leo's too outraged to answer, when she turns into that meddling ol' hyena and snarls at Taddeo, *"You fucking dick."*

The man I just exchanged vows with looks sickened. Unfortunately, I'll never know if it's because he feels incredibly bad for keeping my emails from Leo, or if it's because he got caught. Before I have a chance to ask Taddeo a damn thing, Leo is literally in his face, ordering him to stand up.

Oh boy, this isn't going to end well. I have to do something.

"Leo, we're making a scene. I think we should just—"

"Stay out of this, Chrissy! He messed with my family. He messed with my Goddamn life!"

Directing his attention back to Taddeo, he demands, "Get the fuck up and face me like a man."

Looking about twenty years older than he did when he walked in two hours ago, Taddeo rises from his chair and does what his friend tells him to do.

"I'm only gonna ask you this one time. And don't fucking lie to me, because it'll only take one call to Eric in I.T. to find out the truth. Did you see all of the emails Chrissy wrote and purposely keep them from me?"

"Yes."

Crushed by what his oldest and most treasured friend did to him…the guy he oftentimes referred to as his brother, Leo lets out a very loud and very seething moan.

"WHY, MAN? WHY THE FUCK WOULD YOU DO THAT?"

Oh Christ, now all heads *and* the entire staff from the restaurant kitchen are staring at us.

"I don't know."

"THAT'S YOUR ANSWER? '*I DON'T KNOW!*'"

"I guess I thought I was helping."

"*HELPING*? I had just quit the company *and* that nightmare, Lauren…I told you to your face that I was going to California to get Chrissy back. You kept those emails from me *after* you knew what I wanted. How the fuck is that helping?"

Speechless, Taddeo just shakes his head.

Not done with the verbal beating, Leo continues with, "So tell me, *Bro*, what else have you done to destroy my life?"

Taddeo and I are the only two people in the world who know *exactly* what else he did, or rather, didn't do, and if he wants to keep his face intact, he better keep it that way. He's a big bastard who did a lot of dumb shit, but I believed in the vows he and I just shared. His attitude about me changed when he saw the pictures of Greyson…when he saw what Leo and I created out of love. *I saw his remorse.* I believed, I *still* believe we can be friends. But that will never be an option if he says what I think he's about to say.

Leo presses on with, "This friendship is over, so you might as well spill it—all of it."

As discreetly as possible I shake my head at Taddeo, signifying him to keep his mouth shut, but he speaks anyway.

"Chrissy called me last March."

"I know that. She told me the day I saw her pregnant for the first time in the meditation room. You told her I was moving in with Lauren."

I give Taddeo one last discreet shake of the head to prevent him from proceeding…and then I hang it low when he ignores my silent plea.

"In the phone call she told me she was pregnant. She wanted to know if she should tell you. That's when I told her…I told her you were moving in with Lauren and you were happy. I'm pretty sure I convinced her to move on with her life."

Leo's heavy breathing causes his chest to swell and the veins in his forearms look ready to burst. He's like a Papa Lion on steroids.

"I need to get this straight. You knew Chrissy was pregnant, and you didn't tell me?"

Without giving him the obvious answer to the question, Taddeo clears his conscious of another cruel secret.

"She also called the office looking for you in May. I told her that you knew where she was, and if you wanted anything to do with her and the baby…"

I shake my head one more time to get him to stop. One more time he avoids my plea.

"…you would have something to do with her and the baby. I never told her the real reason you went back to California."

"Let me get this straight…After you read all of her emails to me, ones that sound like she was desperately trying to fix our relationship, you *never* told her I dumped Lauren and that I was trying to start a new business? You NEVER fucking told her I was trying to get my shit together so I could get her back?"

For the second time Taddeo doesn't give him the obvious answer to the question. Instead, he offers up an excuse.

"I'm an asshole and I know it was wrong. She just…she had just made me so mad with all of her fucking around before. I wanted her to get a dose of her own medicine for a change."

Exploding with rage, Leo yells, "IT WASN'T YOUR PLACE TO GIVE HER A DOSE OF ANYTHING!"

"Leo, please…He was only trying to protect you. He just loves you…probably a little more than he should, but I forgive him…Let's just move past this, okay?"

Leo growls, "No. It's not okay, Chrissy. He hurt you…Goddammit, he tried to keep me from my daughter!" And then he warns Taddeo, "Leave before I rip every limb from your body. And you better pray to God I never find out the name of the woman you fall in love with, because you better believe I'll do everything in my power to destroy your relationship with her."

"Dude, I was an asshole, but I…

Leo's voice drops to a venomous whisper when he interrupts him and says "Get the fuck out of my life."

Taddeo mumbles an apology to me and Marti, grabs his jacket, and leaves. Within seconds of his exit the restaurant is back in business. My table...not so much.

Leo pulls a wad of cash from his wallet, tosses it on the table, and tells me he'll meet me at home later, right now he needs to go for a walk.

Contemplating the impact of tonight's dinner on tomorrow's festivities, I worriedly watch Leo leave the restaurant, barely taking notice of Marti who whines, "Great, so does this mean I have to do all of the Godparent stuff on my own?"

Second Chance Barbie

September, 2003

L eo crawled into bed a little after two o'clock in the morning. I'm not sure where he was or what he was doing, and I didn't ask. All I did was wrap my arms around him. He did the same right back and then we fell asleep. Now it's morning, and the birds are chirping, the lighting people are covering every square inch of our backyard in white lights, the caterers are setting up the food, the bartender is setting up the all-important bar, and my oldest little girl is jumping up and down on the bed yelling at her future daddy to wake up.

"Weo! It's the day we make a family! It's the day! It's the day! WAKE UP!"

Frustrated, Kendall turns to me, puts her hands on her hips and gripes, "Mommy, today is our wedding! Why is Weo so sweepy?"

Leo's tired eyes stay closed, but a sliver of a smile forms on his "sweepy" lips.

"It was a long night, Sweetheart. How about you go and check on Gracie Smudge Cakes. I smell a big poopy and I bet Barnana could use some help."

Once Kendall skips away, I settle in next to Leo in my specially-purchased white satin wedding day robe, sway a steaming cup of coffee under his nose, and ask him if he knows where a girl can find a groom this early in the morning.

Groggy, but seemingly happy despite the near murder of his best friend last night, Leo sits up and says, "Right here, Baby. I'm your groom."

He takes a big swig of the coffee while staring at me over the rim of the cup. He knows exactly what I'm thinking and quickly addresses the subject.

"I'm okay, Chrissy. It was a long time coming. I'm just glad we didn't shell out…how much is this shindig per person?"

"Are you gonna be mad?"

"No way, I get to marry you today."

Cringing, I hesitantly admit, "Three hundred and twenty-five a head."

"Can I get some Kahlúa in this coffee?"

"I know it's a lot, but we have a lot to celebrate, right?"

"We do. And I don't want what happened last night to get in the way of our day."

"I feel bad about it, though, Leo. Maybe if we talk to him—"

"It's over, Baby. Never bring him up again, okay?"

"But Leo, please hear me out—"

"Chrissy, remember that quality of mine you used to love so much?"

Tracing my finger up and down the middle of his chest, I quizzically ask, "Which one?"

"My ruthless ability to cut people out of my life and not let it affect me for a second."

"Yes, I remember that one."

The first time I saw it in action was when he essentially told Megan to suck it for intimidating me. Talk about a total turn-on.

"Now more than ever, it's important for you to let me be a master at it."

I nod my head in support of what he's asking.

"I have you and the girls and my business. Life is good, and I don't want to waste another minute of my time talking about him. Okay?"

Worried that he's hiding his pain, but not wanting to compound it by making a fuss over Taddeo, I kiss him on his chest and then say, "Okay."

Gliding his hands across the beautiful fabric I'm wearing, he changes the subject completely by asking, "Is this pretty thing for tonight?"

Raising my eyebrows I shamelessly inform him, "I don't think my husband is gonna be able to handle what I plan on wearing for him tonight."

Speaking of tonight, I have no idea where we're going to spend our first evening as husband and wife. Leo wants it to be a surprise. All I know is, we have until three o'clock tomorrow. That's when we have to be back for Kendall's soccer game. Actually, to call it a soccer game is being generous. It's more like a bunch of girls huddled together in a big dust ball that moves from one side of the field to the other in a giant giggly bundle. Nevertheless, we wouldn't miss it for the world. Plus, a longer honeymoon is out of the question until Greyson is off the boob. So what all of this means is Leo and I have one night. And you can bet your sweet ass I'm going to make every minute count.

Pulling me into his chest he asks, "In that case, can we just get the two minute wedding ceremony, throw a bunch of lobster and over-priced wine at the guests, and get on with our twenty-four hour honeymoon?"

I can talk about sex with Leo until the cows come home, but there is something about today's festivities that concerns me…

"Leo, are you sure you're not a teeny bit sad you're not having a big traditional wedding?"

Lord knows I had one…My Barbie dream wedding to Kurt was over-the-top glamorous. Truly, it was every girl's vision of the perfect day. Sadly, as everyone now knows it was also the gateway to hell. Anyway…I'm a firm believer that every girl should get one Barbie dream wedding in her lifetime, but if that marriage craps out, I'm also a firm believer that all future weddings must be banned to beaches and back yards. It's just proper Barbie etiquette. And since Leo is my Ken…he's banned to beaches and back yards, too. Sometimes it makes me sad that he fell in love with divorced Barbie and has to pay the divorced Barbie second wedding price.

"Baby, you do know who you're marrying, right?"

"I do. It's just that…"

"Chrissy, if it were up to me, no one would be coming over here today to watch us get married. It would just be me and you and the kids. I'm not a showy guy, and I don't need to recite my wedding vows in front of a group of people to make them count for something."

"I feel the exact same way. So tell me again…Why *are* we transforming our backyard into a magical fairyland filled with twinkling lights, and clearing out our bank accounts to feed these people?"

From down the hall Kendall yells, "Mommmmy, is Weo awake yet? I want to show him my fancy dress!"

The man who is to become my husband in nine hours lovingly says, "She's why."

"You're a dream come true, you know that?"

"I'll never get tired of you telling me that, Chrissy."

"And I'd do it all day, but I have to make myself look bridal, so that means *you* have to get out of here. But don't go too far. We're so close to the finish line, I'd hate to lose you now."

Once he leaves the room I hear him lightheartedly yell, "Hey! Where the heck is my family?" and it makes me smile. Then I hear Kendall rush to him (knocking over forty-five things) and yell back, "I'm right here! I'm right here!" The whole exchange causes me to fall back onto the bed and count my lucky second chance Barbie stars.

Husband & Wife

The last nine hours were the polar opposite of the nine hours before my first wedding. I didn't cross anything off of a list, and I wasn't pleasing anyone other than myself. Actually, I stand corrected. I was required to please Gracie with a meal every two hours, and I was required to help Kendall into her fancy dress and do her hair—both tasks a total pleasure. Other than those two things, I spent the afternoon in my bedroom with a basket full of delicious food prepared with love by Barbara, an ice bucket full of champagne compliments of Marti, and a bubble bath that I enjoyed soaking in, as opposed to feeling obligated because a *Modern Bride* magazine told me it was the way I should start my wedding day. I painted my nails, watched an *I Dream of Jeannie* marathon, and even took a thirty minute power nap. There were no bitchy bridesmaids, no mother or mother-in-law to get on my nerves, and no schedule that I had to stick to. It was the kind of wedding day I wish for every woman, and it totally has me convinced that *this* is actually my Barbie dream wedding—not the one I had in 1995.

Standing in front of the bathroom mirror, dressed and ready to marry the man who quite literally (thank Molly-God) changed the direction of my life, I marvel at how smoothly everything came together. My off-the-rack white dress looks custom made, hugging me in all the right places, and my three inch vintage-inspired heels fit like Cinderella's glass slippers. I'm not wearing a bra, underwear, or nylons, taking comfort to an all-time high. And it's like the hair gods decided to totally redeem themselves for my junior prom spiral perm catastrophe, because my low side-swept bun held together with a pretty white gardenia could not look any more naturally stunning. The four hundred dollar ensemble I'm looking at in the mirror right now is a million times more beautiful than anything I've ever worn in

297

my life. I'd cry but I don't want to ruin the makeup I just applied...which I have to say isn't too shabby either. A woman can never go wrong with a dramatic winged eyeliner effect paired with false eyelashes and sultry red lipstick. After a spritz of the same Carolina Hererra perfume I wore the night I met Leo, and a deep breath, I open the bathroom door for the first reaction.

Dropping her *People* magazine along with her jaw, Marti exclaims, "Oh Hunny! You look like a pin up girl! Seriously...A total Alice Faye!"

"*A who?*"

"Alice Faye! She's a bombshell classic! You know, like Marlene Dietrich, Greta Garbo..."

Still clueless, I shake my head and wonder out loud, "Seriously, how old are you, Marti?"

"Oh shut up!" Tapping her finger on her chin, she thinks real hard for a second before declaring, "How do I put this in terms you'll understand?" After thinking even harder she screams, "Got it! You look like Jessica from *Roger Rabbit*, but with blonde hair!"

"Aaaawe, now that's a bombshell *and* compliment I can understand!" Planting a red-stained kiss on her cheek, I gush, "Thank you, Ms. Martha Stewart. You're very sweet."

"I'm also very accommodating."

"How so?"

Pretending to be a poo-poo baby, she whines, "Well, I would've thought twice about the whole best friend thing if I knew it meant I had to be a maid of honor *and* the only Godparent to your child. We're talking about a lot of responsibilities that you'll never have to step up and do. I mean, c'mon, like I'll ever be a bride or a parent! I can't understand why *anyone* would want to be either of those things...Total buzzkills."

This woman's sarcastic rants will never stop making me laugh.

298

"Well my sassy old friend, to clarify, you're not my maid of honor…there are no attendants in our wedding. It's just me, Leo, Kendall, and Gracie doing a little something-something and then we all eat. But, you're point is well taken about the Godparent thing, and I promise I'll make it up to you."

And then I kiss her on the other cheek.

"You can make it up to me by giving me this fabulous lipstick. Seriously Hunny, I can get a lot of action with that stuff. Speaking of action…tell me where you and Leo are going tonight?" Clapping her hands, "Oh, I can hardly wait for the dirty details! It's been like how long for the two of you?"

"Too long."

Our heads snap in the direction of the bedroom door to find Leo, who answered Marti's question. Dressed appropriately for the outdoor occasion, he's the perfect combination of dashing and austere in his dark grey pinstripe suit, and of course his scent is intoxicating, as usual. Totally ignoring Marti, he walks directly to me and begins to trace his hands up and down my waist.

"Oh my God, this dress…*You*. Is all of this really mine?"

"I sure hope so. No one else will want it…it comes with two kids and a mortgage."

"That stuff is what I call *the icing on the cake*."

Marti pokes her mouth back in the conversation with, "If you two will excuse me, I'm going to go and throw up now." And then she leaves the room.

Alone in our bedroom, which I still can't believe I can call "ours," given all of the shit I put this man through, Leo and I stare at each other in disbelief that we're finally actually getting married. It's like we're a couple of deer in headlights waiting for chaos to explode through the door…for someone or something to throw a wrench in today's festivities. But nothing happens.

"Leo, I think we might actually tie the knot today."

"You doubted it?"

"I certainly didn't help the cause."

"Neither of us did. Even so, I always knew I'd find my way back to you."

The crazy thing about that is I did, too. Yep, deep down underneath all of my self-deprecation and thoughts of him living a fabulous life without me, I always knew I'd find my way back to Leo. Our connection was that strong. I believe there is someone like that out there for everyone. The hard part is finding each other. If you think about it, finding true love is a lot like finding a particular grain of sand on the beach. It's damn near impossible. Then, if you're lucky enough to find the grain of sand you have to be at the exact right crossroads in your life to hold onto it. Timing is everything. In fact, I believe bad timing has turned great love story after great love story into romantic tragedy after romantic tragedy, and the thought makes me so incredibly sad.

"Hey, I lost you there for a sec. You okay, Baby?"

I shake off the sadness I feel for all of the unlucky and ill-timed love connections of the world, and turn my focus back to my truly-madly-deeply dream come true.

"I'm great. Better than great, Leo, I feel like the luckiest girl alive."

Dabbing at my watery eyes, I change the subject before I ruin my make-up.

"Is everyone here?"

"Yes, and covered in flower petals."

"I take it Kendall's taking her job of flower girl to extremes?"

"I've never seen her so happy."

"Well then, Mister what do you say we walk out there and shout 'I do' so we can get to wherever we're going tonight and take this dress off."

"I say that's the second best idea you've ever had."

As he takes my hand and at long last leads me outside to our wedding, I ask, "What's the first best idea I ever had?"

"To get this dickhead out of his shell that night at Buckley's."

"You know, I'd have to say that was one of my finest—"

But my words come to an abrupt halt when Leo opens the door that leads to our backyard. The few guests we invited are seated in lace-covered chairs, each adorned with a generous swag of beautiful flowers. The runner leading up to the minister is littered with white rose petals, and every square inch of every bush and tree is covered in twinkling white lights. The second I step down into the yard, a cello, a guitar, and a violin begin to passionately play a version of a song I didn't think could ever sound as intoxicating as the original…but this one is.

"Leo, this music…"

"Do you like it?"

"They're playing 'Crash Into Me.' That's what we listened to in the car on the night we met."

"I know, Baby. That's why they're playing it now."

"Oh Leo…it's the most beautiful thing I've ever heard."

And it is…The seductive rendition literally takes my breath away.

Pointing my attention to the end of the aisle, he whispers, "And how about that for being the most beautiful thing you've ever seen?"

Waiting for the two of us is my sweet little Kendall who, for the first time ever, is holding her baby sister in her arms without assistance. It's an absolutely adorable vision, but also a wobbly one that causes Leo and me to walk toward her a little faster than planned. When we reach her, Leo gently takes Gracie in his arms and kisses Kendall on the cheek. I have never seen her look so proud.

Kelly, can you see this? It's happening…It's really happening.

With Kendall between the two of us, we hold her hands. Leo cradles the baby with his other arm.

Look at us, Kel. We're a family.

While the minister is talking, Kendall continually looks up to Leo and smiles, and then back to me and smiles. It so cute, it has the guests giggling the entire time. The giggles tapper off and things become a little more serious when it comes time to say our vows. As agreed ahead of time, Leo and I keep everything short and sweet.

"Chrissy, my love for you, Kendall, and Greyson is pure and constant, and I hereby commit myself to all of you from this day forward."

He loves all of us, Kelly.

"Leo, my love for you, Kendall, and Greyson is pure and constant, and I hereby commit myself to all of you from this day forward."

It's forever, Kelly.

The minister then kindly asks Kendall if she has anything she'd like to say. After thinking long and hard she very seriously says, "I just have a question."

Kneeling down so that I'm eye-level with her, I ask, "What's your question, Sweetheart?"

"When can I call Weo 'Daddy?' I'm the big sister, and I want to start before Gracie Smudge Cakes."

Leo drops down to one knee so that he's also eye-level and answers her.

"Kendall, it would be my honor if you started today."

More than satisfied with that answer, Kendall grins from ear to ear.

The minister then gestures for us to rise from our kneeling and asks if we have rings to exchange. Now it's me who giggles a little.

Pulling my pewter Banana Republic ring from his pocket, Leo slips it on my finger and asks that I wear it as a sign to the world that I'm his wife.

The ring shopping trip we went on after we left his office in July didn't result in a damn one that made me feel more loved as the one I had to remove to try on more lavish styles. I asked him that day if it would be alright if the ring he bought for me in Mill Valley five years ago could officially be the outward symbol of my inward love for him. While it was always Leo's intent to replace the old pewter ring with something more expensive, he agreed that nothing could ever replace its significance and that it would indeed make the perfect wedding ring.

After I slip Leo's ring on his finger and ask that he please wear it as a sign to the world that he is my husband, we offer a pretty ring to Kendall and ask that she wear it as a sign to the world that she is our daughter. She didn't see that one coming at all, and the surprise has her giddy with excitement.

Concluding our short and sweet ceremony, the minister proudly proclaims, "Inasmuch as you have spoken your love promise to one another in the presence of these witnesses, and each of you has given and exchanged a wedding ring, by the power vested in me by the State of California, it is now my deepest honor to declare that you are husband and wife, *and* mommy and daddy."

Did you hear that, Kel? It's official...we're the whole package.

Leo extends his lips to mine, kisses me sweetly and then whispers in my ear, "I have a million better kisses in store for you tonight...For now must keep it clean in front of my daughters."

Five years, seven months, and twenty-two days after sitting next to Leo at a dive bar, against all odds...he's officially my husband. I'm sure there's a handful of people out there thinking, *God help him.*

Alone we are fine; but when we're two, we are eternal
The moons have aligned our separate lives; here become one
And you would be the last thing I saw coming
("Lovely Tonight," *Joshua Radin*)

Like a Virgin

September, 2003

While Leo carries a sleeping Kendall to her bed, I check on Greyson in her crib one last time before we set out on our now fourteen hour honeymoon. Our tiny wedding ended up as a big party that extended into the evening a lot longer than planned—seriously cutting into our about-to-be-revived sex life. With Barb and Marti's reassurance that they have everything covered at the house, they shoo us out the door a little after midnight, winking and making bwamp-chica-bwamp-bwamp sounds the entire time.

Once in the car, Leo reaches his hand over to hold mine and begins the drive to wherever it is we're going. With dreamlike thoughts of what we just made official, I tilt my head back and close my eyes to rest for a minute.

"Tired, Baby?"

"More like serene. It was a dream come true day, wasn't it?"

"It was. Did you hear Kendall call me Daddy?"

"I did. How did it feel?"

"Surreal. I had to take a minute to myself in the garden."

"And when you were there, how was your conversation with Craig?"

"How did you know?"

"That's what I did when Kendall first started calling me Mommy. I'd always run away and ask Kelly if she was okay with it."

305

"I wish I could've known him a little better. I so badly want to be for her what he wanted to be for her."

Eyes still closed, I squeeze his hand and say, "Wherever he is, Leo, he's smiling. They both are."

Just minutes after leaving the house, the car stops and Leo surprises me with, "And I hope this makes you smile."

I tilt my head back up and open my eyes to find myself back in front of my old cottage.

Very sweetly, he says, "I couldn't think of anywhere else I'd rather be tonight."

Marveling at Leo's romantic disposition, all I can do is shake my head and cry. After he wipes a few tears from my face and kisses the tip of my nose, he opens my car door. But instead of waiting for me to get out on my own, he scoops me into his arms and carries me to the front door and over the threshold. Every move my new husband makes has me feeling like second chance Barbie is the absolute luckiest girl in the world. That feeling is multiplied by a million when my eyes adjust to what I'm looking at inside of my old cottage. Under the guise of remodeling the place for Barbara, Leo spent a month making upgrades for her, but the last few weeks he spent making it beautiful for this evening, even going so far as to hire a professional designer to make it honeymoon-perfect.

First my gaze goes to the floor. Where there was once carpet, there are now hardwood floors.

"These old floor boards are from an old demolished barn in Vermont."

"Leo, they're spectacular."

Where there was once a blank wall, a fireplace insert and mantle have been erected and lit candles litter the space.

"It's not functional, but it adds character, don't you think?"

"It's stunning...How did the candles..."

"The Ho-Bag snuck away from the wedding to light them...and do some other stuff."

The kitchen has been totally gutted and every antiquated appliance is replaced by top-of-the-line products that blend beautifully into the country French theme that's taken over the small house. The only remaining piece of old cabinetry is the door where I carved "I loved here." It's now transformed into a work of art and hanging over the mantle. Everything is calling out for me to go to it and touch it, but the thing calling out the loudest is the lone piece of furniture in the center of the small living room and I slowly step to it.

From behind, Leo explains, "I didn't think it appropriate to…you know, spend the night in Barbara's new bedroom, so I had that put in. It'll be picked up tomorrow and replace the one in our bedroom at home."

Adorned in shiny white satin sheets, the fluffiest down pillows I've ever seen, and the silkiest white duvet cover I've ever run my fingers across, is an enormous rustic pine bed positioned in the middle of the flower petal-covered floor. Hanging dead center above the bed is a chandelier bejeweled with more crystals than I can count. The entire cottage radiates romance.

Leo walks over and opens the French doors revealing a refurbished deck, cozy outdoor furniture, and a brand new custom firepit that's complete with a roaring fire, compliments of The Ho-Bag.

"Leo, I'm speechless…"

And I'm also uneasy. Not about the time that's passed since Leo and I were intimate, especially since I now know he was never with another woman when we were apart. Trust me, there will be nothing uneasy about exposing my body to Leo and him exposing his body to me. The nervous concerns I used to have when we were first together aren't the same as the ones I have right now.

"Baby, what are you thinking about?"

"Just thinking about Gracie."

And not because it's the first time I've left her over night. It's because she came out of the same place Leo wants to go in. *That's* what has me feeling so uneasy.

"She'll be okay, Baby. Barb will—"

"It's not that. It's..."

He calms my nerves when he pulls me into his chest.

"Tell me. What is it then?"

Clinging tightly to him, I confess, "I have to take this...the sex...I have to take it slow. Like it's the first time." Slightly embarrassed, I bury my head into the crook of his arm and confess, "I guess after having Greyson that's kinda what I think it'll feel like."

"You have no idea how happy that makes me, Chrissy."

A little surprised, I wonder, "Why does it make you happy?"

"I always wanted your first time to be with me."

Leo has always had an insane ability to put my worries at ease.

"And even if that first time can't be tonight, the next ten hours will still be perfect..." Taking my hand, "...C'mon, let's start down the hall."

He guides me to the bathroom to show me where the old tub is now replaced by a modernized claw-foot tub. A claw-foot tub that The Ho-Bag already filled with hot bubbly water and surrounded with candlelight.

"It looks big enough for two."

Unzipping the back of my dress, he kisses my neck and whispers, "That was the plan."

As Leo takes a small step back, I let my pretty white wedding dress fall to the floor, revealing the special outfit I had planned for him this evening—no outfit.

"Knowing we were short on time, I thought I'd just go commando."

I'm gently laughing, but he's all business.

"It's the prettiest thing you've ever worn for me."

After assisting me into the tub, he leaves the bathroom, returning minutes later with two glasses and a bottle of champagne. Then he joins me in the water, where thirty minutes turns into an hour, four hot water refills, eight champagne refills, and talk of where we should take our first family vacation. It was the best bath of my life.

As Leo reaches for the hot water knob again, I guide his hand away with my foot.

"Not ready for more?"

"No. I think I'm…I think I'm ready for you, Leo."

He studies my face for a long time before asking, "Are you sure, Chrissy? We don't have to do anything you're not ready to do. We have the rest of our lives."

Though scared about what lies ahead, I slowly rise from the water and profess, "I'm ready for the rest of our lives to start now."

Without saying another word, Leo steps out of the tub, grabs a towel, and proceeds to dry me off, kissing every spot on my body that was once dripping with water, starting with my legs. The direction he travels makes me dizzy, so I rest my hands on his head for balance, my fingers run through his black hair as his lips make their way all the way up to my neck. Like always, each kiss is attentive and adoring. Each touch of his lips makes me less afraid of the unknown feeling that lies ahead and more craving the beauty of it. Sensing my desire, he effortlessly lifts me in his arms and carries me to the bed, which is now shimmering by the light of the full moon.

Before he lays me in the white fluffy cloud, he stares deep into my eyes. They're asking me one last time if I'm absolutely sure.

"Just go slow."

He does just that starting with how gently he lays me on the sheets. And then every move he makes after that is made with tender precision. The kisses on my neck and behind my ear, and the way his fingers trace lightly up and down my inner thighs and then up to my breasts, is done with meticulous care. His entire focus is on ensuring one thing…that I'm ready for him. Concluding by the arching of my back and my deep moaning that he accomplished his goal, he delicately positions himself on top of me and whispers, "As slow as you want, Baby."

Without response, my hands travel down to his backside, dig into his flesh, and pull him into me. But still, he's cautious and

309

pulls back, taking things even slower than I've permitted. And then adding to the sweetness, he asks me every few minutes if I'm okay, and in between those inquiries, he tells me how much he loves me.

The only thing I ask of Leo while we're giving ourselves to each other is, "No more babies, not yet." To which he couldn't agree more.

Every time I've ever made love to Leo, from that first time on the floor of his apartment in Moraga, to the night we called of our engagement at his loft in New York, to this night, our wedding night in my darling old cottage...*every single time has been life-altering*. It literally seems like every single time I make love to Leo, the course of my life changes. It's been an exciting, yet thoroughly exhausting ride, that I'm glad has finally slowed down to merry-go-round speed. With the sun now rising, this is the topic of our conversation as we lay wrapped in each other's arms.

"Look how normal we are now, Leo."

Finding that comment rather amusing, he laughs as he says, "I don't think there's anything normal about us."

"What are you talking about? There's nothing but bottle feedings and soccer games on the schedule today. It doesn't get any more normal than that."

He kisses my neck and jokes, "That's who we are in the daytime...But at night we turn into crazed animals, making it our mission in life to satisfy each other's needs and conquer each other's body."

After we're done laughing, I turn serious with, "Are you a little glad things have slowed down?"

"*Glad*? More like grateful! Two more days at the pace we've been running for the last five years and I would've had a heart attack. Baby, I've been ready for slow since a month after I met you."

"But you hung in there with me."

"Like I always told you, Chrissy, I will always be where I know you are."

"So does that mean you're going to go to work with me every day?"

Sitting up a little he curiously asks, "So you decided?"

Since Leo told me a few months ago that it has been his objective since the night he met me to make my stay-at-home-mom dreams come true, I've been giving the subject a lot of thought. The conclusion I came to didn't surprise me at all.

"I love Forever Young, and I love working with Marti and Barb. Those studios are like my first kids, and I can't imagine my life without them. I most definitely want to continue working."

Chrissy Anderson is a worker bee. She always has been and she always will be. But she's also a little old-fashioned. She needed a man in her life to relieve some of that worker bee pressure. She needed a man to be a man. She got her man.

"But I want you to know something, Leo."

"What's that?"

"That you gave me a choice is like a dream come true."

"That will always be my goal...to make all of your dreams come true."

Trying to contain my delight, I coyly confess, "If that's the case, I have two more requests please."

He jolts up, straddles me, and holds my hands above my head.

Attempting to be serious, he looks down at me and asks, "Oh yeah...Tell me what I need to do to make my wife happy. Tell me about these new demands of yours."

"Well, Hubby...You remember that movie *The Bridges of Madison County*?"

"Never saw it."

"*Never saw it*? Well, now I know what we're doing tonight because my first new dream has everything to do with that movie...and an orchestra."

He's kissing my neck now and without stopping he says, "An orchestra? I'm not following."

311

But now his lips are all over my ear causing me to not follow either.

I tilt my head to lock lips with him and breathlessly mumble, "I'll explain when we're watching the movie tonight. Right now I need you to turn into that crazed animal and make it your mission in life to satisfy me and conquer my body."

Next (adjective)

Something that will exist or happen in time to come.

Anniversary Day

September, 2013

"**M**ommy! *Helloooooo*, earth to Mommy!"
Greyson's voice jolts my thoughts away from the past where they've been dragged for the millionth time this week. I'd love to continue reminiscing about the morning after I finally married Leo and about the new dreams I shared with him in bed that day, but with one of those dreams about to bang on my front door…time to get my head out of my forty-four-year-old-not-quite-yet-sagging ass and get on with the day.

"Mommy, did you hear me? I picked these flowers from the garden for your wedding anniversary party tonight! Do you like them?"

"I love them, Smudgy! White roses are my very favorite."

And they have been ever since they came to represent truly, madly, deeply love for my ex-husband Kurt. When I finally found out who those white roses were for on that day he came to the meditation room, it was the last little bit of reassurance I needed that Kurt's life would be better off thanks to our divorce. I could officially be happy without guilt. Even better…those roses paved the way for him to leave the country, and for me to have Kendall with no strings attached.

"Kendall seems sad, Mommy. Do you think I should give the flowers to her to cheer her up?"

Kendall's sad because of me. She wouldn't be sulking right now if I didn't just make her watch her dying mother's video diary.

"Awe, Gracie…you're such a sweet little girl. I think that's a great idea."

"And I'll sing 'The sun'll come out tomorrow' when I hand them to her!"

It warms my heart to watch my peppy little girl run off to find her big sister…but it also stings it.

Leo and I never had any other kids after Greyson came along. Trust me, there were many drunken nights when the biggest aphrodisiac in the world was me yelling, "Get me pregnant, Baby!" over and over again while he pounded away at me. But better minds (a.k.a. Leo's) prevailed, and to this day we're thankful to be a family of four. But there are times, like right now, when I get a little gloomy that I'm the mother of just two children who are growing up way too fast.

Throughout my marriage to Leo there have been moments of sadness about how much of my pregnancy he missed, but it never made us sad enough to mess with our great balance. We had Greyson and Kendall, each precious gift delivered in *completely* different packaging. Greyson delivered in a conventional package (a.k.a. amazing sex), and Kendall delivered in the most unconventional package imaginable (a.k.a. her parents dying), each package a unique blessing which has produced perfect balance in our lives.

Kendall, who was always a cautious child, has grown into a mature and even more cautious young woman. At fifteen years old now, I believe her father is still the only male to ever kiss her cheek. Boys don't interest Kendall at all yet. Horses are the focus of her attention, and they are what she's spent nearly every weekend of her life doting on—earning her medal after medal in hundreds of equestrian show-jumping competitions. With two million dollars coming her way when she turns eighteen in the form of the trust her deceased parents created for her, I see a lot of horses in Kendall's future…and a barn…and a stable…and ranch hands. She's a naturally stunning beauty with her long brunette hair, bright blue eyes, and tall and slender frame. Most days she looks like she just walked off of a Ralph Lauren photo shoot and I've oftentimes asked her if modeling is something she'd like to try. But she always rolls her eyes and asks me to buy her a horse instead. Aside from an occasional eye roll and being irritated about watching those old videos her deceased

316

mother made for her, Kendall's joy and kindness is infectious. My oldest daughter represents the tranquility in our family.

Greyson, on the other hand, is a bold risk-taker who likes to be the center of attention and would give anything to be on a catwalk. Gee, I wonder where she gets that from. Anyway, she's quite the little actress who's been involved with a children's theatre group since she was five years old, starring as the lead role in almost every production she's in. It's the kind of limelight that her sister and father have a hard time comprehending, but I totally get it and I'm the first to offer a standing ovation in all of her performances. Greyson's an "all in" kinda kid and I'd rather go balls to the wall on her penchant for acting, than be a dumbass who sits idly by and watches her risk-taking daughter get into trouble…as in the form of falling in love too young and going "all in" with her first boyfriend. Gee again, I wonder where her predisposition to *maybe* do that comes from. Anyway, knowing my youngest daughter is a chip off the old block, I keep a very close eye on her. But while Greyson is all me on the inside, she's all Leo on the outside with her dark hair and mystical green eyes. Despite the fact that my baby's need for attention elevates Leo's heart rate and mine, she represents the liveliness in our family and has all of us laughing like crazy every single day.

Over the years Leo and I have had a few serious conversations about having more children, but stopped short of creating one out of fear it would wreck our incredibly tranquil and lively balance. Why risk messing up a good thing? Besides, with Kendall in line to receive a fortune when she turns eighteen, Leo feels compelled to make things even for Greyson. Adding more babies to our family would only add to the millions of dollars he already feels pressure to produce. Neither of has a clue how to work all of this out with the girls, which is why Kendall doesn't even know about her trust yet. Besides that, how do the two of us give to Greyson without giving to Kendall? That doesn't seem fair either. It seems like no matter how we configure things, the monetary scale is always tipped in

Kendall's favor. On top of the trust fund secret…there's an even bigger one. Greyson doesn't even know that she and Kendall aren't biological sisters. It was something Kendall asked me and Leo to keep a secret, and because we never thought of Kendall as anything other than our own, it has been easy. Ugh. I see some rocky roads ahead. But I'll deal with all of those challenges in the next chapter of my life, for now I'm all about enjoying our tranquil and lively balance.

Right now I just want to enjoy my girls, who are the lights of my life. But as I just mentioned, there are moments when I get a little gloomy about not experiencing an entire pregnancy with Leo. I thought once my optimal childbearing years were behind me the heartache would subside. But in actuality it's gotten a tiny bit worse, and I have Hannibal Lecter to thank for that when he reminds me every year that my "fruit is rotting" and at this stage of my life I should be looking forward to becoming a grandparent as opposed to being a really old mom. Why I keep that meanie as my OB is beyond me.

"I swear…sometimes getting old is the same as getting punched in the stomach."

Shocking the hell out of me, my hardworking and still handsome as ever husband pops his head up from the ground, wipes a bunch of sweat off of his forehead, and asks through the window screen, "What's that, Baby?"

"OMIGOD, LEO! I had no idea you were down there! What the heck are you doing?"

I still can't help but marvel at how far we've come, and not just because it's our ten-year wedding anniversary…It's because I *really* can't believe the guy stuck with me after all of the crap I put him through.

"I'm running the power cord for my tenth and final heat lamp. I want everyone to be comfortable tonight."

This is how Leo's been from day one: caring and attentive.

"Babe, it's sweet but it's also eighty-five degrees outside. I think two would've been sufficient."

"My mother and your parents are seventy-five years old…"
Then, jamming the power cord into the outlet, "…Old people get
cold and I don't want their bitching and moaning to ruin our
party. I want tonight to go off without a hitch."

"You're a perfect man, you know that, Leo?"

"No one's perfect, Baby. But I do know one thing…"

"What's that?"

"You and I are the perfect fit."

He makes me smile and forget all about my "rotting fruit."
But the charming moment is quickly blown to bits right along
with our electrical panel.

"Uh-oh…Looks like ten heat lamps is one too many, and I
blew a fuse."

After a quick kiss through the screen window of our
bedroom, Leo runs off to fix the problem. Our talk of being
perfect for each other has me chuckling out loud and thinking
about my wonderful old therapist, Dr. Maria. The memory of
one of my first times on her couch when I was going on and on
about how Leo thought I was perfect makes me chuckle. I
remember she put her hand in the air to stop my crazy talk and
called me stupid, or him an idiot, or some other completely un-
technical psychotherapeutic word that I can't remember at the
moment. She looked me square in the eye and set me straight by
telling me I might be the perfect fit for Leo, but NO ONE is
perfect. And then she said…and I'll never forget, "Chrissy,
when you go from one relationship to another, you just trade in
one set of problems for another. Of course, the hope is that
you're with someone you can actually solve them with."

I wish so badly I could pick up the phone and tell Dr. Maria
how absolutely right she was. Leo's not perfect and Molly-God
knows I'm not either. And we definitely have our fair share of
daily, weekly, and yearly problems to bite us in the ass.
However, we respect each other's imperfect qualities almost as
much as we adore each other's perfect ones, and Leo and I can
solve a problem together faster than one is created. *We are a
perfect fit.* Like I said, it would be great to pick up the phone and

give Dr. Maria the kudos she deserves, but sadly she passed away two years ago after succumbing to a very short battle with lung cancer.

Barbara was the one to deliver the news of Dr. Maria's shocking passing to me. She was still a patient of Dr. Maria's and as always, she was right on time for one of her weekly appointments, which had long since turned into nothing more than a pleasant visit. But instead of being beeped into the back like usual, Barb was approached in the lobby by another therapist who told her that Dr. Maria had stage IV lung cancer that had metastasized to other areas of the body. Dr. Maria died within six days of her diagnosis.

Barb and I attended our cherished therapist's funeral and we grieved right along with many of her other patients, friends, and family members. No mention was made of why Dr. Maria was diagnosed so late or how she even got lung cancer since she wasn't even a smoker. Barb took the news pretty badly, and for a week I hung out with her at the old cottage just to make sure she was okay. Nowadays, whenever I drive through Danville I never stop at my old house anymore, I just take extra time in Dr. Maria's parking lot and stare up at her old office. Oh, and I also flip off every person I see with a cigarette dangling from their lips. To this very day I cringe when I think of what my life would be like if I had never met Dr. Maria. She is dearly missed, and I bet not just by me. Now that she's gone a lot of messed-up housewives are no doubt spiraling out of control.

"Mom, did you have a chance to think about that thing we talked about?"

I whirl around to find Kendall holding the white roses. She's back in my room and standing right next to the box of videos.

"Sweetheart, it's only been like twenty minutes since we had the conversation."

"Isn't that enough time to decide? I mean, do I have to remind you that she just talked about people I've never even met...for like the fiftieth time."

"Kendall, you've met Courtney and Nicole plenty of times."

Of course, all of those gathering were before she turned six. That's when the two of them moved out of state and have never been back simultaneously. Even when they come back solo, it's not very often and for lack of time, they never really see Kendall, only me. In the last ten years, I've seen Nicole just four times in person and Courtney only eight times. They're always good visits filled with a lot of laughter (and alcohol), but everyone has a lot of shit going on and has to get back to their busy life. Courtney finished her project in Zimbabwe, and now lives in Colorado doing her doctor thing, and Nicole is still living in Arizona working in some penitentiary...I mean, junior high school. I'm in the process of closing my Moraga and Alamo studios. There just isn't enough time due to horse functions and theatre productions, and I'm consolidating all business into my first baby, the Lafayette studio, where Club NiCo continues to kick ass. Life is crazy good for all of us, and we'll always have our crazy good times to bond us. But just as I suspected would happen when Courtney and Nicole moved away, the nitty-gritty details of our daily lives have been turned over to our local, more convenient "mom" friends and work associates.

"C'mon Mom, she refers to them as Auntie *Courty* and Auntie *Nicky*. Don't you think it's a little silly?"

I think it's a lot silly considering the most she's ever communicated with those two is via a yearly Christmas card.

"What does Daddy think?"

"He thinks I should leave the decision up to you."

Without looking down she puts her foot on the front of the box and shoves it behind her.

"Okay Hunny, I get it, I get it. Can we make a deal, though?"

"What's that?"

"I'll jump ahead to the last video and if it seems like there's something super important you should hear, will you watch just that section with me?"

She walks to me, wraps her arms around me and says, "Deal. Thank you, Mama. I love you."

321

"Did you just say '*I* love you' and not just 'love you?'"

"Yeah, same thing though, right?"

"Hardly." Looking at my watch and noticing that the clock is ticking on that knock on the front door, I inform her that I'll educate her on the ginormous difference later.

"Okay, but Mom?"

"Yeah, Lovey?"

"Can you watch it now, so I know if I can just be done with it?"

"Kendall, I have guests coming and—"

"*Pleeeeease* Mom? It means more to me than almost anything in the world."

Given all that this little girl had to go through in her early life, I'll always cave into her a little faster than I should.

"Okay, okay. Now scat!"

Once Kendall's out of the room, I walk back to the mirror that I scrutinized my body in front of just thirty minutes ago. I stand and stare at my reflection for a very long time before I lay in on myself.

Can you really do this...*today*?

Which "this" are you talking about, watching Kelly's last video or opening the front door to your past?

Christ, both I guess.

You can postpone the video, but unfortunately it's too late to rescind his invitation to the party. I mean, he's bringing his wife and kid to the shindig. To bail now is just plain rude.

So, you'd rather be a good hostess than a good wife?

Okay, stop right there you self-deprecating douche...You're a great wife! The best! Your reasons for inviting him here were completely selfless and...and...

Face it, Chrissy, your husband won't see it that way. You've opened up a can of worms that probably should've stayed shut forever.

Walking away from the mirror and toward Kelly's box of videos, I silently agree with myself. And the giant knot in my stomach is physical proof that the can most definitely should've stayed sealed shut.

"Well, since I'm in some kind of worm can-opening mode...might as well get this over with."

I reach into the box and grab the very last video Kelly made for Kendall and when I do I notice that something doesn't add up. In the letter Kelly wrote to me—the one I found in Craig's nightstand—she said there were sixteen videos, one made for every year of Kendall's life starting at age three and stopping at age eighteen. Kendall and I just got done watching the fourteenth video, so there should only be two videos remaining, but there are three left in the box. What I'm holding in my hand is a seventeenth video. The words on the video cover are jumbled and barely legible. All I can determine is that the words are not consistent with what is written on the other covers. It has me very worried about what I'm going to see on my television screen, and suddenly very convinced that Kendall is probably right about shoving these things in the attic. The giant knot in my stomach tightens with every step I take toward the VCR.

Do-Over?

"Leo! Come in the bedroom! Hurry!" Rushing in at the speed of light, my "perfect" husband trips over the box of Kelly's videos and spills them everywhere. He even nearly crashes to the floor himself.

Huffing and puffing he asks, "What is it? Are you okay?"

With the remote control still glued to my hand and pointed at the television, I slowly drop down and sit on the edge of the bed.

"I'm stunned…just stunned."

"Baby, what's going on?"

"It's Kelly. She wants a…she wants a do-over."

"A what?"

"A do-over."

Plopping down beside me, he exhales, "I don't mean to be cruel, but isn't it a little too late for her to redo anything?"

"I'm not talking about her life. I'm talking about…Well, just watch."

I press Play on the remote control, and Kelly's feeble body appears on the screen. Her eyes are sunken, almost skeletal, and underlined with dark circles. Her skin is a sickly translucent yellow, her hair completely gone, and apparently the energy to wrap her head in the pretty red scarf she had been wearing since the first video is gone too. Leo, who hasn't seen many of these videos, winces and shakes his head in sorrow at what he's looking at.

"Chrissy, I pray that you pull the biggest Chrissygan of your life and watch this video before all of the others so that you can undo some of my dumb decisions."

"Wait a minute. Why is she talking to you all of a sudden? I thought she made these for Craig and Kendall."

"I thought so, too. Just watch."

"Remember in that talk on my porch a few months ago when I told you change doesn't come easy for me? Well, I'm so stubborn that I made these videos to try and keep Kendall's life exactly how I wanted it to be—I never wanted my expectations of the next eighteen years to change." Struggling to laugh though her jagged breaths, she wheezes, *"I just watched all of these stupid tapes and realized I've been trying to parent from the grave."* Then turning serious again, *"But that was a huge mistake and it cost me time with my family in these last months of my life, and I think it might cost Kendall a lot more than that in the long run."*

"Oh God, Chrissy, is she about to tell you not to show all of these to Kendall...after you already did?"

I just raise my eyebrows and continue to stare at the screen.

"I just got done telling Craig I screwed up. I don't want him to watch these videos and I really don't want a girl who is eight, ten, twelve...eighteen years old and who never even knew me to suffer through them either. I want Craig to figure everything out on his own...I mean, isn't that what parents are supposed to do? And if something should happen to him and you are the one to raise Kendall, I want you to figure everything out on your own, too. I don't want the words of a dying woman to influence the wellbeing of a child she wasn't around to see grow up." Straining to laugh again, she says, *"For Christ's sake, I talk about Courtney and Nicole in these things as if they'll forever be Kendall's closest companions. For all I know Courtney will run off to save the world, and Nicole will slip in a pool of one of her spilt drinks and die herself."*

"Holy crap, Baby, she actually got that prediction half right."

"I dunno…There's still a lot of drinks in Nic's future…a lot of opportunity for a tragic spill."

Appreciating my wit at a time like this, he puts his hand on my knee and gives it a squeeze.

"I told Craig to put the videos in the attic. When Kendall is a grown woman she can decide for herself what she wants to do with them. But Chrissy, in the event that something should happen to Craig, you are the one who will raise Kendall and somewhere in this house is a letter telling you that. That letter also tells you to show Kendall every last one of these stupid videos. Unfortunately, I can't find the letter to edit it. Craig promised to make the changes, but in case he forgets, I made this video for you."

"Looks like someone forgot to make those changes…or unfortunately died before he got around to it."

Oblivious to what Leo just said, I reach for the video cover and examine the words written on it once again—this time more closely.

"I'll be damned. Leo, does this say what I think it says?"

Taking the case, he studies the chicken scratch writing for a few seconds before his eyes widen.

"I think it says, '*For Chrissy.*'"

Snapping my attention back to the television, I hush Leo and say, "This is where I left off when I yelled for you to come in here."

"There are also a few other changes that need to be made to the letter…and to our will."

Leo grabs the remote out of my hands and quickly presses pause.

"What are you doing, Babe?"

"Chrissy, we have to stop watching this."

"*Why?*"

"What if she's about to tell you about some change to the will that never took place—something that would've altered the outcome of where Kendall is at this very moment. We can't know what it was, Chrissy. It'll eat away at you and it could fuck stuff up for her."

"How could it fuck anything up for Kendall?"

"She's only fifteen. Whatever Kelly's about to say is supposed to be in effect until she's eighteen…that's not for three more years, Chrissy."

"But whatever it is, I won't do it. No one other than us will ever know what's on this tape and we'll never tell anyone."

Handing the remote back to me, he rather sternly says, "Baby, I'll never allow a change to our family. Kendall's our daughter and I'm not sharing her with anyone. I have no problem keeping whatever it is Kelly's about to say a secret so that our lives aren't interrupted…but can you?"

I think long and hard about the unexpected letter I found in Craig's nightstand all of those years ago and the confidence Kelly expressed in it about my ability to raise her daughter. And I think about the Will I went over with a fine tooth comb, the Will that made *me* Kendall's legal guardian, giving *me* absolute authority over her upbringing. When I'm done with my internal evaluation I know one thing is for certain…

"Leo, no one is taking our daughter away. In fact, I think we're about to find out we should've had a lot more of her."

Pre-irritated at what I'm fairly certain is about to come out of Kelly's mouth, I press play.

"Our will specifies that if something should happen to Craig, you will be Kendall's legal guardian and Kurt will have weekend visitation. That set-up seemed like a good idea a few months ago. Now…not so much."

Leo looks like he could throw up in anticipation of what Kelly's about to say. Me…I'm pissed because I know *exactly* what she's about to say.

328

"There will be no weekend visitation. And it's not just because the feeling I get from that Kayla girl makes me sicker than chemo, it's because why complicate an already complicated situation? You will have Kendall one hundred percent of the time. Craig is to make this change with the attorney, but you can also show this video to Kurt. I know he'll comply when he hears my wishes."

Because both scenarios made me Kendall's legal guardian, the change to the will would not have altered where Kendall is at the very moment, but the change *most certainly* would've altered my relationship with Leo. He never would've had to "dig deep" to get over Kurt's visitation. I never would've been at Kurt's house on my birthday to drop Kendall off. We never would've broken up. I'm so angry right now I could throw the remote control at my dead friend.

"Baby, I know what you're thinking but—"

With watery eyes, and a cracking voice I interrupt.

"Leo, all of that chaos and keeping the baby from you…it never needed to happen.

"But it did, Chrissy."

"No it didn't. You just heard her. Kurt never should've had Kendall on the weekends. I never needed to be without her *or* you."

"Yes, you did."

"What are you talking about?"

He gently takes the remote control out of my hand, walks me to the window, and points to Greyson, who's helping the caterers set the tables for the party.

"It all needed to happen or else she wouldn't be here."

He's right. Every single argument, screw up, frustration, bad decision, cocktail, video, death, and unfathomable roll in the hay had to happen in order to create Greyson at that exact moment. In fact, everything single experience in my life and Leo's life

329

going all the way back to the day we were born had to happen just as it did for her to exist.

Placing his finger on my chin, my husband guides my gaze to his.

"Chrissy, I wouldn't eliminate one bad thing that ever happened to me, or any stupid decision I ever made for fear it might affect where I am and all that I have at this very moment."

And I can't be mad that I just now found Kelly's request for a do-over. In fact, I should be on my knees kissing the television that I didn't find it until today. Had there never been a visitation agreement with Kurt, I never would've been in Leo's New York loft that day when he broke up with me. I never would've been in his bed having break-up sex. I never would've gotten pregnant with Greyson.

Watching my baby girl through the window pretend to be a queen, and listening to her talk in a dramatic English accent, I quiver at what almost didn't happen.

"I can't imagine my life without her, Leo."

"Me, neither. Thank God you didn't pull one of those Chrissygans and watch these videos out of order."

Taking my hand he leads me back to the edge of the bed.

"C'mon, let's watch the rest of this so we can get on with the rest of our lives."

And then he presses play one last time.

"One last thing and I'll let you go…I guess literally, huh?"

At that sad statement, my eyes fall shut.

"I shouldn't have spent the last few months locked in my room making these videos; I should've been drinking beer with you and Craig on the front porch while we watched Kendall crawl on the front lawn…" And then my old voice of reason does something extremely out of character…she begins to cry. My eyes reopen to take in the extraordinary sight and to cry alongside her. *"…I'd give anything to have these last few months*

330

back. I'd give anything to tell you in person that even if you aren't the one to raise Kendall, you will be the one to shape her. As the emotional core of the A-BOB's I know you're not going anywhere. I know you will help Craig." Clearing her throat and doing her best to compose herself, she presses on with, *"Now, I really, really hope your curiosity gets the best of you and you grab this video first so that you can undo pretty much every dumb decision I made in the last few months. I guess technically, I really, really hope nothing ever happens to Craig, but you get my point."* Just then Craig appears in the background, walks up to Kelly, and kisses the top of her head. *"Look Craigy, I'm talking to Ki-Ki. I'm telling her about all of those changes."* He sweetly tells her not to worry about the changes because nothing will ever happen to him. His tragically wrong words make me and my husband clasp our hands together tightly. *"I really hope you get that Leo guy back so you can have what I have, Chrissy."* Her eyelids begin to drowsily fall shut. *"Promise me you'll go after the whole package..."* Knowing his wife has overexerted herself, Craig reaches toward the video recorder and turns it off.

Processing everything we just watched, Leo and I sit in stunned silence until we're interrupted by a faint knock on the door.

"*Mom?* Daddy...you guys in there?"

Leo scrambles to turn off the television while I mop the mascara off of my face.

"We're here, Kendall. Come on in."

Poking her head into our bedroom she raises her eyebrows and asks, "So...can I take video day off of my yearly list of things to do?"

Leo and I look at each other for a second before the both of us quickly kneel beside the box and start loading up all of the videos that spilt all over the place when he ran into the room. Simultaneously, we confirm her request with, "We're good with that."

Delighted with our decision, she thanks us profusely.

"I should've honored your request sooner, Sweetie. I'm so sorry to have put you through this for so many years."

"You were just being a good friend, Mom. I understand."

Finished with loading up the box, Leo then kisses the top of my head just like Craig just did to Kelly and says, "She was being a *best* friend."

Shaking off the craziness of the twists and turns of video number seventeen, I scoot them both out of the room so that I can get pretty for my ten-year wedding anniversary party. Once they're gone, I shake my fists up at the Heavens and gripe, "I'll talk to you about this later, Kel. Right now I have another can of worms…a *bigger* can of worms to deal with!"

Not Funny

September, 2013

"Oh my gosh, Leo, the yard looks just like it did on our wedding day!"

And it does. Everything from the lighting, to the catering, to the bar is set up exactly how it was ten years ago today.

Walking into his arms, I continue to admire my surroundings.

"Everything is absolutely gorgeous."

And so is he. Just like our wedding day, he's impeccably dressed. While more casual for today's festivities in jeans and a sport coat, he's as dashing as he ever was. Recollecting the first time I ever saw him on that barstool at Buckley's, I think...Yep, he's still my oddly beautiful green-eyed ghost dick boy.

"Do you know how unfair it is that all of your fine lines and specks of grey hair actually make you better looking? Women are so screwed when it comes to that stuff."

Wrapping his arms around my black cocktail dress, he gushes, "Do you know how lucky I am to be married so long to a woman who doesn't have fine lines and grey hair?"

With my arms now around his neck, I remind him, "Do you know how much money it takes every month for that to be the case?"

"Twenty dollars?"

I peck him on the lips.

"Higher."

"Forty?"

I peck him on the lips again.

"Way higher."

"A hundred dollars?"

I peck him again.

"Oh, Baby…You have *noooo* idea what it costs to keep this boat afloat."

"Well, whatever it costs, it's worth it. And look at you in that dress. How about we blow off this party, check into a hotel, and do last night all over again?"

"I don't know if I can stay up that late two nights in a row."

He knows I'm not talking about being tired from our longer than usual sexcapade…I'm talking about how long I had to wait for the sexcapade. As always, the night before our wedding anniversary is a late night for Leo. The long walk he habitually takes alone on September twelfth of every single year got him in the door well after ten o'clock last night. After our bottle of wine my clothes didn't come off until way after midnight. Thanks to my million dollar eye cream my eyes aren't puffy right now, but my husband's *definitely* need a dollop or two.

"You look tired, Leo. Is it because of your heavy thoughts on that walk, or the heavy stuff that happened after you got home?"

He never wants to talk about "the walk." Not for ten years. I know exactly what he's thinking about on that stroll, but he has always kept his thoughts to himself.

Lowering his tired eyes at me, he tries to be funny as he sets the record straight.

"I'm tired because you ruined me last night, Woman!"

Even though I know my moves in the boudoir aren't the reason for his weary eyes, I don't question his excuse. I don't want to frustrate him. There will be enough of that when my surprise guest knocks on the door. I let the subject of the walk go…for now.

"Ruining you is the thing I'm best at, Mister! And just so you know, I've got another sleepover scheduled for both of our girls. Get your beauty sleep, Hubby, because next Thursday night I own you!"

He turns a little more serious when he pulls me back to his lips. For a second I think he might even talk to me about his walk. But I'm wrong.

"Thank you for the best ten years of my life, Baby. Happy anniversary."

They were, in fact, the very best ten years a couple could ever ask for. They were full, and normal, and un-chaotic, and happy…they were everything my Hope List preached, and all that I practiced. But given the bomb that's about to hit the front door, I have a scary feeling the next ten years will be a little rocky. There's even a good chance my husband will be giving me the silent treatment for most of them.

Ha! And you thought you wanted a do-over, Kelly!

Criminy, I'd give anything for my own do-over and take back that invitation right about now. But since I can't, I might as well start planting the seed for the storm that's coming.

"Leo, can you think of one thing that might've made the last ten years better?"

"What are you talking about?"

"I mean, there has to be *one* thing that you sometimes wished for…"

Now it's his turn to peck me on the lips as he boasts, "Nope!"

"Not one single thing?"

"No way, Chrissy. Everything about us…about our life, is perfect."

"You never wished our family was bigger?"

He pulls back a little when he answers that one.

"Like that we had another kid? No. Never."

"Not necessarily a child, I'm talking more about—"

Just then the back gate flies open and the backyard gets loud…very, very loud.

"HEY, HEY, HEY! The hyena is here! The party can start now!"

Knowing full well Marti's arrival means a goody will be given, Kendall and Greyson come running out of the house yelling, "Yay! Auntie M is here! Auntie M is here!"

Greyson is first to receive a tube of shiny pink lip gloss in exchange for payment in the form of a kiss on the cheek.

335

Kendall is next up. Marti pulls two tickets to the race track out of her purse and tells her to keep next Saturday open, she'll pick her up at noon.

Leo laughs and rolls his eyes. I just roll my eyes.

"Marti, if I told you once, I told you a million times, those aren't the kind of horses she's interested in."

"Yeah? Well they're the kind I'm interested in!" And then she yells outside of the gate, "Baggy, hurry the frick up with that thing!"

Coming around the gate is The Ho-Bag and he's carrying the most exquisite cake I've ever seen. It looks like two pearl white gift boxes tied together with a giant sage green bow, and it's embellished with little pink rose buds. The second he places it on the table, Marti lays in on him again.

"Now look what you did, you big Goombah! You got frosting all over the front of your uniform. You'll have to go home and change before your shift starts."

Yep, our little Korean rock yard worker is now a big ol' cop. He was so proud of himself for "saving the day" when Greyson was born, that he decided to put his problem-solving skills to better use than loading useless shit into the backs of trucks. So he took some college classes, joined the police academy, and has been a cocky Korean son-of-a-bitch with a gun ever since.

"Back off, Hyena, or I'll be forced to put the handcuffs on you and make you lick it off!"

She jabs back, "Is that a promise?"

Leo whispers in my ear, "They're gonna give our parents strokes, you know that, right?"

Actually, I'm going to give *him* a stroke and he doesn't know it. Looking at my watch…but he will in thirty minutes. Shit.

Making her way over to me with a big smile, Marti brags, "I'll never get tired of him talking to me like that."

"Are you guys ever gonna admit you're a couple?"

"Hells no! Because we're not! I'm a free agent, Hunny. Always have been, always will be."

336

My Martha Stewart *always has been* and *always will be* one in a million. She's the best friend, the best Aunt, and at fifty-something years old, she's still the best yoga instructor on the planet. And her rock-hard body backs up one out of three of those claims.

"Marti, how is it that you still look exactly the same after all of these years?"

Pointing at herself, she reveals, "What, *this*? Oh this is just a twice a day facial mask and the love of about four thousand really hot guys."

She's also got the best humor…Which I could use a little dose of right now. Bursting at the seams, I have to tell her about my can of worms. She'll make me feel better…She always does.

"Hey Mar-Mar, wanna hear something kinda funny?"

"You know it, Doll. Tell me whatcha got."

"Well I guess it's funny depending on how you look at it."

"Yeah…I'm listening."

"It's not really 'ha ha' funny, it's more like 'get outta here' funny."

"Hunny, Baby, Sweetie…I'm not getting any younger. Just tell me, what's so fucking funny?"

With Leo in listening range, I whisper my not-so-funny story in her ear. When I'm done, she pulls away in dismay.

"Oh Hunny, Hunny, Hunny! There isn't anything funny about that at all." Glancing around the room she inquires, "Where's my Ho-Baggie? I want to be standing near that gun when all hell breaks loose."

"Oh, c'mon…It's not *that* bad."

"*Not that bad?* Doll, I was there. I saw Leo's face. I'll *never* forget that face."

"There was a face?"

"There was a face alright. And if I were you I'd be camping out on your front porch so that when your little guest gets here you can point him back in direction of his car so that none of us ever has to see that face again."

337

She's right and her advice is good advice. Too bad it arrived two minutes too late.

"It's too late to camp out on the front porch."

"Why?"

"Because you left the gate open and he just walked through it."

In the most excruciatingly slow one-two-three sort of dance, I look at the man at the gate, he looks at Leo, and Leo looks at me. Too late for a do-over.

He's *Baaaaaaack*

September, 2013

As she slinks away from me, Marti whispers, "Look at your hubby. *That's* the face I was talking about."

The man standing near the gate is almost unrecognizable with his nearly all grey head of hair and salt and pepper goatee. If it weren't for his dauntingly familiar eyes that are the color of rich soil flecked with black dots, I wouldn't even believe it was him. He notices Leo right away and stops dead in his tracks, reluctant to take another step into the yard without approval. I take my eyes off of him and follow his gaze to Leo's face—his chillingly murderous face—that's looking right at me.

At long last parting from my anxious eyes, my husband looks around to make sure his daughters are happily preoccupied in the house with Marti. When he's sure they can't hear him he very coldly asks, "What the fuck is he doing here?"

"Baby, I'm sorry...I invited him."

"What part of never wanting to see him again didn't make sense to you?"

Holy Moly, I haven't seen this kind of killer look in Leo's eyes since "Lo Siento" night...his college graduation when he eavesdropped on my phone conversation with Kurt and found out I wasn't as close to divorce as I had led him to believe. Who was it I said he reminded me of that night? Oh yeah...Charles Manson and Mike Tyson. I pause before answering Leo's question to examine his rage and search for some kind of leniency. But it doesn't look good for me. Yep, Charles and Mike are back in full force.

"It made sense...It's just that, well...Remember the morning after we got married when I told you about my two new dreams? Well, I knew you wouldn't do anything about this one, so...I kinda did."

339

"I remember, Chrissy, and I also remember I told you *your* dream was *my* nightmare."

Then he looks back over at his nightmare and says, "I don't know what my wife was thinking by inviting you here, and I sure as hell don't know what you were thinking by accepting the invitation. Both were mistakes. Get the fuck off of my property."

Yowza, Charles and Mike are ready to throw down.

"C'mon Leo, can't you just talk to him for a minute, for me?"

"I don't have anything to say to him."

Then he tells the man at the gate to leave again.

Knowing he won't get asked quite as nicely a third time in a row, my guest turns to leave, but I stop him when I yell, "Taddeo...WAIT!"

Leo's childhood best friend, the man he has known since he was two years old, and whom he hasn't seen in exactly ten years and one day, stops and turns to kindly address me.

"Chrissy, don't be mad at him for not wanting me here. He and I are cut from the same cloth...I totally understand why I'm not welcome. But thank you for trying and thank you for accepting my long-overdue apology."

I walk to Taddeo, grab his arm, pull him toward Leo, and announce, "No! You *are* welcome here. I don't care how uncomfortable this is for my husband, but he's gonna listen to what you have to say, dammit."

Once Taddeo is face to face with Leo, I demand the two of them to bury the hatchet. But neither of them speaks.

Standing between the two of them, I throw my hands in the air and yell, "Oh my God, what is it about a man turning forty that magically transforms him into a big giant baby?"

Simultaneously, the two old best friends chime, "*Who's turning forty?*"

Knowing the age bomb would jolt the two thirty-eight year olds away from the debacle at hand and break their silence, I take the opportunity to dive in.

"Guys, it's been a great ten years…for all of us. But looking back, didn't you ever feel like something was missing…Like the only other guy in the world to really get you was just a phone call away?"

Looking Taddeo square in the eye, my husband is first to reply with, "Yeah, and that's where I wanted him to stay." Then he turns to me with, "Chrissy, do I need to remind you what this asshole did to you…what he almost did to *us*? Jesus Christ, he kept my child a secret from me! You think calling him and asking him to come here today can fix the all of the damage he caused?"

"Chrissy didn't call me. I called her."

A little shocked that Taddeo would make the effort, Leo confirms the allegation with me.

"Is that true?"

"It's totally true. He called knowing our ten-year anniversary was approaching. He wanted to tell me he's still sorry for what he did and that his…"

Turning toward Taddeo, I quietly ask, "Is it okay if I tell him?"

He nods his head.

"He wanted to tell me he's still sorry for what he did, and that his life has never been the same without his brother."

As stubborn as ever, Leo just stares into the swimming pool, saying nothing.

"Baby, I know you feel the same. I mean, c'mon…every year on December sixth you take a long walk along the reservoir by yourself. I know that's Taddeo's birthday. And then you always take another long walk on the night before our anniversary, just like you did last night. I know you're not thinking about us, you're thinking about the big blow up that happened between the two of you the night before our wedding. You take those walks because you're sad and I thought—"

"You know what I feel when I take those walks? I feel pissed."

341

And then he surprises everyone when he shoves Taddeo in the chest.

"I feel pissed because you hurt my wife!"

He shoves him again.

"I feel pissed that I never got to read the emails she sent me!"

He shoves him again.

"I feel pissed because you knew about my daughter before I did!"

He shoves Taddeo even harder this time, and his old friend keeps on taking the well-deserved abuse. But with this shove The Ho-Bag takes a concerned cop step closer to the scene. Leo puts his hands in the air and tells his old rock yard/new cop friend he's fine and that he'll stop being pissed when Taddeo leaves.

"But Leo, I'm not hurt anymore because of what Taddeo did, and I haven't been since the night before our wedding. And you found out about Greyson *exactly* when you were supposed to find out about her. Any sooner and…" Twirling my hands around the yard, "…Maybe the outcome wouldn't have been all of this. Baby, like you just told me in our bedroom a few hours ago, we can't eliminate one bad thing that ever happened to us, or any stupid decision we made, or other people made for that matter, for fear that it might affect were we are at this exact moment. In some weird way, Taddeo's choices affected ours, and look where all of those choices got us—to our ten-year wedding anniversary. Leo, we don't *really* know what our lives would be like at this very moment if he hadn't done all of the stupid stuff he did."

My theory is a stretch, but it's a stretch that I can tell is making him think.

"I know your heart has been broken all these years, and for a minute when I was on the phone with Taddeo, I thought asking him here could mend it. Maybe it was stupid to invite him here, but you have to know my heart *and* his just want to fix yours."

Taddeo walks over to me, gives me a hug and says, "Thank you for trying, but I should just go. Really...I don't think I'd forgive me for what I did either."

Just then a teeny tiny woman holding a gigantic gift comes barreling through the open gate. She's dragging a handsome young boy on her other arm and screaming in Italian. She sounds like a deranged lunatic.

Leo asks me who it is, but it's Taddeo who answers as the tiny but mighty woman walks to him.

"This is my beautiful and insanely loud wife, Gianna, and my son, Filipo."

The boisterous woman slaps her husband in the arm for the backhanded compliment, and then immediately asks where Chrissy is. Her inquiry pulls my attention away from Taddeo's son's brilliant eyes and striking adolescent good looks.

A little intimidated by her moxie, I softly admit, "I'm Chrissy."

Charging me like a bull, Gianna Pascali wraps her arms around me and with her thick Italian accent says, "I am so happy to meet you, *il mio dolce*, we have a *tons* in common and a *tons* to talk about. But first, thank you very much for inviting my family here today." Pointing at Taddeo, "This big *bambino* has been sulking about your husband since the day I met him." Now walking toward Leo, she lowers her voice, "And this very handsome man must be the old best friend, *sì*?"

After Leo confirms his identity, she goes on with, "That was a shit thing my husband did to you, no?" Then she yells at her son to cover his ears before continuing with, "...All of my husband's whining about what he did to you would've broken us up if I didn't get knocked up." And then she doubles over in laughter.

Not laughing, Leo asks, "Taddeo told you what he did to us?"

Ignoring her husband's obvious embarrassment, she confesses, "The dumb *bambino* was drunk at a bar going on and on about what an asshole he is..." pointing at herself she giddily boasts, "…and look who decided to sit next to him…and go home with him…and sleep with him to make him feel better!" And then she cackles loudly once again.

I chime in with, "Whoa, whoa, whoaaa! *You guys met at a bar*? That sounds a little familiar!"

Taddeo's cute-as-ever wife quips, "*Il mio dolce*, that's not even the half of what you and I have in common!"

"*Il mio dolce*?"

Taddeo clarifies, "It means 'my sweet' in Italian. Everyone's 'my sweet' to her."

Now more serious, Gianna takes a step closer to Leo and takes his hand in hers.

"My husband tells me for the last ten years that if you were to find out my name you will do everything in your power to destroy our relationship, *si*?"

Not backing down to the little firecracker, my husband jabs, "Should I start now, *Gianna*?"

She stares him down for a scary amount of time before she bursts out in amused laughter, points at my husband, and squeals, "I like this one!" Then after her laughter dies down, she very coolly says, "You can try to destroy us, Mr. Leo, but my love for this big man standing next to me is as solid as yours is for that little woman standing next to you. You will fail just as he failed. Your efforts will be as futile as my husband's were." Then, after she kisses him on both cheeks, she advises my husband to, "Have a cocktail and let it all go, *il mio dolce*."

Then she drops Leo's hands, takes hold of mine, and begins to guide me to the bar area.

"Come on, my Chrissy, let's go and pop a bottle of something special and get to know each other better. These boys need to solve their own problems. If they are meant to be solved, they will be solved. Sometimes…*not often*…but sometimes, the women need to stay the fuck out of the way, *si*?"

Worried that leaving "the boys" alone to solve their problems will land one of them in the pool, I pretend I have to light a few candles. I send Gianna and Filipo into the house to drop their jackets, and tell them I'll be inside in a minute…And then I slump down low to the ground behind a table to eavesdrop on the old friends.

Surprisingly, Leo breaks the silence.

"Your wife, she's…she's something."

"She's a lot of things. Mostly, she's the only one who's ever been able to whip me into shape."

"A bar, huh?"

"Yeah, I went on a little bit of a drinking binge when I got back to New York after that night all of that shit went down between us. She was the only who sat long enough to hear the whole disgusting story, and *didn't* throw a drink in my face."

"When was that?"

"About a month after I last saw you."

"And you guys stayed together?"

"Who knew you could randomly meet your soulmate at a bar?"

From behind the table, I smile at Taddeo's facetious remark. I certainly appreciate the wit, but my fingers are literally crossed that Leo accepts the comment as a long overdue compliment about our relationship, and doesn't shove him in the chest again. The good news is Leo doesn't shove him in the chest, but the bad news is he also doesn't say anything. Nervous about what will happen next, I reach up to the table top, grab an open bottle of wine, and begin to chug it.

Taddeo finally breaks the silence with, "Anyway, three months after that she was pregnant."

After an even longer uncomfortable silence, Leo awkwardly asks, "So your son…Filipo…"

"I was being way too proper earlier. He actually goes by Fili."

"So that makes Fili about a year younger than Greyson?"

"Yep. He just turned nine."

"How nice for you to be around for your wife's entire pregnancy."

Leo's snide comment and my concern for where this conversation is headed cause me to take another gigantic swig from the bottle and hunker down until shit hits the fan.

"Actually, it was a little crazy. We didn't get married until after Fili was born...we had to wait for Gianna's divorce to be final."

And on that news I spit out the gigantic swig, stand up and holler, "Hooooold on! You met your *married* wife in a bar?"

Gianna startles me from behind when she says, "I told you we had a *tons* and a *tons* in common. I was going to start with my age, but it looks like these *cogliones* got a head start on my story."

Leo asks Taddeo what a *coglione* is, and he tells him it's a dick, or a prick, or a testicle...he can't remember which one. I ignore the foreign word altogether, and skip right to the good stuff.

"*Your age?*"

Taking the wine bottle out of my hand, and replacing the space with a giant martini, she seductively admits, "Like you, I am also six years older than my husband. These *cogliones* don't realize the power we have over them, do they, *il mio dolce*?"

Near full-on hysterical laughter at the way Taddeo's life has somehow mirrored the one he used to give Leo so much grief about, I turn to my *coglione* and mischievously ask, "I don't know...Do I have power over you, Darling?"

Shaking his head at the lunacy that's unfolding all around him, he says, "You must have some kind of power over me because this guy is still standing here in one piece."

Taddeo digs back with, "I can still kick your ass too, you know. I'd just hold back right now because I deserve everything I have coming to me."

The five-foot-five-inch Ho-Bag walks up to the six-foot-three-inch guys, pats his gun, and brags, "And I could kick both of your asses without even breaking a sweat."

Our Korean cop's comical comment came at just the right moment, providing us all with a much needed gentle laugh.

346

Then, exploring my "power," I ask my husband, "Baby, it might take some time for things to mellow out between you and Taddeo, but can the Pascali family please stay for the party? Can we give these relationships a second chance? I mean, that is what you and I are so good at, right?"

"You know it goes against one of my most coveted qualities to revitalize someone after I make them dead to me…"

"I know, but you revitalized me like seven hundred times and look how good we turned out."

"You know what, Chrissy?"

Nervous because of how sternly Charles/Mike just asked that, I cringe and mutter, "What?"

"You have more power over me than you'll ever know." And then turning to his former best friend, he moans, "C'mon, asshole, let's go get a couple of shots of whiskey. Hell, if anything comes out of tonight, at least maybe I'll find out why your hair turned grey so fast."

Following Leo to the bar, Taddeo whispers back, "You did just meet my wife, right?"

As the two *cogliones* walk away from their wives, Gianna and I tap glasses to our immense, yet ballsy, power.

—————

~~Francesca~~

September, 2013

It was a risky move to invite Taddeo to the west coast, let alone to my anniversary party. But after a decade of witnessing Leo's bi-annual long walks where I knew he was stewing over the demise of his oldest friendship, this wife had to take matters into her own hands. And it was a risk worth taking. From the garden, tucked away behind an overgrown bougainvillea plant, I spy on the two old friends having a long-overdue serious conversation over a bottle of whiskey. Then, after adjusting my vantage point, I see a few tears drop down Taddeo's face. And then I get goose bumps as I watch one of the sweetest things ever…Leo patting his old grieving friend's back, comforting him, and at long last, forgiving him.

My focus then turns to my parents who are making small talk with Leo's mom. Even though the sun has long since set, my mom still has on her big black sunglasses, doing all that she can to hide from the world. Those sunglasses used to break my heart, now they just crack me up. The three of them have been pretty decent grandparents which is a giant step up from the pretty sucky ones I thought they'd be. I love them for participating in our lives when I ask them to, and I love them even more for staying the hell away the rest of the time.

Marti and The Ho-Bag are canoodling in the corner, most likely making plans to hook up/lick stuff off of each other after his night shift is over. I don't think either of them will ever fully realize how much their tenacity changed my life and Leo's life. If it wasn't for my old Slutty Co-worker dragging me into Buckley's, and Leo's old cigarette-behind-the-ear-wearing-rock-yard-worker-friend doing the same to him, we wouldn't be celebrating this evening. In fact, Leo and I wouldn't even know each other. They're incredibly special to us, and we call them our family. Although never officially labeled Greyson's Godfather, The Ho-Bag stepped up and assisted Marti with every single Godparent duty. Though I'll always feel sad that Taddeo missed out on the opportunity, I can't imagine things being any different than they are for Greyson...or as The Ho-Bag calls her, Grey-Bag.

My lifesaver, Barbara, arrived about an hour ago and is now straightening up the bar area...No wait! She's...*Oh my goodness, is Barb flirting*? Making my way over to the lush tomato plant, I peek through the vines and catch sight of something I never thought I'd see in a million years—sixty-something-year-old Barb getting some action from the old fart we hired to work the bar. Would you look at that...*he's got googly cataract eyes for her*! I crouch down low and cover my mouth to silence my delight. Perhaps this evening is more than a celebration of my ten years of marriage, perhaps it's a celebration of Barb getting her groove back! I cannot wait to get her alone in the kitchen and sing my own version of bwamp-chica-bwamp-bwamp! Heck, if she takes that dude back to the cottage after the party I might even grab Kendall's old night vision goggles, run over, and spy. With that thought my hands cover my mouth again to drown out my giggles.

My focus then turns to the rest of the crowd and to who *isn't* here this evening. There's no Courtney or Nicole, but really no sadness about it. Like Kelly, they're always with me in spirit. But whose absence does make me sad is Megan's. Not sad like I want to cry, just sad that I don't know her anymore. The very last time I saw Megan in person was the day she quit the studios to embark on her valiant crusade to raise Nepalese orphans. I remember asking her on that last day, "It's not forever though, right?" Well, turns out it was. During our last conversation on the phone, when I gave her relationship with Kurt my blessing, I think we both realized we had to go our separate ways...and she took my ex-husband with her.

When Kurt first told me the news about their move to Nepal, I couldn't quite figure out what the picture would look like when they returned. You know…the two of them back from their adventure…popping in and out of my life…for the rest of my life. But Kurt and Megan never came back. I only heard directly from Kurt once in the last ten years, and that was in the form of a wedding gift. The wedding gift was the dog he and I had together when we were married. I lost my dog, Pup, in the divorce. Technically, there was no custody battle over Pup. I gave him to Kurt free and clear after he told me it was the least I could do for ruining his life. But when I came home the day after my fourteen-hour honeymoon, I found my sweet Pup tethered to my front porch with a big white bow attached to his collar, a bowl of water by his side, and a note that said…

Hi Mom, I'm your wedding present. Dad went to Nepal. Not sure when he'll be back.

Walking to a patch of wildflowers, I pick a bunch, and then place them on Pup's gravesite. Kendall and Greyson made the burial place five years ago when he died of old age. He lived a good life with our family, and up to the end he spent every day going to the studios with me, and every weekend doing laps with Leo in the pool.

While I've had no direct contact with Kurt and Megan, Kendall has loosely kept in touch with them over the orphanage's Facebook page. About three years ago, she showed me a picture of the two of them jumping out of a dilapidated twin prop plane with what looked like Mt. Everest in the background. They were holding hands and Megan had on a veil. I felt nothing but extreme happiness for the both of them, and liberation from a life that scared the crap out of me. To celebrate their nuptials and my hard-fought freedom, Forever Young, Inc. sent a sizable care package to their seventy-five *thousand* Nepalese kids…and to this day my company continues to make yearly anonymous donations. What can I say…I'm a softy (from a comfortable Western civilization distance) when it comes to the orphans.

Making my way through the vegetable garden to rejoin my family and friends, I lovingly tap a handmade wooden sign that says, "Armstrong Family food grown here." Leo made it the day Kendall officially changed her last name. It was eight years ago, and also the day Leo and I formally adopted her. She's now Kendall Wilson-Armstrong. A decision made by her and overwhelmingly approved by us.

Looking up at the Heavens, I say, "And approved by you too, huh Kel?"

My beloved old voice of reason hasn't been back in my dreams for over ten years now. The last time was during that night I ended up in the hospital. You know, when I thought Kurt told me the baby was his, and then I farted and fainted. Her last words to me as I slept were, "She comes first…She needs you." I woke from the dream to the sound of Kendall's voice calling me "Mommy" for the first time ever. It was beautiful. I also think it was Kelly's way of officially saying goodbye to me. I visit Craig and Kelly at the cemetery just once a year now. I tidy up the space and leave a bottle of beer on each tombstone. Other than thanking them for my unexpected gift, I don't have much else to say.

Looking back up at the Heavens, I gripe, "Until now, you big do-over dumbass!"

I shake off the annoyance at my old voice of reason and decide to just put it in the attic with all of those damn videos. Kendall was right all along…they should've been in the attic. Well, maybe not the videos for ages three, four, and five. *My* dumb ass actually learned a lot from those years.

Looking back into the fray of the party and at all of the people I love so much, I thank Molly-God that I had the courage to jump ship on my stupid life list and start over. Had I not abandoned the wedding vows I made to Kurt, I wouldn't know most of the people here today, and as my eyes land on Greyson, I shiver as I think…*my baby girl wouldn't even exist.* The other thing I thank Molly-God for is that I didn't have children when I was married to Kurt. It was one thing to be without kids and confront the big three I never wanted to be—a failure, a cheater, and a bad guy—but I can't even fathom what it would be like to face the big three with little ones around. There's just no freaking way I could've justified leaving a man who was a good guy for a man who made me feel like a good woman. There is absolutely no doubt in my mind that if I had a child with Kurt, I'd still be with him today, and that is a *very* sobering thought. I'd like to say these kinds of thoughts rarely cross my mind, but in actuality, they cross my mind every single day…when I'm at the kid's school, at the market, walking around the reservoir, and at cocktail parties. I see the women who met their Leo, but stayed married to their Kurt. Some know my chaotic and convoluted love story and they confide in me, and others, well I can just see the letdown in their eyes. Maybe because I got so close to becoming one of them, I have some kind of Francesca-detector, who knows? The one thing I don't do when I see these women is judge. I relate and I'm sympathetic. All I want to do is hug them and tell them they're not crazy, they're human. Occasionally I'll overhear a mini-Chrissy talking about how perfect her life is with a husband/fiancé who doesn't pay an ounce of attention to her. I want to butt in and rescue her from inevitable heartbreak, but you can't tell a young woman what you think without being asked for your opinion. Them's stubborn bitches. I know this because I used to be one of them.

When I met Leo in that bar back in 1998, every choice I had to make surrounding my relationship with Kurt seemed so daunting. But looking back, I think I knew the big three wouldn't kill me; it was becoming Francesca that would. My crushing fear of becoming her kicked the big three's asses. For others it might be the other way around…Everyone's tolerance for pain is different. Thank Molly-God mine was exactly what it was.

Speaking of Molly-God…I often thank her for my wonderful life. But ever since that first conversation with her after I gave birth to Greyson, I never talked directly to her ever again. That was the only conversation I ever needed. (Truth be told, I'm more comfortable with my ghosts.) I remember in one of my first sessions with Dr. Maria she said, "…When we start asking meaningful questions to any kind of higher power, ghosts included, we subconsciously start to look for the answers ourselves." The conversation I had with Molly-God that day was really a conversation with myself. And as long as I continue to stay true to the commitments I made in that conversation, I have no doubt that Leo will be committed to me forever.

In the distance I hear Kendall yell, "Mom, where are you?" Then I look to Greyson, who's whispering something in her daddy's ear. When she's done talking, I see the two of them scan the yard. My family is looking for me. Time to rejoin my party…Time to rejoin my truly, madly, deeply life.

Lover of Horses

September, 2013

"Geez Mom, I've been looking all over for you! Where the heck were you?"

"Just taking a little time out in the garden. Is everything alright?"

"You *have* to do something about that Fili boy. He's following me wherever I go, and talking about some kind of future he expects us to have together. It's really grossing me out. I mean, he's just a kid!"

Trying to contain my laughter, I calm her down.

"Kendall, it's cute. Besides, you're a beautiful girl…It's natural that he'd have a crush on you."

"He should have a crush on Greyson. She's his age!"

"There are no age rules when it comes to crushes. Just look at me and your father."

"Okay, one…gross! And two, get this…he says we're meant to be because I love horses and his name, *Filipo*."

"I'm not following."

"He says it means 'lover of horses' in Italian. Big whoop!"

"How cute though, right? You love horses, too."

She stomps her foot on the ground for me to take her seriously.

Guiding her away with my hand I assure her, "Okay, okay, okay…I'll steer him in Smudgy's direction."

But it's too late. The lover of horses is making a bee line for my oldest daughter and he's got a cupcake for her. Directly behind him is Greyson and it looks like she's got a cupcake for him.

"Looks like we might have some trouble on the horizon if we decide to keep the Pascali family in our lives."

355

I whirl around to find Leo who's observing the same cupcake conundrum as me.

"It's cute though, right?"

"When you're a dad, it's never cute to see a boy chasing your daughter...or your daughter chasing a boy. I don't care if the boy is nine years old."

"You know what, Mister?"

"What?"

"I think you're a pretty cute dad...and a forgiving friend. I saw you and Taddeo over there on those barstools. Did my honeymoon dream come true, is all forgotten?"

"Let's just say there's hope."

"Let's just say that makes me a very happy woman."

"I just have one question. Why was it so important to you that I let him off the hook?"

I've had ten years to think about this and the answer is simple.

"He did what he did out of love. I know better than anyone what it's like to make stupid decisions out of love, and I also know what it's like to be forgiven for those stupid decisions. Let's just say I wanted to pay it forward."

He nods his head in understanding of my reasoning before saying, "I realized two things after my conversation with Taddeo."

"What's that?"

"I missed him, a lot."

"What was the other thing?"

"Someone's wife has some serious *cogliones*!"

"Oh, I know! Gianna certainly is a little firecracker!"

"I wasn't talking about her!"

After our laughter subsides, Leo whispers in my ear, "Meet me in front of the house in five minutes." And then he pats my butt and walks away leaving me alone to once again take in the beauty of the evening. But the time to appreciate my surroundings is cut short.

"Ah! There you are, *il mio dolce*! Why are you standing her all alone on this very special night?"

"Just taking it all in…" Pointing at some of my convenient mom friends from the neighborhood who are dancing like clowns to eighties music, I reveal, "I saw you out there earlier. You've got some good moves, Mrs. Pascali."

After studying me long and hard she lets out a loud sigh, followed with, "I am a little disappointed in this evening."

"Oh, I'm sorry! Is it the food? I'm sure the caterers can whip up something—"

Cackling loudly she roars, "No, not in the food, *il mio dolce*! It's that I thought *I* was the luckiest woman in the world, but after meeting you and watching the way your husband cherishes you, you are giving my love with Taddeo some competition, *sì*?"

Cackling a little myself, I reassure her, "No competition. It's not my intent to rub what I have with Leo in anyone's face. In fact, I wish what I have with him on every woman alive. You and me…we're very lucky women, *sì*?"

Pulling me in for a hug she roars again, "*Sì, sì, sì!*"

Then she pulls back and asks to have a look at my wedding ring. That's when her smile vanishes.

"*Il mio dolce*, what in the fuck is this, some kind of gypsy toy?"

Looking down at my Banana Republic ring I tell her, "This is what I call love." And then I explain the significance of the pretty pewter piece. By the time I'm done with the story she has tears in her eyes.

"So no diamond for you….never?"

"A diamond isn't what makes a marriage. I had to learn that lesson the hard way."

Cackling louder than ever before, Gianna bellows, "You really are something, aren't you, Mrs. Chrissy Armstrong?"

"Now that's a question I haven't heard in a lot of years, Gianna!"

"You know what, my new great friend? I think you and I are going to know each other for a very long time. *Sì*?"

357

Agreeing with her prediction, I shout, "*Sì!*"

Realizing I'm late for my rendezvous with my husband, I kiss my new sassy Italian girlfriend on each cheek and bolt.

Sweet Symphony

September, 2013

"**I** thought you wanted to meet in the front of the house?"
On my way to the front door to look for Leo, he startles me by pulling me into the coat closet.

"I changed my mind."

Nudging me up against the wall he kisses me like he's twenty-two again and just met me last night at Buckley's. His hands go up my dress, squeeze my ass, and then back out several times to rub whatever he can grasp. The passion is almost more than I can take. It's wildly reminiscent of the red-hot stuff we experienced when we were first together, and it takes me by absolute surprise.

Breathless, I break away and ask my still potent as ever love-drug, "Baby, what's gotten into you? Is it the whiskey?"

"Not the whiskey at all. I've been watching you all night and I just feel so damn lucky."

"*I'm* the lucky one, and given the hell I put you through, I don't think there's a soul out there who would disagree."

"I'll tell you what hell was. Hell was not knowing you, hell was thinking I had lost you, and hell was wondering if I'd ever get you back."

With his lips all over my neck, I wonder out loud, "Leo, why do you think we're this way?"

"What way?"

"All truly, madly, deeply."

Abruptly stopping the kisses and looking deep into my eyes, he explains, "Because before meeting each other we had never been around another person in our entire lives that made us feel

359

special for who we were—who we *really* were. That's it. Pure and simple."

And the only reason we figured that out was because we were vulnerable with each other. The stuff Leo and I talked about in my car on the night we met...it wasn't normal. It was emotional and heavy stuff that I don't think a lot couples even reveal over the course of their entire relationship for fear of judgment, ridicule, or an argument. (Note...If you can't be vulnerable with the person you claim to be in love with because you fear those things, then you're not in a relationship, you're in a fakeship.) But heck, I didn't care what Leo's reaction was to my vulnerability because I was freaking married, and he didn't care what my reaction was to his vulnerability because he didn't give a shit about anyone or anything. On top of those two things, neither of us was looking for love! But man, because we were vulnerable with each other, *and* adored each other's vulnerabilities, we sure found it. *That night we found each other's particular grain of sand on the beach.* Moreover, we knew if we lost the grain of sand we'd never be lucky enough to find a more perfect one to take its place. That's what always brought us back together. That's what makes Leo and Chrissy truly, madly, deeply.

Now back to kissing my neck, he divulges more thoughts on his theory.

"But I also think we're truly, madly, deeply because we don't care what anyone else thinks."

My husband is absolutely right. You can't care what other people think of whom you choose to love, or *not* love. When it comes to your love life, it's NOT the time to be satisfying other people's opinions. The difference between what's good for you and what's good for everyone else is happiness. Take it from me, the sooner you realize that, the better off you'll be.

"Hey Baby, remember the night we met...when I told you I was ready to drive to Vegas and lock it down with you?"

"How could I forget?"

"I always wondered…if you weren't already married to someone else, would you have taken me seriously."

I think back to that magical morning when the sun was rising. We had spent the entire night getting to know each other and our final hour at daybreak making out like sex-starved maniacs. Without knowing it at the time, he was just what the doctor ordered to salvage the rest of my life, and it killed me to drive away from him knowing it was forbidden to ever see him again.

"My heart tells me 'yes,' but my mind says 'no freaking way!' Babe, I only knew you for eight hours."

"If I had this in my hand do you think it would've changed your mind?"

I look down to find Leo holding a small box. I know exactly what's in it, and my gaze goes right to my Banana Republic ring that I'm pretty sure is about to get it's ass kicked. I feel sad for it.

After he turns the light on over our heads he tells me to open it. Which I do, and upon first glance at the contents, I actually feel no sadness for my Banana Republic ring, only happiness that it has a buddy—a two carat diamond-encrusted beauty of a buddy.

Looking up at my gem of a husband, I explain that there's no way he could've had this rock in his hand the night we met because it cost more than four cans of chili.

After a little laugh by the both of us, I tell him, "I feel bad though, Babe."

"That's not the reaction I was looking for."

"No! I love it, Leo. It's stunning. I feel bad because all I got you for our ten year anniversary was a forty-year-old Italian bastard."

"Thirty-eight!"

After another little laugh, my husband takes my old ring off and replaces it with the new one and says, "I know the ol' Banana is special to you, but this is the one I want my wife to wear every day now. You deserve it."

Like a grain of sand, my husband, Leo, truly is one in a zillion.

"Oh and there's just one more thing…"

With my eyes glued to my new hunk of metal, Leo opens the closet door, guides me to the front door, and opens it. It isn't until he loudly clears his throat that I look up.

For a second I can't quite figure out what I'm looking at. I mean, I can see it…the rows upon rows of chairs, the men and women in black formalwear holding their instruments, the conductor front and center of them all, but it isn't until I hear the light tap of a stick and the instruments begin to play the theme song to *The Bridges of Madison County* that I wrap my brain around what is happening on the street in front of my house…which is an orchestra making musical magic. In awe of the spectacle, my hands clasp my mouth, my eyes pool with tears, and my body trembles almost uncontrollably.

The sound of the sweet symphony causes our guests from the party to filter into the front yard, neighbors as far as I can see down the road in all directions flow out of their homes in wonderment, and every car driving along the street pulls over and the passengers disembark their vehicles to see and hear what's going on.

With tears in his own eyes, Leo whispers in my ear, "If memory serves, my wife told me about *two* dreams on that fourteen-hour honeymoon of ours."

Not able to speak, all I can do is nod my head at Leo's recollection of that morning in bed. I remember I had just got done thanking him for making all of my stay-at-home-mom dreams come true, but told him I had decided to keep working anyway. That's when he asked to hear more of my dreams—new ones he wanted to make come true. After we finished making love, I told him what those dreams were. One, I wanted him and Taddeo to make up, and two, I wanted to hear an orchestra play the theme song to my favorite scary movie of all time, *The Bridges of Madison County*. Never, and I mean NEVER, did I think those two dreams could ever come true, and I sure as hell never thought they'd come true at my home and on the same day. But as I listen to the sweet symphony playing in my front yard, and watch Taddeo embrace his vibrant wife, I'm reminded that dreams really can come true.

My one in a zillion extends his hand out to me and asks, "May I have this dance?"

I take it and cling tightly to his chest as he sways me from side to side.

"Baby, look up...Look at what's happening."

All around, in every direction, on front lawns, in the middle of the street, alongside parked cars...the guests from our party and strangers everywhere embrace and sway to the beautiful music. Barb is cuddled up to the bartender, who's beginning to look like Mr. Second Chance, The Ho-Bag is nuzzled into Marti's chest, mostly because he's a good three inches shorter than her, and Taddeo and Gianna are holding each other tight and kissing like Leo and I just were in the coat closet. My parents are even enjoying the moment, and so is Leo's mom who's dancing with Greyson. Other than the awkward exchange Kendall is having with Fili as she tries to decline his offer to dance, love is everywhere.

Grandpa, Kelly, Craig, Dr. Maria, Pup...Can you hear the music? Are you dancing, too?

Closing my eyes, I see all of them in a beautiful meadow and they're dancing, and they're smiling, and they're waving to me. It's a beautiful sight that I don't want to lose, but I also don't want to miss what's going on all around me. I open my eyes and envision my two oldest friends, Courtney and Nicole, and their husbands swaying to the music along with everyone else. Court's husband is burping and Nic's shirt is covered in red wine stains; nevertheless, they're happy as ever, too. I even see Kurt and Megan twirling around recklessly in the street. They look, and I presume smell, like shit, but yes...I can see them, too, and they are happy and in love. Everyone and everything I ever loved in my life and love now is here with me and I feel all of it...*I can feel the sweet symphony of my life.*

Shaking me out of my dreamlike state, Leo asks, "Do you like it, Baby?"

"Oh Leo…it's breathtaking. How did you make all of this happen?"

"Just call me the dream-giver."

"Something tells me the dream-giver spent more on this night than he did on our wedding."

"Dream-receiver would be correct in that assumption."

After swaying from side to side and soaking in the symphony for a few minutes, he whispers in my ear again.

"Okay Baby, lay it on me."

"Lay what on you?"

"The new dreams."

"You do realize it's been like ten years since you asked me that question."

"I know, and it has me a little nervous. I have a feeling you've racked up more than two this time."

"Actually, I just have one and it won't cost you a dime."

"No do-over Porsche?"

"Nothing like that at all. My dream, Leo, is all I ever wanted from the first night I met you. All I want is to grow old with you."

Kissing my forehead he assures me, "Mine, too, Baby. Mine, too."

Spinning his wife in our direction, Taddeo yells out, "Guys, looks like we've got a little love triangle on our hands."

Pointing over to Fili and Kendall, who are surprisingly dancing, we see Greyson trying to cut in. Kendall's quick to accommodate her request, but Fili ain't lettin' go of the goods.

I gush, "I think it's sweet."

"I do too, *il mio dolce!*"

Watching the awkward moment play out with the kids, I look a little more closely at the googly eyes…the googly *green* eyes Fili has for Kendall. And then something jolts me…

Curious, I ask the Italian Stallions, "Hey guys, how old did you say Fili was again?"

"Ah, *il mio dolce*, my *bambino* is nine years old, why is it you ask?"

"Oi vey."

Puzzled, Leo asks, "Why the oi vey?"

"Hun, Kendall's fifteen…"

"What are you getting at, Baby?"

"Green eyes…six years younger than Kendall?" Speaking to the whole group now, "…The three of you don't see an alarming resemblance here?"

Trying to decipher my words, Leo, Taddeo, and Gianna all turn their heads to examine our children who are semi-dancing under the stars to the sweet sounds of the symphony. It looks as if Fili's young 'lover of horses' mystique has worked on teenage Kendall, because she's actually teaching him how to dance and seemingly enjoying it; the three of them appear to finally catch onto my observation.

Surrounded by the beauty of the evening, the elegance of all of our guests, and strangers alike, dancing to the most enchanting love song ever composed, we turn back to each other, and exhale all at once as we mutter, "*Oh shit.*"

("Catch My Breath," *Kelly Clarkson*)

The End

THE LIST TRILOGY

The Life List
The Unexpected List
The Hope List

www.askchrissy.net
@askchrissy
www.facebook.com/chrissyandersonbooks

"If we open our hearts and minds, I mean really open them to the point that it feels uncomfortable to do so, even in the midst of tragedy, there's an opportunity to find some good stuff that we never knew existed." -Dr. Maria

Acknowledgements

Because I'm extremely committed to my tagline, "the difference between doing something and doing nothing is everything," I feel it's necessary to acknowledge those who have offered me love, genuine encouragement, and selfless guidance while writing *The List Trilogy*.

First and foremost, I want to thank my husband. The irreplaceable love I have for him is the inspiration behind every word I write. From the moment I met him, I felt compelled to write about our love story. And once I started, I became obsessed with sharing it. I hope I've made him proud, for his love and respect means everything to me. My daughter, who was four at the time I began writing Part I of *The List Trilogy*, is nine now. My baby has demonstrated a level of patience with my "hobby" that blows my mind and warms my heart. *The List Trilogy* is for her to read with an open mind and a willingness to learn…when she's an adult, of course!

There were many times over the last five years when I almost chickened out of publishing my work. If it wasn't for my best friend, Eva, who took my panicked phone calls, stressed out texts, and rambling (*almost psychotic*) emails about how stupid I think I am, and turned them into rejuvenating and motivating therapy sessions, *The List Trilogy* would never exist. Thank you, my dear old friend, for all of your recommendations, and for protecting me *once again* from making a total ass of myself. It's also essential that I acknowledge my pal, Vikki. As busy and professional as this woman is, she's the only one of my friends who appeared on my doorstep with tears streaming down her face after she read the last word of *The Life List*. To this day she continues to inundate me with marvelous marketing ideas to take my trilogy to the next level. I have to thank my poker group gals, (Lisa H., Lisa S., Nat, and Ang) for the most genuine of genuine laughter and encouragement. The shit that comes out your *almost*-middle-aged mouths after seventeen bottles of wine has inspired my writing more than any of you will ever know. Just like I wish every woman had a "Leo" in her life, I wish every woman had the kind of genuine encouragement *all* of my girlfriends have given to me with regard to my work.

I have to acknowledge Peter Baxter for the work he's done on my website, www.askchrissy.net. Like me, Peter is one of those freaky left-brain/right-brain people. He's an accomplished author of several works of non-fiction about smart stuff like Africa and he's a web developer. *Who even thought a species like that existed?* Our style of writing could NOT be more different, yet he's offered me subtly valuable advice that's no doubt taken my work to a more polished level.

And speaking of polished level…I'd be a total literary laughing stock if it weren't for author Amy Metz, and professional wordsmith and editor, Margie Aston (http://margieaston.com). Both of these incredibly selfless women picked-up first editions of *The Life List* at random, read it, and loved it. But they could've loved it even more if I knew how the hell to use an ellipsis or how to spell "fuck's sake," so each of them contacted me to offer their professional and much needed support. Words can't express how indebted I am to these two women for their brains, generosity, and overall conviction that I had a really great story that could become phenomenal if I knew how to punctuate…and spell, for fuck's sake! (They'd be so proud.) I keep a list of people that I swear to God I will reward for kindness and at the top of it are Amy and Margie.

Lastly, I have to thank all of the mini-Chrissys and forsaken-Francescas out there. While "Leo" was my inspiration for my convoluted and chaotic love story, you gave me the ultimate courage to tell it. I don't want anyone to ever feel as lonely, scared, or confused as I felt during those years of my life. No matter if you're at the beginning of an arduous relationship, or deep into one that you wish you left a long time ago, I hope I've made you feel sane and supported. I want you to know you have a friend. Maybe those things will be *your* difference between doing something and doing nothing. And if they aren't, well no one knows why better than me.

Oh wait…there is one more very important thing. If you've read this far, please tell me why. Reviews are the breath of life for authors and every single one left on Amazon will increase the visibility of my work. Without your review *The List Trilogy* will most definitely get lost in a book abyss. I'm begging you to not let that happen. Please click to Amazon right now…two minutes of your time is all it will take to make a staggering difference.

Xoxo,
Chrissy

Next up for Chrissy Anderson...

The Truth Trinity

56200458R00232

Made in the USA
Lexington, KY
17 October 2016